Wolf Who Rules

Baen Books by Wen Spencer
Tinker
Wolf Who Rules

Wolf Who Rules

Wen Spencer

WOLF WHO RULES

This is a work of fiction. All the characters and events portrayed in this book are fictional, and any resemblance to real people or incidents is purely coincidental.

Copyright © 2006 by Wen Spencer

A Baen Books Original

Baen Publishing Enterprises
P.O. Box 1403
Riverdale, NY 10471
www.baen.com

ISBN 10: 1-4165-2055-4
ISBN 13: 978-1-4165-2055-9

Cover art by Kurt Miller

First printing, April 2006

Distributed by Simon & Schuster
1230 Avenue of the Americas
New York, NY 10020

Library of Congress Cataloging-in-Publication Data

Spencer, Wen.
Wolf Who Rules / by Wen Spencer.
     p. cm.
  "A Baen Books original."
  ISBN-13: 978-1-4165-2055-9 (hardcover)
  ISBN-10: 1-4165-2055-4 (hardcover)
  1. Elves--Fiction. I. Title.

PS3619.P4665W65 2006
813'.6--dc22
                              2005037946

Printed in the United States of America

10 9 8 7 6 5 4 3 2 1

To Ann Cecil,
In many ways, elf-like.

Thanks to
Greg Armstrong, David Brukman,
Ann Cecil, Gail Brookhart, Kevin Hayes,
W. Randy Hoffman
Nancy Janda, Kendall Jung,
Don Kosak, June Drexler Robertson,
John Schmid, Linda Sprinkle,
Diane Turnshek, Andi Ward,
Joy Whitfield and
Thorne Scratch, who let me steal
her lock, stock and barrel

PROLOGUE: CUP OF TEARS

Elves may live forever, but their memories do not. Every elfin child is taught that any special memory has to be polished bright and carefully stored away at the end of a day, else it will slip away and soon be forgotten.

Wolf Who Rules Wind, viceroy of the Westernlands and the human city of Pittsburgh, thought about this as he settled before the altar of Nheoya, god of longevity. It was one more thing he would have to teach his new *domi*, Tinker. While clever beyond measure, she had spent her childhood as a human. He had only transformed her genetically into an elf; she lacked the hundred years of experience that all other adult elves lived through.

Wolf lit the candle of memory, clapped to call the god's attention to him, and bestowed his gift of silver on the altar. Normally he would wait to reach perfect calmness before starting the ceremony, but he didn't have time. He'd spent most of the last two days rescuing his *domi*, fighting her oni captors, and discovering how and why they had kidnapped her away. In truth, he should be focusing on his many responsibilities, but the fact that his *domi* had been restored to him on the eve of Memory made him feel it was important to observe the ritual.

He picked up the cup of tears. As a child, he couldn't understand why anyone would want to cling to bad memories. It had
taken the royal court, with all its petty betrayals, to teach him the
importance of bitterness; you needed to remember your mistakes
to learn from them. For the first time, however, he did not dwell
on those affairs of the heart. They all seemed minor now. His
assistant, Sparrow Lifted by Wind, had taught him the true meaning of treachery.

He replayed now all her betrayals, slowly drinking down the
warm saltwater. He did not know when she had started working
with the oni, perhaps as early as the first day the human's orbital
hyperphase gate had shifted Pittsburgh to Elfhome. He knew for
sure that she'd spent the last few weeks subtly detouring him away
from the oni compound. She had arranged for his blade brother
Little Horse to be alone, so the oni could kidnap him and use him as
a whipping boy. So many lies and deceptions! Wolf remembered the
blank look on her face as she talked on her cell phone on that last day.
He knew now the call was from the oni noble, Lord Tomtom, alert-
ing her that Tinker and Little Horse had escaped. What excuse had
she used to slip away in order to intercept them? Oh yes, a member
of the clan needed someone to mediate between them and the
Pittsburgh police. He had thanked her for sparing him from such
small responsibilities so he could focus on finding the two people
most important to him. Too bad Little Horse gave her such a clean
death.

Dawn was breaking, and the cup of tears was drained, so he set
aside his bitter memories. As light spilled into the temple, he lifted
the cup of joys.

Normally he would dwell for hours on his happy childhood in
his parents' household, and then, with a few exceptions, skip over all
the lonely years he spent at court, and start again as he built his own
household and settled the Westernlands. He did not have time
today. In celebration of their safety, he thought only of Tinker and
Little Horse.

Sipping his honeyed tea, he remembered Little Horse's birth
and childhood, how he grew in leaps and bounds between Wolf's visits
back home, until he was old enough to be part of Wolf's household.

He brought with him the quiet affection that Wolf missed from his parents' home. Bitterness at Sparrow tried to crowd in, but Wolf ignored the temptation to dwell on those thoughts. He had only a short time left, and he wasn't going to waste it on her.

He turned his thoughts to Tinker. A human, raised on Elfhome, she was a delightful mix of human sensibility steeped in elfin culture. They had met once years ago, when she had saved him from a saurus. She had saved him again from a recent oni assassination attempt. The days afterward, as she struggled to keep him alive, she proved her intelligence, leadership, compassion, and fortitude. Once he realized that she was everything that he wanted in a *domi*, it was as if floodgates had opened in his heart, letting loose a tide of emotions he hadn't suspected himself capable of. Never had he wanted so much to protect another person. The very humanity that he loved in her made her butterfly fragile. The only way to keep her brightness shining was to make her an elf. At the time, he had regretted the necessity, but no longer. As a human, Tinker would have either been taken away from the home she loved by the NSA, or she wouldn't have survived Sparrow's betrayal. If he had any regrets it was trusting Sparrow and underestimating the oni.

Much as he'd have liked to continue dwelling on the good memories of his beloved, there was too much to do. Reluctantly, Wolf Who Rules blew out the candle, stood, and bowed to the god. The oni had forced his *domi* into building a gateway between their world and the neighborhood of Turtle Creek. Since the oni were gaining access to Earth (and ultimately Elfhome) via the orbital hyperphase gate, Tinker had used her gate to destroy the one in orbit. Unfortunately there were side effects not even his beloved could explain. Pittsburgh was now stuck on Elfhome. Turtle Creek had melted into liquid confusion. And something, most likely the orbital gate, had fallen from the sky like shooting stars. It left them with no way to return the humans to Earth, and an unknown number of oni among them.

1: GHOST LANDS

＊━━◯◖━◗━━＊

There were some mistakes that "Oops" just didn't cover.

Tinker stood on the George Westinghouse Bridge. Behind her was Pittsburgh and its sixty thousand humans now permanently stranded on Elfhome. Below her lay the mystery that at one time had been Turtle Creek. A blue haze filled the valley; the air shimmered with odd distortions. The land itself was a kaleidoscope of possibilities—elfin forest, oni houses, the Westinghouse Air Brake Plant—fractured pieces of various dimensions all jumbled together. And it was all her fault.

Color had been leached from the valley, except for the faint blue taint, making the features seem insubstantial. Perhaps the area was too unstable to reflect all wavelengths of light—or maybe the full spectrum of light wasn't able to pass through—the—the—she lacked a name for it.

Discontinuity?

Tinker decided that was as good a name as any.

"What are these *Ghostlands*?" asked her elfin bodyguard, Pony. He'd spoken in Low Elvish. *Ghostlands* had been in English, though, meaning a human had coined the term. Certainly the phrase fit the ghostly look of the valley.

4

So maybe Discontinuity wasn't the best name for it.

A foot taller than Tinker, Pony was a comforting wall of heavily armed and magically shielded muscle. His real name in Elvish was *Waetata-watarou-tukaenrou-bo-taeli*, which meant roughly Galloping Storm Horse on Wind. His elfin friends and family called him Little Horse, or *tukaenrou-tiki*, which still was a mouthful. He'd given her his English nickname to use when they met; it wasn't until recently that she had realized it had been his first act of friendship.

"I don't know what's happening here." Tinker ran a hand through her short brown hair, grabbed a handful and tugged, temptation to pull it out running high. "I set up a resonance between the gate I built and the one in orbit. They were supposed to shake each other apart. They did."

At least, she was fairly sure that they had. Something had fallen out of the sky that night in a fiery display. Since there were only a handful of small satellites in Elfhome's orbit, it was a fairly safe bet that she had somehow yanked the hyperphase gate out of Earth's orbit.

"This was—unexpected." She meant all of it. The orbital gate reduced to so much space debris and burnt ash on the ground. Turtle Creek turned into Ghostlands. Pittsburgh stuck on Elfhome. Even "sorry" didn't seem adequate.

And what had happened to the oni army on Onihida, waiting to invade Elfhome through her gate? To the oni disguised as humans worked on the gate with her? And Riki, the tengu who had betrayed her?

"Is it going to—get better?" Pony asked.

"I think so." Tinker sighed, releasing her hair. "I can't imagine it staying in this unstable state." At least she hoped so. "The second law of thermodynamics and all that."

Pony grunted a slight optimistic sound, as if he was full of confidence in her intelligence and problem solving. Sometimes his trust in her was intimidating.

"I want to get closer." Tinker scanned the neighboring hillsides, looking for a safe way down to the valley's floor. In Pittsburgh, nothing was as straightforward as it appeared. This area was mostly abandoned—probably with help from the oni to keep people away from their secret compound. The arcing line of the Rim, marking where Pittsburgh ended and Elfhome proper began, was diffused by advancing elfin forest. Ironwood saplings mixed with jagger bushes—elfin trees colliding with Earth weed—to form a dense impenetrable thicket. "Let's find a way down."

"Is that wise, *domi*?"

"We'll be careful."

She expected more of an argument, but he clicked his tongue, the elfin equivalent of a shrug.

Pony leaned out over the bridge's railing; the spells tattooed down his arms in designs like Celtic knots—done in Wind Clan blue—rippled as muscle moved under skin. The hot wind played with tendrils of glossy black hair that had come loose from his braid. Dressed in his usual wyvern-scaled chest armor, black leather pants, and gleaming knee boots, Pony seemed oblivious to the mid-August heat. He looked as strong and healthy as ever. During their escape, the oni had nearly killed him. She took some comfort that he was the one thing that she hadn't totally messed up.

As they had recuperated, she'd endured an endless parade of visitors between bouts of drugged sleep, which gave the entire experience a surreal nightmare feel. Everyone had brought gifts and stories of Turtle Creek, until her hospice room and curiosity overflowed.

Thanks to her new elfin regenerative abilities, she'd healed far faster than when she was a human; she'd awakened this morning feeling good enough to explore. Much to her dismay, Pony insisted on bringing four more *sekasha* for a full Hand.

Yeah, yeah, it was wise, considering they had no clue how many oni survived the meltdown of Turtle Creek. She was getting claustrophobic, though, from always having hordes of people keeping watch over her; first the elves, then the oni, and now back to the elves. When she ran her scrap yard—months ago—a lifetime ago — she used to go days without seeing anyone but her cousin Oilcan.

As viceroy, her husband, Wolf Who Rules Wind, or Windwolf, held twenty *sekasha*; Pony picked her favorite four out of that twenty to make up a Hand. The outlandish Stormsong—her rebel short hair currently dyed blue—was acting as a Shield with Pony. Annoyingly, though, there seemed to be some secret *sekasha* rule— only one Shield could have a personality at any time. Stormsong stood a few feet off, silent and watching, in full bodyguard mode while Pony talked to Tinker. It would have been easier to pretend that the *sekasha* weren't guarding over her if they weren't so obviously "working."

The bridge secured, the other three *sekasha* were being Blades and scouting the area. Pony signaled them now using the *sekasha's* hand gestures called blade talk. Rainlily, senior of the Blades, acknowledged—Tinker recognized that much by now—and signaled something more.

"What did she say?" Tinker really had to get these guys radios. She hated having to ask what was going on; until recently, she had always known more than everyone else.

"They found something you should see."

The police had strung yellow tape across the street in an attempt to cordon off the valley; it rustled ominously in a stiff breeze. Ducking under the tape, Tinker and her Shields joined the others. The one personality rule extended to the Blades; only Rainlily got to talk. Cloudwalker and Little Egret moved off, searching the area for possible threats.

"We found this in the middle of the road." Rainlily held out a bulky white, waterproof envelope. "Forgiveness, we had to check it for traps."

The envelope was addressed with all possible renditions of her name: Alexander Graham Bell, "Tinker" written in English, and finally Elvish runes of "Tinker of the Wind Clan." The *sekasha* had already slit it open to examine the contents and replaced them. Tinker tented open the envelope and peered inside; it held an old MP3 player and a note written in English.

I have great remorse for what I did. I'm sorry for hurting you both. I wish there had been another way. Riki Shoji.

"Yeah, right." Tinker scoffed and crumpled up the note and flung it away. "Like that makes everything okay, you damn crow."

She wanted to throw the MP3 player too, but it wasn't hers. Oilcan had loaned it to Riki. The month she'd been at Aum Renau, Oilcan and Riki had become friends. Or at least, Oilcan thought they were friends, just the same as he thought they were both human.

Riki, though, was a lying oni spy, complete with bird-feet and magi-cally retractable crow wings. He'd wormed his way into their lives just to kidnap Tinker. She doubted that Oilcan would want the play-er back now that he knew the truth; it would be a permanent reminder that Oilcan's trust nearly cost Tinker her life. But it wasn't her right to decide for him.

She jammed the player into the back pocket of her shorts. "Let's go."

Rage smoldered inside her until they had worked their way down to the Discontinuity. The mystery of the Ghostlands deep-ened, drowning out her anger. The edge of the blue seemed uneven at first, but then, as she crouched down to eye it closely, she realized that the effect "pooled" like water, and that the ragged edge was due to the elevation of the land—like the edge of a pond. Despite the August heat, ice gathered in the shadows. This close, she could hear a weird white noise, not unlike the gurgle of a river.

She found a long stick and prodded at the blue-shaded earth; it slowly gave like thick mud. She moved along the "shore" testing the shattered pieces of three worlds within reach of her stick. Earth fire hydrant. Onihida building. Elfhome ironwood tree. While they looked solid, everything within the zone of destruction was actually insubstantial, giving under the firm poke of her stick.

Pony stiffened with alarm when—after examining the stick for damage done to it and finding it as sound as before—she reached her hand out over the line.

Oddly, there was a resistance in the air over the land—as if Tinker was holding her hand out the window of a moving car. The air grew cooler as she lowered her hand. It was so very creepy that she had to steel herself to actually touch the dirt.

It was like plunging her bare hand into snow. Bitterly cold, the dirt gave under her fingertips. Within seconds, the chill was painful. She jerked her hand back.

"*Domi?*" Pony moved closer to her.

"I'm fine." Tinker cupped her left hand around her right. As she stood, blowing warmth onto her cold-reddened fingers, she gazed out onto the Ghostlands. She could feel magic on her new *domana* senses, but normally—like strong electrical currents—heat accompanied magic. Was the "shift" responsible for the cold? The presence of magic, however, would explain why the area was still unstable—sustaining whatever reaction the gate's destruction created. If her theory was right, once the ambient magic was depleted, the effect would collapse and the area would revert back to solid land. The only question was the rate of decay.

Pony picked up a stone and skipped it out across the disturbance. Faint ripples formed where the stone struck. After kissing "dirt" three times, the stone stopped about thirty feet in. For a minute it sat on the surface and then, slowly but perceivably, it started to sink.

Pony made a small puzzled noise. "Why isn't everything sinking?"

"I think—because they're all in the same space—which isn't quite here but isn't really someplace else—or maybe they're everywhere at once. The trees are stable, because to them, the earth underneath them is as stable as they are."

"Like ice on water?"

"Hmm." The analogy would serve, since she wasn't sure if she was right. They worked their way around the edge, the hilly terrain making it difficult. At first they found sections of paved road or cut through abandoned buildings, which made the going easier. Eventually, though, they'd worked their way out of the transferred Pittsburgh area and into Elfhome proper.

On the bank of a creek, frozen solid where it overlapped the affected area, they found a dead black willow tree, lying on its side, and a wide track of churned dirt where another willow had stalked northward.

Pony scanned the dim elfin woods for the carnivorous tree. "We must take care. It is probably still nearby; they don't move fast."

"I wonder what killed it." Tinker poked at the splayed root legs still partly inside the Discontinuity. Frost like freezer burn dusted the wide, sturdy trunk. Otherwise it seemed undamaged; the soft mud and thick brush of the creek bank had cushioned its fall so none of its branches or tangle arms had been broken. "Lain would love an intact tree." The xenobiologist often complained that the only specimens she ever could examine were the nonambulatory seedlings or mature trees blown to pieces to render them harmless. "I wish I could get it to her somehow."

The tracks of both trees, Tinker noticed, started in the Ghostlands. Had the willow been clear of the Discontinuity at the time of the explosion—or had the tree died after reaching stable ground?

"Let me borrow one of your knives." Tinker used the knife Pony handed her to score an ironwood sapling. "I want to be able to track the rate of decay. Maybe there's a way I could accelerate it."

"A slash for every one of your feet the sapling stands from the Ghostlands?" Pony guessed her system.

"Yeah." She was going to move on to the next tree but he held out his hand for his knife. "What?"

"I would rather you stay back as much as possible from the edge." He waited with the grinding power of glaciers for her to hand back his knife. "How do you feel, *domi*?"

Ah, the source of his sudden protectiveness. It was going to be a while before she could live down overestimating herself the night of the fighting. Instead of going quietly to the hospice, she'd roamed about, made love, and did all sorts of silliness—and of course, fell flat on her face later. It probably occurred to him that if she nose-dived again, she would end up in the Ghostlands.

"I'm fine," she reassured him.

"You look tired." He slashed the next sapling, and she had to admit he actually made cleaner, easier-to-see marks than she did, robbing her of all chance to quibble with him.

She made a rude noise. Actually, she was exhausted—nightmares had disrupted her sleep for the last two days. But she didn't want to admit that; the *sekasha* might gang up on her and drag her back to the hospice. That was the problem with bringing five of them—it was much harder to bully them en masse—especially since they were all a foot taller than her. Sometimes she really hated being five foot nothing. Standing with them was like being surrounded by heavily armed trees. Even now Stormsong was eyeing her closely.

"I'm just—thinking." She mimed what she hoped looked like deep thought. "This is very perplexing."

Pony bought it, but he trusted her, perhaps more than he

should. Stormsong seemed unconvinced, but said nothing. They moved on, marking saplings.

With an unknown number of oni scattered through the forest and hidden disguised among the human population of Pittsburgh, Wolf did not want to be dealing with the invasion of his *domi's* privacy, but it had to be stopped before the queen's representative arrived in Pittsburgh. Since all requests through human channels had failed, it was time to take the matter into his own hands.

Wolf stalked through the broken front door of the photographer's house, his annoyance growing into anger. Unfortunately, the photographer—paparazzi was the correct English word for his kind, but Wolf was not sure how to decline the word out—in question was determined to make things as difficult as possible.

Over the last two weeks, Wolf's people had worked through a series of false names and addresses to arrive at a narrow row house close to the Rim in Oakland. The houses to either side had been converted into businesses, due to their proximity to the enclaves. While the racial mix of the street was varied, the next door neighbors were Chinese. The owners had watched nervously as Windwolf broke down the photographer's door, but made no move to interfere. Judging by their remarks to each other in Mandarin, neither did they know that Wolf could speak Mandarin in addition to English, nor were they surprised by his presence—they seemed to think the photographer was receiving his due.

Inside the house, Wolf was starting to understand why.

One long narrow room took up most of the first floor beyond the shattered door. Filth dulled the wood floors and smudged the once white walls to an uneven gray. On the right wall, at odds with the grubby state of the house, was video wallpaper showing recorded images of Wolf's *domi*, Tinker. The film loop had been taken a month ago, showing a carefree Tinker laughing with the five female *sekasha* of Wolf's household. The image had been carefully doctored and scaled so that it gave the illusion that one gazed out a large window overlooking the private garden courtyard of Poppymeadow's enclave. Obviously feeling safe from prying eyes, Tinker lounged in her nightgown, revealing all her natural sexuality.

Wolf had seen the still pictures of Tinker in a digital magazine but hadn't realized that there was more. Judging by the stacks of cardboard boxes, there was much more. He flicked open the nearest box and found DVDs titled *Princess Gone Wild, Uncensored.*

"Where is he?" Wolf growled to his First, Wraith Arrow.

Wraith tilted his head slightly upward to indicate upstairs. "There's more."

At the top of the creaking wooden stairs, there was a large room empty of furniture. A camouflage screen covered the lone window, projecting a blank brick wall to the outside world. A camera on a tripod peered through a slit in the screen, trained down at the enclaves. This room's video wallpaper replayed images captured this morning, a somber Tinker sitting alone under the peach trees, dappled sunlight moving over her.

Wolf moved the camera, and the device's artificial intelligence shrank Tinker's image into one corner and went to live images as the zoom lens played over Poppymeadow's enclave where Wolf's household was living. Not only did the balcony provide a clear view over the high stone demesne wall but into the windows of all the buildings, from the main hall to the coach house. One of Poppymeadow's staff was changing linens in a guest wing bedroom; the camera automatically recognized the humanoid form and adjusted the focus until she filled the wall. The window was open, and a microphone picked up her humming.

"I haven't done anything illegal," a man was saying in the next room in English. "I know my rights! I'm protected by the treaty."

Wolf stalked into the last room. His *sekasha* had broken down the door to get in. The only piece of furniture was an unmade bed that reeked of old sweat and spent sex. His *sekasha* had a small rat of a man pinned against the far wall.

On the wall, images of Wolf's *domi* moved through their bedroom at Poppymeadow's, languidly stripping out of her clothes. "You want to do it?" she asked huskily. Wolf could remember the day, had replayed it in his mind again and again as his last memory of her when he thought he had lost her. "Come on, we have time."

She dropped the last piece of clothing on the floor, and the camera zoomed in tighter to play down over her body. Wolf snarled

out the command for the winds and slammed its power into the wall.
The wall boomed, the house shuddering at the impact, and the wallpaper went black. Tinker's voice, however, continued with a soft
moan of delight.

"Hey! Hey!" the man cried in English. "Do you have any idea
how expensive that is? You can't just smash in here and break my
stuff. I have rights."

"You had rights. They've been revoked." Wolf returned to the
balcony and knocked the camera from its tripod. The wallpaper
showed a somersault of confusion as the camera flipped end over
end. When it struck pavement, it shattered into small unrecogniz-
able pieces, and the wallpaper flickered back to the previously
recorded loop of Tinker sitting in the garden.

"Evacuate the area," Wolf ordered in low Elvish. "I'm razing
these buildings."

Apparently the man understood Elvish, because he yelped out,
"What? You can't do that! I've called the police! You can't do this!
This is Pittsburgh! I have rights!"

As if summoned by his words, a commotion downstairs
announced the arrival of the Pittsburgh police.

"Police, freeze," a male voice barked in English. "Put down the
weapons."

Wolf felt the *sekasha* downstairs activate their shields, blooms
of magic against his awareness. Bladebite was saying something low
and fast in High Elvish.

"*Naekanain*," someone cried in badly accented Elvish—*I do not
understand*—while the first speaker repeated in English, "Put down
the weapons!"

Wolf cursed. Apparently the police officers didn't speak
Elvish, and his *sekasha* didn't speak English. Wolf called the winds
and wrapped them about him before going to the top of the stairs.

There were two dark-blue-uniformed policemen crouched in
the front door, keeping pistols leveled at the *sekasha* who had their
ejae drawn. The officers looked human but, with oni, appearances
could be deceiving. Both were tall enough to be oni warriors. The
disguised warriors favored red hair while one policeman was pale
blond and the other dark brown. The blond motioned with his left

hand, as if trying to keep both his partner and the elves from acting.

"*Naekanain*," the blond repeated, and then added. "*Pavuyau Ruve*. Czernowski, just chill. They're the viceroy's personal guard."

"I know who the fuck they are, Bowman."

"If you know that," Wolf said, "then you know that they have the right to go where I want them to go, and do what I want them to do."

Bowman flicked a look up at him and then returned his focus on the *sekasha*. "Viceroy, have them put down their weapons."

"They will only when you do," Wolf said. "If you have not forgotten, we are at war."

"But not with us," Bowman growled.

Czernowski scoffed, and it saddened Wolf that he was closer to the mark.

"The oni have been living in Pittsburgh as disguised humans for years," Wolf said. "Until we're sure you're not oni, we must treat you as if you were. Lower your weapons."

Bowman hesitated, eyeing the *sekasha* as if he was considering how likely it was that he and his partner could overwhelm Wolf's guard. Wolf wasn't sure if Bowman's hesitation was born from overestimating his own abilities, or total ignorance of the *sekasha's*.

Finally, Bowman made a show of cautiously holstering his pistol. "Come on, Czernowski. Put it away."

The other policeman seemed familiar, although Wolf wasn't sure how; he rarely interacted with the Pittsburgh police. Wolf studied the two men. Unlike elves, where one could normally guess a person's clan, humans needed badges and patches to tell themselves apart. The officers' dark blue uniforms had shoulder patches and gold badges identifying them as Pittsburgh police. Bowman's brass nameplate read *B. Pedersen*. Czernowski's nameplate was unhelpful, giving only a first initial of *N*.

"I know you," Wolf said to Czernowski.

"I would hope so," the officer said. "You took the woman who was going to be my wife away from me. You ripped her right out of her species. You might think you've won, but I'm getting her back."

Wolf recognized him then—this was Tinker's Nathan, who bristled at him when Wolf collected his *domi* from the Faire. The uniform had thrown Wolf; he hadn't realized the man was a police officer.

At the Faire, Czernowski had acted like a dog guarding a bone. Even though Tinker had stated over and over again that she was leaving with Wolf, Czernowski had clung to her, refusing to let her leave.

"Tinker is not a thing to be stolen away," Wolf told the man. "I did not *take* her. She chose me, not you. She is my *domi* now."

"I've seen the videotape." Nathan indicated the open box of DVDs. "I know what she is, but I don't care. I still love her, and I'm going to get her back."

"Who gives a fuck?" the thrice-damned photographer shouted behind Wolf. "It doesn't give these pointed-ear royalist freaks the right to break down my door and trash my stuff. I'm a tax-paying American! They can't—"

There was a loud thud as he was slammed up against his broken wall to silence him.

"Sir, can you step aside?" Bowman started cautiously upstairs before Wolf answered.

Wolf stepped back to make way for the two policemen.

The policemen took in the open window, the recording of Tinker in the garden, the smashed-down door, the broken wallpaper now stained with blood, and the broken-nosed paparazzi in Dark Harvest's hold.

"It's about time," the photographer cried. "Get these goons off me!"

"Please step away from him," Bowman told Dark, his hand dropping down to rest on his pistol. He repeated the order in bad Elvish. "*Naeba Kiyau.*"

"He's to be detained." Wolf wanted it clear what was to be done with the photographer before relinquishing control of him. "And these buildings evacuated so I can demolish them."

"You can't do that." Bowman pulled out a pair of handcuffs. "According to the treaty—"

"The treaty is now null and void. I am now the law in Pittsburgh, and I say that this man is to be detained indefinitely and these buildings will be demolished."

"The fuck you are." Czernowski spat the words. "In Pittsburgh we're the law and you're guilty of breaking and entering, assault and battery, and I'm sure I can think of a few more."

Czernowski reached for Wolf's arm and instantly had three swords at his throat.

"No," Wolf shouted to keep the policeman from being killed. Into the silence that suddenly filled the house, Tinker's recorded voice groaned, "Oh gods, yes, right there, oh, that's so good."

Bowman caught Czernowski as the policeman started to surge forward with a growl. "Czernowski!" Bowman slammed him against the wall. "Just deal with it! He's rich and powerful and she's fucking him. What part of this does not make sense to you? He drives a Rolls Royce and all the elves in Pittsburgh grovel at his feet. You think any bitch would pick a stupid Pole like you when she could have him?"

"He could have had anyone. She was mine."

"The fuck she was," Bowman growled. "If you'd scored once with her, all the bookies in Pittsburgh would know. You were always a long shot in the betting pool, Nathan. You were too stupid for her—and too dumb to realize that."

Czernowski glared at his partner, face darkening, but he stopped struggling to stand panting with his anger.

Bowman watched his partner for a minute before asking, "Are we good now?"

Czernowski nodded and flinched as Tinker's recorded voice gave a soft wordless moan of delight.

Bowman crossed to a section of the broken wall and pressed something and the sound stopped. "Viceroy, none of us like this any more than you do, but under international law, as of five years ago, this scumbag is within his rights to make this video."

"He's under elfin law now, and what he has done is unforgivable."

"Your people don't have technology capable of this." Bowman waved a hand at the wallpaper. "So you don't have laws to govern capturing digital images."

Wolf scoffed at the typical human sidestepping. "Why do humans nitpick justice to pieces? Can't you see that you've frayed it apart until it doesn't hold anything? There is right and then there is wrong. This is wrong."

"This isn't my place to decide, Viceroy. I'm just a cop. I only know human law, and as far as I last heard, human law still applies."

"The treaty says that any human left on Elfhome during Shutdown falls under elfin rule. The gate in orbit has failed; it is currently and always will be, Shutdown."

Bowman wiped the expression off his face. "Until my superiors confirm this, I have to continue to function with standard protocol and I can't arrest this man."

"Then I'll have him executed."

"I *can* put him in protective custody," Bowman said.

"As long as protective custody means a small cell without a window, I'll agree to that," Wolf said.

"We'll see what we can do." Bowman moved to handcuff the photographer.

Wolf felt a deep yet oddly distanced vibration, as if a bowstring had been drawn and released to thrum against his awareness. He recognized it—someone nearby was tapping the power of the Wind Clan Spell Stone. Wolf thought that he and Tinker were the only Wind Clan *domana* in Pittsburgh—and he hadn't taught Tinker even the most basic spells . . .

As the vibration continued, an endless drawing of power from the stones, cold certainty filled him. It could only be Tinker.

Tinker and her *sekasha* had neared the far side of the Ghostlands, crossing once again into Pittsburgh but on the opposite side of the valley. The road climbed the steep hill in a series of sharp curves. As they crossed the cracked pavement, Stormsong laughed and pointed out a yellow warning street sign. It depicted a truck about to tip over as it made the sharp turn—a common sight in Pittsburgh—but someone had added words to the pictograph.

"What does it say?" Pony asked.

"Watch for Acrobatic Trucks," Stormsong translated the English words to Elvish.

The others laughed and moved on, scanning the mixed woods.

"You speak English?" Tinker fell into step with Stormsong.

"Fuckin' A!" Stormsong said with the correct scornful tone that such a stupid question would be posed.

Tinker tripped and nearly fell in surprise. Stormsong caught Tinker by the arm and warned her to be careful with a look. Most of

Tinker's time with Windwolf's *sekasha* had been spent practicing her High Elvish, a stunningly polite language. Stormsong had just dropped a mask woven out of words.

"For the last twenty-some years, I pulled every shift I could to stay in Pittsburgh—" Stormsong continued. "—even if it meant bowing to that stuck-up bitch, Sparrow."

"Why?" Tinker was still reeling. Many elves first learned English in England when Shakespeare still lived and kept the lilting accent even if they modernized their sentence structure and word choice. Stormsong spoke true *Pitsupavute*, sounding like a native.

"I like humans." Stormsong stepped over a fallen tree in one long stride and paused to offer a hand to Tinker; the automatic politeness now seemed jarringly out of place. "They don't give a fuck what everyone else thinks. If they want something that's right for them, they don't worry about what the rest of the fucking world thinks."

The warrior's bitterness surprised Tinker. "What do you want?"

"I had doubts about being a *sekasha*." She shrugged like a human, lifting one shoulder, instead of clicking her tongue like an elf would. "Not anymore. Windwolf gave me a year to get my head screwed on right. I like being *sekasha*. I do have—as the humans say—issues."

That explained the short blue hair and the slight rebel air about her.

Stormsong suddenly spun to the left, pushing Tinker behind her even as she shouted the guttural command to activate her magical shields. Magic surged through the blue tattoos on her arms and flared into a shimmering blue that encompassed her body. Stormsong drew her ironwood sword and crouched into readiness. Instantly other *sekasha* activated their shields and drew their swords as they pulled in tight around Tinker. They scanned the area but there was nothing to see.

They were in the no-man's-land of the Rim, where tall young ironwoods mixed with Earth woods and jagger bushes in a thick, nearly impassable tangle. They stood on a deer trail, a path only one person wide, meandering through the dense underbrush. For a moment no one moved or spoke. Tinker realized that the birds had gone silent; even they didn't want to draw the attention of whatever had spooked Stormsong.

Pony made a gesture with his left hand in blade talk.

"Something is going to attack," Stormsong whispered in Elvish, once again becoming the *sekasha*. "Something large. I'm not sure how soon."

"*Yatanyai?*" Pony whispered a word that Tinker didn't recognize. Stormsong nodded.

"What does she see?" Tinker whispered.

"What will be." Pony indicated that they should start back the way they had come. "We're in a position of weakness. We should retreat to—"

Something huge and sinuous as a snake flashed out of the shadows. Tinker got the impression of scales, a wedge-shaped head, and a mouth full of teeth before Pony leaped between her and the monster. The creature struck Pony with a blow that smashed him aside, his shields flashing as they absorbed the brunt of the damage. It whipped toward Tinker, but Stormsong was already in the way.

"Oh, no, you don't!" The female *sekasha* blocked a savage bite at Tinker. "Get back, *domi*—you're attracting it!"

A blur of motion, the beast knocked Stormsong down, biting at her leg, her shield gleaming brilliant blue between its teeth. The Blades swung their swords, shouting to distract the creature. Releasing Stormsong, the creature leapt to perch high up the trunk of an oak. As it paused there, Tinker saw it fully for the first time.

It was long and lean, twelve feet from nose to tip of whipping tail. Despite a shaggy mane, its hide looked like blood red snake scales. Long-necked and short-legged, it was weirdly proportioned; its head seemed almost too large for its body, with a heavy jawed mouth filled with countless jagged teeth. Clinging to the side of the tree with massive claws, it hissed at them, showing the teeth.

Its mane lifted like a dog's hackles, and a haze shimmered to life over the beast, like heat waves coming off hot asphalt. Tinker could feel the presence of magic on her *domana* senses, like static electricity prickling against the skin. The second Blade, Cloudwalker, fired his pistol. The bullets struck the haze—making it flare at the point of impact—and dropped to the ground, inert. Tinker felt the magic strengthen as the kinetic energy of the bullet fed into the spell, fueling it.

"It's an oni shield!" Tinker cried out in warning. "Hitting it will only make it stronger."

Stormsong got to her feet, biting back a cry of pain. "Go, run, I'll hold it!"

Pony caught Tinker by her upper arm, and half carried her, half dragged her through the thicket.

"No!" Tinker cried, knowing that if it weren't for her safety, the others wouldn't abandon one of their own.

"Domi." Pony urged her to run faster. "If we cannot hit it, then we have no hope of killing it."

Tinker thought furiously. How do you hurt something you can't hit but could bite you? Wait—maybe that was it! She snatched the pistol from the holster at Pony's side and jerked out of his hold. Here, under the tall ironwoods, the jagger brushes had grown high, and animals had made low tunnel-like trails through them. Ducking down, Tinker ran down a path, the gun seeming huge in her hands, heading back toward the wounded *sekasha*. The thorns tore at her bare arms and hair.

"Tinker *domi!*" Pony cried behind her.

"Its shield doesn't cover its mouth!" she shouted back.

She burst into the clearing to find Stormsong backed to a tree, desperately parrying the animal's teeth and claws. It smashed aside her sword and leapt, mouth open.

Tinker shouted for its attention, and pulled the gun's trigger. She hadn't aimed at all, and the bullet whined into the underbrush, missing everything.

As the beast turned to face her, and Stormsong shouted warning—a wordless cry of anger, pain, and dismay—Tinker realized the flaw in her plan. She would need to shove the pistol into the creature's mouth before shooting. "Oh fuck."

It was like being hit by a freight train. One moment the beast was running at her and then everything become a wild tumble of darkness and light, dead leaves, sharp teeth, and blood. Everything stopped moving with the creature pinning her to the ground with one massive claw. Then it *pulled*—not on her skin or muscle, but something deeper inside her, something intangible, that she didn't even know existed. Magic flooded through her—hot and powerful as electricity—a seemingly endless torrent from someplace unknown to the monster—and she was just the hapless conduit.

She had lost the gun in the wild tumble. She punched at its head, trying to get it off her as the magic poured through her. The massive jaws snapped down on her fist, and suddenly the creature froze—teeth holding firm her hand, not yet breaking skin. Its eyes widened, as if surprised to see her under it, her hand in its mouth. She panted, scared now beyond words, as the magic continued to thrum through her bones and skin. Her hand seemed so very small inside the mouthful of teeth.

A sword blade appeared over her, the tip pressing up against the creature's shields, aimed at its right eye. The tip slid forward slowly as if it was being pressed through concrete.

"Get off her," Pony growled, leaning his full weight onto his sword, little by little driving the point through the shields. "Now!"

For a moment, they seemed stuck in amber—the monster, Pony, her—caught in place and motionless. There came a high thrilling whistle from way up high, bursting the amber. The creature released her hand and leapt backward. She scrambled wildly in the other direction. Pony caught hold of her, hugging her tight with his free hand, his shields spilling down over her, encompassing her.

"Got her!" he cried, and backed away, the others closing ranks around them.

The whistle blew again, so sharp and piercing a sound that even the monster checked to look upward.

Someone stood on the Westinghouse Bridge that spanned the valley, doll-small by the distance. Against the summer-blue sky, the person was only a dark silhouette—too far away to see if he was man, elf, or oni. The whistle trilled, and, focused on the sound, Tinker realized that it was two notes, close together, a shrill discord.

The monster shook its head as if the sound hurt and bounded away, heading for the bridge, so fast it seemed it teleported from place to place.

The whistler spread out great black wings, resolving all

question of race. A tengu, the oni spies created by blending oni with crows. Tinker could guess which one—Riki. What she couldn't guess was why he had just saved them, or how.

"*Domi.*" Pony eclipsed the escaping tengu and his monstrous pursuer. He peered intently at her hands and then tugged at her clothing, examining her closely. "You are hurt."

"I am?"

"Yes." He produced a white linen handkerchief that he pressed to a painful area of her head. "You should sit."

She started to ask why, but sudden blackness rushed in, and she started to fall.

2: GO ASK ALICE

Tinker fell a long time in darkness.

She found herself at the edge of the woods near Lain's house, the great white domes of the Observatory gleaming in moonlight. The ironwood forest stood solemn as a cathedral before her. Something white flickered through the night woods, brightness in humanoid form. Like a moth, Tinker was drawn toward the light, entering the forest.

A woman darted ahead of her, wearing an elfin gown shimmering as if formed of fiber optics tapped to a searchlight—brightness weaving through the forest dimness. She was so brilliant white that it hurt to look at her. A red ribbon covered her eyes and trailed down the dress, bloodred against the white. On the ground, the ribbon snaked out into the distance.

It came to Tinker, knowledge seeping into her like oil into a rag, that she knew the woman and they were searching for someone. In the distance was a thumping noise, like an axe biting into wood.

"He knows the paths, the twisted way," the woman told Tinker while they searched for this mystery person. "You have to talk to him. He'll tell you how to go."

"We're looking in the wrong place," Tinker called.

23

"We fell down the hole and through the looking glass," the woman cried back. "He's here! You only have to look!"

Tinker scanned the woods and saw a dark figure flitting through the trees, keeping pace with them. It was a delicate-boned woman in a black mourning dress. A blindfold of black lace veiled her eyes. Tears ran unchecked down her face. At her feet were black hedgehogs, nosing about in the dead litter of the forest floor. In the trees surrounding Black and the hedgehogs was a multitude of crows. The birds flitted from limb to limb, calling "Lost! Lost!" in harsh voices.

"Black knows all about him." Tinker said. "Why don't we ask her?"

"She is lost in her grief," White breathed into Tinker's ear. "There is no thread between you. She has no voice that you will listen to."

The thumping noise came from the direction that they needed to head, speeding up until it sounded like helicopter rotors beating the air.

"Wait!" Tinker reached out to catch hold of White, to warn her. She missed, grabbing air. "The queen is coming. You've murdered time. It's always six o'clock now."

"We can't stand still!" White caught Tinker's hand and they were flying low, like on a hoverbike, dodging trees, the ground covered with a checkerboard design of black and red. "We have to run as fast as we can to keep in the same place. Soon we won't be able to run at all and then all will be lost!"

"Lost! Lost!" cried the crows and Black flew like a silent shadow on Tinker's other side. They had left the hedgehogs behind. The red ribbon of White's blindfold raced on ahead of them, coiling like a snake.

"He eats the fruit of the tree that walks." White stopped them at the edge of a clearing. The ribbon coiled into the clearing and its tip plunged into the ground. "Follow the tree to the house of ice and sip sweetly of the cream."

Feeling with blind fingers, White followed the ribbon, hand over hand, out into the clearing. The bare forest floor was black, and grew blacker still, until the woman was sheer white against void with red thread wrapped around her fingers. Tinker took hold of the thread and followed out into the darkness. Beyond the edge of the clearing, she started to float as if weightless. Tinker tried to grip tight to the red ribbon, but it was so thin that she lost track of it and started to fall upward. The woman caught hold of her, pulling her close, and wrapped the red thread tight around her fingers, making a cat's cradle. "There, no matter what, you can always find me with this."

Turning away, the woman pulled on the ribbon, and pearls started to pop out of the ground, strung on the thread. "It starts with a pearl necklace."

Tinker was drifting upward, faster and faster. Black and her crows flew up to meet her in a rustle of wings, crying, "Lost, lost."

Tinker opened her eyes to summer sky framed by oak leaves. Acorns clustered on the branches, nearly ready to fall. A cardinal sang its rain song someplace overhead.

With a slight rustle, Pony leaned over her, bruised and battered himself, worry in his eyes. "*Domi*, are you well?"

Tinker blinked back tears. "Yes, I'm fine." She sat up, trying to ignore the pain in her head. "How is everyone else?"

"Stormsong is hurt. We have called for help but we should start for the hospice in case it returns . . ."

"Its eyes are open," Stormsong said from where she lay on her side, a bloody bandage around the leg that the creature had bitten. "It's not coming back."

"What the hell does that mean?" Tinker asked.

"It means what it means," Stormsong groaned.

"There is no sign of the beast," Rainlily said.

"Okay," Tinker said only because they seemed to be waiting for her to say something. How did she end up in charge?

Almost in answer, a sudden roar of wind announced the arrival of Wolf Who Rules Wind, head of the Wind Clan, also known as her husband, Windwolf. Riding the winds with the Wind Clan's magic, he flew down out of the sky and landed on the barren no-man's-land of the Rim. He dressed in elfin splendor. His duster of cobalt-blue silk, hand-painted with a stylized white wolf, whipped out behind him like a banner. He was beautiful in the way only elves could be—tall, lean, and broad-shouldered with a face full of elegant sharp lines. With a word and gesture, he dismissed his magic. Released, the winds sighed away.

Beauty, power, and the ability to fly like Superman—what more could a girl want?

"Beloved." Windwolf knelt beside her and folded her into his arms. "What happened? Are you hurt? I felt you tap the clan's spell stones and pull a massive amount of power."

The "stones" were granite slabs inscribed with spells located on top of a vastly powerful ley line that the *domana* accessed remotely via their genome. Until Windwolf unleashed his rage on the oni, Tinker hadn't realized the power that the stones represented. In one blinding flash of summoned lightning, it suddenly became clear why the *domana* ruled the other elfin castes. Somehow, the monster had tapped and funneled the power through her.

"Oh, is that what the fuck it did to me?" And with that, she lost control of the tears she'd been keeping at bay. What was it about him that made her feel so safe in a way not even Pony could? She hugged him tightly, trusting he would make it right. As she wallowed in the luxury of being sheltered by the only force besides nature that seemed larger than herself, Windwolf turned his attention to Pony.

"Little Horse, what happened?" Windwolf's voice rumbled in his chest under her head, like contained thunder. "Is anyone hurt?"

"We were attacked by a very large creature." Pony went on to describe the fight in a few short sentences, ending with, "Stormsong took the brunt of the damage."

"We need to get her to the hospice." Tinker pulled free of Windwolf's hug, smeared the tears out of her eyes, and started for Stormsong. "The thing bit her in the leg."

Windwolf crossed to Stormsong in long strides, beating Tinker to the *sekasha's* side. The forest floor was annoyingly uneven; after stumbling slightly, Tinker slowed to baby steps. Pony hovered protectively close as if he expected her to pitch face first into the dead leaves. The big gray Rolls Royce they'd left on the other side of the valley and an ambulance had picked their way through the shattered streets to stop fifty-odd yards short of their location.

"Considering how fucked we were, I'm fine." Stormsong

slapped Windwolf's hands away from the bloody bandage on her leg. "We didn't stop it—it just left."

Heat flushed over Tinker, and the sounds around her went muffled, as if someone had wrapped invisible wool around her head. It was dawning on her that she'd been stupid and nearly got them all killed. By returning to Stormsong, she'd pulled the other *sekasha* back to a fight that they should have lost. She should be dead right now. So fucking dead.

Stormsong glanced up at Tinker, frowned, and murmured something to Windwolf, giving him a slight push away from her. Windwolf looked up at Tinker and stood to sweep her off her feet and into his arms.

"Hey, I can walk!" Tinker cried.

"I know." He carried her toward the Rolls Royce. "I have seen you do it."

Tinker sighed at the nuances lost in the translation. This was how she ended up married to Windwolf—she accepted his betrothal gift without realizing he was proposing to her. "There is nothing wrong with my legs."

He eyed her bare legs draped over his arm. "No. There is not. They are very nice legs."

She studied him. All told, they had spent very little time with each other and she was still getting to know him. She was beginning to suspect, though, that he had a very subtle but strong sense of humor. "Are you teasing me?"

He said nothing but the corners of his eyes crinkled with a suppressed smile.

She smacked him lightly in the shoulder for teasing her. "You don't have to carry me!"

"But I like to."

"Windwolf," she whined.

He kissed her on her forehead. "You might think you are well, but you are in truth pale and wobbly. You have done what was needed. Let me care for you."

If she insisted on walking, she ran the risk of falling flat on her face. What harm could letting him carry her do, except to her pride? Like so often since he charged into her life, Windwolf left only bad choices for her to make in order to protect her sense of free will—and she was too smart to choose stupidity. Sighing, she lay her head on his shoulder and let him carry her.

He tucked her into the Rolls and slid in beside her. Pony got into the front, alongside the *sekasha* who was driving.

She noticed that her T-shirt was shredded over her stomach. Under the tattered material, five shallow claw marks cut across her abdomen; barely breaking the skin, the wounds were already crusted over with scabs. A fraction of an inch deeper, and she would have been gutted. She started to shake.

"All is well, you are fine," Windwolf murmured, holding her.

"I felt so helpless. There was nothing I could do to hurt it. I wish I could do the things you do."

"You can. I gave you that ability when I made you a Wind Clan *domana*."

"I know, I know, I have the genetic key to the Wind Clan spell stones." Which was how the monster sucked power through her. "What I don't know is *how* to use the spell stones. I want to learn."

"I was wrong not to teach you earlier." He took her hand. "I allowed myself to be distracted from my duties to you at Aum Renau; I should have started to teach you then."

"You'll teach me now?"

"Tomorrow we will start your lessons." He kissed her knuckles. "You will also have to learn how to use a sword."

"Shooting practice with a gun would probably be more useful."

"The sword is for your peers, not your enemies. Currently you have the queen's protection. No one can call insult on you or challenge you to a duel. But that protection will not last forever."

"*Pfft*, like random violence solves anything."

"True, it rarely does, but you need to know how to protect yourself and your beholden."

She made another noise of disgust. "What you elves—" She saw the look on his face and amended it. "—we elves call civilized. Can I still have the gun?"

"Yes, beloved, you may have the gun too. I will find comfort knowing you can defend yourself."

"Especially with a monster running around that sees me as

some kind of power drink." She winced at her tone—he wasn't the one she was upset with.

"Reinforcements should be arriving soon, but until then Pittsburgh will not be safe."

"What reinforcements?"

"After you and Little Horse were kidnapped, I realized that there were more oni in the area than Sparrow previously led me to believe. I sent for reinforcements; the queen is sending troops via airship from Easternlands. They should arrive shortly. Unfortunately, this will pull the Fire Clan and probably the Stone Clan into the fight—which is why I'm thinking you should learn how to use a sword."

"Why is it a bad thing that other clans are going to help fight the oni? Isn't this everyone's problem?"

"We hold only what we can protect." Windwolf squeezed her hand; she wasn't sure if it was to comfort her or to seek comfort for himself. "By admitting that we need help, we have put our monopoly on Pittsburgh at risk. The other clans might want part of the city for services rendered in fixing this problem. The humans will fall under someone else's rule."

"You've got to be kidding! Why?"

"Because we cannot protect all of Pittsburgh from the oni. The crown will mediate a compromise."

"Couldn't your father, as head of the Wind Clan, have sent us help?"

"He has. He sent *domana* to Aum Renau and the other East Coast settlements. It is a great comfort to me to know that they are protected. The *domana* aren't that numerous, and the clans that can help are limited to those who have spell stones within range of Pittsburgh."

"This is all my fault," Tinker whispered.

"Hush, this battle is part of a war that started before even I was born."

She snuggled against him, logic failing to squash the guilty feeling inside of her. She was distracted, however, by something very hard under her. "Do you have something in your pocket? Or are you just happy to see me?"

"What? Oh, yes." Windwolf pulled a small fabric bundle out of his pants pocket. "This is for you."

"What's this?" Tinker eyed it tentatively. Accepting a similar package from Windwolf had indicated her acceptance of his marriage proposal—when she didn't realize the significance of his gift. She still had mixed feelings about being married to Windwolf. As a lover, Windwolf was all that she would want— warm, gentle, and caring wrapped in a sexy body—and she loved him deeply.

It was the whole marriage thing—having someone else's will and future joined to hers. They were building "their home" for "their people" and someday, maybe, "their children." Being the viceroy's wife, too, came with more responsibilities than she wanted; people were entrusting her with their lives. So far, the good outweighed the bad—but with elves "till death do us part" meant a very long time.

"Before the queen summoned me from Pittsburgh, I ordered clothes and jewelry to be made for you. I know that they are not of the style you might pick for yourself. It is important, though, that you look your best in front of the crown and the other clans."

"Okay." She pulled loose the bow and unwrapped the fabric. Inside were four small velvet pouches with drawstring pulls. She opened the first to the glitter of gems. "Oh!"

She gasped as she poured diamonds out into her palm. Over a foot of necklace studded with pea-sized diamonds. "Oh my! They're gorgeous!"

As she lifted them up, the afternoon sun prismed into a million tiny rainbows.

"They will look lovely against your skin." Windwolf dropped a kiss on her throat.

The second bag spilled rubies into her hand like fire, but as she lifted up the strand, it reminded her of the red ribbon in her dream. The third bag held a matching bracelet.

"They're beautiful," she said truthfully, but still put them away.

The fourth bag held a pearl necklace. She couldn't keep the dismay off her face.

"You don't like them?"

"I had a bad dream after the beast knocked me out. I was looking for something in a forest with this woman. She had a long red ribbon tied around her eyes and on the other end of it was a pearl necklace."

She'd wanted him to say, "It was just a dream," but instead he said, "Tell me all of your dream."

"Why?"

"Sometimes dreams are warnings. It is not wise to ignore them."

So she said, "It was just a dream." How could he rebuke her so easily with just his eyes? "I'm still me. I'm still mostly human—not elf. I would know by now if I had the ability to see the future."

"In elves it is carried by the female line; being that humans and elves can interbreed with fertile results, we must be very similar." He put away the pearl necklace. "It is the nature of magic to splinter things down to possibilities. Even humans without magic can see where the splintering will happen, and the possible outcomes. Humans call it an 'educated guess.' In the past, where magic would leak through natural gates from Elfhome to Earth, there were often temples with oracles predicting the future."

"So it doesn't matter if I'm mostly human or partly elf?"

"Tell me your dream." Windwolf ran the back of his hand lightly down her cheek.

So she described what she could remember. "Both women are someone I know but not really. Movie stars or something like that— I've only seen pictures of them."

"Both women wore blindfolds? The *intanyei seyosa* wears one when she's predicting. It helps block out things that would distract her from her visions, but also it is a badge of her office."

Tinker remembered then her one encounter with the queen's *intanyei seyosa*, Pure Radiance. The oracle had worn a white dress and red blindfold.

"So I'm dreaming that they're dreaming? That's very Escheresque."

Windwolf looked confused.

"Escher is a human artist that my grandfather liked; his pictures are all tricks of perspective."

"I see."

"Well, I don't. What does it mean?" She prodded the bags with a finger. "That you were going to give me jewelry? What is so dangerous about the necklaces?"

"Dreams are rarely straightforward. Most likely the necklaces represent something else."

"Like what?"

"I do not know, but it might be wise to find out."

3: NUTS AND BOLTS

Wolf spotted Wraith at the fringe of the Ghostlands when he flew back to Turtle Creek. He'd left his *domi* in the care of his household at Poppymeadow's enclave and returned to help deal with the beast that attacked her. He dropped down to land beside his First.

"I don't know what Storm Horse was thinking," Wraith growled in greeting. "How did he end up with all the babies?"

Little Horse had chosen the five youngest *sekasha* to make up the Hand that accompanied Tinker into Turtle Creek; not one of them was over three hundred. True, any death would have been grievous, but to lose the five youngest would have been a blow to the close-knit band of warriors.

"They are the ones my *domi* is most comfortable with." Wolf knew that Wraith was truly rattled if he was using the nickname, as some of the "babies" were in truth older than Wolf. His First Hand didn't like to remind him that he was impossibly young for his level of responsibilities.

"Oni, they could have handled," Wraith allowed and then handed a sheet of paper to Wolf. "But not an oni dragon. I'm amazed any of them are still alive."

Wolf recognized Rainlily's fluid hand in the drawing. The

low-slung creature looked like a cross between a ferret and a snake. "An oni dragon? Are you sure?"

Wraith clicked his tongue. "It's much smaller than the one we fought when we closed the gate between Earth and Onihida, and the coloring is different. It might be just a less dangerous relative, like we have the wyvern cousins to our dragons, or perhaps a hatchling. It would explain how they survived."

The oni war had been shortly before Wolf was born. A Stone Clan trading expedition had discovered the way from Earth to Onihida by accident. When the survivors managed to return to Elfhome with their tale of capture and torture, the clans united to send a force to Earth to stop the oni spreading from Onihida to Earth, and then, possibly to Elfhome. Wraith Arrow and others of Wolf's First Hand had been part of the battle.

"Are oni dragons that dangerous?" Wolf folded the paper and tucked it away. He would have to let the Earth Interdimensional Agency know of this new threat if they couldn't kill the beast quickly. The EIA could best spread warnings through the humans.

"We lost two dozen *sekasha* in the caves to the beast. We couldn't hurt it. It could—" Wraith frowned as he searched for a word. "—*sidestep* through walls as if they didn't exist, and it called magic like you do."

"How did you kill it?"

"When the Stone Clan pulled down the gate and the connection between the worlds broke, its attack pattern totally changed. It dropped its shield and became like a mink in a chicken coop, stupid with bloodlust. We boxed it in so it couldn't turn and we hacked it to pieces."

"Maybe the oni were controlling it magically. Little Horse said that the tengu used a whistle to call it off them—perhaps the sound only triggered a controlling spell. Earth doesn't have magic."

"So their control over it vanished and we were fighting the true beast?"

Wolf nodded. "Perhaps."

"So the key is to kill the controller first."

"Perhaps." Wolf didn't want to fall into a wrong mind-set. He crouched beside the torn earth and spilt blood to find the monster's tracks. They were as long as his forearm, with five claw marks splayed like a hand. Pressed into the dirt at the center of one track was one of Tinker's omnipresent bolts, a bright point of polished aluminum glittering in the black earth. It must have fallen from her pocket during the fight. Wolf picked it out of the dirt, realizing for the first time the size of his beloved compared to what had attacked her. Gods above, sometimes he wished her sense of self-preservation matched her courage; she couldn't keep leaping into the void and swimming back. One of these times, the void was going to drink her down. He rolled the bolt around his palm to shake off the dirt, thinking he should talk to her about being more careful, only he didn't want to fall into the trap of becoming her teacher.

Wraith crouched beside Wolf, and stirred his fingers through the dirt. "*Domi* showed great courage in protecting Little Horse. She needs, though, someone who can steer her away from the dangers. Little Horse is lost at summer court."

From Wraith's tone, the *sekasha* also thought that Windwolf was too deep in the first throes of love to think clearly. Perhaps he was. "Are you volunteering?"

Wraith tilted his head. "Do you want me to?"

Wolf considered, tumbling the bolt through his fingers. Wraith was not the first to come forward in the last two days and let him know that they'd be willing to change allegiance to Tinker. He'd given them all permission to advance their case to Tinker since she needed at least four more sekasha to make a Hand. Wraith, though, was his First, and Wolf depended heavily on him. Without Sparrow, losing Wraith would cripple Wolf. "No. I need you. Others plan to offer, she will have plenty to choose from."

"Yes, but will they guide her?"

Do I want her guided? That was the true question. He'd benefited greatly by choosing *sekasha* who had served his grandfather, but they had brought subtle pressure to bear on him at all times. This conversation itself was a perfect example of their influence on him. Their persuasion extended out to the rest of the household, reinforcing the caste differences so that Wolf was always correctly above everyone. When the queen summoned Wolf to Aum Renau, he'd left Little Horse behind to guard over Tinker. The youngest of the *sekasha*, his blade brother had also been raised in a household where the caste lines had been allowed to blur. Little Horse would be open-minded, affectionate, and the least likely to try and change Tinker. Wolf had hated the necessity to make her elf in body—he didn't want to force her, even by subtle persuasion, to become elf in mind and habit.

No, I do not want her guided in the way that Wraith would.

He would speak with Tinker, but not point her toward the older *sekasha*. He would allow her and Little Horse to find those they were most comfortable with.

"On this, I will act." He let Wraith know that the conversation was closed, that he would not discuss it farther. He turned his attention back to the oni dragon.

The main fight area was a chaos of torn earth and blood. The *sekasha* might be able to read the course of events, but to him it was only churned earth. The bark of surrounding trees was gouged in the dragon's five-clawed pattern.

"It had *domi* pinned. Little Horse attempted to penetrate its shield." Wraith pointed at a spot on the ground, and at the nearest scored tree. "It leapt to that tree. Rainlily said that the tengu was on the bridge, so that tree there"—Wraith pointed to a distant tree with claw marks halfway up the towering trunk—"is the next set."

The leap meant the creature was stunningly powerful without magic.

"Let's see where the trail leads."

The railing of the bridge was scored deep by the dragon's claws. After that, however, the track became impossible to follow with the naked eye. The *sekasha* considered the bridge deck, scuffing it with their boots.

"Too much metal." Wraith voiced the *sekasha*'s collective opinion.

Wolf nodded; he'd thought as much. Using magic to track was rarely possible in Pittsburgh with its omnipresent web of metal in the roads, the buildings, and the power lines overhead.

There was whistle from the rear guard, indicating the arrival of a friendly force. Still, the *a* around him went alert when a limo belonging to the EIA pulled to a stop at the far end of the bridge. The oni had infiltrated every level of the UN police force; they could no longer automatically assume the EIA was friendly.

With a cautiousness that made it clear that he understood his position, Director Derek Maynard got out of his limo and walked the rest of the distance to Wolf. Apparently Maynard had spent the morning dealing with humans, as he was in dressed in the dark solid suit that spoke of power among men. Wolf thought it might be the way they perceived color.

"Wolf Who Rules *ze Domou.*" Over the years, Maynard had picked up much of the elfin body language. He projected politely constrained anger as he bowed elegantly.

"Director." Wolf used his title without his name to mildly rebuke him.

Maynard bowed his head slightly, acknowledging the censure. He paused for a minute, nostrils flared, before speaking. He looked worn and tired. Time wore Maynard down at an alarming rate; in twenty short years he had gone from a young man to middle-aged. Gazing at him, Wolf realized that in a few decades he'd lose his friend.

If I could have only made him an elf too. But no, that would have destroyed Maynard's value as a "human" representative.

"Windwolf." Maynard chose to continue in English, probably because it placed him in the less subservient role. "I wish you would have warned me about declaring the treaty void."

Wolf sighed, it was going to be one of those conversations. "You know the terms. Pittsburgh could exist as a separate entity only while it continued to return to Earth."

"You've said nothing in the last two days about voiding the treaty."

"And I haven't said anything about the sun setting, but it has and will."

"The sun setting does not cut me off at the knees."

Wolf glanced down at Maynard's legs, and confirmed that they were still intact. Ah, an English saying he hadn't heard before. "Derek, pretend I don't understand human politics."

"The treaty is between the humans and the elves." Maynard followed the human tendency to talk slowly and in short sentences in the face of confusion. It made the time to enlightenment agonizingly long, even for an elf. "But the treaty is the basis for many agreements between the United States and the United Nations. It makes Pittsburgh neutral territory controlled by a UN peacekeeper force—the EIA—for the duration of the treaty."

"Ah, with the treaty void, Pittsburgh reverts to control of the United States."

"Yes!"

"No."

"No?" Maynard looked confused.

"Pittsburgh now belongs to the Wind Clan, and I decide who will be my representative with the humans and I choose you."

Maynard took a deep breath as he pressed his palms together, prayerlike, in front of his mouth. He breathed out, took another breath. Windwolf was starting to wonder if he was praying. "Wolf, I thank you for your trust in me," Maynard said finally. "But for me to continue acting as director of the EIA, it would require me to disregard all human laws—and I cannot do that."

"There are no human laws anymore. Humans must obey elfin laws now."

"That's not acceptable. I know you're the viceroy, and as such Pittsburgh falls under your control, but the humans of Pittsburgh will not accept you unilaterally abolishing all human laws and rights."

"These were conditions agreed to by your own people."

"Well, shortsighted as it might have been, it was assumed that if something happened to the gate that Pittsburgh would return to Earth."

"Yes, it was." Wolf did not point out that humans were typically shortsighted, rarely looking past the next hundred years. "But we knew that sooner or later we would have to deal with humans wanting to or needing to remain on Elfhome."

"Yes, of course," Maynard said dryly. He gazed down at the blue paleness of the Ghostlands. "Is your *domi* sure that we're truly stranded? We're still a week before scheduled Shutdown."

"Something fell from orbit. She believes it to be the gate."

"But she could be wrong."

"It's unlikely."

"Let us say that we wait a week to be sure before calling the treaty null and void."

"A week will not make any difference."

"Ah, then it will be no problem." Maynard spread his hands and smiled as if Wolf had agreed.

In that moment, Wolf could see the tactfully charming young officer he had hand-selected out of the UN security force to act as the liaison between human and elf. Maynard had been so young back then. Wolf smiled sadly. "And if I agree to a week?"

"During this week, we draw up an interim treaty that basically extends the original treaty."

"No." Windwolf shook his head. "We could create an interim treaty but the original treaty can not stand. It makes humans too autonomous."

"Pittsburgh has existed as an independent state for thirty years."

"No, not Pittsburgh, humans. All elves belong to a household and to a clan. They hold a very specific position within our society. They are responsible to others, and others are responsible for them. It's the very foundation of our culture, and if humans are to be part of our world, then they must conform to our ways."

"You mean—you want humans to form households? Set up enclaves?"

"Yes. It's imperative. All of our laws are structured on the assumption that the people under our laws are part of our society. You can't be as independent as most humans are and still be part of us."

They searched late into the evening but found nothing more of the dragon. Storm clouds had gathered throughout the day, and as dusk became night, it started to rain. Unable to track the dragon farther, Wolf and his *sekasha* returned to the enclave. He checked first to see how his *domi* was doing. Tinker lay in the center of their shared bed, a dark curl of walnut on the cream satin sheets. Wolf paused beside the footboard to watch his beloved sleep. Despite everything, he found great comfort in seeing her back where she belonged, safe among the people who loved her.

A *saijin* flower sat on the night table, scenting the warm air with its narcotic fragrance. Little Horse slept in a chair beside the bed. The hospice healers had stripped off his wyvern armor; fresh bruises and healing spells overlaid the pale circles of bullet holes from two days ago.

I almost lost them both to the oni, Wolf thought and touched his blade brother's shoulder. "Little Horse."

The *sekasha* opened his eyes after a minute, rousing slowly. "Brother Wolf. I only meant to sit down for a moment." He looked drowsily to the flower beside him. "The *saijin* must have put me asleep."

The narcotic was starting to color Wolf's senses with a golden haze, so he opened the balcony doors to let in rain-damp air.

"Are you well?" Wolf took the other chair, waiting for Little Horse to wake up from his drugged sleep, wondering if he'd made a mistake pairing his blade brother with Tinker. They were both so young to go through so much.

"I'm bruised, that is all." Little Horse rubbed at his eyes. "My shields protected me."

"Good."

"I was thinking about the oni leader, Lord Tomtom, before I drifted off. He checked on our progress either at noon or at midnight. Some days he would make two inspections. It occurred to me that he was rotating between compounds, overseeing two or three of them."

"So the number of oni warriors in the area might be much greater than the sixty you counted?"

Little Horse nodded. "From what I observed, though, the warriors are like sea wargs." His blade brother named a mammal that gathered in colonies on the coast; the male animals fought to gather harems of females, and any cub left unprotected was usually killed and eaten by its own kind. "Command goes to the largest of the group and he rules by cruelty and fear. They fight among themselves, but I saw no weapon practice or drills. I believe that not one of their warriors would be a match for a *sekasha.*"

"That is good to know." It backed what Maynard had told him

at one point. Warned by Tinker, Maynard had begun to secretly sift through his people two months earlier. Using Tinker's description of "cruel and ruthless people with no sense of honor" he found the hidden oni fairly simple to find. So far intensive magical testing had proved his guesses correct.

Little Horse glanced toward the bed and a smile stole onto his face, making him seem younger still. "Despite their large size and savageness, she terrorized them."

Wolf laughed. Little Horse yawned widely, so Wolf stood up and pulled his blade brother to his feet. "Go to bed. The others can keep watch."

"Yes, Brother Wolf." Little Horse hugged him. It was good, Wolf decided, that he paired Tinker with his blade brother. They would protect each other's open and affectionate natures from the stoic older *sekasha*.

After steering Little Horse to his room, Wolf detoured to check on Singing Storm. He expected to find her sleeping when he cracked her door. She turned her head, though, and slit open her eyes. A smile took control of her face. Still she greeted him with a semiformal, "Wolf Who Rules."

He lowered the formality between them. It was her ability to see him as nothing more than a male that made him love her so. "How is my Discord?"

Her smile deepened. "Good and just got better."

"I'm glad." He leaned down and kissed her. She murmured her enjoyment, running her hands up his chest to tangle in his hair. She tasted candy sweet from her favorite gum.

"I've missed you," she whispered into his ear. She meant intimately, like this, because she had guarded over him every day for the last two months. Taking Tinker to be his *domi*, however, had meant an abrupt change in their relationship. They hadn't even had a chance to discuss it afterward.

"I'm sorry."

She nipped him on the earlobe in rebuke. "No matter who, if they were the right one, you would have wanted this."

"It was graceless." He had given her only a few hours warning of his intention to offer for Tinker. She knew him well enough to know that he would want a monogamous relationship as long as Tinker was willing to give him one.

"When did we start to care about grace? Wasn't that the whole point of leaving court, all the false elegance? I like that we're honest with one another—and I like her—which is not surprising since I like humans."

"She's an elf now," Wolf gently reminded her.

"In the body, but not in the mind. She speaks Low Elvish as if she was born to it, yes, but she doesn't know our ways, Wolf. If you don't have time to teach her, then get her a tutor."

Wolf found himself shaking his head. "No. I don't want a stranger trying to force her into court elegance."

"Are you afraid that she will lose all that makes her endearing to you?"

Only Discord would dare to say that to him—but then—that was another reason he loved her. She would risk annoying him to make him face what needed to be faced. For her, he sighed and considered the possibility.

"No," he said after thinking it through. "Yes, I love her humanity and I'll mourn it if she loses it completely, but she is so much more than that."

"Then have someone teach her. She nearly got us all killed today because she couldn't bear to sacrifice me."

He knew better than to argue with Discord on that but was pleased with Tinker's decision. It was Tinker's courage and ability to pull off the impossible that had initially attracted him to her, and he would have been deeply saddened to lose Singing Storm. "I'm trying to find a solution to this. I know she needs to be taught our customs, but I don't want her to necessarily conform."

"I never said anything about conforming." Discord nuzzled into his neck. "Conforming is for chickens."

He laughed into her short blue hair. "That's my Discord." He kissed her and drew away to consider her. From her hair to her boots, Discord challenged everything elfin. Yet of all his *sekasha*, she was the only one that had grown up at court and had high etiquette literally beaten into her. There was no one more knowledgeable, yet less likely, to force those skills on Tinker.

"What is it that you want of me?" she asked.

"You know me too well." He tugged on her rattail braid. "I want you to keep close to my *domi* and be there when she needs guidance."

"Pony is her First." Discord switched to English, a sign that she wanted to be bluntly truthful. "I'll be stomping all over his toes. I don't want to piss him off. He's one of the few that never said shit to me about being a mutt."

"Pony is not the type to put pride before duty. He loves Tinker, but he knows that he doesn't fully understand her. He hasn't spent enough time in Pittsburgh, away from our people . . ."

"Like me?" It was a point of sadness between them. For decades they had ignored all the little signs that they could not be more than *domou* and beholden. The fact that she would choose Pittsburgh over being with him had made clear that while they were good together, they were not right.

"Like you." Wolf took her hand, kissed it, and moved on. "Humans are still mysterious to him."

She thought for a moment and then returned to Elvish. "As long as it does not anger Storm Horse, I will be there for her."

4: ON GOSSAMER DEATH

The next morning, shortly after dawn, the oni made their first attack. Wolf heard a muffled roar and then the loud anguished wail of a wounded gossamer. Luckily, his people were already awake and ready. Only Tinker, having been drugged the night before, still slept.

"Have Poppymeadow lock down the enclave," Wolf told Little Horse. "I'm leaving you just with her guards and Singing Storm. Everyone else with me."

Wolf arrived at the airfield, though too late to scry the direction of the attack. All he could do was watch the gossamer die in the pale morning light. The great living airship wallowed on the ground, its translucent body undulating in pain. The remains of the gondola lay under it, crushed by the massive heaving body. The clear blood of the gossamer pooled on the ground, scenting the air with the ghost of ancient seas.

"We can't get close enough to heal the wound." The gossamer's navigator was weeping openly. "Even if we could, I doubt we could save her. It's a massive wound, and she's lost too much fluid. My poor baby."

The gossamer let out a long low breathy wail of pain.

"Did you see where it came from?" Wolf wasn't sure what "it" was because none of the crew had seen the attack clearly.

The navigator shook his head. "I felt it hit before I heard anything. She shuddered, and then started to go down, and I jumped clear."

"Here comes another one!" Wraith shouted as he pointed at some type of rocket flashing toward them.

Wolf flung up his widest shield, protecting the crew and *sekasha* surrounding him. "Stay close!"

The rocket struck his wind wall and exploded into a fireball that curved around them, following the edges of his shield. The deflected energy splashed back in a wave of pulverized earth, like a stone thrown into mud.

A piece of metal skimmed overhead and struck the gossamer. The shrapnel smashed the gossamer sideways, blasting through the nerve center of the creature. The airship gave one last agonizing wail and collapsed.

Wolf shifted carefully to maintain his shield and did a wind scry. The scrying followed the disturbance of the rocket path through the air, making it visible to him. It pointed back to a window a few houses down from the paparazzi's spy perch. The Rim had razed all the buildings between the airfield and the street at the first Startup, so he had an equally clear shot back at the sniper.

Wolf summoned a force strike and flung it along the scry. The power arrowed away, plowing a furrow in a straight line to the human structure. The force strike punched its way through the building, reducing the structure instantly to a cloud of dust and a pile of rubble strewn into the alley behind it.

"Have someone escort the crew to safety," Wolf told his First. "The rest, come with me."

Maintaining his shield forced him to move slowly toward the human buildings, following the rut carved out by the force strike. The dust expanded, shrouding the area as he crossed the no-man's-land of the Rim.

"Keep the winds close," Wraith murmured as they reached the street. "There may be more than one nest."

Wolf nodded his understanding. The *sekasha* activated their shields and moved out of his protection. The house had been two stories tall. It made a large hill of rubble, capped by the broken rooftop. If there were any survivors, they'd have to be dug out.

Maynard emerged out of the dust, followed by a score or more of his people in EIA uniforms. All of the EIA were spell-marked, verifying that they were human.

"Wolf Who Rules." Maynard bowed and signaled his people toward the rubble.

"Maynard." Wolf nudged his shield slightly so it wrapped Maynard in his protection.

"What happened?" Maynard eyed the rubble as his people started to sift through it.

Wolf indicated the dead airship with his eyes; maintaining his shields limited his ability to motion with his hands. "Someone fired on what is mine. I returned fire."

Maynard glanced at the distortion around them. "How long can you keep up your shields?"

"There is no reason for concern." The Wind Clan's spell stones rested on a powerful *fiutana* that provided unlimited magic. "My gossamer is dead, but my crew is safe. For that I am thankful."

A call came from the EIA digging through the rubble. Most of the roof had been shifted off. In the debris of the second floor was a female huddled under a sturdy table. She appeared human, as small and dark as Wolf's *domi*. Old bruises, like purple and yellow flowers, marked her face and arms; someone beat her on regular occasions.

She gazed at Wolf with fear. "Don't let them have me! We're like cockroaches to them! Razing this neighborhood is just the start of them stomping us out!"

The human workers moved reluctantly aside to let the *sekasha* claim her. Wraith took out his leatherbound spell case, slipped out a *biatau,* and pressed it to the female's arm.

She whimpered and one of the watching EIA said, "It doesn't hurt. We've all had it done to us."

The simple spell inscribed onto the paper of the *biatau* was merely the first of the spells that the EIA had been subjected to, but it was the quickest and easiest to use as a first screening process. The oni had relied on an optical disguise spell that let them appear human; the *biatau*, when activated, would shatter the illusion and allow their true form to show.

Wraith spoke the verbal command and the spell activated. There was, however, no change to the woman's appearance.

Maynard sighed deeply, as if he saw all the dangerous complications that the woman presented. "She's human."

"Unfortunately." Wolf motioned that the EIA should take her prisoner.

"Here's another one," Bladebite called.

The second person was a large male, badly hurt. Wraith took out another *biatau* with the same spell and used it on the male. There was a ripple of distortion and the male's features shifted slightly to a more feral looking face with short horns protruding from his forehead.

"Oni." Wraith growled out the word.

"He's badly hurt," Maynard said. "The prison has a medical ward. We can take him there."

Wraith jerked the oni up onto his knees.

"Wolf," Maynard said quickly and quietly. "We have protocols on how prisoners are to be treated. The Geneva Convention states that the wounded and sick shall be collected and cared for."

"We do not accede," Wolf said, "to your Geneva Convention."

In one clean motion, Wraith unsheathed his sword and beheaded the oni.

The woman shrieked and tried to launch herself toward the dead body.

"Wolf, you can't do this!" Maynard growled.

"It has been done," Wolf said.

Maynard shook his head. "The treaty, which the elves signed, states that you will adhere to the Geneva Convention in the treatment of prisoners."

"For human prisoners," Wolf said. "We will not take oni prisoners."

Maynard frowned. "That is the only option you're entertaining? A massacre of all the oni?"

"They breed like mice," Wolf said. "We do not fight for today, or this year, or even this century, but for this millennium—and to do so, we must be ruthless. If we leave a hundred alive, in a few years they will be several thousand in number, and in a thousand years, millions. We can not allow them to live, or they will crowd us out of our own home."

"You can't let the elves do this!" the woman wailed. "If we don't stop the elves, they'll turn on us next."

"It's their world." Maynard leveled his gaze and words at his watching men, aiming his words at them alone. "Not ours."

"It was their world!" the woman shouted. "We're stuck here now, so it's ours too."

There was a flaw in Maynard's logic. The old arguments that Maynard could have used to counter her were useless now. Her railing, unfortunately, could lead the humans to dangerous ground, so Wolf interceded.

"We are willing to share with humans. We do not wish to share with oni. A full contingent of royal troops is on its way to Pittsburgh. When they arrive here, their goal will be to find and kill every oni that ever set foot on Elfhome. My people have committed genocide before and have full plans to do it again. I strongly caution you not to put the human race between the royal troops and our enemy."

Whatever impact his words had, however, were lost when the woman suddenly looked past Wolf and shrieked. Wolf turned to see what she was focused on. One of the EIA workers had a small squirming creature in his arms. As the man neared, Wolf realized that the creature was a child, species so far undetermined, but human looking, perhaps four years old.

Wolf sighed. He had hoped it wouldn't come to this; that he would only have to deal with adult oni. Certainly among all of the elves, there were no children. In fact, he was fairly sure that—not counting his *domi*'s unusual status—Little Horse was the youngest elf in Pittsburgh. Unfortunately, when one could breed like mice, one did.

The name tag of the EIA worker holding the child read "U. D. Akavia."

"The child needs to be tested, Akavia," Wolf said.

Akavia's brown eyes went wide; he hadn't considered that the child was anything but what it appeared to be.

"No!" the woman sympathizer cried. "Don't give those monsters my baby!"

Akavia glanced to the woman and then down at the child whimpering in his arms. "She's just a little girl."

"We need to know if she is human or oni." Wolf tried to pose the statement in a nonthreatening way.

"She can't hurt anyone." Akavia covered the girl's small head with a protective hand. His eyes went past Wolf to the *sekasha* behind him.

Of course the human saw only the child, not the female that would be an adult in a decade, nor the army she could produce in the years to come. In truth, even to Wolf, she looked small and helpless.

"Let us test her," Wolf said. "If she is human, we will give her back."

Akavia's eyes narrowed in suspicion. "And if she's oni?"

Yes, Wolf thought as he scanned the hostile faces of the heavily armed EIA force that outnumbered his *sekasha*, that would be a problem.

He sensed the tension going through his *sekasha*, who were growing impatient. He had no doubt that his people would walk unscathed away from a fight with the EIA, but the EIA might not understand this, and he needed all the allies he could muster.

Maynard moved between Wolf and Akavia. Maynard's face set into hard lines, as if bracing himself for a fight. With Wolf or with his own people? "Let us test her."

He left unsaid: *Let us at least find out if we have cause to fight.* Wolf nodded. "That is acceptable."

"Uri David." Maynard motioned to Akavia. Wolf shifted his shields to include the EIA subordinate so Maynard could take the girl into his arms.

"Wraith." Wolf indicated that the *sekasha* was to hand Akavia the *biatau*.

Akavia placed the spell against the child's bruised and dusty arm. When the spell activated, there was no change to the girl's appearance. Relief went through the EIA.

"It proves nothing," Wraith growled. "It's probably mixed blood. The female has all but admitted that she's coupled with the monster."

Maynard's gaze skipped to Wraith and then came back to Wolf. *Please*, his eyes implored, *let her go.*

Wolf studied the child. She gazed at him with eyes as brown and innocent as his *domi's*. He didn't want to kill this child. Wolf steeled himself and forced himself to remember that an oni wouldn't waver in killing an elfin child or a human child. His people counted on him to do the right thing, no matter how difficult the right thing might be.

How could he winnow the monster from the human?

"Little one, what's your name?" Wolf asked the girl.

"Zi." The girl pointed to the woman. "Mommy's sad."

"Yes, she is. So am I." Wolf let his face show his inner sorrow.

Zi considered him gravely, and then leaned out to pat him gently on the cheek. "Don't be sad. Everything will be a-okay."

Wolf threw out his hand to keep the *sekasha* from reacting. "She has compassion; oni don't have that capacity."

Wraith slowly took his hand from his sword hilt. "So human empathy is a dominant trait?"

"So it seems." Wolf gave the girl a slight smile. "Yes, Zi, everything will be A-okay."

5: TREE THAT WALKS

The dying echoes of thunder pulled Tinker out of the dark sludge of drugged sleep. She opened her eyes to see shadows moving across an unfamiliar ceiling.

Where am I?

For one panicked moment, she thought she was back in the oni compound with the kitsune projecting illusions into her mind. She fought her sheets to sit up, heart pounding, to scan the luxurious bedroom. *Saijin*-induced sleep still clung to her like thick mud, making it hard to think. It took Tinker a minute of comparing all the various places she had slept in the last two months to finally recognize the room. It was the bedroom she and Windwolf had shared a month ago at Poppymeadow's enclave. She remembered now the massive four-poster bed, the carved paneling, and the view to the courtyard orchard. The window stood open to a warm summer morning, letting in air sweet with ripening peaches. Dappled sunlight played across the walls and ceiling. Tinker flopped back into the decadent nest of satin sheets and down pillows, tempted to go back to sleep.

But if she did, she'd probably have another nightmare.

Her groan summoned Pony from his attached bedroom.

"Good morning, *domi*."

Eyes still closed, she grunted at him. "It's not fair to expect me to be polite before I'm fully awake. Where's Windwolf? Did he get back safely last night?"

"He was needed at the Faire Grounds this morning. He took everyone except Stormsong with him."

"How is Stormsong?"

"Her leg bothers her slightly, but she is whole. She is practicing in the swordhall."

That was good news.

Tinker heaved herself back up and rubbed a heavy crust of sleep from her eyes. "Gods, I hate *saijin*. It turns my brain to taffy. What's that for?"

That being one of the *sekasha*'s pistols. While the gun itself was of human make, the black tooled leather holster and belt were elfin. Pony laid it on the bed, a coil of dangerous black on the sea of cream.

"Wolf Who Rules wished you to have it."

Oh, yeah, I asked for a gun.

"It is specially made for the *sekasha*." Pony settled on the bed beside her. "Only parts of it are metal, and those are insulated with plastic, so they don't interfere with our shields. Once you learn magic, it will be important that you don't wear metal."

There was an elaborate system of wood buckles, D-rings, and ties to support the weight of the pistol on the hip without metal. In place of a metal snap, the belt maker had used a heavy plastic substitute.

"Is it loaded?"

"Not yet. I thought you would like to get comfortable with it first."

So they played with the gun. Taking it apart. Putting it together. Strapping on the holster (although it had a tendency to slide on her long silky nightgown.) Drawing the pistol smoothly. Holding it with both hands to keep it steady. Aiming it. And finally, loading and unloading it.

"Wolf Who Rules wants you to start the basics of the sword fighting," Pony said. "It would be unwise for you to wear a sword until you are able to use it. Guns are simple. Point and pull the trigger."

"I'm fine with that." She had no interest in swords. They relied too much on brute force. At five foot nothing, it didn't matter how smart she was, she wasn't going to win a sword fight with an elf. "Okay. I think I'm ready to face the day."

"In that?" Pony indicated her current nightgown and holster outfit.

"I thought I'd start a new fashion statement." Nevertheless, she started to look for the clothes she'd had on the day before. She was going to have to do something about clothes. After being kidnapped twice, she was left with only one T-shirt and one pair of shorts. Everything else in her closet was elfin gowns.

Pony guessed what she was looking for. "They took your clothes to be cleaned."

"Oh no." She went to the window and looked out. Beyond the orchard wall was the kitchen garden and the clothes lines. Windwolf's household staff was hanging up the laundry. Her jeans dangled between several pairs of longer legged pants. Her T-shirt? Oh yes, that had been cut to ribbons by the dragon. "Oh pooh."

Well, she could wear a dress and just go clothes shopping. Of course she didn't have any cash in hand, nor did she ever receive the promised replacements for the ID that the oni stole the night she saved Windwolf's life. It could be sitting in her mailbox back at her loft—if the EIA had been so stupid as to mail it out after she was kidnapped by the oni. Oh gods, what if she'd been declared legally dead after the oni "staged" her death?

She did have Windwolf's entire household at hand. Surely one of the elves was savvy enough to go to the store and buy her clothes. She considered the elves in the garden washing clothes— by hand—in large wooden tubs. Okay, she had clothes at her loft.

Was it a good thing or a bad thing that she was now fashion aware enough to know that those clothes were too scruffy?

Tinker sighed. "I really don't want to run around Turtle Creek in a dress."

"*Domi*, I would rather wait until we could gather a Hand. It would not be wise for us to go alone."

Tinker wasn't getting the hang of the elfin "we" despite having had Pony at her side every moment for nearly two months. She was thinking of just trotting over by herself and seeing how much the Ghostlands had shrunk. Well, she supposed that could wait.

She used her walk-in closet as a dressing room, stripping out of the gun belt and her nightgown. She considered her informal gowns, called day dresses. She had bullied the staff into taking off the long sleeves, but the dresses still had bodices that accented her chest, tight waists, and flowing skirts. Her choices were sable brown, forest green, or jewel red, all in gleaming fairy silk that clung to her like wet paint. The red one, at least, had pockets and a shorter skirt. She had to admit that she looked fairly kicky with her new gun belt riding low on her hip. She added her polished black riding boots and the ruby jewelry that Windwolf had given her. She practiced drawing her pistol and pointed it at the mirror. "You looking at me? Uh? You looking at me?"

"No, *domi*, I cannot see you," Pony said from the other side of the closet door.

She laughed, holstering the pistol. "Did Windwolf find the monster that attacked me and kill it?"

"No."

"Okay." She came out of the closet. "Since we can't do anything about Turtle Creek, let's focus on the monster."

"*Domi*, I do not think we should go after the dragon alone."

"Dragon?"

"It was an oni dragon and very difficult to kill."

"Well, yeah, which is why I should figure out how to kill it. The oni probably have more than one. There has to be a way to take down its shields so anyone with a gun can kill it."

Pony looked at her nervously, as if he suspected she was going to hunt down the oni dragon and poke it with sticks.

Tinker felt the need to reassure him that she didn't have anything that radical in mind. "I want to start with Lain; she's a xenobiologist. When you've got a problem outside your field of specialty, you go to an expert."

⁘

A flatbed semi trailer sat parked in front of Lain's stately

Victorian mansion. A yellow canvas tarp covered something lumpy. The xenobiologist stood on the trailer, leaning on her crutch, watching Tinker park the Rolls. Something about Lain's face made Tinker suspect that somehow the trailer was her fault.

"I thought you might turn up today," Lain said.

"Well, apparently I need a small army to go back to Turtle Creek, and Windwolf has all the *sekasha* today except Pony and Stormsong."

Said *sekasha* had already split up into Blade and Shield. Stormsong had moved off to scout the area as a Blade. Pony trailed behind Tinker, acting as Shield.

"So, I thought I'd come talk to you about the monster that attacked me yesterday," Tinker said. "The *sekasha* are saying it's an oni dragon."

"Ah." Lain made a sound of understanding. "I suppose I should thank you for your present."

"Present?" Tinker eyed the trailer apprehensively. What had she done now without realizing it?

Lain flipped up one corner of tarp to reveal limp willowy branches. "They told me that you sent it."

The black willow! *"He eats the fruit of the tree that walks."* Tinker shivered as recognition crawled down her spine. It was just too weird having another part of her dream show up with her name attached to it. "I sent it?"

"That's what they told me," Lain said.

Tinker could remember finding the tree, but she—she didn't order this. Or had she? She turned to Pony. "Did I ask . . . ?" His look of concentration made her realize that she had been so rattled that she was still speaking English; she switched Elvish. "Did I ask to have the black willow brought here?"

"You said you would love to give it to Lain."

That apparently that had been enough of an order for Pony. Tinker really had to keep in mind that the *sekasha* took her word as law. While she had been smothered in attention, the elves had bound up the long limp branches and sturdy trunk-feet and hauled it to the Observatory. Once at Lain's, however, they'd abandoned it—trailer and all.

Lain had warned her once about elves bearing gifts. Tinker winced, realizing that she had become one of said elves.

"I'm sorry, Lain." She made sure she was speaking English, afraid that she might insult Pony for her own stupidity. "I didn't know they were going to bring it here and dump it on you."

"It's a matter of gift horses and teeth, I suppose." Laying her crutch down, Lain nimbly swung down off the trailer, her upper body muscles cording to make up for her weakened legs. On the ground, Lain reached up for her crutch, and then turned to rap Tinker smartly on the head with her knuckles. "Learn to think before you open that mouth of yours."

"Ow!" Tinker winced. "I'm bruised there."

"You are?" Lain tilted Tinker's head to examine her scalp, combing aside her short hair with gentle fingertips. "What from? That creature that attacked you?"

"Yeah."

Lain smelt as always of fresh earth and crushed herbs and greens. "Ah, you'll live." She rubbed the sore area lightly. "Give the nerve receptors something else to think about."

Tinker mewed out a noise of protest and pain at the treatment.

Lain held her at arm's length then and looked down over Tinker, shaking her head. "I never thought I'd see you in a dress. That's a beautiful color for you."

Tinker showed off her rubies and her pistol, making Lain laugh at the contrast. "Do you want the tree?"

"A fully intact specimen? Of course!" Lain let her quiet scientific glee with the black willow show. "I saw my first black willow my first Startup; they flew me in on an Air Force jet to look at the forest where Pittsburgh had been the night before. I didn't want to come; I was still wrapped up in being crippled. Then I saw that wall of green, all those ironwoods as tall as sequoias. Out of the forest came a black willow, probably seeking a ley line, and the ground shook when it moved. God, it was instant nirvana—an alien world coming to me when I could no longer go to it."

A hot heady mix of delight and embarrassment flushed through Tinker; she wanted to hear more about how thoughtful she been, yet she knew how little she had actually contributed toward getting the tree moved. "I thought you might like it."

"I love it! But not necessarily here." Lain motioned toward her house. "I'm not totally convinced that the willow is dead. It might be just dormant after a massive system shock. I'd rather not have it reviving on my doorstep."

The tree that walks . . . "Yeah, that might be a bad idea. I can get a truck and move the trailer . . . someplace."

"What would be best is storing it at near freezing temperatures. The cold will keep it dormant if it's still alive."

Tinker eyed the fifty-three-foot semi trailer. "Well, getting it off the trailer wouldn't be hard—I can get a crane to do that—but shoving it into something refrigerated—that's going to be hard."

"I have faith." Lain limped toward her house, calling back. "I know you'll be able to figure it out."

Ah, the disadvantages of being well-known.

Stormsong was on the porch. She flashed through an "all clear" signal and indicated that she hadn't been inside the house.

"Let us clear the house first, *domi*," Pony said.

She wanted to whine, "It's just Lain's house." The *sekasha* had risked death for her, though, so she only sighed and sat down on the porch swing. "Can I have the willow cut up?"

"No," Lain said.

"I didn't think so. That would make life too simple." Tinker swung back and forth, the wind blowing up her skirt in a cooling breeze. "It would be easiest if we could keep the tree on the trailer and put it all into one large refrigerator. I could build one, but not quickly. Is there a large freezer unit that we can borrow?"

"There's Reinholds," Lain said.

"The ice cream factory?"

"I doubt they're using all their warehouses."

"That's true." The hundred-year-old company was one of the many Pittsburgh businesses that had survived being transplanted to another universe. Elves loved ice cream. Being stranded on Elfhome, however, limited Reinhold's production. Things such as sugar and chocolate all needed to be shipped in from Earth.

Pony reappeared at the door, and indicated with a nod and hand sign that the house was clean of menace. The *sekasha* took up guard at the doors, giving Tinker the privacy she was beginning to treasure so much.

It had been two months since Tinker had last been in Lain's house, the longest time in her life between visits. It was comforting to find it unchanged—large high-ceilinged rooms full of leather furniture, stained wood, leaded glass, and shadows.

Lain made a call to Reinholds to check on their freezer capacity. Apparently Reinholds shuffled her through various departments, as she repeated herself between long pauses. Tinker raided her fridge for breakfast. There were strawberries and fresh whipped cream, so Lain wasn't kidding when she had said that she'd expected Tinker to arrive.

The call ended with Lain hanging up with a sigh. "They have one large unit that has been shut down for some time. They're still trying to find someone that knows something about it; they'll call me back." She picked up the teakettle and limped to the sink to fill it. "You cut your hair again."

"Yeah, I cut it." It annoyed Tinker that her voice suddenly shook. When she had taken a razor to her hair, her oni guard had mistaken it for a suicide attempt; the following struggle came close to getting Pony killed. Immediately afterward, she had gone back to dipping circuit plates—it was stupid that tears now burned her eyes. She concentrated on stabbing a strawberry in the whipping cream.

"I know you hate it when people pry," Lain said quietly. "God knows, between myself, your grandfather, and that crazy half-elf Tooloo as role-models, it's no wonder you insist on keeping everyone at arm's length."

Tinker could guess where this was going. "I'm fine!"

Lain busied herself with teacups, the faint ring of china on china filling the silence between them. The teakettle started to rattle with a prewhistle boil. "God, I wish children came with instruction manuals. I only want to do what's best for you—but I don't know what that is. I never have."

"I'm fine." Tinker actually managed to keep her voice level

this time.

The teakettle peeped, a final warning before a full scream. Lain turned off the fire and stood there a moment, watching the steam pour out of the shimmering pot. Taking a deep cleansing breath, she sighed it out and asked, "Lemon Lift or Constant Comment?"

"The Lemon Lift," Tinker said.

"The EIA made Turtle Creek off-limits when the fighting broke out." Lain moved the teacups carefully to the table, and changed the subject with equal deftness. "No one has been able to get down to look at these Ghostlands. What did you find?"

Tea was only a medium to transport honey, so while Tinker coaxed it to maximum viscosity, she told Lain about what she found.

"Can you fix it?" Lain asked.

"I'm a genius—not a god. I don't even know what *it* is. But by the laws of thermodynamics, it should collapse. I had Pony score the trees around the edge. Once I can go back into the valley, I'll check on the rate at which it's decaying."

Tinker sipped her tea and then changed the subject. "What I really came here to talk to you about is the monster that attacked me. It's an oni dragon."

"There were warnings on the television last night and the radio this morning. Yet another beastie for us to worry about."

Tinker knew that she shouldn't feel responsible—but she did anyhow. She had made the Discontinuity that the dragon had passed through to get to Pittsburgh. "The dragon generates a magical shield that protects it. According to Pony and Stormsong, Windwolf's First Hand fought one of these things *nae hae*."

The elf phrase, meaning "too many years to count," dropped out of Tinker's mouth like she had been born to the concept of living forever. She found it a little disturbing. "Apparently the shield also protects it from magical weapons like spell arrows. They think Windwolf will be able to kill it—but he can't be everywhere at once. We need a more mundane way of dealing with the beastie."

"Do you know if it's a natural creature or a bioengineered one?" Lain took out her datapad and opened a new file to take notes.

"No. The oni didn't mention anything to me about the dragon, and the *sekasha* don't know. What's the difference?"

"The result of creatures evolving in an environment full of magic is they often can use magic to their own benefit. Take the black willow; it's mutated from a tree with all the standard limitations to a highly effective mobile predator. By and large, though, the bioengineered creatures tend to be more dangerous than the randomly mutated creatures."

"Like the wargs?" Tinker knew that the wolflike creatures had been created for war but now ranged wild in the forest surrounding Pittsburgh.

"Yes. The wargs not only have the frost breath, but they show no signs of aging or disease and their wounds heal at a speed that suggests a spell somehow encoded at the cellular level. They're massive, intelligent, and aggressive in nature."

"So the question is, how much did the oni dragons get in their DNA gift baskets?"

"Yes. But let's start with the basics. We've never encountered an Elfhome dragon—we only know that they exist because the elves keep telling us that they do, and that we really don't want to study them closely."

Tinker laughed at that comment.

"Is this dragon mammal or reptile?" Lain asked.

"I'm not sure. It had scales, but it also had some sort of weird mane. It was long, and lean, with a big square jaw." Tinker put her hands up to approximate the size of the head. "Short legs with big claws that it could pick things up with."

Lain got up to put the teakettle back on the stove. "Beware the Jabberwock, my son! The jaws that bite, the claws that catch!"

It took Tinker a moment to identify the quote, a poem out of *Alice Through the Looking Glass*.

"*We fell down the hole and through the looking glass.*"

The sudden connection with her dream was like a slap. White's face jolted into her mind again. With the addition of the book title, though, she remembered where she had seen White before.

"You know, I had the oddest dream about Boo-boo Knees."

Lain whipped around to face her. "Boo?"

"At least, I think it was Boo-boo."

"H-h-how do you know about Boo's nickname?"

"The picture. It has her name on the back of it."

"Which picture?"

"The one in the book." When Lain continued to stare at her in confusion, Tinker went to scan the bookcases until she found the book in question: *The Annotated Alice.* Complete in one book were both *Alice in Wonderland* and *Alice Through the Looking Glass and What She Found There,* with copious footnotes that explained layers upon layers of meaning in what seemed to be just a odd little children's story. Tinker had discovered the book when she was eight. Lain apparently had forgotten the photo tucked into the book, but Tinker hadn't.

It was an old two-dimensional color photo of a young woman with short purple hair. She hovered in midair, the Earth a brilliant blue moon behind her. She challenged the camera with a level brown-eyed gaze and a set jaw, as if she were annoyed with its presence. On her right temple was a sterile adhesive bandage. Written on the back was "Even in zero gravity, I find things to bang myself on. Love, Boo-boo Knees."

At the point Tinker had found it, she'd never seen a two-dimensional photograph; neither her grandfather or Lain were ones for personal pictures. From its limited perspective to the name of Boo-boo Knees, she'd found it fascinating. She stared at it until—ten years later—she could have drawn it from memory.

The picture was where she had carefully returned it, marking the place where one story ended and another started.

"Oh!" Lain took the photo. "I'd forgotten about that."

"Who is she?" *Why am I dreaming about her?* Tinker flipped through the book, remembering now forgotten passages echoing back from the dream. The tea party with the Mad Hatter murdering time, leaving his watch stuck at six o'clock. The checkerboard layout that they had flown over. Alice and the Red Queen hand in hand, like Tinker and White had been in the dream, racing to stay in place.

"That's Esme." Lain identified White as her younger sister.

"It is?" Tinker reclaimed the photo. She had always imagined Esme as a younger version of Lain, but Esme looked nothing like her. Come to think of it—Tinker had never seen a picture of Esme before, not even her official NASA mission photo.

"I'm not surprised you're dreaming of her," Lain was saying as Tinker continued to search the photo for the cause of her dreams. "You're bound to be upset about the gate and the colonists."

Was that the true reason? The dream seemed so real compared to the rest of her nightmares. She didn't know Boo-boo Knees was Lain's sister, and Lain had many retired astronauts as friends, so Tinker had had no reason to assume that this was a picture of a colonist. And why all the *Alice in Wonderland* references? Were they just reminders of where the photo was stored— or that the colonist had dropped into a mirror reflection of Earth? Certainly there was nothing to say that Earth had only two reflections: Elfhome and Onihida.

"Lost, lost," the crows had cried.

According to Riki, the first colony ship, the *Tianlong Hao*, was crewed entirely by tengu. If Black was a tengu female, that would explain the crows—but what about the hedgehogs? Tinker flipped through the book, found a picture of Alice with a flamingo and a hedgehog. The queen was screaming, "Off with his head!" Was this some oblique reference to the queen of the elves?

"Oh, this is going to give me a headache," Tinker murmured.

Down the hall, the phone rang. Lain gave her an odd, worried look and went to answer it.

Tinker found herself alone with the photograph of Lain's younger sister, looking defiantly out at her. "Why am I dreaming of you? I don't know where you are. I don't know how to save you. Hell, I don't even know how to save Pittsburgh."

Lain limped back into the kitchen. "That was Reinholds. The freezer in question is shut down because the compressor needs to be repaired. They said if I have someone repair the unit, we could store the tree there. They'll even throw in some free ice cream."

"He eats the fruit of the tree that walks," Tinker suddenly

remembered all of what White—Esme—had said. *"Follow the tree to the house of ice and sip sweetly of the cream."*

"I'll go look at the compressor." Tinker kept hold of the book. She had a bad feeling she was going to reread the silly thing. "And see if I can fix it. I think I *have* to do this. Can you do me a favor in the meantime? See if you can find out anything about this oni dragon." Tinker described the magical shield that the dragon generated. "If we have to fight it again, I want to be able to hurt it."

6: LIVELY MAPLE FLAVOR

For years, Tinker had thought of herself as famous. The invention and mass production of the hoverbike made Tinker's name well-known even before she started to race. True, few people realized that the girl in the "Team Tinker" shirt *was* the famed inventor/racer; still, she often got a reaction when she introduced herself.

But she wasn't prepared for the welcome she received at the Reinholds' offices.

The receptionist looked up as Tinker and her bodyguards entered. "Can I help . . ." the woman started, and then her gaze shifted from Pony to Tinker, and her question ended in a high squeal that drew everyone's eyes. "Oh, my god! Oh, my god! It's the fairy princess!"

Tinker glanced over her shoulder, hoping that there would be a female in diaphanous white behind her. No such luck. "Pardon?"

"You're her!" The woman jumped up and down, hands to her mouth. "You're Tinker, the fairy princess!"

Other office people came forward. One woman had a slickie in hand, which she held out with a digital marker. "Can you autograph this for me, Vicereine?"

64

Vice-what? Tinker felt a smile creeping onto her face in response to all the brightly smiling people gathering around her. The slickie was titled, *Tinker, the New Fairy Princess.* The cover photo was of Tinker, a crown of flowers disguising her haphazard haircut, looking fey and surprisingly pretty.

"What the hell?" Tinker snatched the slickie from the woman. When in god's name was this taken? And by whom?

She thumbed the page key, flipping through the pictures and text. The first half-dozen photographs were of Windwolf, taken across seasons and at various locations, looking studly as usual. The text listed out Windwolf's titles—viceroy, clan head for Westernlands, cousin to the queen—and added Prince Charming.

"Oh, gag me." She flipped on and found herself. It was a copy of the front cover. When was it taken? She couldn't remember any time appearing in public with a crown of flowers. The only time she had flowers in her hair like this was . . .

Oh, no! Oh, please, no. She frantically flipped on, hoping that she was wrong. Two more head shots, and then there it was— her in her nightgown, the one that looked like cream poured over her naked body. Oh, someone was so dead meat.

The morning after returning from the queen's court, she had breakfasted in the private garden courtyard of Poppymeadow's enclave. She had been alone with the female *sekasha*—and some pervert with telephoto lens. Thankfully, because of the distance involved, the photo was 2-D with limited pan and zoom features.

"Can you sign it, Vicereine?" the owner of the digital magazine asked.

"Sign?" Tinker slapped the slickie to her chest—she didn't even want to give it back.

The woman held out her marker. "Could you make it out to Jennifer Dunham?"

Tinker stared at the marker, wondering what to do. Certainly she couldn't ask her bodyguards—she suspected that they would not take the invasion of her privacy well. Not that the picture was all that indecent, but more that they had failed to protect her. She fumbled with getting the slickie back to its cover picture without flashing it at her bodyguards, scribbled her name in the corner, and thrust it back.

"I'm here about the broken freezer unit that Lain Shanske called about." Time to escape to something simple, understandable, and easily fixed. This freezer repair sounded like a good greasy project to let her forget all the big, unsolvable problems. "You said that if it was fixed, she could use it."

"That was me that she talked to." One man separated himself from the crowd. "Joseph Wojtowicz, you can call me Wojo, most people do. I'm the general manager here." Halfway through his handshake, he seemed to think he'd made a blunder in etiquette and bowed over her hand. "Yes, if you can get the unit working, she's more than welcome to it."

"Well, let's go see it." Tinker indicated that they should go out of the office, away from the crowd of people who were showing signs of producing cameras. "I want to see if it's actually big enough to hold the tree."

Thus they managed to escape, no picture taken, through the offices and to a backstreet. Stormsong led the way, moving through the maze of turns as if she worked at the offices. Pony trailed behind, keeping back the curious office staff with dark looks.

"I heard about the monster attacking you yesterday." Wojo didn't seem to notice her *sekasha*, focusing only on Tinker as they rounded a corner and took a short flight of cement steps up onto a loading dock. "Are you okay? It sounds like you had a nasty fight on your hands."

Gods, first Lain and now him. How many people had heard about the fight at Turtle Creek? "I'm fine."

"That's good! That's good! I knew your grandfather, Tim Bell. He was—" Wojo paused to consider a polite way to describe her grandfather. "—quite a character."

"Yeah, he was."

"This is it, here." He stopped before a large door padlocked shut. He pulled out a key ring and started to sort through the keys. "It was our main building before Startup. After that, it was so unpredictable that we only used it for overflow. Four years ago, we stopped being able to use it at all."

By Startup, he meant the first time Pittsburgh went to

Elfhome. In typical fashion, Pittsburghers used Startup to mean that first time, and each consecutive time, after Shutdown returned Pittsburgh to Earth. Shutdown itself was a misnomer because the gate never fully shut down, only powered down sharply, a fact that she had counted on when she set out to destroy it. The oni could have stopped the resonance only by completely shutting off the orbital gate, something it wasn't designed to do easily. The poor crew that maintained the gate probably had no clue what was happening or how to stop it. Tinker tried not to think of the poor souls trying to save themselves before the gate shook itself to pieces. Had they abandoned the structure? Were there ships in orbit around Earth that could rescue them? Or had they, too, phased into space over Elfhome, doomed to rain down with the fiery pieces of the gate?

I've killed people, she thought with despair, and I don't even know how many, or what race they belonged to.

"Well, I'll be damned." Wojo turned away from the door, frowning at his key ring as if it had failed him. "None of these keys fit the lock. I guess the key was taken off this ring when we stopped using the building. I'll be right back."

Pony and Stormsong were conferring in whispers. Tinker caught enough to realize that Stormsong was translating for Pony. Was having her *sekasha* understand *everything* worth the convenience of not having to repeat herself?

A slight chiming caught Tinker's attention. Across the street sat a small shrine to a local ley god, its prayer bells ringing in the slight breeze.

The gods of the ley were all faces of the god of magic, Auhoya, the god of chaos and plenty. Tinker was never sure how he could be many different gods and yet still be one individual, but she'd learned that with gods, one didn't try to understand like one would with science. They were. Auhoya was shown always with a horn and a two edged-sword. She supposed in some ways, magic was a lot like science, used to make or destroy.

She clapped her hands to call the gods attention to her, bowed low, and added a silver dime to the hoarde already littering the shrine.

"Help me to make things right." Adding a second dime, she whispered, "Help me to never mess up this badly again."

"Tinker *ze domi*," someone said behind her, using the formal form of her title.

She turned and found Derek Maynard, head of the EIA, standing behind her. If Windwolf was prince of the Westernlands, then Director Maynard was prince of Pittsburgh. Certainly, there was a similarity in their appearance, as Maynard was elf-tall and elf-stylish. He kept his hair in a long, blond braid and wore a painted silk duster, and tall, polished boots. She noted that while he was primarily in white, his accents—earrings, waistcoat, and duster—were all Wind Clan blue.

"Maynard? You're about the last person I expected to run into here. Is the EIA out of ice cream?"

"I'm here to see you." Maynard bowed elegantly, weirding her out. For years she had been terrified of the EIA, and now its director was treating her like a princess.

"Me?" To her annoyance, the word came out as a squeak. Obviously, someone wasn't completely over her fear.

"I heard of the attack on you yesterday . . ."

"Hell, does everyone in Pittsburgh know about that?"

"Possibly. It made the newspaper. How are you feeling?"

"I wish people would stop asking."

"Forgiveness." He swept a critical gaze down over her, taking in her silk dress, black leather gun belt, and polished riding boots. "I am glad to see you well."

"You chased me down just to see how I was?"

"Yes." He motioned toward the shrine. "Did you convert after Windwolf made you an elf?"

"I was raised in the religion," she said. "My grandfather was an atheist or agnostic, depending on his mood. Tooloo often babysat me when I was a child; she thought if I wasn't watched over by human gods, I should be protected by elfin ones."

"Has anyone ever taught you about human religion?"

"Grandpa taught us to exchange Christmas presents, and Lain lights candles at Hanukkah."

"Lain Shanske? I take it that she's Jewish."

"By blood, although not totally by faith. It seems a weird compulsion that she fights, like she doesn't want to believe, saying she's not going to do Hanukkah, but at the last minute, she pulls out the candles and lights them."

Maynard nodded, as if Lain's behavior wasn't bizarre. "I understand."

"I don't. If you try to talk to her about the Jewish God—one minute she's saying that her god is the only true god, and the next minute, she'll be telling me that scientifically, her creation story is impossible. It's like she wants me to know her religion, but doesn't want me to believe it, because she doesn't believe it—but she does."

"Things that you're told as a child—your fear, your religion, your bigotry—become so much a part of you that's it hard to remove them when you grow to be an adult. Sometimes you don't realize such things are there until the moment of truth, and then they're suddenly as impossible to miss as a third arm, and as hard to cut off."

"You talk like you've been through it."

"There have been a few times when all I could do was kiss dirt and pray."

Stormsong scoffed, reminding Tinker that this wasn't a private conversation. On the heels of that, she remembered that this was the second most important person in Pittsburgh after Windwolf— and he had come looking for her.

"You didn't come here to ask me about my religion."

"Actually, in a way, I had," Maynard said. "You do realize that Pittsburgh's treaty with the elves is now null and void?"

"No. Why would it be void?"

"The basic underlying principle of the treaty is that Pittsburgh was a city of Earth only temporarily visiting Elfhome. Every article was written with the idea that humans would and could return to Earth."

"Shit! Okay, I didn't realize that." She frowned at him, wishing she wasn't so tired. Surely this conversation had to be making some kind of sense, but she was missing the connection. What did her religion have to do with the treaty?

"Little one." Stormsong took out a pack of Juicy Fruit gum and offered Tinker a piece. "He wants to know how human you are after everyone has had a chance to fuck your brain over for the last few months. He needs your help but he doesn't know if he can trust you."

Ooooh. Tinker took the gum to give herself a moment to think.

"Succinct as ever, Stormsong." Maynard also accepted a piece.

"That's why you love me." Stormsong stepped back out of the conversation, becoming elfin again.

The last time Tinker remembered talking with Maynard was before she'd been summoned by the queen. She'd warned him about the oni. Slowly unwrapping the gum, she tried to remember if she had seen Maynard after that. No, the oni had kidnapped her while she was on her way to see him. Yeah, she could see why he might be concerned she'd been somehow—damaged.

That still begged the question of what the hell he expected her to do in regard of negotiating a new treaty. As a business owner, she found all of the regulations set up in the original one to be baffling, perplexing, mystifying, bewildering . . . and any other word that meant *confusing.*

"Look, I can help with junkyards, hoverbike racing, and advanced physics." She sighed and put the gum in her mouth. For a moment the taste—not Juicy Fruit as she remembered but something similar, only a hundred times better—distracted her. It was like getting kicked in the mouth. "Wow." She checked the bright yellow wrapper in her hand. Oh yes, she was an elf now, and things tasted different.

Maynard was frowning, waiting for her to finish her point.

"Um—" What had she been saying? Oh yes, her areas of expertise. "But I've discovered that I know very little about anything else."

"You're Windwolf's *domi.*"

"And this makes me an expert on—what? I don't know you well enough to discuss my sex life and quite frankly, the only place I get to see my husband is in bed."

"Whether you like it or not, *ze domi*, that makes you a player in Pittsburgh. There are sixty thousands humans that need you on their side."

"Fine, I'm on their side. Rah, rah, rah! That still doesn't give me a clue on how to help. Fuck, I tried to help the elves and look at the mess I made. You can't screw up much more than Turtle Creek."

"A lot of elves see this as a win-win situation. If you had permanently returned Pittsburgh back to Earth, it would have been perfect."

"Some of us would have been pissed," Stormsong said.

Maynard gave Stormsong a look that begged her to be quiet.

"Look," Tinker said. "If shit hits the fan, I promise I will move heaven and earth to protect the people of this city, but I am not a political animal. At this point in time, I don't even want to try to tackle anything that can't be solved with basic number crunching."

Maynard was still gazing at Stormsong, but in a more intent fashion now. Stormsong wore an odd stunned look, like someone had hit her with a cattle prod.

"Stormsong?" Tinker scanned the area, looking for danger.

"You will," Stormsong murmured softly in a voice that put chills down Tinker's spine.

"I will *what*?" Tinker shivered off the feeling.

"Move heaven and earth to protect what you love," Stormsong whispered.

"What the hell does that mean?" Tinker asked.

Stormsong blinked and focused on Tinker. "Forgiveness, *ze domi*," she said in High Elvish, disappearing behind her most formal mask. "My ability is erratic and I'm untrained. I—I am not certain . . ."

"If that's the case, I'm satisfied." Maynard acted as if Stormsong had said something more understandable. "Forgiveness, *ze domi*, I must take my leave. *Nasadae*."

"*Nasadae*," Tinker echoed, mystified. What the fuck just happened? Maynard bowed his parting. Stormsong had gone into *sekasha* mode. And the conversation had been in English, so asking Pony would be pointless.

Wojo returned with the keys. "I see you've found the cause of all our problems." He indicated the shrine marking the ley line. "As soon as the magic seeped into the area after the first Startup, the whole unit went whacky. It was the weirdest thing I'd ever seen—including waking up the day before."

"Huh?" She was having trouble switching gears. *That's it, I won't fight any monsters today and will go to bed early.*

Wojo misunderstood her grunt of confusion. "I lived out in West View right on the Rim—almost didn't come with the rest of the city. My place looked down on I-279. Every morning, I'd get up, have coffee, and check traffic out my back window. That first Startup, I looked out, and there was nothing but trees. I thought maybe I was dreaming. I actually went and took a cold shower before going back and looking again."

Tinker added a shower and maybe a nightcap to her "must get sleep" list—if she could find either.

"I never realized how noisy the highway was until afterward," Wojo continued blithely. "When the forest is still, it's absolute quiet, like the world is wrapped in cotton. And the wind through the trees—that green smell—I just love it."

Tinker bet Stormsong would know where to find booze and hot water.

"But between the wargs, the saurus, and the black willows, West View was just too isolated—I was way out past the scientist commune on Observatory Hill. It's all ironwood forest now. I have a nice place up on Mount Washington, beautiful view of the city, and it's much safer up there. And hell, with gas prices what they are, it makes sense to take the incline down the hill and take the light rail over."

"Yeah, yeah," Tinker agreed to shut him up and indicated the door. "Let's see what you have."

Wojo unlocked the padlock, freed it from the bolt, and opened the door.

Before her transformation, ley lines seemed nearly mystical—lines of force running like invisible rivers. The little shrines erected by the elves on strong ley lines served as the only warning for why the normal laws of physics would suddenly skew off in odd directions, as the chaos of magic was applied to the equation. "I hit a ley" embedded itself into the Pittsburgh language, blaming everything from acts of nature to bad judgment on the unseen presence.

But now, as a *domana*, she could see magic. The door swung open to reveal a room filled with the shimmer of power.

"Sweet gods," she breathed, earning a surprised look from Wojo and making the *sekasha* move closer to her.

The magic flowed at a purple on the far end of the visible spectrum, lighting the floor to such near-invisible intensity that it brought tears to her eyes. The high ceiling absorbed most of that light, so it stayed cloaked in shifting shadows. Heat spilled out of the room, flushing her to fever hot, and seconds later, the sense of lightness seeped up her legs, slowly filling her until she felt like she would float away.

"What?" Wojo asked.

"It's a very strong ley line," Tinker said.

Wojo made a slight surprised *hrumpf* to this.

She considered what she was wearing. An active spell with this much force behind it, snarled by something metal on her, could be deadly. She wasn't sure how dangerous this much latent magic might pose. "You might want to empty your pockets."

She pulled off her boots, emptied her pockets into them, and took off her gun belt. Since the *sekasha* caste couldn't sense magic, she told Pony and Stormsong, "This ley seems almost as strong as the spell stones."

"The shrine indicates a *fiutana*," Pony explained. "Like the one that the spell stones are built on."

"What's that?" Tinker asked.

Pony explained, "A single point where magic is much stronger than normal, welling up, like spring waters."

"If you're coming in," she told the two warriors, "strip off all metal. And I mean all."

The *sekasha* started paper, scissors, stone to see which was going in, and which would stay behind with the weapons.

There was a light switch by the door; Tinker cautiously flipped it on, but nothing happened.

"Lightbulbs pop as soon as you carry them into the room," Wojo explained, "so we stopped installing them."

"We need a light source shielded from magic." Tinker flipped the switch back to off. "I don't think even a plastic flashlight would work."

"No, they pop too." Wojo took out two spell lights and held out one to her. "These are safe, but you'll want to watch—they're really bright."

With this much magic around, that wasn't surprising.

She wrapped her hand tight around the cool glass orb before activating it. Her fingers gleamed dull red, her bones lines of darkness inside her skin. Carefully, she uncovered a fraction of the orb, and light shafted out a painfully brilliant white.

Stormsong won paper, scissors, stone and opted for coming inside. She ghosted into the room ahead of Tinker, her shields outlining her in blue brilliance, her wooden sword ready. Tinker waited for Stormsong to flash the "all clear" signal before entering the warehouse.

The cement floor was rough and warm under her stocking feet. She walked into the room, feeling like she should be wading. It lacked the resistance of water, but she could sense a current, a slow circular flow, and a depth.

Wojo followed, oblivious to magic. "This is the space. Is it big enough? If we can get the refrigerator unit to work?"

Tinker considered the loading dock, the wide door, and the large room. They would have to transfer the tree from the flatbed to something wheeled, then shift both back onto the flatbed to get the tree up to the loading dock height and still be able to shift it into the cooler. Given that they'd have to fit a forklift in to help with the transfer, it would be a tight fit, but certainly doable.

"Yeah, this will do." Of course they would have to drain off the massive excess of magic. Strong magic and heavy machinery did not mix well. "You had the cooling unit running for, what, ten years? I'm surprised you managed to keep it running that long."

"More like fourteen," Wojo said. "Your grandfather, actually, came over just after Startup and set us up so it worked fine for years. It didn't break down until after he died."

The machine room was off the back of the refrigerated room, through a regular-sized door in the insulated wall. The compressor itself was normal. The cement around it, however, had been inscribed with a spell. A section had overloaded, burning out a part of the spell. She'd never seen anything like it.

"My grandfather did this?" Tinker asked.

"Yes." Wojo nodded. "He heard about the trouble we were having and volunteered to fix it. We were a little skeptical. Back then, no one knew anything about working magic. People are picking magic up, but still, no one had a clue how to fix what he did when it broke."

Tinker's family had the edge that they were descended from an elf who had been trapped on Earth. Her father, Leonardo Dufae, developed his hyperphase gate based off the quantum nature of magic after studying the family's codex. It was the main reason Tinker had been able to build a gate when no one on Earth had yet figured out how to copy her father's work.

"Define *wacky*," Tinker asked.

"What?" Wojo said.

"You said that it went wacky after the first Startup."

"Ah, well, the compressor seemed to work like a pump. The magic was so thick that you could see it. It blew every lightbulb on the block. The forklifts kept burning out but then they'd skitter across the room, just inches off the floor. Loose paper would crawl up your leg like a kitten. It was just weird."

Yes, that fell under wacky. She knew that the electric forklifts had engines that could short to form a crude antigravity spell—it was what had given her the idea for hoverbikes. The loose paper was new. Perhaps they had something printed on them that had animated them.

"We finally just shut it down and gave all the ice cream to the queen's army." Wojo waved his hand to illustrate emptying out the vast storage area. "Kind of an icebreaker—pardon the pun. A thousand gallons of the cookie batter, chocolate fudge, and peanut butter. Luckily, the Chinese paid for the inventory loss and it hooked the elves on our ice cream."

Tinker sighed, combing her fingers back through her short

hair. "Well, first I'll have to drain off the magic; by building a siphon that funnels magic to a storage unit. I have one set up for my electromagnet since a ley line runs through my scrapyard." She used to think of it as a strong ley line, but it was just a meandering stream compared to this torrent. "But that won't handle a flood like you're talking about."

"Whatever your grandfather did worked for years."

The question was—what had her grandfather done? To start from scratch would take time she didn't have, not with the black willow warming in the sun. Luckily, he had kept meticulous records on anything he ever worked on. "I'll go through his things and see if I can find a copy of the spell."

7: THINGS BETTER LEFT BURIED

The treaty between the elves and humans banned certain humans from Pittsburgh as it traveled back and forth between the worlds: criminals, the mentally insane, and orphans. When her grandfather had died, her cousin Oilcan had been seventeen and Tinker had just turned thirteen. Facing possible deportation, dealing with her grandfather's things had been the last thing on Tinker's mind. Truth be told, she'd run a little mad at the time, resisting Lain and Oilcan's attempts to have her move in with them. She had roamed the city, hiding from her grief, and sleeping wherever night found her. Terrified that she was going to lose the only world she'd ever known, she had drunk it down in huge swallows.

Only when Oilcan had turned eighteen, able to be her legal guardian, had they settled back into a normal life. With money from licensing her hoverbike design, she had set up her scrap yard business, moved into a loft, and laid claim to a sprawling garage between the two. Her grief, however, had been too fresh to deal with her grandfather's things; Oilcan and Nathan Czernowski had packed them up and stored them away in a room at the back of the garage.

Even now—looking at the small mountain of boxes, draped in plastic, smelling of age—it was tempting to just shut the door on the emotional land mines that the boxes might hold.

"*Domi*," Pony said quietly behind her. "What are we looking for here?"

"My grandfather created the spell at the ice cream factory. I need to find his notes on it so I can fix it quickly. I figure it's in one of these boxes."

Pony nodded, looking undaunted by the task. "How can we help?"

Backing out of the whole tree mess wasn't really an option; she already had too many people involved. The dust, however, was making her nose itch.

"Can you take these boxes out to the parking pad?" She waved toward the square of sunbaked cement. "After I look through a box, you can put it back."

The first box she opened was actually some of their old racing gear. Inside were a dozen of their FRS walkie-talkies, heavily shielded against magic. She'd upgraded the team to earbuds, and mothballed the handheld radios.

"Score!" she cried. "This is just what I wanted!"

"What are they?" Pony picked one up. "Phones?"

"Close. I want to make it so the Hands can communicate over distance better. These are a little bit clunky but they're easy to use." Oddly, Stormsong thought this was funny. She took the box, saying mysteriously, "This should be interesting."

Tinker supposed it could be worse. Her grandfather had been methodical in organizing his things. Oilcan kept everything carefully separated as he packed the boxes. Still she couldn't find anything filed under "Reinholds", "Refrigeration", "Ice Cream", or the type of compressor that Reinholds used.

"*Ze domi*," Stormsong murmured politely.

Tinker sighed. Random searching wasn't going to work. "What is it, Stormsong?"

"I want to thank you for yesterday."

"Yesterday?" Tinker found the Aa-Ak box and sat down beside it. "Can you put these boxes in alphabetical order?"

Stormsong started to rearrange the boxes, but switched to

English, losing her polite mask. "Look, little one, you're a good kid—
your heart is in the right place—so I guess I do have to thank you for
that stupidity you pulled yesterday. If you hadn't come back, I'd be
dead. But I had made my peace with that—being *sekasha* is all about
choosing your life *and* your death—so don't ever pull that shit again.
You really fucked up. When that thing hit you, you should have been
so much dead meat—and that would have been a huge waste,
because you are a good kid. The kind I would have been happy
dying to protect—do you understand?"

Tinker blinked at her for moment, before finding her voice. "I
thought I figured out a way to kill it."

"It wasn't your place to kill it."

"What? I lost at paper, scissors, stone?"

"You know what I hate about being a *sekasha*? It's the *domana*.
We *sekasha* spend our lives learning the best way to handle any
emergency. We train and train and train—and then have to kowtow
to some *domana* who is just winging it because they've got the big
guns. Do you know what? Just because you've got the big brains, or
the kick-ass spells, doesn't mean you know everything. Next fight,
shut the fuck up and do what you're told, or I'm going to bitch slap
you."

It took Tinker a moment to find her voice. "You know, I think
I like you better when you speak Elvish."

Stormsong laughed. "And I like you better when you speak
English. You're more human."

Tinker controlled the urge to stick out her tongue. She
deserved Stormsong's criticism because she had screwed up. Still,
she suddenly felt like crying. Oh joy. The last few weeks had left her
rubbed raw. Instead, she pushed the Aa-Ak box toward Stormsong,
saying, "I'm done with this one," and moved on. At least, having had
her say, Stormsong took the box away without comment.

Under "Birth" Tinker found birth certificates for everyone in
the family but herself. She pulled Oilcan's and had Stormsong put it
in the car. Under "Dufae" she found the original Dufae Codex carefully sealed in plastic. She'd only worked with the scanned copy that
her father had made.

"Wow." That too she pulled out and had put in the Rolls to

take home with her. The next box started with E's, and toward the back was a thick file folder marked simply "Esme." "What the hell?"

Tinker pried the file out of the box, flipped it open, and found Esme Shanske looking back. She ruffled quickly through the file. It was all information on Esme. NASA bios. Newspaper clippings. Photographs. It threw her into sudden and complete confusion.

"What are you doing here?" she asked Esme's photo. "I wasn't looking for you. What was I looking for?" She had to think a moment before remembering that she wanted to find her grandfather's notes on the spell at Reinholds so the walk-in freezer could function again so she could store the black willow. But why? "Why am I doing this again?"

Lain wanted the black willow (thus the whole reason it was salvaged in the first place) and it might revive—good reason to lock the tree in the cooler. The cooler was broken. She needed to fix it. They were all nice, sane, and logical links in a chain.

What made it all weird were her dreams and Esme popping up in odd places. It jarred hard with Tinker's orderly conception of reality. It pushed her into an uncomfortable feeling that the world wasn't as solid and fixed as she thought it was. She wanted to ignore it all, but Windwolf had said that it wasn't wise to ignore her dreams.

Perhaps if she dealt with them in a scientific manner, they wouldn't seem so—frighteningly weird.

She got her datapad and settled in the sun to write out what she remembered of the dream, and what had already materialized. The pearl necklace headed the list, since it was the first to appear. Second was the black willow and the ice cream. She considered the hedgehogs of the dream and the flamingoes in the book's illustrations and decided her future might be decidedly weird.

And who was the Asian woman in black? She felt that the woman had to be tengu because of the crows. She had felt, however, that she knew the woman, just as she knew Esme. Perhaps she was another colonist, which was why the birds kept repeating, "Lost." Riki had told her that the first ship was crewed by tengu.

Then it hit her—Riki lied about everything. She flopped back onto the sun warm cement and covered her eyes. Gods, what was she doing? Trying to apply logic to dream symbols was not going to work! So how was she going to figure out the future with only dreams and possible lies?

"Domi." Pony's voice and the touch of his hand on her face yanked Tinker out of her nightmare. "Wake up."

Tinker opened her eyes and struggled awake. She lay on the warm, rough cement of the parking pad. Stormsong was doing a leisurely prowl in the alley. Pony knelt beside her, sheltering her from the sun. She groaned and rubbed at her eyes; they burned with unshed tears.

"What is it?"

"You were having a nightmare."

She grunted and sat up, not wanting to fall back to sleep, perchance to dream. Lately dreaming was a bitch. The oni had really force-fed her id some whoppers, not that her imagination really needed it, no thank you.

"Domi?" His dark eyes mirrored the concern in his murmured question. "Are you all right?"

"It was just a bad dream." She yawned so deep her face felt like it would split in half. "How can I sleep and wake up more tired?"

"You've only been asleep for a few minutes." He shifted so that he sat beside her. "Nor was it restful sleep."

"You're telling me." In her dreams, she hadn't been able to save him from being flayed of his tattoos. She leaned against his bare arm, his skin and tattoos wonderfully intact, glad for the opportunity to reassure herself without making a big deal of it. *Just a nightmare.*

He smelled wonderful. After weeks together, she knew his natural scent. He was wearing some kind of cologne, an enticing light musk. She felt the now familiar desire uncoil inside her. Gods, why did stress make her want to lick honey off his rock-hard abs? Was this some kind of weird primitive wiring—most of us are going off to be eaten by saber-toothed tigers, so let's fuck like crazy before the gene pool lessens? Or was she uniquely screwed up?

Every night with Pony among the oni had been a torture of temptation. There had been only one bed and she had been stupid enough to insist that they share it. She would lay awake, desperately wanting to reach out to him—to be held, to be made love to, to be taken care of. She managed to resist because of a little voice that reminded her that she would swap Pony for Windwolf in a heart-beat—that it was her husband she really wanted. There had been no way to kick Pony out of the bed without admitting how much she wanted him, so he and her secret temptation stayed.

Even now she fought the urge to plant little kisses on his bicep. *I'm a married woman. I'm married and I do love Windwolf.* She couldn't even imagine being married to Pony, although she wasn't sure why—he was to-die-for cute. Unfortunately, she could imagine having hot sex with him. She sighed as her curiosity stirred to won-der what running her tongue up the curve of his arm would taste like. *Now I've done it—it will eat me alive wondering . . .*

"*Domi*, what is it?"

Embarrassment burned through her. "N-n-nothing. I'm just tired. I haven't been sleeping well."

"Have you found what you needed?" he asked.

"No." She shook her head and yawned again. She saved her notes on the datapad and handed Esme's file to him. "Put this in the Rolls. I'll get back to work."

Luckily the information she was looking for was in the F's, under "Flux Compression Generator". *Huh?* Normally compressing a magnetic field would generate more amperes of current than a lightning bolt and cause an electromagnetic pulse. What in hell was her grandfather thinking? But there was no mistaking the Reinhold floor layout, and the accompanying notes on the spell. With the folder, it should be fairly simple to recreate her grandfather's spell.

She heard the scrape of boots on the cement behind her. The *sekasha* were probably bored to tears.

"This is what I was looking for." She got to her feet and brushed the dust from her skirt. She looked up and was startled to find the *sekasha* forming a wall of muscle between her and Nathan Czernowski. The sight of him put a tingle of nervousness through her. "Nathan? What are you doing here?"

"I saw the Rolls and figured that it had to be you."

"Yeah, it's me." She busied herself with the boxes as an excuse not to look at him, wondering why she felt so weird until she remembered where they'd left off. Last time she'd seen him, he—he—she didn't even want to assign a word to it.

Nathan had been like an older brother to her and Oilcan. He'd hung around the garage and scrap yard on his off hours, drinking beer with them, and shooting the breeze. On racing days, he acted as security for her pit. She knew all his sprawling family members, had attended their weddings and funerals and birthday parties. There wasn't another man in Pittsburgh that she would have let into her loft while she was dressed only in a towel. Nobody else she would have thought herself utterly safe with.

Then he'd held her down, torn off her towel, and tried to push into her.

In one terrifying second, he'd become a large, frightening stranger. She had never considered before how tall he was, how strong he was, or how easily he could do anything he wanted with her.

He hadn't actually done—it. He'd stopped. He seemed to be listening to her. She would never know if he actually would have gotten off her, and let her up, and gone back to the Nathan she knew, because Pony had come to her rescue.

A day later she'd been snatched up by the queen's Wyverns, dragged away to attend the royal court, and then kidnapped by the oni, where she witnessed true evil. She hadn't thought of Nathan once in all that time. She wasn't sure what she felt now.

"I heard about the monster—" Nathan started.

"You and all of Pittsburgh. I'm fine!"

"I see." Nathan gazed her wistfully. "You look beautiful."

"Thanks." She knew it was mostly the jewel red silk dress. She also knew that it clung to her like paint where it wasn't exposing vast amounts of skin. Suddenly she felt weirdly under-dressed.

They stood a moment in nervous silence. Finally, Nathan wet his lips and said, "I'm sorry. I went way over the line, and I'm—so—sorry."

She burned with sudden embarrassment; it was like being naked under him again. "I don't want to talk about it."

"No, I'm ashamed of what I did, and I want to apologize—though I know that really doesn't cut it." His voice grew husky with self-loathing. "I would have killed another man for doing it. That I was drunk and jealous excuses nothing."

"Nathan, I don't know how to deal with this."

"I just loved you so much. I still do. It kills me that I lost you. I just don't want you to hate me."

"I don't hate you," she whispered. "I'm pissed to hell at you. And I'm a little scared of you now. But I don't hate you."

At least she didn't think she did. He had stopped—that counted for something, didn't it? More than anything, she felt stupid for letting it happen. Everyone had told her that things wouldn't work out between her and Nathan—and she had ignored them.

They stood in awkward silence. It dawned on her that the *sekasha* were still between her and Nathan, a quiet angry presence. She realized that Pony must have told Stormsong who Nathan was and what he'd done, and embarrassment burned through her. Once again she was having her nose ground into the fact that she was being constantly watched. She pushed past the *sekasha* and Nathan, wondering how much detail had Pony told Stormsong. She could trust Pony with her life, but not her privacy; she wasn't even sure he understood the concept.

When she reached the Rolls, she was tempted to climb in and drive away, but that would mean leaving the storage room half unpacked. She dropped the file in the back of the car, beside the other things she'd set aside to take home. Nathan and the *sekasha* had trailed her out to the Rolls. Somehow, out in the alley, she felt more claustrophobic, their presence made unavoidable by the fact that they had followed her en masse.

"I have what I need," she told Pony and then realized she had said that already. "Everything else needs to be put back."

"Yes, *domi*." Pony signaled to Stormsong to return to the storage room; he remained with Tinker.

Nathan stayed too. His police cruiser sat behind the Rolls. For some reason the Pittsburgh police had doubled up and Bue Pedersen waited patiently for Nathan to finish.

"Bowman." Tinker nodded to Bue.

"Hiya, Tinker." Bue nodded back.

"They tell me that you're his *domi*." Nathan meant Windwolf.

"Yeah." She fiddled with the bracelet. She had no wedding ring to flash as proof. Elves apparently didn't go for those kinds of things.

"You know, everyone's going on and on as if you got married to him and you're a princess now, but Tooloo says that you're not his wife."

Her heart flipped in her chest. "What?"

"Tooloo says that Windwolf didn't marry you."

She stared at him dumbfounded for a minute before she thought to say, "And you believed her? Tooloo *lies*. You ask her five times in a row when her birthday is and she'll tell you a different date each time!"

He looked down at her bare fingers. "Then why was there no wedding? Why no ring?"

She tried to ignore the weird cartwheeling in her chest. "Nathan, it's not—they—they don't do things like we do."

He gave a cold bitter laugh. "Yeah, like changing someone's species without asking them."

"He asked!" she snapped. She just hadn't understood.

"Come on, Tink. I was there. You had no idea what he had done to you. You still don't know. You think you're married. Hell, half the city thinks you're married. But you're not."

She shook her head and clung to the one thing she knew for sure. "Tooloo lies about everything. She hates Windwolf. She's lying to you."

"Tink—"

"I don't have time for this bullshit! Stormsong, we're leaving! Just lock the door and come."

"The humans farm—grass?" Bladebite prodded the green rectangle of sod laid down in the palace clearing.

"Convenient, isn't it?" Wolf pointed out, although he suspected that his First Hand wouldn't see it as such.

"It's unnatural," Bladebite grumbled. "Grass already grows quickly—why would they want it to instantly appear?"

Wolf rubbed at his temple where a headache was starting to form. "Quickly," of course, was all a matter of perspective. The palace clearing was still a raw wound of earth from cutting down the ironwoods and tearing up the massive stumps. Until the dead gossamer could be removed from the faire grounds, the clearing would have to double as an airfield. Wolf knew his First Hand reflected what most elves would think of the sod. It couldn't be helped. After last night's rainfall, the clearing was turning into a pit of mud.

Wolf had delegated cleaning up the gossamer body to Wraith Arrow, an imperfect match of abilities and task, but currently the best he could hope for as Tinker had apparently found some project on the North Side that was taking up her time. Reports were drifting back, along with a box of walkie-talkies.

His First Hand viewed the devices with the same open suspicion as the sod. Luckily, while Wraith dealt with the gossamer, Cloudwalker filled the fifth position. The "baby" *sekasha* was cautiously prodding the buttons on the walkie-talkie.

While his Hands kept alert for trouble, Wolf focused on getting the clearing ready for the arrival of the queen's troops. The settlements on the East Coast reported that a dreadnaught had passed overhead, so it would be arriving soon.

"You're not going to take down the oaks—are you?" The human contractor pointed out the massive wind oaks. "That would be a crying shame."

Wolf hated the idea of cutting down the trees for a single day's use of the clearing. While the trees were spell-worked to be extremely long-lived, their acorns rarely sprouted hardy saplings, and thus the trees continued to be quite rare. Wolf had been sure that finding five so close to Pittsburgh was a sign of the gods' blessings. He had chosen the site because of the trees and planned to build the palace around them.

He paced the clearing, trying to remember the dreadnaught's size. Would there be room for it to land without taking down the trees? While he did, he wondered about the oni's attack. Why kill the gossamer? Thinking with a cold heart, he realized that it would have made more sense for the oni to attack Poppymeadow's in the middle of the night. The ley line through the enclaves wasn't strong enough to support aggressive defense spells. The rocket would have triggered the alarms, but Wolf wouldn't have been able to call his shields in time.

One would think that the oni would have realized by now that Wolf was their strongest adversary. But maybe he was overestimating their grasp on the situation. Taking himself out of the equation, he considered the question again. Why the gossamer? There had been a second gossamer in plain sight, waiting for mooring. True, that airship had fled the area and it would probably take hours for its navigator to coax the beast back to Pittsburgh. Perhaps the oni hoped to isolate Wolf by killing both his ships before he could react. Perhaps they didn't realize that he had already sent for support.

While the gossamer's death was a pity, he was glad that the oni attacked it and not the enclaves. He had lost two of his *sekasha* this century. He did not want to lose another.

Wolf became aware that the *sekasha* had stopped a human from approaching him while he was thinking. He focused on the man with pale eyes and a dark goatee. "What is it that you want?"

"I'm the city's coroner." The man took Wolf's question as permission to close the distance. Bladebite stopped the human with a straight arm and a cold look.

"I am not familiar with that word," Wolf said.

"I'm—I'm the one that deals with the dead."

"I see." Wolf signaled to his Hand to let the man advance. Sparrow had dealt with this man, since Wolf had been wounded the two times his people had been killed.

"Tim Covington." The coroner held out his hand to be shaken.

Wolf considered the offered hand. The other *domana* would not allow such contact—a broken finger would leave them helpless. Humans needed to be schooled in day-to-day manners—but was now the time to start? He decided that today, he would keep to human politeness and shook Covington's hand. At least the man introduced himself first, which would be correct for both races.

"Wolf Who Rules Wind."

"I was down the street, dealing with the oni bodies, and they said you were here."

"We only executed one oni."

Covington looked away, clearly disturbed. "They unearthed two more dead males when they brought in the backhoe."

"Why do you seek me out? I have no dead."

"I've been coroner for nearly ten years. I dealt with both Lightning Strike and Hawk Scream." Covington named the two fallen *sekasha*.

"They have been given up to the sky."

"Well, I prepared Sparrow but no one has come for her. The enclaves—they have no phones. I wasn't sure what to do."

Bladebite recognized Sparrow's English nickname. He spat on the ground in disgust.

"No one will come for Sparrow." Wolf turned back to pacing the clearing.

"What do you mean?" Covington fell in step with Wolf.

"Sparrow betrayed her clan. We will have nothing to do with her now. Deal with her body as if she was an oni."

Cloudwalker suddenly trotted up to them, looking concerned. "*Domou!* We have a problem."

"What is it?" Wolf cocked his fingers to call the winds.

Cloudwalker pointed to the oak trees. Humans had chained themselves to the massive trunks.

"How did they get there?" Wolf glanced around at the three Hands of *sekasha* scattered across the clearing.

Cloudwalker blushed with embarrassment. "We—we tested them and they were not oni. They had no weapons."

They did have a banner that read, "Save the oaks." Wolf had heard of this type of lunacy, but never seen it in action. How did they get organized so quickly?

"We did not realize that they were not part of the human work crew," Cloudwalker finished. "So we let them pass. What do you want us to do with them?"

Wolf didn't completely trust his *sekasha* to solve the problem without involving swords. He didn't want dead peaceful protesters. "Call Wraith Arrow—he has the EIA helping him. Have them send the police to arrest these humans."

Covington waited as if there was more he needed. Wolf turned to him.

"I'm not sure what to do with the oni," Covington continued their conversation. "Do you know their practices?"

"I am told that in times of plenty, they feed their dead to their hounds," Wolf said. "In times of famine, they eat both their dead and their dogs."

"I don't believe that's true. That's the kind of sick propaganda that always gets generated in a war."

"Elves do not lie." Wolf paused to consider the areas he had just paced off. He believed that the one section of the clearing was large enough for the dreadnaught to land easily, even in high winds. The other sections, however, were deceptively small—they should mark the areas in some manner.

"Everyone lies." Covington demonstrated in two words the humans' greatest strength and weakness. They were able to look at anything and see it as human. It gave them great ability to empathize but it also kept them from seeing others clearly.

"Our society is built on blind trust," Wolf said. "Lying is not an option for us."

But Covington couldn't see it. Perhaps it was too big for him to grasp. The need for truth came from everything from their immortality to their fragile memory, to the ancient roots of the clans, to the interdependency of their day to day lives. Tinker, though, seemed to understand it to her core.

"Treat Sparrow as you see fit." Wolf knew that Covington would be true to his human nature, and treat her with respect, but unknowingly consign the dead elf to the horrors of embalming fluid, a coffin, and a grave instead of open sky. "Ask the EIA what to do with the oni bodies. Be aware that there will be more. Many more."

Tinker's grandfather always said that you needed a plan for everything from baking a cake to total global domination. He taught her the minutia of project management along with experimental and mathematical procedure. Over the years, she had put the skill to good use, from starting a small salvage business at age fourteen, to thwarting the oni army with just her wits and one unarmed *sekasha*.

The truly wonderful thing about focusing on a complex project was there wasn't time to think of messy, extraneous details like elfin wedding customs. Just trying to drain the buildup of magic out of the cooler required creative scavenging for parts and guerilla raids across the city for workers. She designed four jury-rigged pumps that used electromagnets to siphon magic into steel drums of magnetized iron fillings. Unfortunately, the drums would slowly leak magic back out, so they would have to rotate them out, letting them sit someplace until inert. While the siphons were inside the cooler, she sat the drums outside, so whoever changed them didn't need to enter the locked room. The walls seemed solid enough—she would have to check the architectural drawings to be sure, but certainly reinforcing the door wouldn't hurt.

The more she considered safety procedures, the less sure she was this was a good idea. The project, however, was rampaging beyond her ability to stop it. The Reinholds employees were searching out drawings and adding bars to the door, the EIA was sending a tractor-trailer truck to Lain's, a dozen hastily drafted elves were gathering to help with the move, and she'd given out her promises like Halloween candy.

Why was she doing this again? Was her only reason some nonsense out of a dream? Or was she really focusing on the tree so she didn't have to consider that Tooloo was right?

Afraid that she'd fry any of her computer equipment, she had stuck to low-tech project management. Settling on the loading dock's edge, she wrote "*domi*" on her pad of paper and then slowly circled it again and again as her thoughts spun around the question.

Without question, she was Windwolf's *domi*—the queen herself had confirmed that. Tinker had assumed that *domi* meant "wife"; for a long time she simply translated it as "wife." Later, she had sensed that it didn't mean quite the same thing. And Windwolf never used the English word "wife" or for that matter, "married." He'd given her some beans, a brazier, and a *dau* mark. She rubbed at her *dau* between her eyebrows, feeling the slight difference in skin texture under the blue glyph. What the hell kind of wedding ceremony was that? And nothing else? Hell, when Nathan's cousin Benny had been married by the justice of the peace, they still had a wedding reception afterward. Surely the elves did *something* to celebrate a marriage—so why hadn't there been *something*?

If *domi* didn't mean "wife," what did it mean? When she had talked to Maynard two months ago about it, she'd gotten the impression it meant she was married, but now she couldn't recall the exact words that Maynard had used. What she remembered distinctly was how Maynard had been carefully trying to keep his balance on the fence between the humans and the elves. Had she heard only what she wanted to hear? Certainly it would make a neater package for Maynard if Windwolf had married Tinker instead of just carried her off to be a live-in prostitute.

Whispering in the bottom of her soul was a small voice that called her a glorified whore. She couldn't ignore the fact that the only thing she did with Windwolf was have sex. Great sex. Wives did more than that—didn't they? Nathan's mother and sisters went grocery shopping, cooked for their husbands, and cleaned up the dirty dishes but Lemonseed handled all that for Windwolf. Wives washed clothes—Nathan's sisters actually had long discussions on the best ways to get out stains. Dandelion, however, headed the laundry crew.

Without thinking about it, she started a decision tree, branching out "wife" and "whore." What difference did it make to *her*? She never worried about being a "good girl" but at the same time, she had always been contemptuous of women who were either too dumb or too lazy to do real work, using their bodies instead of their brain to make a living. Could she live with all of Pittsburgh knowing that she was a glorified whore?

Stormsong squatted down beside her, took the pencil from her hand, and scratched out "whore" and "wife" and wrote "lady." "That, *domi*, is the closest English word. It means 'one who rules.' It denotes a position within the clan that oversees households that have allegiance to them but are not directly part of their household."

"Like the enclaves?"

"Yes, all the enclaves of Pittsburgh owe fidelity to Wolf Who Rules. He chose people he thought could function as heads and supported the building of their households. It is a huge undertaking to convince people to leave their old households and shift to a new one. To leave the Easternlands—to come to this wilderness— to settle beside the uneasy strangeness of Pittsburgh—"

Stormsong shook her head and switched to English. "You have no fucking idea how much trust these people have in Wolf."

"So why did he choose me? And why do these people listen to me?"

"I think that he sees greatness in you and he loves you for it. And they trust him."

"So they don't really trust me?"

"Ah, we're elves. We need half a day to decide if we need to piss."

"So—I'm not married to him?"

Stormsong tilted her head side to side, squinting as she considered the two cultures. "The closest English word is 'married' but it's too—small—and common."

"So, it's grand and exotic—and there's no ceremony for it?"

Stormsong nodded. "Yup, that's about it."

A hoverbike turned into the alley with a sudden roar. Stormsong sprang to her feet, her hand going to her sword. Pony checked the female *sekasha* with a murmur of "*Nagarou*" identifying Tinker's cousin Oilcan as the sister's son of Tinker's father.

Oilcan swooped around the extra barrels and dropped down to land in front of the loading dock where Tinker sat.

"Hey!" Oilcan called as he killed his hoverbike's engine. "Wow! Look at you."

"Hey yourself!" Tinker tugged down her skirt, just in case she was flashing panty. Gods, she hated dresses. "Thanks for coming."

"Glad to help." He leaned against the chest-high dock. Wood sprites were what Tooloo had called them as kids—small, nut brown from head to bare toes, and fey in the way people used to think elves would look. Beneath his easy smile and summer stain of walnut, though, he seemed drawn.

"You okay?" She nudged him in the ribs with her toe.

"Me?" He scoffed. "I'm not the one being attacked by monsters every other day."

"Bleah." She poked him again to cover the guilty feeling of making him so worried about her. "It's like—what—nearly noon? And there's not a monster in sight."

"I'm glad you called." He pulled out a folded newspaper.

"Otherwise I might have been worried. Did you see this?"

"This" was a full front-page story screaming "Princess Mauled." She hadn't seen a photographer yesterday when Windwolf carried her through the coach yard but apparently one had seen her. She flopped back onto the cement. "Oh, son of a turd."

Oilcan nudged against her foot, as if seeking the closeness they had just moments before. "I'm sorry, I shouldn't have shown it to you."

"You didn't take the picture." Lying down felt too good, like she could easily drift to sleep. She sat back up and held out her hand for the paper. "Let me see how bad it really is."

She looked small, helpless, and battered in Windwolf's arms, covered with an alarming amount of blood. The picture caption was "Viceroy Windwolf carries Vicereine Tinker to safety after she and her bodyguards were attacked by a large wild animal."

"What the hell is a vicereine?" she asked.

"Wife of the viceroy."

"Oh." There, she was married, the newspaper said so. "It still sounds weird."

"Vicereine?"

"All of it. Vicereine. Princess. Wife. Married. It seems unreal for some reason."

She scanned the story. It was odd that while it was she and the five elf warriors in the valley, all the information came from human sources. It listed her age and previous address, but only gave Stormsong's English name, not her full elfin one of *Linapavuata-watarou-bo-taeli* which meant Singing Storm Wind. And the *sekasha* were labeled "royal bodyguards." Was it because the reporter didn't speak Elvish, or was it because the elves didn't like to talk about themselves? She learned nothing except that the news had a very human slant. It was odd that she hadn't noticed before.

"Even after all this time, you don't feel married?" Oilcan asked. She made a rude noise and nudged him again in the ribs with her toe. "No. Not really. It doesn't help that Tooloo is spreading rumors that I'm not."

"She is? Why?"

"Who knows why that crazy half-elf does anything?" Tinker

wasn't sure which was worse: that Tooloo was considered an expert on elfin culture, or that the people Tinker cared about most all shopped at Tooloo's general store. Her lies would spread out from McKees Rocks like a virus with an authenticity that the *Pittsburgh Post-Gazette* couldn't touch.

"Hell," she continued. "It was like three days before I even figured out that I was married—I don't even remember what I said when he proposed."

"Does he treat you well?" Oilcan asked. "Doesn't yell at you? Call you names? Try to make you feel stupid?"

She made the kick a little harder. "He's good to me. He treats me like a princess."

"Ow!" He danced away, laughing. "Okay, okay. I just don't want to see you hurt." He sobered, and added quietly. "My dad always waited until we were home alone."

His father had beaten his mother to death in a drunken rage. When Oilcan came to live with them, he was black-and-blue from head to knees, and flinched at a raised hand.

"Windwolf isn't like your dad." She tried not to be angry at the comparison; Oilcan was only worried about her. "If nothing else, he's a hell of a lot older than your dad."

"This is a good thing?"

Tinker clicked her tongue in an elfin shrug without thinking and then realized what she'd done. "The elves have been so much more patient than I could ever imagine being. Windwolf has moved his whole household to Pittsburgh to make me happy, because to them, living here for a couple decades is nothing."

"Good."

"Now, are you going to help me with this tree?" she asked.

"I'll think about it." He grinned impishly.

8: CALLING THE WIND

—•→⟹ ⟸←•—

She had to learn not to be surprised when Windwolf popped up at odd times.

She was stretched out on the back room's floor, making a copy of her grandfather's spell. Her attempts with a camera had failed, the magical interference corrupting the digital image. After what it had done to the camera, she had decided against bringing in her datapad to scan it. Instead she had Reinholds find a roll of brown packaging paper. She had covered the floor with paper, and now was making a tracing by simply rubbing crayons lightly across the paper, pressing harder when she felt the depression of the spell tracings. Working with the damaged spell made her nervous, and her dress was driving her nuts, so she had stripped down to underwear and socks and Oilcan's T-shirt.

She'd worn the black crayon out, so she upended the box, spilling the rest of the crayons out onto the floor beside her. The array of colors splayed out on the floor shoved all other thoughts from her mind. She used to make magic pencils by mixing metal filings into melted crayons, pouring them into molds and then wrapping them with construction paper. The only bulk supply of crayons were the packs of sixty-four different shades, which she would separate into the eight basic colors: red, orange, yellow, green, blue, purple, black, and white. It got so she could look at a spray of crayons and see those eight—but she was seeing twelve now.

Since becoming an elf, she knew she saw the world slightly differently. Things she thought were beautiful had been suddenly nearly garish or clashed weirdly. This was the first time that she had proof that Windwolf had somehow changed her basic vision.

"There you are." Windwolf's voice came from above her.

She glanced up to find him standing beside her. "What are you doing here?"

"I was told that you were here, drawing pictures—mostly naked."

"*Pfft.*" She focused back on the paper, not sure how she felt about knowing that her vision had been changed. In a way, it was like getting glasses—right? "I only took my boots, bra, and dress off."

"I see."

She glanced over her shoulder at him and blushed at how he was looking at her. "Hey!"

He grinned and settled cross-legged besides her, resting his hand on the small of her back. "This is an odd beast."

It took her a moment to realize he meant the damaged spell, not her.

"Do you recognize it?"

"In a manner of speaking. It is not a whole spell." He studied the circuits. "This is only an outer shell—one that controls effects put out by another spell."

She had been focusing on the various subsections and hadn't realized that they didn't form a complete spell. Her knowledge of magic came solely from experimentation and her family's codex, which itself seemed to be an eclectic collection of spells.

"It's possible that this machine sets up a spell-like effect." Windwolf motioned to the compressor. "And this shell modifies that effect."

"Oh, yes. The heat exchanger could be acting like a spell."

"These are Stone Clan runes. See this symbol?" He traced one of the graceful lines. "This subsection has to do with gravitational force—which falls within earth magic."

"I didn't realize it was Stone Clan."

"Where did you learn it?" he asked.

"My family has a spell codex that's been handed down for generations."

"This means that your forefather was a Stone Clan *domana*."

"How can you be so sure?"

"Such spells are closely guarded. The clan's powers rest on the control of their element."

"Maybe he stole it." That appealed to her, a master thief as an ancestor.

"With your family's sense of honor, that is unlikely."

That pleased her more. She abandoned the tracing to roll over and smile up at him. "So my family is honorable, eh?"

He put his warm palm on her bare stomach to rub lazy circles there. "Very. It shows in everything you and your cousin do."

"Hmm." She enjoyed the moment, gazing up at him. The look in his eyes always made her melt inside. It still stunned her that someone could be directing such love toward her. How did she get so lucky? Of course her brain cared more about puzzles. "But I couldn't feel magic before you made me your *domi*."

Windwolf shook his head. "The magic sense is a recessive trait. It would have quickly vanished in the following generations of mating with humans."

"Would I be able to use their spell stones?"

"I doubt it very much." Windwolf shook his head. "Only part of that is ability, though; the rest is politics. Even if you somehow retained the needed genes, the Stone Clan will not train my *domi*."

"That's a bitch."

There was a slight noise and Windwolf glanced toward it. One of the *sekasha* who came with him, Bladebite, took up post by the door from the machine room into the warehouse. The pallets with the black willow filled the dim room now. The door out to summer was just a distant rectangle of light on the other side of the tree. For a moment, all of their attention was on the still tree. Thankfully, the siphons were working—she could sense no overflow of magic—and the tree remained dormant. She needed to finish up so they could kick on the compressor and take the refrigeration room down to freezing.

"I do not like you working close to that thing," Windwolf said. "The *sekasha* would not be able to kill it if it roused."

"I know. It usually takes dynamite and a bulldozer to take one down. But I think my dreams are saying that it's a key to protecting what we have."

"Dreams are hard to interpret."

"Yeah, yeah, I know. That's one thing I did learn with the whole pivot stuff—this dream stuff is counterintuitive. What feels like the wrong thing is sometimes the right thing."

The queen's oracle, Pure Radiance, had foreseen that Tinker would be the one person who could block the oni invasion of Elfhome—the pivot on which the future would turn. Oracles seemed to operate on the Heisenberg Uncertainty Principle; apparently telling Tinker how she was going to stop the oni would keep Tinker from doing it. Considering Chiyo's mind reading ability and Sparrow's betrayal, it was just as well that the oracle had been obscure. Thinking back, though, Pure Radiance must have known more than she told Tinker; having Tinker dragged to Aum Renau and kept there for three weeks allowed Tinker to strengthen her body, build a strong relationship with Pony, and learn skills she needed to kill Lord Tomtom, the leader of the oni.

Nevertheless, the key to stopping the oni had been doing what they wanted her to do—which seemed to completely defy logic.

"At least travel with a full Hand," Windwolf said. "Chose four more—any one of them would be proud to pledge to you."

"I don't want to take your people from you. Besides, didn't you say that once I took Pony that I couldn't set him aside without making him look bad? How could you give me yours without insulting them?"

"I cannot give them to you. They must offer themselves to you. It is their hearts, which I cannot rule, which you accept."

There were times she felt like the conversation had been run through a translator one too many times. "How can I just choose four at random? Wouldn't that be me asking and you giving?"

"They have let me know that if you need them, they would be willing to go. I have released all of them from their pledge so that they are free to go."

"All of them?"

Windwolf nodded. "With the exception of Wraith Arrow. I need him. You have gained much respect with the *sekasha*. And I am greatly pleased."

"Wow."

"What do you think of Stormsong? Do you fit with her?"

Fit with her? That was an interesting choice of words. Not "like her," which was what she expected Windwolf to ask. "She's a pistol. Sometimes it seems like she's two different people, depending on which tongue she's speaking."

"A language can govern your thoughts. You cannot think of something if you have no words for it. English is a richer language than Elvish, infused with countless other tongues over time. And in so many ways, English is freer. Elvish is layered heavily with politeness to enforce the laws of our society."

Tinker considered. Yes, politeness came more readily to her when she spoke Elvish. It was only when she was using the very formal, very polite High Elvish that she noticed—and then it was because it felt like being handcuffed into being nice.

"I like speaking English with you," Windwolf said. "I feel like I can just be me—the male that loves you, and not the lord and ruler of our household. That we show each other our true faces when we talk like this."

"Yeah, I noticed that when Stormsong drops into High Elvish, it's like she puts on a mask."

"We speak so little High Elvish here compared to court. My mother says that this rough country is making me uncouth—I'm too plainspoken after being around humans so long. She expects me to come home wrapped in bearskins."

She couldn't believe that anyone could think of him, and all his smooth elegance, as uncouth. "Oh, please."

"If you're determined, you can be eloquently insulting in High Elvish. Court makes an art out of it. I don't have the patience for that—which has earned me a label of boorish."

"Idiots, they deserve a bloody nose."

"My little savage." He pulled her into his arms and kissed her soundly. "I love you dearly—and don't ever lose your fierce heart—but please, pick no fights, not until you've learned to defend yourself."

She skirted promising him anything by kissing him.

"Are you done here?" he asked much later.

"With this part." Reluctantly she slipped out of his arms to lift up the paper that had been covering the spell. "I dug through my grandfather's things and found his notes on this project. I need to compare this to what he has and then fix it. I'll finish it up tomorrow."

"Good," Windwolf said. "There is much we have to do and things I want to do. For instance, I want to talk to you about what direction we're going with the computing center."

"The what?" she asked before remembering. When she had returned to the Pittsburgh area during Shutdown, she had realized that technology on Elfhome was nonexistent. From electrical power to Pittsburgh's limited Internet, everything went with the city when it returned to Earth. In a fit of panic, she'd razed ten acres of virgin forest and drafted a small army to start work on building infrastructure. Since she had been kidnapped only hours into the project, she hadn't even gotten the chance to ask belated permission, let alone finish it. "Oh. That. I wasn't sure—you know—if you even considered it a good idea."

"I think it's an excellent idea."

"I haven't even thought about it since that morning."

"You left quite detailed plans." He brushed his hand along her cheek. "I made a few changes and had it finished. I'd like to expand it, though we probably should wait until the oni have been dealt with."

"But Pittsburgh is kind of stuck here now. What's the point?"

"The point is that Pittsburgh, right or wrong, feels too human for elves to make technology their own. It's like our cooks in Poppymeadow's kitchen; they can cook there, but it's not their kitchen, so they bow out and eat whatever Poppymeadow's staff makes. The changes I made to the computing center were ways to make it more comfortable for our people to use."

"Wow, I never thought of that." In truth, she hadn't been thinking about anyone but herself that morning. "How long do you think we can keep this level of technology, though, without Earth?"

"Once the oni are dealt with, we will find a way back to Earth." Windwolf promised with his eyes.

"Pittsburgh is never going back. The only way to affect all of Pittsburgh is from orbit. Even if we managed to start a space program, we'd have to get the alignment perfect so the enclaves stay here, and then sending Pittsburgh to the right universe . . ." She shivered. "I don't want that kind of responsibility."

"You and I can shake the universe until we find a way." He kissed her brow. "But first things first. Come, get dressed, and let me teach you magic."

Much to her surprise, he took her to the wide-open field where they had been building the new viceroy's palace. Oddly, a gossamer was moored here instead of at the Faire Grounds. They pulled to the edge of the abandoned project and got out of the Rolls. The entire thirty acres had been covered with sod.

"Why here?" She swung up onto the gray Phantom's hood. The windswept woman of its hood ornament— the spirit of ecstasy— seemed so appropriate for the Wind Clan. She wondered if that was how Windwolf had ended up with the Rolls Royce.

"The spell stones represent massive power." Windwolf settled beside her on the hood. "Poppymeadow would probably be annoyed if you lost control of the winds in her orchard."

There was a typical Windwolf answer. Did he sidestep the real question on purpose or was he teasing her with his very dry humor or did they just simply have a fundamental miscommunication problem?

"You're going to teach me how to fly?"

"No," he said slowly. "You will learn how, someday, but not from me, not today."

Her disappointment must have showed, as he actually explained more.

"I have sent for a *sepana autanat*," Windwolf told her. "But arrangements must be made, and such things take time."

"A what?"

"He trains the clan children in magic." He paused to search out the English word. "A teacher."

"Oh." She'd had so few teachers in her life that the idea of a total stranger teaching her was unsettling. "Can't you just teach me yourself?"

"I wish I could, but there are things I don't remember of the early lessons. And there were so many silly learning games we played that even now I don't understand why we did them. I suspect that they were to teach focus and control."

"What kind of games?"

He gave an embarrassed smile. "You will laugh." He stood up, squared his shoulders, and closed his eyes. Taking a breath, he raised his hands to his head, and eyes still closed, splayed out his fingers like tree branches waving in a breeze. "Ironwood stand straight and tall." He dropped his hands slightly so his thumbs were now in his ears, and he flapped the hands. "Gossamer flies over all." Hands to nose this time. "Flutist plays upon his pipe. Cook checks to see if fruit is ripe." He touched index fingers together. "Around and around, goes the bee." He spun in place three times. "Yeah, yeah, yeah, yeah, yeah."

He clapped five times and launched into the song again, faster this time, and then again, faster still. Windwolf was right; she had to giggle at him. He was so regally beautiful, yet he purposely used a childish singsong voice as he wiggled his fingers, spun in place, and clapped his hands. After the third round, he collapsed beside her, laughing. "Well, you're supposed to do that faster and faster, until you're too dizzy."

"What is that supposed to teach you?"

"I don't know." He lay back onto the warm hood to watch the clouds roll overhead, considering. "I think—it might have been staying aware of where your body is regardless of what you're doing. That is very important in controlling magic. There is much for you to learn, and not all of it has to do with controlling the winds."

She scoffed at that understatement. "I thought I knew a lot about elves, about clans and everything, but I'm finding that I don't know anything at all. Like I didn't know each clan had their own spells."

Windwolf considered her for a moment, sadness gathering at the edges of his eyes. "Yes, there is so very much you need to learn. I suppose some history can not hurt, and probably help make sense of our people."

She had heard one long history lesson from Tooloo, but Tooloo tended to twist things to her own unique way of looking at things. "Yeah, it might help."

"In the beginning all elves were much like humans, as evidenced by the fact that we can still interbreed," Windwolf started. "Perhaps—there is a chance—that the first elves were humans, lost through the gateways from Earth to Elfhome—or maybe humans are the ones that became lost. We were tribes scattered, hither and yon, and in our homelands, we practiced the magic that was strongest. Back then, magic was considered holy, and those that used magic were our priests, and they were the first of the clan leaders."

This was different than what Tooloo had told her, in tone if not in fact.

"I don't understand," Tinker asked. "I thought all magic is the same. It's just a general force harnessed by the mechanics of a spell, right?"

"Yes and no. The Wind Clan spells have been refined for millennia, but they are based on certain natural properties. The Wind Clan, according to legends, started in the high steppe lands. For countless generations, those freeborn tribes used their magic, and were slowly changed by it. That's where the genetic stamp developed that allows you to key to one set of spell stones or another."

"But didn't the Skin Clan gather all those tribes together and force them to be the same?"

"They tried. They would conquer a tribe and do all they could to stamp out its culture. Burning temples. Killing the leaders, the scholars, and the priests. Skin Clan were ruthless masters, but we were not totally helpless. We managed to hide away some of our priests, keep them hidden for centuries. We formed secret societies that evolved into the clans. As slaves all we had to call our own was our life, our honor, and our pledge to protect and to serve. But those were weapons strong enough to overthrow the Skin Clan."

"So—since everything had to be kept secret—ceremonies like weddings were a big no-no?" If so, then her marriage to Windwolf made a lot more sense.

"Yes, we could not afford to be discovered. Simple words, whispered between two people, were all we could trust."

"How did the *domana* end up ruling?"

"The clan leaders realized that the only way we could win against the Skin Clan was to use their greatest abilities against them. Once the Skin Clan became immortal, they ordered all their bastards killed. We started to hide away healthy babies, offering up stillborn and deformed infants in their place. They were protected by the clan so that they could protect the clan."

Tooloo had told her a version of this, only somehow not as noble, not so desperate. Quick Blade, Windwolf's great-grandfather, had been one of the babies hidden away and had died fighting for his adopted clan's freedom.

"After we won the war with the Skin Clan, we suffered a thousand years of war among ourselves. Clan against clan. Caste against caste. Elf against elf. We had lived so long in slavery that we had no idea how to be free. It was the *sekasha* that held us together—they demanded that the clan structure be maintained when the other castes would have abandoned it."

"I would have thought it was the *domana* that kept the clans intact."

"The other castes feared that we would become cruel monsters like our fathers. The *sekasha* guard us—from harm and from ourselves. More than one *domana* has been put down by his own Hand."

"Why did *sekasha* want the *domana* in charge instead of just taking power themselves?"

It was as if Windwolf never considered the "why" of it. He

frowned and thought for a minute. "I am not sure. It is the way they wanted it. Perhaps it was because with the *domana's* access to the spell stones, the *sekasha's* choices were limited to putting the *domana* in power, destroying the stones, or killing all the *domana*. While they are *sekasha* first, they are fiercely loyal to their clans. It is their nature to be so. And as such, it would go against their nature to weaken their clan."

"So the spell stones and the *domana* stayed."

Windwolf nodded. "And we have had what passes as peace for thousands of years—because of the *sekasha*."

Tinker glanced over to where Pony and Stormsong stood. Close enough to protect. Far enough away to give her and Windwolf a sense of privacy. Who was really in charge? On the surface, it would seem she was—but if she was—why was she stuck with *sekasha* watching her when she would rather be alone?

"In the Westernlands, the Wind Clan has only the spell stones at Aum Renau." Windwolf returned to his magic lesson. "On the other side of the ocean, there are other sets.

"What's the range of a set?"

"The stones can reach one *mei*; Pittsburgh is one-third *mei* from the coast."

It finally explained one mysterious elfin measurement. Unlike human measurements which were exact, the *mei* was said to be roughly a thousand human miles but subject to change. At Aum Renau, Windwolf had shown her how he cast a trigger spell. It set up a quantum level resonance between him and the spell stones, in essence a conduit for the magic to follow. Power *jumped* the distance. It had been his demonstration at Aum Renau that had given her the idea of how to destroy both gates. Magic, though, could be influenced by the moon's orbit and other factors, so the exact distance would be variable—which fit the quantum-based system.

The distance limit also explained why only two clans were coming to help them deal with the oni.

"So, the Stone Clan and Fire Clan each have a set of stones within a *mei*?"

"Yes."

"And spell stones from different clans can overlap." Tinker wanted to be sure she had it right.

"Yes. The *domana's* genetic key determines which one they pull from. The spells are slightly different. In the terms of battle, the Stone Clan is much weaker in attack, but they are superior in defense. Their specialty is mining, farming, and architecture."

Architecture was the forefather of engineering. It kind of made sense—her being Stone Clan and a genius in the hard science.

"Do we actually fight with them?"

"Yes and no. There has been no open warfare between the clans for two thousand years, not since the Fire Clan established the monarchy. To a human, that might seem like lasting peace, but my father saw battle as a young man, and our battles have merely become more covert. Fighting is limited to assassinations and formal duels."

The concept of elves wanting her dead was somewhat unnerving.

"You are under the queen's protection," Windwolf continued. "So you will be fairly safe from the other clans for the time being. I want to teach you, however, a shielding spell so you can defend yourself."

"Oh cool."

He laughed and distanced himself from the Rolls. "Have you been taught the rituals of prayer?"

She nodded.

"Good. First you must find your center, just as you do for a ritual." He stood straight and took a deep cleansing breath.

"Hold your fingers thus." He held out his right hand, thumb and index rigid, middle fingers cocked oddly.

She copied the position and he made minute changes to her fingers.

"Each finger has several degrees. *Laedin.*" He tucked her index finger into a tight curl, and then, gliding his finger along the top of hers, showed her that there needed to be a straight line from the back of her hand to the knuckle. "*Sekasha.*" He uncurled her finger to the second knuckle and corrected a slight tendency to bend at the first knuckle. "*Domana.*" He had to hold her finger straight so she only bent the tip. "Full royal." This was a stiff finger.

"Bows to no one," Tinker said.

"Exactly. You must be careful with your hands. A broken finger can leave you defenseless.

"The first step is to call on the spell stones. You use a full suit—king and queen." These were thumb and pinkie held straight out. "*Domana, sekasha, laedin.*"

Tinker laughed as she tried to get her fingers to cooperate.

"There are finger games you can play to get them to do this fluidly." He patiently corrected small mistakes in her hands. "In the base spells, correct positioning is not as vital, but later, a finger out of place will totally change the effect of your spell."

"This does get easier?"

"Yes, with practice.

"To call winds and cast the spells, you need to hold your hand before your mouth." He raised his hand to his mouth and demonstrated the desired distance and then dropped his hand to continue speaking. "Don't touch your face with your hand, but you should feel as if you're almost touching your nose. Also if you were to breathe out, like you were blowing out a candle, the center point of your breath would hit this center joint of your fingers."

"Okay." She held up her hand and found it was harder to not touch her nose than she thought.

"When I was little, my brothers and I would practice fighting with each other and in the heat of battle, sometimes we ended up punching ourselves in the nose."

Tinker laughed.

"Now, listen to the command to call the winds, and then to cancel." He raised his right hand to his mouth. "Daaaaaaaaaaaaaaaaaae."

Tinker felt the tremor in the air around Windwolf, like a pulse of a bass amplifier, first against her magic sense, and then against her skin.

Mentally, she knew that his body was taking the place of a written spell; his voice started the resonance that would establish a link between him and the spell stones, over three hundred miles away. Despite everything she knew, his summoning of power out of thin air somehow seemed more magical than any act she'd ever witnessed.

He dismissed the power with another gesture and spoken command.

"Now, you try it."

She felt the magic resonance deep in her bones, and then it bloomed around her, enveloping her. Carefully she dismissed it.

"Very good. Once you tap the stones, you are connected to them. That means you need to immediately use the power, or dismiss it. Casting a spell that you hold, like a shield, keeps the connection open until you end the spell. Casting a spell like a force strike breaks the link immediately."

She nodded her understanding, trusting that when he taught her the various spells, he would tell which category they fell into.

"The shielding spell I'm going to teach you is the most basic of all the spells, but it is very powerful. With the power that the spell stones tap, it is nearly impenetrable."

"Nearly?"

"I do not know anything that could breach it, but I am afraid that *you* might find something—so I put in a cautionary note."

She stuck out her tongue at him. "You make me sound like a troublemaker."

"You do not make trouble—it finds you. And it is always sorry when it does."

She laughed. "Flattery will get you everywhere."

He kissed her then, making her melt against his body. They spent a few pleasant minutes kissing, and then he set her firmly down.

"You need to learn this, my love. You need to be able to protect yourself and your beholden."

"Yeah, I know. Teach away. I'm all ears."

"You summon the power and then shape it." He called forth the power, paused deliberately, and then changed the position of his hand and spoke a new command. The magic pulsing with potential changed, distorting the air around them so they stood inside a transparent sphere.

He held his stance. "Nothing can get in unless you allow it. It will last as long as you desire—but you must be careful with your movements." He moved slowly around to demonstrate the range of motion desired to maintain the shield. "Notice you must keep your hand in the correct position. If you shift your fingers or move your hand too quickly, you lose the connection for the shield."

He flapped his hands loosely and the shields vanished.

"Ugh!" Tinker cried. "It seems dangerously easy to lose your shield when you least want to."

"There are weaker shields that don't require you to hold your position. The *sekasha* spell, for example, allows them to continue fighting without disrupting their shield. The difference in strength is—" He paused to consider a comparison. "—an inch of steel versus a foot."

"Oooh. I see." That messed with her head. She had assumed that *sekasha* provided protection to the *domana* during battle—keeping them safe as they called down lightning and such. It seemed that the truth was that the *domana* were heavy tanks during fighting. They were able to take massive damage as well as deal it. It seemed that the *sekasha* must be for day-to-day life, allowing the *domana* to sleep and eat without fear.

Windwolf called up the shield again and this time showed her how to properly cancel the shield. "It is best for you to get into the habit of intentionally dropping the shield rather than just relaxing your position."

It seemed easy enough, once you got past bending your fingers into pretzels. Tinker managed to initialize the resonance conduit, trigger the shield spell, hold it for a minute, and then cancel the shield spell.

"What about air? If you keep up the shield, do you run out of air?"

"No. Air slowly leaches in, as does heat and cold. The shield will protect you for a period of time in fire, but eventually the heat and smoke will overcome you."

"Ah, good to know."

"Someone comes," Stormsong murmured softly, looking east.

The *sekasha* pulled in tight as they watched the eastern skyline.

"Listen," Wraith Arrow said.

After a moment, Tinker heard the low drone of engines in the distance.

"It has to be the dreadnaught," Windwolf said.

"They're coming," Tinker murmured, wondering who "they" might be.

"Yes." Windwolf tugged on her wrist. "We need to return to the enclave."

Tinker glanced at him in surprise. She would have thought they would stay to greet the newcomers.

"I am not sure who the queen has sent," Windwolf explained. "I want to look our best. Can you change quickly?"

She supposed it depended on your idea of quickly. "I think I can. What should I wear?"

"The bronze gown, please."

"That's not the most formal one I have."

He smiled warmly at her. "Yes, but I love to see you in it."

She blushed and tried not to worry about how she was going to get into the dress quickly.

As they got into the Rolls, a shadow passed overhead accompanied by the low rumble of large engines. A dreadnaught slid out from behind the hill to hover near the treeline. She'd forgotten how massive the blend of airship and armored helicopter was; it dwarfed the ironwoods, its four massive rotor blades beating a storm of leaves out into the meadow. Barrels of heavy guns bristled from the black hull, like the spiked hide of a river shark. The gossamer moored at the clearing stirred nervously in the presence of the large predator-like craft. As they watched, the mooring lines were cast off and the gossamer gave way to the dreadnaught.

The thumping of the rotors suddenly echoed into her memories of her dream. In the background, constantly, had been the same sound.

She shivered at the foreknowledge, and wondered what her dream had been trying to warn her of.

9: TRUE FLAME

At Poppymeadow's enclave, she discovered one of the *sekasha* had called ahead. Half the females of Windwolf's staff ambushed her at the door and hurried her to her room. She tried not to mind as they clucked and fussed over her, pulling her out of clothes, washing her face, neck, and hands, and pulling the formal gown over her head. Certainly she wouldn't be able to dress quickly without them, but their nervousness infected her.

At least she was confident about how she looked. The dress was a deep, rich, mottled bronze that looked lovely against her dusky skin. Over the bronze silk was another layer of fine, nearly invisible fabric with a green leaf design, so that when the bronze silk moved, it seemed like sunlight through forest leaves. Unfortunately, it still had long sleeves that ended in a fingerless glove arrangement and the dainty matching slippers.

"Oh please, can I wear boots?"

"You'll be outside, so the boots are appropriate," Lemonseed proclaimed, and her best suede ankle boots were produced, freshly brushed.

Tinker stepped into the boots, the females fastened the row of tiny hooks and eyes made of cling vine and ironwood down the back of the gown, and she was dressed.

Windwolf waited by the car, wearing the bronze tunic that matched her underdress and a duster of the leaf pattern of her overdress. His hair was unbound in a shimmering black cascade down his back.

"Where is your jewelry?" he asked.

"They wanted me to wear the diamonds." She held out both necklaces. "But I thought the pearls would look better. I told them I'd let you pick."

"The pearls do look better." Windwolf took the diamond necklace and fastened it in place. "But the diamonds are for formal occasions such as this. The pearls would be for more intimate times, such as a private dinner party."

Sighing, she surrendered the pearls to Lemonseed for safekeeping. "We're just going out to the clearing and saying 'howdy,' aren't we?"

"We are greeting the queen's representatives who can strip us of everything if they deem us unable to protect what we hold. Appearance is everything."

"They can't *really* take everything—can they?"

"It is unlikely." Windwolf swept her into the Rolls. "Please, beloved, be on your best behavior. Keep to High Elvish—and forgive me, but speak as little as possible, since your High Elvish is still weak."

Great, the queen's representatives hadn't even landed and already she was being made to feel like a scruffy junkyard dog. Her annoyance must have shown on her face, because Windwolf took her hand.

"Beloved, please, promise me to keep that cutting wit of yours sheathed."

"I promise," she growled, but silently reserved the right to kick anyone who truly pissed her off.

Tinker could see why Windwolf had opted to dress first. True, the dreadnought had landed and its many gangplanks were lowered. There was, however, no sign of the queen's representatives. A sea of Fire Clan red moved around the ship as the queen's

Wyverns secured the area with slow thoroughness. Their Rolls was checked at the entrance to the clearing where Wyverns had already erected a barrier. After their identities were verified, the Rolls was directed to a shimmering white tent of fairy silk. An ornate rug already carpeted the tent. Servants were setting up a teak folding table, richly carved chairs, a map chest, and a tea service.

Leave it to elves to do everything with elegance.

The queen's Wyverns were tall, with hair the color of fire pulled back and braided into a thick cord. Like the Wind Clan *sekasha*, they wore vests of wyvern-scale armor, and permanent spell tattoos scrolled down their arms; both were done in shades of red that matched their hair.

All of Windwolf's *sekasha* had come with them and formed two walls of blue in the sea of red. Seeing all the *sekasha* en masse, Tinker realized not only how much alike the Wyverns looked, but also how much the Wind Clan *sekasha*—slightly shorter with black hair—looked the same. Only Stormsong stood out with her short blue hair.

"Are the *sekasha* of the various clans separate families?" Tinker whispered to Windwolf as she held out a hand to him, so he could help her out of the car. Experience had taught her that the long skirts loved to wrap tight around her ankles as she got in and out of cars and carriages—she had nearly gone face-first into the dirt several times.

"Hmm?" Windwolf steadied her as she scrambled out.

"They look alike." Once out, she twitched her skirts back into place.

"The Skin Clan liked their *sekasha* to match—like coach horses. They would bioengineer a generation to suit them and then breed them one to another. They would kill all the children that didn't express the desired traits, weeding out stock until it bred true, like drowning litters of puppies when a mutt gets into a pure breed's kennel."

"That's horrible!"

"That's why we rebelled against them. Why we will have nothing to do with the oni who are so much like them."

"This one has the domana *genome?" Lord Tomtom had said when he held her prisoner. "Perhaps I'll get my own litter on her."* Tinker shivered as she remembered Tomtom's clinical gaze on her. No wonder the elves hated and feared the oni so much.

Alertness spread through the Wyverns, like ripples in a pool, moving outward. A figure in white and gold emerged from the dreadnaught. With the focus of every person on the field tight on him, the tall male strode across the meadow to join them at the tent. He wore a vest of gold scale, white leather pants, and a duster of white fairy silk that flared out behind him as he walked.

He ducked into the tent and nodded to Windwolf. "Viceroy."

Windwolf bowed. "Prince General."

Prince? He had the queen's glorious beauty—the radiant white skin, the vivid blue eyes and oh-so-gold hair twisted into a *sekasha*-like braid.

Tinker carefully followed Windwolf's suit as to how low to bow. Not that she needed to worry, for the elf prince didn't even glance in her direction. The duster settled around him, revealing that it had a delicate white-on-white design of wyverns and flames.

"Well, it took a hundred and ten years." Surprisingly, the prince general used Low Elvish. He had a deep voice with a hint of rasp, as if he'd spent the day shouting. "But as I said, it was only a matter of time before you would be calling for help and then I would have to come save your sorry ass. Of course you never could do things small—you had to go find a nest of oni for me to wrestle."

Windwolf grinned hugely. "True!"

"Young pup!" The prince returned the smile and gave Windwolf a rough hug. "It is good to see you again. It has been too long."

"I have been busy."

"So I've heard."

"True Flame, this is my *domi*, my beloved Tinker of the Wind Clan. Beloved, Prince General True Flame of the Fire Clan."

The prince turned his vivid gaze onto her and his eyebrows arched up in surprise. "So this is your child-bride. They said she was little . . ."

"Spare her your razor truth, please, True. I love her dearly and do not wish to see her hurt."

True Flame snorted. "She better learn to guard her heart. Those vultures at court will rip her to shreds."

"I don't plan to take her to court . . ."

"Can we stop talking like I am not here?" Tinker matched True Flame's Low Elvish. A look from Windwolf told her that regardless of what True Flame did, she was expected to speak High Elvish.

"Certainly, cousin," True Flame said.

"Cousin?" Tinker glanced to Windwolf in confusion.

"My mother is the youngest daughter of Ashfall," Windwolf said, and then, seeing Tinker's blank look, added. "Ashfall was our first king."

True Flame gave Windwolf a look that clearly asked, *"She doesn't know that?"*

"Grandfather has been dead for *nae hae*," Windwolf said.

"We've only had three rulers," True Flame said. "Ashfall, Halo Dust, and Soulful Ember."

"Yes, my knowledge of all things elfin is lacking," Tinker acknowledged and managed to bite down on "I'm sure, however, you're equally ignorant of buckyballs." *Be nice to the male who can take everything away from you*, she reminded herself, and managed to force her mouth into a slight smile. Thank gods, Windwolf seemed to be friends with him.

True Flame took in the weak smile and turned back to Windwolf with a slight look of distaste.

"Once you come to know her, True, you will see why I chose her."

True Flame clicked his tongue and waved toward the table. "Time will tell. Most of your choices continue to mystify me. Sit. Let us discuss this mess you're in."

He pulled a map from the chest and spread it on the table. It showed the city of Pittsburgh and the surrounding areas of Elfhome in detail.

"First, what is happening here?" True Flame pointed at Turtle Creek on the map. "The whole area seems—wrong."

Windwolf explained the events that had led to Tinker creating the Ghostlands.

True Flame looked at Tinker with slight surprise, sweeping a look down over her, before saying, "She's surprisingly destructive for her size."

"That's part of her appeal," Windwolf agreed.

She kicked Windwolf under the table, which earned her another warning look. She gave the look back at him. Being nice was one thing, having them gang up on her was another.

"Can the oni cross from their world to ours through this unstable area?" At least True Flame asked her directly.

"I don't know," Tinker said. "I need to study the area more. In theory, there should not be enough energy to keep it unstable."

"We think at least one creature has come through." Windwolf said. "My *domi* was attacked in the valley yesterday by what we believe is an oni dragon. It is unlikely that the oni could have smuggled such a creature across all the borders on Earth—so it stands to reason that it's a new arrival."

"Then we will have to wait until this area is secure"—True Flame tapped Turtle Creek on the map—"before you can continue your study."

"If the oni can come through, then we're in trouble," Tinker said. "They had an army poised to come through my pathway. With a few hours of study, I can—"

"Child, you will stay out of this valley until I give you leave," True Flame said.

"I am not a child," Tinker snapped.

"You have learned your *esva*?" True Flame asked.

Tinker didn't know the word. She glanced to Windwolf.

"No, she hasn't," Windwolf said quietly, as if holding in anger. "You know it takes years of study."

"A *domi* protects her warriors as they protect her," True Flame said. "Until we know the enemy's strength, we will not endanger any of our people by pushing them onto the front lines with a helpless child to protect."

Windwolf put a hand to her shoulder as if he expected her to say something rude. Tinker, however, found herself glancing at Stormsong and Pony standing with the Wind Clan's *sekasha*. She hadn't been able to protect her people—she'd nearly gotten them killed. She looked away, embarrassed by True Flame's correct reading, and that she had failed Pony and the others so completely.

True Flame took her silence as agreement and moved on. "Have you been able to determine any other oni stronghold?"

"Not yet. Tinker killed their leader, Lord Tomtom, but the size of their organization and the type of operations that they were carrying out suggested a number of subordinates, which we haven't identified or located."

True Flame grunted and signaled for tea to be poured. A servant moved forward to fill the delicate china tea bowls. After a month at Aum Renau, Tinker knew that talking was a no-no without Windwolf's glance in her direction; some elf bullshit about appreciating the act of being civilized. She distracted herself with the honey and milk. True Flame studied the map of the sprawling Earth city and expanse of Elfhome wilderness, ignoring the tea. Silence would rule until True Flame, as highest ranked person at the table, spoke.

"The oni weakness has always been their own savagery," he said finally. "To keep his underlings in check, an oni keeps his people weak and in disorder. There is no chain of command. Once you killed this Lord Tomtom, it was each dog for himself until one could emerge as strongest."

True Flame locked his gaze on Tinker. "Each elf knows who is above them, and who is beneath them, and that neither relationship is stronger than the other. Those who serve are to be protected, those who protect are to be served. We are not wild animals thinking only of ourselves, but a society that works only when we each know our position and act accordingly."

Tinker forced herself to sip her tea and chose her words carefully. "Having seen the oni up close, there is no need to convince me which is better."

She expected another angry look from Windwolf, but his eyes filled with sorrow, which only made her more uncomfortable than his annoyance would have. She focused on her tea instead.

"The rest of my force will be arriving on gossamers shortly," True Flame said. "I was afraid that you'd be overrun before they could arrive, so I came on ahead."

"Thank you," Windwolf said. "If my beloved's aim had not been true, all would have been lost before you arrived."

"Tonight, we can bivouac in this field, and tomorrow, we'll start securing the city." True Flame ran his hand over the great expanse of wilderness. "The Stone Clan is traveling under escort of my force. I will have no choice but to reward them for their service."

"I know that," Windwolf said in a carefully neutral tone.

It hurt to see him sit there and take it. She couldn't just sit there and watch him bow his head and have the Stone Clan swoop in to take what he had carved out of raw wilderness. "Wolf Who Rules didn't summon Pittsburgh here. And there was no way he could have kept the humans off Elfhome—not even killing every last human would have done that—because then there would have been retaliation. The door was open to the oni by no fault of his."

"I know that," True Flame said.

"Then why should he be punished and the Stone Clan rewarded? You claim that our society works because everyone works together. What benefit would the Stone Clan reap if the world was flooded by oni? Wolf Who Rules has put everything on the line—where is his reward?"

"Because it is the law of our people: you hold only what you can protect. It is the law that kept the peace for thousands of years."

"Beloved," Windwolf said quietly. "It is not as unfair as it seems. We are making a choice. Does the city fall to Stone Clan, who are honorable elves, or to oni?"

"I wouldn't turn over a—a—a—warg to the oni." That was an unfortunate choice of words as it reminded her of the warg at the oni camp and poor, poor—but hopefully dead—Chiyo. How could someone she hated trigger such remorse? One thing was certain—she cried much too easily lately. "This sucks," she snapped in English, wanting to blot the evidence of tears out of her eyes, but the damn fancy sleeves of her gown were in the way. She turned away from True Flame; she didn't want him to see her crying. Yeah, yeah, impress the elf on how grown up you are and bawl like a baby.

There was movement beside her and she realized Pony had moved up to her side. It took everything she had not to reach for him.

"If I may be excused." She hated that her voice shook. "I wish to go back to the enclave."

"You may go," True Flame said.

She reached for Pony's arm. He got her up and away smoothly, almost as if tears weren't blinding her. So much for appearances.

A full Hand peeled off to accompany her and Pony back to the enclave. Somehow, just having Pony there clearing a path to her bedroom refuge made it possible to blink back the tears and get herself under control. Still she was fumble-fingered with emotion as she tried to undo the hooks of her dress.

She finally gave up. "Can you undo me?"

Pony stood behind her and unhooked the tiny fasteners down the back of her dress. "*Domi*, do not be upset. True Flame can see that your heart is in the right place."

She groaned at the echo of what Stormsong had said to her. "They will put that on my gravestone. 'Here lies Tinker, her heart was in the right place, but her foot was in her mouth and god knows where her brain went.'"

He chuckled. "Usually we judge ourselves harsher than anyone else does."

It was a relief to let the dress slither down to the floor. She stepped out of the pool of silk and picked it up, not wanting it to be ruined. She had messed up enough things already today.

"So, Wolf Who Rules' mother is—" Tinker paused to recall the various words the elves used to denote relationships. This was made tricky because she wasn't sure if True Flame's mother or father was the connection. If True Flame was Soulful Ember's brother, then his father was King Halo Dust. What was the word for paternal aunt? "—father's sister to True Flame?"

"Yes. Longwind and Flame Heart formed an alliance of the Wind Clan and Fire Clan. Wolf Who Rules spent his doubles at court under the queen's care, learning the fire *esva*. It was there that he gained the favor of his royal cousins."

"What is that? *Esva*?" She hung up the dress and considered what was in the closet to wear—all elfin gowns and the sexy white nightgown that she didn't feel like wearing. She wanted the familiar comfort of cotton. Had her shorts dried yet?

"An *esva* is all the spells scribed into a clan's spell stones."

"Wait. Fire? Wolf Who Rules is Wind Clan."

"He is both. He is the only one of his family who can access both Clan's spell stones. It was expected that he would choose to be Fire Clan, but he chose Wind Clan instead."

"Why?" She found the T-shirt she had borrowed off of Oilcan and sniffed at it. It was a little stinky. She wondered when Oilcan had last washed it.

"I can guess it was because he was born and raised in the Wind Clan," Pony said. "Such things are hard to ignore, but I cannot be sure. You will have to ask him."

The bedroom door opened and another of Windwolf's *sekasha*, Bladebite, stepped into the room. His gaze went down over Tinker; it was the heated calculating look a male gives a female. Suddenly the bra, underwear, and diamond necklace that had been plenty of clothes with Pony felt like nothing.

She clutched the T-shirt to her chest. "What is it, Bladebite?"

"It is time you finished your First Hand. I came to offer myself to you."

Oh shit. What should she do? She'd managed to screw up every single one of these encounters over the last two months, entering relationships with a careless "yes." After the look he'd given her, though, she didn't want to say yes—but would "no" be a deadly insult? She started to turn toward Pony, but Bladebite caught her arm, forcing her to look at him.

"This is between you and I, not him." Bladebite said. "You're making your preferences fairly clear to us all, but they're not wisely thought out. I have the experience you need. You should fill your Hand with strong males, not mutts like Singing

Storm."

"What the hell is wrong with her?"

"Since you obviously have no taste for Galloping Storm Horse . . ." Bladebite used Pony's true elfin name.

"I love Pony," she snapped, and blushed red as she realized it was true. When did that happen? "Things have changed since we left Aum Renau. We've been through a lot together."

"And if a fruit is tempting, you take a bite when you're most hungry."

What the hell did that mean?

"I offer all of me to you," Bladebite continued. "Do you accept?"

"I—I—I," she stammered. *I don't know what the hell to say.* The bedroom's dressing mirror was behind Bladebite. She could see Pony; his jaw was clenched but he made no move to interfere. Apparently Bladebite was right—it was up to her to say yes or no. Her reflection reinforced that she was nearly naked, the glitter of diamonds the only thing visible besides the T-shirt clutched to her chest. She never thought of herself as short, either, until something like this forcibly reminded her that the elves were all a foot taller.

"I can't make that decision now," she finally managed to force out. "I'm upset and not thinking clearly."

"You don't need to think. Just accept me."

Not think? Gods, he might as well be saying not breathe. "No." And then seeing the look on his face. "Not now. I'm too upset."

"We can't afford another spectacle—" Bladebite started.

But apparently she'd said the magic words. Pony's "on duty" light went on, and he shifted from behind Tinker to between her and Bladebite.

"Tinker *ze domi*" Pony used her most formal title and High Elvish, "said that she is upset and will decide later. Please, Bladebite, go."

The words were polite but Pony's tone was cold as steel.

Bladebite gaze locked with Pony's. For a moment, she was afraid that the older *sekasha* would draw his sword. He nodded though and bowed slightly to her. "Good night then, *ze domi*."

She started to shake when the door closed behind him.

"I am sorry, *domi*. Until you refused him, I could not act."

"Was I right to say no?"

"I am disappointed only in him. He has the years to know that you were upset and could not make such decisions."

She got dressed, annoyed that her hands still shook. Why was she veering all over the place emotionally? Maybe she was going to get her period. Usually she wasn't this hormonal, but she hadn't had one as an elf yet. Oh, she hoped that wasn't the case; thousands of years like this would drive her mad. How often did elves get periods? It had been over two months since her last one as a human. Oh gods, what if she was pregnant? Of course that made her feel weepy again.

"I need something to drink," she said. "Can you ask Poppymeadow to find us a bottle of—" What was that stuff called again? "Ouzo?" Wait, if she was pregnant, should she be drinking? And if she was just getting her period, what did elves use? Pads? Tampons? Magic? Hopefully a period only lasted the normal five days—surely even elves couldn't do—that—for more than a week. Damn it, when Windwolf made her an elf, he should have given her an owner's manual for her new body.

She fumbled with her necklace and failed to get it off. "Oh please, Pony, get this off me."

Pony undid the necklace. "I will get you something to eat and drink, and then perhaps you should take a nap. You have been through much lately, *domi*, and you are worn down."

"I want to practice magic." She needed to learn how to protect her people.

"It would be difficult and dangerous the way you are now."

She supposed that was true. "Okay, okay. Something to eat and a nap—and I need to talk to Stormsong about—female—things."

10: STORM WARNINGS

Wolf had watched his *domi* retreat with concern. He had expected her to be gnawing at the prince's ankles instead of breaking down into tears. He felt guilty for chiding her as he had. The oni must have affected her more deeply than he originally thought. He felt badly too that he had been pleased that she hadn't bedded Little Horse while they were prisoners together; he wanted her to himself as long as possible. Perhaps, if she had slept with Little Horse, she would have fared better.

At least she had turned to her beholden when she lost control of her emotions. As much as Wolf wished he could have taken her back to the enclave and comforted her, all of his people and the humans of Pittsburgh needed him to stay and deal with Prince True Flame.

Is this how the humans lived all their life? Having things that they desperately wanted to do—comfort their love ones, teach them what they needed to know—but with no time to do it? No wonder they seemed to rail at life so.

True Flame sat watching him, expression carefully neutral. "Being the pivot—" Wolf sighed and shook his head. "It has subjected her to extraordinarily difficult choices. She's only had hours to recover her center."

"This is recovered?"

"No, and it worries me."

True Flame glanced away, as if embarrassed by what he saw on Wolf's face. "Forgiveness, Wolf. We get along because we both have no need for empty politeness – but I remember now that politeness can render much needed gentleness to the soul. I will keep my sword sheathed from now on."

"Thank you."

"There will be nothing that I can do when the Stone Clan arrives except to remind them that she is under my sister's protection. She will have to interact with them, and they will take advantage of her."

Wolf nodded unhappily. "It will be like trying to keep wargs from the lambs at this point. I wish there was some way I could keep her safe until she has had time to heal from whatever the oni have done to her."

True Flame shook his head. "They'll arrive tomorrow with my troops. I can delay the *aumani* a day, on the pretense of giving them time to settle in."

"Thank you." In their current situation, a day was the most he could have hoped for. "Who have they sent?"

"Earth Son, Jewel Tear, and Forest Moss."

Wolf breathed out; the threesome was tailored for hostile opposition to him. He knew nothing of Forest Moss and thus could not foresee what danger lay there. Judging by the others, there was a good possibility, however, that this was an ancient member of the Stone Clan, to offset Wolf's youth. Earth Son's father was one of the three children of King Ashfall used to ally the strongest of the clans to the crown via marriage. Obviously Earth Son's inclusion was to eliminate Wolf's advantage with True Flame—at least in theory.

The Stone Clan had always misunderstood the nature of the alliance, and considered it a failure. The alliance had only produced Earth Son. While he showed his father's gene type in his height, his eyes, and his temper, his gene expression did not include attunement to the spell stones. Earth Son could not use the fire *esva*. When Earth Son came to court, he treated his Fire

Clan cousins as strangers, and was regarded as such by them.

In comparison, Wolf's parents produced ten children, half of which inherited their mother's genome and pledged to the Fire Clan. Wolf grew up seeing the royal family as an extension of his own and when he went to court, he fell under his older brothers' and sisters'protection. Earth Son seemed to fail to understand the slight differences in their position. He only saw the younger elf being rewarded with favor he thought he was due, and held it against Wolf.

The Stone Clan could barely find a delegate more ill-suited to deal with Wolf—but they had managed. Wolf spent a decade at summer court, thinking he and Jewel Tear were soulmates, the other half of each other, and all the other lyrical nonsense you thought while blindly in love. A hundred years and meeting Tinker had taught him that he'd been wrong about the entire nature of love. He and Jewel Tear had drifted apart soon after he came of age and his ambitions took him to the wilderness of the Westernlands. That the Stone Clan included her in the delegation probably meant he misjudged their relationship.

So these three were coming to his holdings and dealing with his people?

True Flame looked out at the sod-covered clearing and the dense forest of tower ironwoods beyond. "What in the god's name were you thinking of, leaving everything behind for this wilderness?"

"I was thinking of leaving everything behind for this wilderness."

"I've never understood why you're wasting yourself here."

"What would I be doing at court? Nothing has changed there since we last interacted with humans. We had completely stagnated. We had the same base of technology as the humans, and yet we didn't develop the car, or the computer, the telephone, or the camera."

"We have no need of them."

"It doesn't bother you that we sat completely still for hundreds of years while they raced ahead?"

"Less than three hundred years, pup. It passed like a lazy summer afternoon in my life."

Wolf clenched his jaw against this. He'd heard the like all his life from elves younger than True Flame's two thousand years. "Every agricultural advance since the days of poking holes in the ground with sharp sticks, we've stolen from the humans. The plow. Crop rotation. Fertilization. You're old enough to remember the great famines."

True Flame gave him a look that would have silenced him as a child.

Wolf refused to be rebuked. The events of the last three decades had proved him right. "It's as if we get locked into one mind-set—"this is how the world is," and can't conceive or desire something more. I tracked back all our advances while I was at court—"

"I've heard this theory of yours, Wolf."

"Have you? Have you really listened to my words and thought it through?"

"True, there were times of famine, and yes, we went to Earth and saw how to increase crop production and put those techniques to use. But we have lived in peace for thousands of years with all that we could want—why should we clutter up our lives with gadgets?"

Wolf sighed. "You never listened. Not to anything I ever said, did you? I told you over a hundred years ago that sooner or later, the humans would come to us. And I'm telling you now, it's only a matter of time before another race finds us."

One instructional conversation with Stormsong, one stiff drink, one mystery meal of panfried wild game (what in gods' name had drumsticks that size?), and one short nap, and Tinker was feeling much better.

According to Stormsong, her emotional swings were from exhaustion. It would be a year before Tinker would need to worry about a period. Nor, Stormsong said as she poured a generous round of ouzo, could Tinker be pregnant. "Drink, eat, sleep," Stormsong repeated Pony's advice, only more succinctly.

It was fairly clear that *discussions* had taken place while Tinker was asleep. There was an undercurrent running through the *sekasha* and they were metaphorically tiptoeing around her as if she would break. She wasn't sure which was more annoying: that they felt that they needed to tiptoe, or that they were doing such a horribly obvious job at it. At least it kept Bladebite from hounding her, although he was clearly sulking.

Much to Tinker's disgust, Stormsong coaxed her out to the enclave's bathhouse. She went only because the enclave had no showers and the last time she done more than wallow in a sink was at the hospice. She was starting to stink even to herself. She thought she hated elfin bathing—the cold water prescrub gave new meaning to the word unpleasant—but when she discovered that the bathhouse was both communal and mixed sex, she decided to loathe elfin bathing. As far as she was concerned, if the gods wanted them naked, they wouldn't have invented clothing.

The bath at least was stunning, done in jewel-toned mosaics with marble columns and a great skylight of beveled glass. Minerals had been added to the hot water, so it was hazy to the point that it gave a small level of privacy. And the *sekasha* seemed well-practiced in using the towels to keep themselves discreet until the water covered them. Thankfully Bladebite didn't join them, though, surprisingly, Pony did. The eye candy of Pony covered only by steaming water, however, didn't outweigh the negative of being the shortest, darkest, smallest-breasted female present.

"Relax." Stormsong had proved to be naturally a pale-white blond—a fact Tinker hadn't really wanted to know. "We won't eat you."

"At least we won't." Rainlily smiled with a glance toward Pony.

Tinker stood up, realized that she was flashing them all, and sat back down to hide in the hazy water. "I am not amused."

Stormsong splashed Rainlily. "Shush, you."

"If we don't tease her," Rainlily said, "she'll think elves are just as prudish as humans. I've never understood how they can be so blatant with their sexual imagery, and yet in relationships with one another, they are so narrow-minded. As if a heart can hold only one love at a time, and you have to empty out one before there's room for another."

"Let her cope with one thing at a time." Pony watched Tinker with a worried gaze.

"I'm fine," she told him and wondered why she had to say that so often lately.

"One lover gets boring after thirty or forty years," Rainlily said. "It's like peanut butter on a spoon, it's really good, but with chocolate sometimes, it's even better."

Tinker knew that elves loved peanut butter as much as they loved Juicy Fruit gum and ice cream. Considering her experience with the gum, she really had to track down a jar of peanut butter.

Stormsong moaned at the suggestion of peanut butter and chocolate. She added, "Or peanut butter and strawberry jam on fresh bread."

"Peanut butter on toast." Sun Lance held up her hand as if she held a piece of toasted bread by its crust. "Where the bread is crunchy and the peanut butter is all hot and runny."

"Raisin bread toast." Tinker modified Sun Lance's suggestion to her favorite way to eat peanut butter before she became an elf.

"Peanut butter, pretzels, chocolate," Rainlily listed out, "and that marshmallow fluff all mixed together."

"Oh, that explains Cloudwalker and Moonshadow at the same time," Stormsong murmured.

"*Nyowr*," Rainlily growled with a smile, which was the Elvish version of a cat's meow.

"Peanut butter on apple slices," Sun Lance said.

"On a banana," Tinker said.

"On Skybolt," Rainlily said knowingly.

"Oh yes, that's nice," Stormsong agreed.

Tinker was going to need a scorecard to track the *sekasha's* relationships.

"Peanut butter ice cream," Pony said.

"Peanut butter ice cream!" The females all sighed.

"Unless *domi* takes another *sekasha*, though, then her options are limited." Rainlily pointed out. "There's Pony, and then there's Pony."

"That's still peanut butter and—" Stormsong thought a moment, before finishing. "—virgin honey."

Rainlily eyed Pony and smiled. "Definitely virgin honey."

Pony blushed and looked down.

"And Wolf Who Rules is peanut butter ice cream," Sun Lance said.

That triggered a chorus of agreement from the females. Tinker had one moment of feeling pleased that she married the prize male and then realization hit her like a two-by-four to the head. She gasped out in shock.

"*Domi*?" All four *sekasha* instantly reacted, moving toward her as they scanned the building for enemies.

"Windwolf! You've all slept with him?"

The female warriors exchanged glances.

"Well?" she pressed.

"Yes, *domi*," Stormsong said quietly. "But not since he's met you."

Was that really supposed to make her feel better? Well, giving it a moment to sink in, yes it did. She knew that Windwolf had to have had lovers before her—she just didn't expect to be naked in a tub with them at any point. There were two other female *sekasha*. Tinker supposed they were ex-lovers too. Windwolf's household numbered seventy-five—she didn't even know how many were female, but most of the sizeable kitchen staff was. The possible number staggered her. "Any females from the rest of the household?"

The *sekasha* blinked at her in surprise.

"No, *domi*, that wouldn't be proper." Was it a good thing or a bad that Stormsong was keeping to Elvish?

"Only the *sekasha* are *naekuna*," Pony explained.

"You're what?"

"*Naekuna*." Pony sat up slightly in the water to point at a tattoo on his hipbone. She blushed and looked away. "We can turn on and off our fertility."

"It is considered best if a *domi* and *domou* chooses among their beholden *sekasha* for their lovers." Stormsong had a similar tattoo on her hip. "The security of the household is not compromised and we're *naekuna*."

Tinker had one moment of relief until she realized that she had to interact with the five female *sekasha* on a daily basis. She stared at Stormsong, Sun Lance, and Rainlily, unsure how to cope with the sudden knowledge that these females had slept with Windwolf. They knew what a good lover he was—had probably helped him perfect his technique. What if—as the whole peanut butter conversation had suggested—Windwolf wanted variety? How did one deal with that? The crushing weight of inevitability that you would have to share? With such drop-dead beautiful females no less?

Elves always were so focused on today. You couldn't get them to talk about the past. *Nae hae,* too many years to count, it happened long ago, why bother? The future was the future, why stress over it bearing down on you?

Given long enough time, the smallest probability became reality. Sooner or later, you would live through all the possible futures. Nor would the past really be a true indicator of the future as you worked through one unlikely chance to the next.

Did the elves wear blinders just to keep sane?

"Are you all right?" Pony asked.

"Um, let me get back to you about that."

"*Ze domou.*" Wraith Arrow was operating at maximum respect now that the Fire Clan had arrived. Or more specifically, since the Wyverns had arrived. Wolf found himself wondering if perhaps the *sekasha* had chosen their king based on his Hands rather than his clan. "Forest Moss is one of those who traveled to Onihida when the pathway was found. He and the *sekasha,* Silver Vein in Stone, were the only two who managed to survive their capture by the oni."

At one time, certain caves and rock formations had created pathways that let a person walk from one world to the next. Anyone without the ability to detect a ley line could search closely for the pathway, even to the point of stepping in and out of worlds, and never find it. The dangers of traveling to Earth were great. The pathways themselves came and went like the tides of the ocean, apparently affected by the orbit of the moon. Earth had no magic, leaving the *domana* powerless and the *sekasha* without their shields. Still, all the clans sent out *domana* and their *sekasha* to barter silk and spices for steel and technology. To circumvent the dangers, the pathways were mapped out carefully, and traders crossed back to the safety of Elfhome as often as possible. In one remote area on Earth, a new pathway was discovered, and eagerly explored.

Unfortunately it was a pathway that led to Onihida. Of the twenty that went on the expedition, only two returned to Elfhome.

Wolf considered what he knew of that doomed expedition, which was very little since it happened before he was born. Unlike humans who seemed to be driven to chronicle their life and make it public, elves kept such things private. Everything he knew about the oni and Onihida came from questioning his First Hand. He had selected Wraith Arrow and the others for their knowledge of the humans and Earth, not thinking he'd ever need their familiarity with the oni.

"So you've met him?" Wolf asked.

Wraith nodded. "They had tortured him, healed him, and then tortured him again. It broke his mind."

That was two hundred fifty years ago. Had Forest Moss recovered?

It made Wolf wonder about Tinker and her time with the oni. What had they done to her to change her so much? Wolf felt a wave of sadness and anger. His *domi* had been so brave, trusting, and strong.

Wraith continued his report. "Silver Vein did not look to Forest Moss. The Stone *domou* had a vanity Hand, which he lost. Last that I heard, he had not gained another Hand."

"He's coming here without *sekasha*?"

Wraith nodded.

What game was this? Why include someone who lacked the most basic abilities of building a household? Did this mean that the Stone Clan didn't intend to create holdings in Pittsburgh?

⊷═◗ ◖═⊷

"I'm not sure you should be trying to call the spell stones." Stormsong was the only one who actually voiced the doubt all of them were clearly thinking as they followed her through the enclave's enclosed gardens.

"I'm fine," she said for what seemed the millionth time in the last three days.

"You spent a month working around the clock," Stormsong started. "And you haven't—"

"Shhh!" Tinker silenced her and worked to find her center. Getting her fingers into the full-suit position took a moment of concentration. Bringing her hand to her mouth, she vocalized the trigger word. The magic spilled around her, pulsing with potential. Carefully, she shifted her fingers to the shield position and spoke the trigger. The magic wrapped around her, distorting the air.

"Yes!" Without thinking, she threw up her hands in jubilation and the shield vanished. "Oops!"

The *sekasha* were too polite to comment. Finding her center was harder while burning with embarrassment. Her heart still leapt up when she called up her shield but she managed not to move this time. She held it for several minutes and then practiced at looking around, and then moving, without forgetting to maintain her hand positions.

"Okay," Tinker said. "Can I talk? Can you hear me?"

Pony grinned at her. "We can hear you. As long as you don't have your hands near your mouth, you can talk—but it's not always wise."

She dismissed the magic. Only after the power drained completely away did she celebrate. Laughing, she hugged Pony. "I did it!"

He surprised her by hugging her tightly back. "Yes, you did."

The walkie-talkie chirped and Stormsong answered with a "Yes? It is nothing—she is only practicing."

Tinker grimaced. She had forgotten Windwolf would notice her tapping the spell stones. "That's Wolf Who Rules?"

"Yes, *ze domi*," Stormsong said.

"Sorry, Windwolf!" Tinker called. "But I did it! I called the shields!"

Stormsong listened for a moment and then said, "He says, 'Very good,' and wants to know if you plan to continue practicing?"

"For a while." It occurred to her that the stones might only support one user. "That isn't a problem for him—is it?"

"No, *domi*." Pony answered the question. "Both of you can use the stones at the same time."

Stormsong listened and then said good-bye. "Wolf Who Rules merely wanted to be sure you were fine. Practice away, he said."

So she did until she momentarily forgot how to dispel the magic. When at last the magic washed away, Pony came and took her hands in his.

"Please, *domi*, go to bed. You can do more tomorrow."

Tinker woke from her nightmare to a dark bedroom. For a moment, she couldn't figure out where she was. She'd fallen asleep in so many places lately. She eyed the poster bed, wood paneling, and open window—oh yes—her bedroom at Poppymeadow's. Even awake, her dreams crowded in on her. She put out a hand and found Windwolf's comforting warmth. It was all she needed to push away the darkest memories.

Sighing, she snuggled up to her husband. This was one of the unexpected joys of being married, her secret treasure. She had never realized how lonely she was at night. Back in her loft, any light noise had her out of bed, and once awake, she often found herself getting dressed and wandering out into the sleeping city, in search of something she'd couldn't name or identify. Before Windwolf, if asked, she would have said she was perfectly happy— but if she had been, how could she be so much happier now?

She was just noticing something hard digging into her side, when she realized it was Pony beside her, not Windwolf. While Pony wore his loose pajamas, he slept on top of the blankets beside her, instead of under them with her. It was his sheathed *ejae* beneath her—she'd rolled on top of it when she cuddled up to him.

"Pony?" She tugged the sword out from under her, dropped it behind him. His presence confused her.

"What is it, *domi*?" he asked sleepily.

It took her another minute to sort through memories and dreams to know what reality should be. They weren't still prisoners of the oni and her husband *really* should be in bed with her. "Where's Windwolf?"

Pony rubbed at his face. "Hmmm? He's probably still with Prince True Flame. There was much to do before the troops arrived tomorrow."

"I had a bad dream about Windwolf. He couldn't see Lord Tomtom. I could but the black willows were holding me—I couldn't move—couldn't warn him."

"Hush." Pony hugged her loosely. "Tomtom is dead. Wolf Who Rules is safe. It was only a dream—nothing more. Go back to sleep."

"What if the oni attacked?" She started to get up but he tightened his hold.

"No, no, Wolf would want you to sleep. You're exhausted, *domi*. You're going to make yourself sick if you do not sleep."

She groaned because she was so very tired but the nightmare pressed in on her. "I can't go back to sleep. Windwolf could be in trouble."

"He's fine."

"How do you know? We were asleep. He could be fighting for his life right now." Oh gods, she was turning into such a drama queen. *Go to bed, go to bed, go to bed*, she told herself, but she couldn't banish the memories.

"Oh, *domi*," Pony crooned. "When I was little and my mother was out with Longwind—Windwolf's father—I'd be worried just like you are now. And my father would say, 'Look at the clear sky, see the stars? If the Wind Clan fought tonight, the wind would throw clouds around, and lightning would be everywhere.'"

She relaxed onto his bare shoulder, gazing out the bedroom window at the peach trees beyond, standing still against a crystalline sky. "What did you do when it stormed?"

Pony chuckled, a good warm sound that did much to banish away her fears. "Ah, you've spotted the weakness in my father's ploy."

It puzzled her that his mother was out with Longwind when he was fighting until she realized that both of Pony's parents would have been *sekasha*. Pony's mother must be beholden to Windwolf's father.

"What is your mother like?" she asked.

"Otter Dance? She is *sekasha*," Pony said as if that explained everything. Perhaps it did. "We of the Wind Clan *sekasha* are known to be playful and lucky where the Fire Clan *sekasha* are considered hot tempered and rude. When we come together in large cities, we of the Wind Clan like to gamble and win, and the Fire Clan tends to lose and start fights. Almost every night ends in a brawl, everyone black-and-blue."

He smelt wonderful. His braid was undone and his hair was a cascade of black in the moonlight. As if it had a mind of its own, her hand drifted down over his chest, feeling the hard muscles under the silk shift.

"Hmmm," was all she managed as exhaustion—thankfully—was beating out desire.

"I do not know which my mother loves more: to gamble or brawl." Pony went on to expand on his mother's adventures in both, but she slipped back to sleep.

Tinker woke twice more that night. The second time was another nightmare, this of being chased by Foo lions through the ironwoods. Pony was there again to soothe away her fear. The third time was Windwolf finally returning home, but by then she could barely stir.

"How is she?" Windwolf whispered in the darkness.

"She woke twice with nightmares of oni." Pony's voice came from near the door.

The bed shifted with the changing of the guard.

"Thank you, Little Horse, for keeping her well."

"I wish I could do more," Pony whispered. "But I could not keep the dreams from her. May you have more luck than I. Good night, Brother Wolf."

11: PAPER SCISSORS STONE

"I would be happier if one of the other heads took them." Ginger Wine eyed the trucks arriving with the Stone Clan luggage.

Wolf nodded, staying silent. In truth, none of the heads of households wanted the Stone Clan taking up occupancy at their enclave. Ginger Wine, however, lost the decision because not only was she was the juniormost head, but her enclave was also the smallest, meaning she would put the smallest number of Wind Clan folk out when the Stone Clan turned her enclave into a temporary private residence. The households of the three incoming *domana* were reported to be fewer than forty people combined. Ginger Wine's enclave had fifty guest beds, thus a loss of only ten beds.

"I've never hosted someone from the Stone Clan before," Ginger Wine said. "I hope they eat our food. We don't have spices or the pans to cook Stone dishes, but I will not have them in my kitchens."

Wolf could not understand the fanaticism with which the enclaves defended their kitchens. He had had to settle several disputes between his own household and Poppymeadow's. He had learned, though, that there was only one correct answer. "If they will not eat, they will not eat."

Ginger Wine chewed on one knuckle, watching as the luggage was unloaded onto the pavement. The first trunks off, logically for a war zone, were the *sekasha's* secondary armor. Sword and bow cases followed. As Ginger Wine's people struggled to lift the shipping containers holding spell arrows, she murmured around her finger, "I want double my normal remuneration."

"Done."

Wolf had arranged to have his Rolls Royces ferry the Stone Clan *domana* from the palace clearing. The first pulled up in front of Ginger Wine's and a single male got out. As there were no *sekasha* attending the male, this had to be Forest Moss. Wolf couldn't tell if the male was pure Stone Clan genome. Forest Moss had the clan's compact build and dusky skin tone. His hair, though, fell shocking white against his dark skin. The lids of his left eye were sewn shut and concave, following the bone line of his skull, showing that the eye had been fully removed. Scars radiated around the empty socket, as if something thin and heated had been dragged from the edge of his face to just short of the eye. The scar at the corner of the eye, however, continued into his eye. After a score of near misses, that last one had burned out the eye.

The right side of Moss' face was smooth and whole, including the brown eye that glared at Wolf.

"Forest Moss on Stone." Moss gave a coldly precise bow.

"Wolf Who Rules Wind."

Moss' one good eye flicked over him and scanned the *sekasha*. Without the matching eye, Wolf found it difficult to read the male. "Yes, you are. And these are your lovelies. Very, very nice."

Wolf took the comment as a compliment and acknowledged it with a nod. There seemed, however, something more to it—like oil mixed in water, invisible until they separated.

"Otter Dance's son," Forest Moss said. "He comes of age this year, does he not?"

What did this battered soul want of Little Horse? "Yes."

"Tempered Steel." Forest Moss named Little Horse's paternal grandfather as he held up his left hand. He lifted his right hand, saying, "And Perfection." Who was Otter Dance's mother. He put his hands together and kissed his fingertips. "What a creature the Wind Clan has crafted."

It had been a mistake to respond to Forest Moss' first comment; Wolf would not repeat his mistake. While the *sekasha* could be ruthlessly practical, it was insulting to suggest anything but chance had brought the two most famous *sekasha* bloodlines together in one child.

Wolf gave him a hard stare, warning him not to continue on the subject.

"What a look! But I am mad. Such looks are seen only by my left eye." Forest Moss touched his ruined cheek to indicate his empty eye socket. He cocked his head, as something occurred to him. "The last thing I saw from this eye was Blossom Spring from Stone being drowned in the pisshole by her First, Granite. The oni had raped all the females from the start. The *sekasha* had their *naekuna* but the *domana*—" Forest Moss sighed and whispered. "Those mad dogs are so fertile they can even spawn themselves on us. Of course, a half-breed child would have given the oni access to the *domana* genome—so the *sekasha* had to act. The oni had taken Granite's arms and right leg, one bone at a time. They thought they had made him helpless, but still he managed to pin Blossom facedown in the sewage. She thrashed beneath him for so long—I would have thought drowning was faster. It was quiet. So very quiet. None of us daring to say a word until it was over. Shhhhh. Quiet as mice, lest the oni hear and realize that their rabid seed had taken and carry her off to bear their puppies."

Wolf steeled himself to keep from stepping back a step from the elf. Was Forest Moss as mad as he seemed, or was this an act to let him be as rude as he wanted? Or was the male deluding only himself, thinking that he was "acting"?

"What of your *domi*?" Forest Moss leaned close to whisper, his one eye bright. "Did those rabid beasts fuck her? Fill her up with their seed? Will there be puppies to drown in the pisspot?"

Wolf would not validate this conversation by explaining that Tinker would be infertile from her transformation long after the danger of pregnancy was past—regardless of what the oni did to her. "You will not speak of my *domi* again."

"I am not the one to fear. All your lovelies standing around you are the ones to fear. They hold our lives in their holy hands, judging every breath we take. They have to be strong because we're so weak. I fully expect that someday one of them will decide I'm too damaged to live."

"Hopefully soon."

Forest Moss laughed bitterly. "Yes, yes, actually, soon would be nice. I'm too afraid to do it myself. I am a coward, you know. Everyone knows. That's why I have no *sekasha*."

Ginger Wine had heard the whole exchange. A gracious host, she bowed elegantly and offered to escort Forest Moss to his room, but a tightness around her eyes meant she was keeping fury in check. Wolf's people might not know Tinker, but she was *his domi*, and they wouldn't take criticism of her lightly.

While he suspected the humans might blame Tinker for Pittsburgh being stranded, the elves always knew it was only a matter of time before the odd cycle of Shutdown and Startup would end. Humans never continued anything for long. As long as the Ghostlands didn't present them with more problems, most elves would see Tinker's solution as a good one.

Alertness went through his Hand, and Wolf turned to find Jewel Tear standing there.

She wore the deep green that always looked so beautiful on her. Her dark hair was braided with flowers and ribbons, most likely taking an hour to create. She had two spell spheres orbiting her. One cooled the air about her. The other sphere triggered favorite scent memories in those around her. The spheres always had made him leery. He knew that it was impossible for the spheres to collide with anything, but he always flinched when they got too near his head. Nor did it help that the one always made Jewel Tear smell like his blade mother, Otter Dance.

Around them the *sekasha* acknowledged each other's presence and waged their still and silent dominance battle. Not that it was much of a contest—Jewel had only been able to recruit a vanity hand of recent doubles. Against his First Hand, they were just babies.

"Wolf Who Rules Wind." Jewel Tear smiled warmly at him, and bowed lower than necessary, almost spilling her breasts out of her bodice.

"Jewel Tear on Stone." He bowed to her, wondering what her flagrant display meant. Was this strictly a personal invitation, however improper, or was the Stone Clan making use of her?

She stepped forward, rising up on her toes as if she meant to kiss him. He stopped her with a look. The spell spheres orbited them as she stood frozen in place.

"Wolf," she whimpered.

"You are not my *sekasha*, nor are you my *domi*."

"I should be!" She jerked her chin up and glared at him. "You asked me! I told you that I needed time to consider it. I finally make my decision, pack my household to join you here in the Westernlands, and I get your letter saying that you were taking a human—a human—as your *domi*."

"I gave you a hundred years. When I was at court last, thirty years ago, we did not even speak to one another."

"I—I was busy, as were you. And a letter? You could not come and tell me yourself?"

"There was no time." He wondered what she hoped to gain with this tactic. He would not break his vow to Tinker, no matter how guilty Jewel tried to make him feel. Because Jewel never responded, she had no legal recourse.

She reached out to neaten his sleeve. "We courted for years—that slow exquisite dance of passion. The boat rides on Mist Lake with the whiting of swans. The picnics in the autumn woods. The winter masquerades. We took the time that is proper, to learn each other, to know that we were right for each other. What do you know of this—this—female? How can you know anything?"

He knew even if he tried to explain how a lifetime of understanding could be distilled out of twenty-four hours, she would not believe him. The elves never did—with the exception of Little Horse. "I knew enough. This is not court, where you have eternity to decide, because nothing changes. I was willing to risk whatever may come because if I did not put out my hand, and take her then, she would have been lost to me forever."

"What of your commitment to me?"

Wolf controlled a flash of anger. "I waited. You did not answer. I moved on."

"I needed time to think!" she cried and then looked annoyed that she had raised her voice. "I thought you knew me well enough to understand my position. I do not have your resources as the son of the clan leader—a favored cousin to the queen. You would have been forgiven for taking a *domi* outside your clan. Both Wind and Fire want you merely because of the other clan's interest; Wind would never turn you out for the Fire to take in. I do not have your luxury. I had to consider long and hard my responsibilities to my household before committing to you. I couldn't risk not being able to support them if neither Wind nor Stone sponsored me."

"If you had come to me, told me your concerns, I could have done something to guarantee that you would always have Wind Clan sponsorship." Even as he said it, though, he knew that it was better that she hadn't. He had made a mistake in asking her to be his *domi*. When he brought her to the Westernlands, dismay had spread across her face when she realized they would spend the rest of their lives in the wilderness, far from court. It had opened his eyes; he had fooled himself about how well they suited each another. He'd been willing to honor that commitment a hundred years ago, even after that realization. Even as recently as thirty years ago, he might have still taken her as his *domi*. In the last two decades, though, he had considered himself released of his pledge.

Jewel tried to make it all seem his fault. "I was supposed to trust you to take care of me when you couldn't be bothered to explain anything to me? You would go off and leave me with no idea what you had planned, what you were doing, when you were going to come back."

"I trusted you to do what you needed to do. I thought you trusted me."

A look flashed across her face before being hidden away, but he knew her too well not to recognize it and could guess her thoughts. One thing you learned well at court was to trust no one.

Not only did she not trust him, she thought him weak for expecting it.

But this left one question. "What made you finally decide?" he asked.

Her nostrils flared and she glanced away from him. "Things have not gone well for me. Some of my ventures failed, I had miscalculated the risks involved on one, and in trying to cover my losses, things—cascaded. I was forced to give up my holdings." Her voice dropped to a whisper. "My household was losing faith in me."

So coming to him was not an act of love but of desperation. It would also explain what she was doing here now—without holdings, she would lose her household and then her clan sponsorship. Jewel Tear was too proud and ambitious to live under someone else's rule. If she was that destitute, though, she wouldn't have the funds to set up a holding at Pittsburgh; it could only mean that the Stone Clan chose her and advanced her stake money.

Did the Stone Clan think that if something happened to Tinker, he would turn to Jewel Tear? How far were they willing to go to put their theory to the test? He knew Jewel well enough to know that she would let nothing stand in the way of her ambitions. That had been one of the things he loved about her.

Tinker wished the machine room didn't feel so much like a trap. Whoever designed the room had never considered that there would be anything as dangerous as the black willow between the back room and the front door. Being around the black willow made everyone nervous. There were no signs, however, of it reviving despite a full day of summer heat. Oilcan rotated the steel drums of metal filings, taking the ones saturated with magic to some place to drain, and replaced them with fresh drums. Tinker could see no overflow of magic. Still, the *sekasha* all kept their shields activated just to use up local ambient magic.

She had the old spell jackhammered out of place. She was now carefully prepping the site to lay down the new spell and cement it into place.

Stormsong settled beside her, her sheathed *ejae* across her knees, her shields a blue aura around her. "Do you mind if we talk?"

"Isn't that what we're doing?"

Stormsong gave a slight laugh, and then continued with great seriousness. "It's not my place to advise you. It should be Pony, as your only beholden, or Wraith Arrow, who is Windwolf's First, but—" Stormsong sighed and shook her head. "Wraith Arrow won't cross that line, and Pony—that boy has a serious case of hero worship for you."

"Pony?"

"You can do no wrong in his eyes. You know all, see all, understand all—which leaves you up the shit creek because you really don't and he won't tell you squat, because he thinks you already know."

"So you're going to tell me?"

"You'd rather walk around with your head up your ass and not know it?"

Tinker groaned. "What am I doing wrong *now*?"

"You need to choose four more *sekasha*, at minimum."

Tinker sighed. "Why? Things are working fine this way."

"No, they're not, and you're the only one that doesn't see that. For instance, Pony is just a baby to the rest of us."

"He's at least a hundred." She knew he was an adult, although just barely, like she had been as an eighteen-year-old human. Unfortunately, now she fell into a nebulous zone of being just barely adult for years and years.

"He just left the doubles this year." Meaning last year, he could use two numbers to indicate his age. "Only half of Windwolf's *sekasha* are in the triples—the rest are older."

"How old are you?" Tinker was fairly sure Stormsong was one of the younger *sekasha*. She was starting to be able to look at elves and see their age indicators. It was odd, to have her concept of Windwolf slowly change from "adult" to "her age" as her perception of all elves changed.

"I'm two hundred." Which made her Pony's age, because to the elves that hundred year difference barely counted.

"So we're all approximately the same age."

"You wish." Stormsong took out a pack of Juicy Fruit gum and offered her a stick. "Yeah, physically Pony and I are like human teenagers, but we've still had a hell of a lot longer than you to figure out people."

Tinker took the gum and let the taste explode in her mouth. "What's your point? Is Pony old or young?"

"That is my point." Stormsong took a piece for herself and put away the pack. "He's the youngest of the *sekasha*, but he's your First."

"Are you trying to confuse me?"

"Anything regarding you, Pony is in charge, but he's the youngest of the *sekasha*."

This was starting to make her head hurt. "Are you talking . . . seniority?"

"Seniority. Seniority." Stormsong took out a small dictionary, flipped through it, and read off the entry for *seniority*. "Precedence of position, especially precedence over others of the same rank by reason of a longer span of service."

"Oh that's not fair," Tinker complained. "You get a dictionary. I want one for Elvish."

"We don't have such things." Stormsong put away the dictionary. "They would be too useful."

Tinker had to put "Elvish dictionary" on her project list.

"Yes," Stormsong continued. "Pony needs seniority over those he commands, which he doesn't have because none of us are yours. What's more, when the bullets start to fly, we need to know which way to jump. Pony doesn't need to think. But the rest of us—we have pledged our lives to Windwolf; it's him we should be thinking of—but we know that only Pony is watching over you."

"I told Windwolf I'd think about this."

"Humans have a wonderful saying: *assume* is making an ass out of 'u' and me. Windwolf assumes that Pony will guide you in your choice, and Pony assumes that you know all."

"So you're doing it."

"Hell, someone has to."

"If it's Pony's job, shouldn't I just tell him that I don't know shit?"

Stormsong gave her a look that Tinker recognized from years of being a child genius.

"Oh gods," Tinker cried. "Don't look at me that way!"

"What way?"

"The 'what a clever little thing' look. It horrifies me how long I'm going to have to put up with that now that I'm an elf."

Stormsong laughed, and then lapsed into Low Elvish, sounding properly contrite. "Forgiveness, *domi*."

"Oh, speak English."

"Yes," Stormsong said in English. "You should talk to Pony, since those you hold need to work well with him. Let me give you pointers he might not think of—he is still new at this. Blind leading the blind and all that shit."

"You're not going to take 'later' as an answer?"

"Kid, how splattered with shit do you need to get before you realize it's hitting the fan? We're fuck deep in oni, Wyverns, and Stone Clan. Now is not the time to be worrying about chain of command."

Stormsong had a way of driving the point home with a sledgehammer. Tinker just wished she wasn't the one being hammered. "Fine, point away."

"What all *sekasha* want is seniority. To be First. Failing that—in the First Hand." Top five, she meant. "Forever at the bottom is a bitch. Pony was wise to seize the chance to be your First once he saw what you were made of. You've proved yourself with keeping both Windwolf and Pony safe from the oni— that's what a good *domi* does—so all of us are willing to fill your Hand."

"But . . ." Tinker swore she could hear a "but" in there somehow.

"It would be best for all—" Stormsong paused and then added, "—in my opinion—that you don't choose from Windwolf's First Hand."

"Why not?"

"Most *domana* fill their First Hand with *sekasha* just breaking their doubles. The *domana* want the glory a Hand gives them, and the *sekasha* see it as a way to be in First Hand. We call it a vanity Hand. The thing is that most *domana* can't attract a Second Hand because not only is the incentive of being First gone, the *sekasha* of the Second Hand have to be willing to serve under the First Hand. Likewise the Third Hand knows that they will be junior to the First Hand and the Second. Adding into this is the personality of the *domana*: does the positive of being beholden to that *domana* outweigh the negative of not having seniority? Many *domana* can only hold vanity Hands."

"Okay." Tinker had assumed that all *domana* had multiple hands. Apparently not.

"Windwolf's grandfather, Howling, helped tear us away from the Skin Clan and form the monarchy that keeps the clans from waging endless war. When he was assassinated, his *sekasha* became Longwind's—but not as his First or Second, since those were already filled."

"Ouch." Tinker wondered how this related.

"Yes, it was a step down for them—but they saw it as fitting since they had failed Howling," Stormsong said. "Windwolf wanted his First Hand to advise him on setting up in this new land, setting up new towns and lines of trade, something he didn't think doubles could help him do. So he approached the *sekasha* of his grandfather's Hands and they accepted. It would make them First Hand again, but more importantly, they believed in him. Wolf Who Rules has always lived up to his name."

"So, the First Hand, they're all thousands of years old?"

"Yes."

"Okay." So maybe she wasn't so good at guessing age—none of the *sekasha* struck her as older than late twenties in human terms. Tinker finished setting the nonconductive pins that would hold the spell level. "Can you take down your shield? I'm going to set the compressor spell into place."

Tinker didn't want to risk brushing the spell tracing up against an active spell. Stormsong spoke the command that deactivated her shields. A slight pricking that Tinker hadn't really noticed vanished, making her aware by its absence that she had been feeling the active magic.

"Thanks." Tinker took the filigreed sections of the spell out of their protective packing and fit them into place.

Stormsong watched her for a few minutes before continuing her explanation. "It was his First Hand that let Windwolf pull a Second and Third Hand made up of triples and quads."

"So why—" Tinker paused to make sure all the pieces of the spell were stable and level. "Why shouldn't I take any of Windwolf's First? Wouldn't that help me, like it helped him?"

"It would help at a cost to Pony. There's no way he could be First to one of Windwolf's First Hand. Also, the First Hand are the ones that see you most as a child that needs firm guidance until you finish growing up. Lastly, they're all technophobes."

"Ick!" Tinker picked up her cordless soldering iron and started to tack together the pieces of the spell with careful, practiced solders.

"The younger *sekasha* won't bring you as much honor as those from Windwolf's First Hand but they'll be the ones that 'fit' with you best. When Pittsburgh appeared, Windwolf realized that he needed *sekasha* willing to learn technology—and that recent doubles would be the most open-minded. That's when he picked up his Fourth Hand."

"You don't think Pony will know that they'll fit best?"

Stormsong sighed. "Pony's mother, Otter Dance, is Windwolf's blade mother."

"His what?"

"Otter Dance is Longwind's favorite lover among his *sekasha*." Stormsong explained.

Tinker was missing the significance. "Pony is Windwolf's brother?"

"Genetically? no. But emotionally? yes, in a way."

"Oookay." Tinker wondered what Windwolf's mother felt about it. Did she see her husband having a lover as some kind of a betrayal? Or did the fact there was even a special name—*blade mother*—mean that it was somehow expected! Certainly Stormsong seemed to think this was nothing hugely remarkable.

"It has been assumed since Pony's birth that he'd look to Windwolf," Stormsong continued. "In my opinion—that assumption did what all assumptions do."

"Make an ass out of you and me?"

"Yes. Pony is fucking amazing, but neither Windwolf nor Pony seem to realize it. Windwolf still sees Pony as a child, and he's not!"

Tinker thought about Pony doing exercises up in their oni cell, wearing only his pants—chiseled muscles moving under silken skin dripping with sweat. "My husband needs his eyes checked."

Stormsong laughed. "I'm glad you snatched Pony up. As long as you don't do something to fuck him up, maybe he'll one day realize how special he is. Until then, he's going to overcompensate for what he sees as his own weakness. Pony might point you toward someone from the First Hand and then try to bow out—all in the name of doing right by you."

Tinker focused on the last of the solders, clenching her jaw in annoyance at Stormsong's comments about Pony and Windwolf. It felt wrong to hear anything negative about either one of them, like she was being disloyal. Really, what did she know about Stormsong other than she was one of Windwolf's trusted bodyguards? Besides the fact that she nearly died for Tinker?

Tinker sighed as she forced herself to consider that maybe Stormsong was right about all this—that it was vital she pick out four more guards immediately and that Pony needed a good slap upside the head. She found herself remembering that Pony had waited without comment for her to decide to accept Bladebite.

"Is Bladebite from Windwolf's First Hand?" Tinker tried to sound casual about it.

Stormsong nodded.

And if Tinker hadn't dodged the question, she would be stuck with Bladebite trying to control her. She sighed. "How do I tell Bladebite no?" Surely she didn't have to tell him "yes" just because he had offered. That would be a stupid system—but the elves never struck her as completely logical. "Can I tell him no?"

"You can say that you don't think you fit with him. That's copasetic."

Copasetic. Tinker shook her head, remembering the days immediately after she had become an elf—everything made more confused by the fact that Pony didn't speak English or understand the differences between the two cultures.

"When the queen called Windwolf to Aum Renau," Tinker said, "why didn't Windwolf leave you with me?"

"My mother is Pure Radiance and my father is the queen's First. They have not seen me for a hundred years and wanted me there. Windwolf thought it unwise not to bring me."

Tinker stared at the elf in amazement. "The oracle and a Wyvern? What the hell are you doing with Wind Clan?"

"I had—issues—with court. Windwolf offered me a chance to escape all that and I jumped. Considering what my mother named me, she probably wasn't totally surprised."

Yes, Stormsong sounded more like a Wind Clan name than Fire Clan.

It occurred to Tinker then what "fit" was about. She felt comfortable sitting and talking with Stormsong. Annoying as the truth was, Tinker trusted her judgment. And it would be good to have someone who understood what it felt like to be the outsider.

"So," Tinker said to Stormsong. "Are you offering?"

Stormsong looked puzzled a moment, and then surprised. "To be yours?"

"Yeah. I—I think we work."

Stormsong blinked at her a few moments before standing, the scrape of her boots on the cement loud in the silence that fell between them.

"I can understand if you don't want to." Tinker busied herself checking the solders. All that was needed was to cement the spell into place, wait for the cement to cure, and the black willow could be safely stored indefinitely. Or at least, until she figured out what her dreams meant.

"I want to be honest with you." Stormsong paced the perimeter of the room in her long-legged stride. "But it's like opening a vein. It's a painful, messy thing to do."

Tinker lifted her hand to wave that off. "I don't think I can deal with painfully messy at the moment."

"You should know stuff like this before you ask. That was the whole point of the conversation. You have to make informed choices."

Tinker made a noise. "I've been doing fairly well lately blindly winging it through mass chaos."

Stormsong scoffed and then sighed. "I'm probably the most misbegotten mutt puppy ever born to the elves. Most people think my mother made a horrible mistake having me. I don't fit in any-where."

"At least you stayed an elf, instead of jumping species like I did."

Stormsong laughed. "There have been times I wished I could. Just be human. Lose myself among them. But a hundred years of *sekasha* brainwashing made that impossible. I can't walk away from it. I tried, but I can't. I like being *sekasha* too much."

"Not to belittle your difficulties, but I really don't get the problem. You're a *sekasha*. I need *sekasha*. We work together well—at least I think we do. Or is it that you hate my guts?"

"I would die for you."

Tinker wished that people would stop saying that to her. "I'll take that as a 'no, I don't hate you' and frankly, I'd rather you didn't die. Now, *that's* painful and messy, and not just for you."

Stormsong laughed and then bowed low to Tinker. "Tinker *domi*, I would be honored to be yours. I will not disappoint you."

12: TEARS ON STONE

At first glance, Turtle Creek seemed the same to Tinker. Sunlight shafted through the Discontinuity in rays of blue. Mist rising off the chill gathered into banks of blue haze and then drifted out of the valley, existing momentarily as white clouds, before burning away in the summer heat. True, royal troops showed up as splashes of Fire Clan red—thus the lifting of the ban on Turtle Creek—but otherwise nothing seemed to have changed. It remained one big hole in reality.

Tinker led her Hand down into the valley to where they'd marked the trees. The first sapling they found had nine slashes in its bark—which should have meant it would be nine feet from the edge of the Discontinuity.

"That looks like only five feet to me." Tinker fingered the mark, wondering if someone might have added slashes after they left.

"Barely five." Pony pointed at the next tree along the edge of the blue.

The tree was marked with seven slashes but the blue came almost to its roots.

"This is bad." Tinker murmured.

"*Domi*." Pony had moved on ahead and pointed now at a tree inside the effect.

She joined him at the edge of the blue; there were four slashes in the bark of the ghostly tree. "Shit, the Discontinuity has grown. How is that possible?" She motioned to the *sekasha* that they were leaving.

"Now what?" Stormsong asked.

"I'm going to need some equipment, then we're coming back."

Tinker scanned the valley with her camera's infrared attachment over the valley, watching the screen on her workpad instead of looking through the eyepiece. In one window, the video feed showed the thermal picture, and in other windows, programs reduced the images to mathematical models. At the center of the Ghostlands, she spotted a familiar circle.

"Something wrong, *domi*?" Pony asked.

She realized that she had gasped at her discovery. "Oh—this here—this looks like our gate. See, here is the ironwood ring and here is the ramp over the threshold."

"It is lying on its side?"

"Yes. The current probably toppled it, though I'm not sure what is causing the current. It might be simple—" Her Elvish failed her. Did they have a word for convection? "Heat rises and cold falls. Basic science. It's what makes the winds blow. I think this is the same thing on a microscale—like a pot boiling."

"Why not like a pond freezing?"

"I don't know. Perhaps because there's a pool of magic below this, heating the bottom, but it's losing massive amounts of energy before it hits the surface—thus the reason for the cold."

"Ah." Pony nodded like he understood.

"Do you see this point here? Right where the gate is lying. Can you shoot this arrow to that point?"

"With the line and weight attached?"

"Yes."

Pony considered for a moment. "Stormsong would be better."

Among the *sekasha*, Pony was considered the better archer. Her surprise must have shown as Pony waved over Stormsong and explained what Tinker wanted.

"When I have to make a shot, I do it with my eyes closed," Stormsong said. "I see where the arrow needs to be."

"Oooookay." Tinker handed her the end of the line.

Stormsong attached the line to an arrow, nocked it in her compound bow, pulled taut the string, and closed her eyes. For a moment she stood there, aiming blind, and then let loose the bowstring. The arrow soared straight and true as if it had nothing weighing it down or trailing behind. The reel whizzed as the line snaked out after the arrow, the numbers on the meter blurring as they counted up the feet. Near the point Tinker wanted, but not exactly, the arrow shot into the ghost ground of the Discontinuity. It appeared on Tinker's screen as a dot of red heat compared to the arctic cold of the land, too far to the right. The reel fell quiet and the line ran taut out into the Discontinuity.

Tinker sighed. "Close enough for horseshoes and discontinuities."

"It's where it has to be," Stormsong defended her shot.

"I'm trying to see how deep the Discontinuity runs. I figure it is deepest at the gate—it's close enough for that."

Tinker clicked on her mouse and the meter fed its number into the computer: 100 yards. Already the arrow chilled to blue, blending into the rest of the chilled landscape.

"Why does it matter how deep it is?" Pony asked as the reel started to click out as the arrow sank.

Tinker shrugged. "Because I don't know what else to do at the moment. I'm just fiddling around, poking at it until something comes to me."

"Will not the current affect this measurement?" Pony asked.

"Oh, damn." She muttered in English, and then dropped back to low Elvish. "Yes, it will." He was right. There was no way to know what was drift and what was the weighted end sinking. "I'll have to measure the drift and correct the measurements."

At least it gave her an excuse to reel in the arrow and try again to thread it through the heart of the gate. She flipped on the winch. The slack reeled in quickly but then the line went taut, and the winch slowed.

"Well, I'll be damned," Tinker said.

"What is it, *domi*?" Pony asked.

"The arrow hit something."

"The arrow went where it was needed," Stormsong repeated.

There were times Tinker really hated Elfhome—magic screwed with everything. "I didn't think anything would be solid enough to catch on the line."

"The line is solid."

"Yes, it is." She gasped as the implications dawned on her. "Pony, you're a genius. The line is solid."

"I cannot be that smart, *domi*, because I do not understand why that excites you."

"Well, it is an important observation. An object from this reality stays in this reality even after sinking into the Discontinuity."

"How is this important?"

"I do not know, but it is something I did not know before."

"Ah. I see."

The object appeared on the thermal scan, an oddly shaped mass of slightly lighter blue. By the naked eye, she could make out a boil of disturbance beyond where the line cut into the earth, creating a sharp V-shaped wake.

"It is big, whatever it is," Tinker said.

Pony unsheathed his sword.

"I doubt if it is anything living." Tinker backed up regardless. Gods knew what she was dragging in from between realities. "It is at—at . . ." She had to teach Pony English or learn more Elvish. What was Elvish for absolute zero? "It is frozen."

The thing hit shore. For a moment she thought it was a large turtle, and then the line kept reeling, rolling it. Long-fingered webbed hands and a vaguely human-looking face heaved out of the earth, rimmed with frost.

"Oh gods!" Tinker leapt back and the other *sekasha* drew their swords. The reel protested the sudden heavy load as the frozen body hit solid earth, the line vibrating. She killed the power before the line could snap. "Don't touch it!"

"I think it is dead." Pony had his sword at its throat just in case.

"The cold itself is dangerous. Don't touch it directly, but get it out."

Tinker kept her distance. The *sekasha* looped straps carefully around the outstretched limbs and hauled the thing out of the liquid earth. The creature was half Tinker's height and had a turtle shell, but also long scaly limbs and webbed feet and hands. Long straight black hair fringed a bare, depressed spot on a humanlike head, and its face was a weird cross of a chubby monkey's and a turtle's. It wore a harness of leather with various pointy things that could be weapons attached to it.

Pony pricked the creature with his sword, eyed the wound. "It does not bleed. It is indeed frozen."

"Ooookay," Tinker said. "It is probably safe to assume that it will stay dead, even if it thaws out."

"An elf would." Pony sheathed his sword.

"What do you think it is?" Tinker asked.

"It's a kappa." A voice called from above them.

Tinker and her Hand turned, looking upwards. Riki perched on branches of an ironwood, high overhead. He ducked back, behind the trunk, as the *sekasha* pulled out their pistols.

"Wait, don't fire," Tinker ordered. "Riki! Riki! What the hell is this?"

"I told you." He peered out around the trunk. "It's a kappa. Ugly little brats aren't they? In Japan, it's believed that they get their great strength from water in that brain depression and if you can trick them into bowing and spilling out the water, they have to return to the water realm to regain their strength."

Stormsong signed "Kill him?" in blade talk. Tinker signed back "Wait."

"It's an oni?" Tinker asked. "Or an animal?"

"That's a blurred line with the oni," Riki said. "I think you would call it oni—they're fairly clever in a homicidal way. The greater bloods made them by mixing animals with lesser bloods, just like Tomtom did with Chiyo. Legend has it that they used monkeys and turtles—a pretty sick mix, if you ask me."

"I didn't see any while we were making the gate."

"There aren't any in Pittsburgh. They're clever, but not enough to pass as a human."

"So you're saying it came through the gate?"

"The oni use them for special ops; they're strong swimmers and wrestlers."

Tinker looked back into the Discontinuity, the slow drift of blue mist. What were the oni up to? Were they just testing these strange waters to see where they led—or were they trying to salvage the gate?

Then again, was Riki telling the truth that there were no kappa in Pittsburgh?

"What are you doing here, Riki?"

"I need to talk to you."

"Talk? Talk about what? How can I even trust anything that comes out of that lying mouth of yours?"

"I'm sorry, Tinker, about everything that happened. I really am. I know you're pissed as hell at me, but I need to talk to you about the dragon."

"What dragon?"

"The one that attacked you. The one I pulled off you. The one that might have killed you and all your people if I hadn't called it."

"So it was a dragon?"

"Not an Elfhome dragon, but yes, a dragon."

"An Onihida dragon?"

"What does it matter where it's from? It's a freaking dragon. Can we just move on?"

"Just answer the fucking question!" she shouted at Riki. "It's rather simple. Was it an Onihida dragon?"

Riki paced the limb like an agitated crow. "For a long, long time dragons were worshipped as gods, both on Earth and Onihida. They lived in 'the heavens' and had great powers that they often used to help humans and tengu alike. All the legends about dragons go on about the heavens and traveling from to Onihida or Earth and back. What that mystical shit might have actually been talking about is travel between universes. So dragons may be native to Onihida—or might be from someplace else. I don't know."

If Riki had told her the truth about his childhood, he was

raised on Earth and probably was less in tune with the mystical than she was. Not that she was particularly "in tune."

"The dragon cast an oni shield spell." She pointed out the flaw in Riki's "not from Onihida" logic.

"No, that's not oni magic, it's dragon magic. The oni true bloods figured out how to enslave dragons and stole their magic."

So he said—but how could she know if he was telling the truth? "Dragon magic? Oni magic? What's the difference?"

"Originally oni magic was only bioengineering, just like the elves."

"So the solid hologram stuff? Like your wings?"

"That's dragon magic."

"And the tengu? They're both oni and dragon magic?"

Riki did an angry little hop. "Tinker! I just want to ask you one simple question, not give you a history lesson."

"What do you want, Riki?"

"The dragon—when it attacked you—did it mark you with a symbol or tattoo or something like that?"

"Strange that you ask, but yeah, it put one right here." She half turned and patted her butt cheek. "It says, 'Kiss my ass.'"

Stormsong snickered.

"I know how pissed you must be, Tinker. Believe me, if this weren't important, I wouldn't come anywhere near you."

She scoffed at that. "What does this mark do?"

"So it marked you?" Judging by the excitement in his voice, it was very important to him.

Stormsong shoved Tinker suddenly behind her and activated her shields with a shout. At the movement, Riki jerked back out of sight. A second later, a bullet struck the tree trunk where Riki had been standing, ricocheted, and struck Stormsong's shield.

"Shields, *domi*." Pony triggered his own and pulled his sword.

Tinker felt a kick of magic from the west. She forced herself to find her center and cast the trigger spell. Her heart was pounding as the wind wrapped around her.

Sekasha emerged from the forest shadows; their wyvern

armor and tattoos were the black of the Stone Clan. Five in all—
a full Hand, the back two acting as Shields, which meant they had
someone to guard. They halted some twenty feet off, tense and
watchful.

"Lower your weapons," a female shouted in High Elvish.

"Lower yours! This is Wind Clan holding!" Tinker shouted
angrily.

"It's a royal holding," The Stone Clan's *domi* came out from
behind one of the ironwoods. "And you're conversing with the
enemy."

The *domi* was short for an elf, several inches shorter than
her *sekasha*, but willowy graceful as any other high-caste female
Tinker had ever seen. She wore an emerald green underdress and
an overdress with a forest of wildly branching trees over it. Her
hair was gathered into elaborate braids, dark and rich as otter fur,
twined with emerald ribbons and white flowers. Two small
gleaming orbs circled around her, like tiny planets caught in her
gravity.

"Yeah, I was talking to him." Tinker almost dropped her
shield but then she realized that her *sekasha* hadn't put away their
swords. "It's a good way to find out things you don't know. Like
who are you?"

"Hmm, short and vulgar—you must be Wolf Who Rules'
domi. What was your name again? Something unpronounce-
able."

"This is one of my issues from court," Stormsong murmured in English. "Lowest ranking introduces themselves first;
it's a matter of honor. You outrank her, so she should go first.
She's trying to provoke you since she can't call insult; you are still
under the queen's protection."

"Fuck that. Who the hell is she?"

"Her name is Jewel Tear on Stone. She and the rest of the
Stone Clan arrived this morning."

"Is she right about this being a royal holding now?"

"Unfortunately, yes."

"Shit!"

"You are talking to me, not her." Jewel Tear picked her way

gracefully toward Tinker. Despite the sweltering heat and her long gown, there was no sweat on her creamy white skin. "You are Wolf Who Rules' *domi*? Tinkle? Thinker?"

Screw this. "Can you introduce us, Stormsong?"

"Me doing it would be a breach of etiquette and be considered extremely rude."

"Good. Do it."

Stormsong executed an elegant bow and said. "Jewel Tear on Stone, this is our Beloved Tinker of Wind."

Amazing how they all reacted as if she had slapped Jewel Tear. All the Stone Clan *sekasha* moved forward as if to attack.

"Hold," Jewel Tear snapped. She glared at Tinker for a moment, but then murmured, "You are such a rude little beast. I don't know if I should be flattered or horrified that Wolf Who Rules chose you after I cut him loose."

Tinker glanced to Stormsong, who nodded slightly, confirming that yes this was an old girlfriend of Windwolf's. Well, if it was a battle of wits that this bitch wanted, she'd come to the right place. "That proves what they say."

"Which is?"

"Only an idiot would turn down Wolf Who Rules."

"Your arrogance is only matched by your ignorance."

"I'd rather be unlearned than moronic—since it's so much easier to cure."

"When Prince True Flame learns of your treason, he will cure that arrogance too."

"I might have been talking to the tengu—but you let him get away." Tinker pointed out.

Jewel Tear spoke a spell and made a motion, and magic pulsed underfoot, pushing up through the ground, the low ferns, and then the trees to the very ends of the leaves. Tinker *felt* the ten *sekasha* standing around them, even Rainlily standing behind her. She and Jewel Tear *echoed* differently—their *domana* shields creating the change, or maybe their innate magical talents. Around them there were birds and animals unseen but now *sensed*.

She didn't, however, *feel* Riki—and by her angry look,—neither did Jewel Tear.

"Horse piss!" Jewel Tear hissed quietly.

"I was trying to get as much information out of the tengu as I could." Tinker rubbed Jewel Tear's nose in it. Interestingly, the female didn't take it gracefully.

"The oni subverted you when they held you prisoner."

"No, they did not." Pony answered the charge. "I stand as witness to my *domi*: by my blood and my blade, she never bowed her will to them."

There was noise of something coming through the woods toward them. Jewel Tear triggered her sonar spell again and the forest was alive with *sekasha* moving toward them, and at least two other *domana*. Tinker was going to have to learn that spell.

"True Flame is coming. We'll see what he has to say."

A wave of red washed around them as Wyverns surrounded them, and then, comfortingly, a tight knot of blue as True Flame and Windwolf entered the clearing. Jewel Tear dropped her shields, so Tinker followed suit.

True Flame glanced at the kappa all but forgotten on the ground, and then to Tinker and Jewel Tear. "What is going on here? Where did that kappa come from?"

"I pulled that out of the Ghostlands." Tinker stepped forward and gave it a slight kick to demonstrate it was frozen solid. "The Ghostlands must have instantly sucked the body heat out of it."

"She was talking with a tengu." Jewel Tear indicated the empty treetops.

"Yes, I was." Tinker saw no point in denying it. "We have a history together. He betrayed me to the oni and I beat the snot out of him for it. He found me and started the conversation."

"What did you speak about?" True Flame asked.

"I'm not sure what he wanted—they nearly killed me shooting at him."

Windwolf had moved between Jewel Tear and Tinker just as a *sekasha* would, his shields still up so he seemed to shimmer with anger. With Tinker's explanation, he took a step toward Jewel Tear. "How dare you?"

Jewel Tear jerked up her chin. "That was an unfortunate and unforeseeable accident. Forgiveness, Tinker *ze domi*."

Tinker nodded but Windwolf shook his head.

"If you harm my *domi*," Windwolf growled, "It will not be the Fire Clan that you'll be answering to."

"Wolf Who Rules—" True Flame snapped.

"I will not suffer future 'unfortunate' accidents. There will be no forgiveness."

True Flame studied Windwolf for a moment and then nodded. "That is your right."

Windwolf caught Tinker's hand. "Come." And he pulled her out of the clearing.

"Wait, my stuff."

"Leave it."

"No!" She jerked her hand free. "I'm not done here."

"You are for right now."

"No, no, no. I'm sick of this. Come here, go there, do this. My grandfather died five years ago, thank you, and I was happy making decisions for myself."

"These are royal holdings now." Windwolf swept a hand to take in the whole valley. "I cannot make her leave."

"So you're making me?" Tinker cried.

"Yes."

"No."

"Beloved. I do not trust her. I cannot stay here and watch over you now and I cannot make her leave."

As always, he seemed to cover all the options—leaving her no good choice but to do what he wanted.

This time she shook her head. "No. Again and again, you don't tell me enough to form my own options. All I know are your options and I'm not playing that anymore."

"Be reasonable."

"Reasonable? What is reasonable about taking the smartest person in this city and making them deaf and blind? I'm supposed to walk away from my work, leaving behind my currently irreplaceable equipment, because some female from the other side of the world is not playing nice in my backyard?"

"I told you that I cannot stay and I cannot make her leave."

"And those are the only options because they're the only

ones you have thought of? You know, if I had a level playing field I could come up with options of my own."

"I do not have time to explain it all."

"Of course not. You never have time."

"Beloved . . ."

"Don't 'Beloved' me. Did you know that—until Pony told me, I didn't know the name of your mother? That I didn't know that you—and I—could use Fire Clan spell stones? I don't even know when I'm going to have a period! I'm stuck in this stranger's body and no one tells me diddly. And when did I agree to be called Beloved Tinker? I think I should at least be able to pick out my own name."

Windwolf looked stunned at her outburst and after a moment, said quietly, "Your name is . . . short."

"Tinker isn't my real name. My real name is Alexander Graham Bell."

"It is? I did not know that."

"Score one for me."

"Beloved—Tinker—Alexan . . . der?" He floundered for a moment. "Isn't that considered a male name?"

"I can hold my own with Jewel Tear. I'm not done here, and I'm not leaving my stuff."

"No, you cannot hold your own." Windwolf caught her by her shoulders. "Do not ever think that you can. Only you can sense her magic—so it is possible for her to attack you without your *sekasha* knowing it. She could make a tree fall, the ground give way, dozens of little ways that you *do not know*."

"You really think she would try to kill me?"

"Yes."

"Any one of us," Stormsong added in English, "can make a bullet ricochet and hit a target. The tengu was a convenient excuse."

Tinker turned to her and saw in her eyes that none of her *sekasha* took the event as an accident. They hadn't relaxed until Windwolf and True Flame appeared.

"But why?" she asked.

"Because the Stone Clan stands to gain much if you are dead

and I'm distracted. Because she is a self-centered, ambitious bitch."

That was unnerving. Tinker kicked at the dirt, not wanting to leave, hating that once again she was bowing to his limited options. "Can we can get True Flame to order her out of the area?"

"No, we must let her try and fix this valley."

Tinker laughed. "With what?"

"Magic."

She doubted that greatly, but she was up against the wall of her own ignorance. "I'm the one that made this mess. I'll be the one that fixes it."

"That is quite possible. Stone Clan, however, has assured True Flame that they can quickly fix the Ghostlands, while you said you needed to study it further. Everyone knows that you were being realistic—but True Flame had to believe the Stone Clan or it would be an insult to them."

"God forbid he insults them." Tinker growled and looked back toward the Discontinuity's edge and her abandoned equipment.

"*Domi*, I will bring your things," Stormsong offered. "I am not totally ignorant of these computer things."

Since Stormsong could manage the Rolls Royce and the walkie-talkie, she should be able to disconnect the equipment and carry it back to the enclave unharmed. Tinker sighed and nodded. "Okay. Thank you."

Windwolf signaled that Cloudwalker would accompany Stormsong, and the two *sekasha* moved off.

"There is so much I need to know," Tinker said to him. "And if we're really going to be husband and wife—you need to take the time for me. How do you expect me to trust you when you keep throwing me in the pool to sink or swim?"

He sighed deeply and scrubbed his hands over his face. "I want to be there for you—protect you—but I can't. It's killing me that you're in the water and floundering—but the only other option I have is to lock you away someplace safe, and that would only kill you faster. The only thing that has kept me sane so far is

knowing that you're actually very good at finding your own way
out of the water."

After seeing his *domi* safely back to Poppymeadow's, Wolf
went in search of Earth Son to lodge his complaint. He found
Earth Son at the palace clearing, pacing it out as if he planned to
claim the piece of land for himself. Apparently the Stone Clan
domana had expected the *aumani* as soon as they arrived in
Pittsburgh; Earth Son wore a full tunic of rich green silk and a
gold burnt velvet duster with a stone horse pattern. Like Jewel,
he had a spell orb keeping him cool in the muggy Pittsburgh
summer.

Wolf closed the distance between them. "Earth Son, I will
have a word with you."

Earth Son had inherited his father's height, so he was slightly taller than Wolf. He tried to use it to look down on Wolf, but
then ruined the effect by doing a sketchy bow. "Wolf Who Rules."

Wolf was too angry to acknowledge the veiled insult of
Earth Son's greeting. "Has the Stone Clan all run mad? We do
not know the number of the oni forces, and the way between our
worlds is not fully shut, and you're already asking for a clan war."

"Us?" Earth Son feigned confusion.

"I may be young, but I spent my doubles at court. I recognize power maneuvering when I see it."

"You are seeing things that are not there—like your so-
called oni." Earth Son's First, Thorne Scratch, tried to silence her
domou with a hand on his shoulder. Earth Son flicked the female
sekasha's hand away. "I have been out for hours doing scrys." He
waved toward the forest beyond the clearing. "And found nothing remotely resembling an oni. 'I can see the shadows of the oni
on the wall,' is that not what you said at court? Apparently that's
all that you've seen—shadows! You're jumping at phantoms if
you ask me."

Wolf didn't even bother with magic. He stepped forward
and caught Earth Son by the throat. "Listen, you little turd, my
domi is under the queen's protection, which means you are not to
attack her. But if you can't get that through that rock skull of

yours, then understand this—if she is hurt in any way, I will hunt you down and tear out your throat."

"You would not dare," Earth Son managed to whisper.

"I started with nothing here. I can do it again. If my *domi* is killed, I will let the crown strip me bare to have my revenge. Do not think our royal cousin will protect you either—after you shit all over the queen's commands, True Flame will not stop me."

"I cannot be held accountable for what that the others—"

"You are clan head for this area and I will hold you responsible."

"Forest Moss is mad!"

"If you didn't want the disadvantages that the mad one brings with him, you shouldn't have chosen him."

"I didn't choose him."

Earth Son's Hand looked relieved as the clearing filled with Wyverns.

"Wolf." True Flame followed on the wash of red. "Let him go."

Wolf released Earth Son, turning over this new piece of information. He knew that Earth Son did not have considerable standing in the Stone Clan, but he thought that Earth Son would have at least been party to picking out the clan *domana* that would be under him. Now that Wolf had talked with Forest Moss and Jewel Tear and learned their situations, their inclusion seemed less a personal attack on the Wind Clan, and more a statement of the Stone Clan's assessment of Pittsburgh. They had sent two of their most disposable *domana*. Or was the count three?

In the clans, birth did not guarantee rank. It was acknowledged, though, that children of the clan leaders learned much from observing their parents. Genetically, too, the leaders were the best that the clans had to offer. True, barring accident or assassination, it was unlikely clan heads would ever change—but as his mother's only child, Earth Son was a likely future leader. Then again, he had arrived with only one Hand. Was he escort for the other two, or fellow exile? If the latter, what had Earth Son done to be sent to Pittsburgh?

"I did nearly a hundred scrys," Earth Son reported to True Flame while he rubbed his throat. "There's no oni here."

"The oni are savage but not stupid," Wolf snapped. "Acting quickly is not to their advantage. They are hiding themselves well and waiting for the best time to strike."

Earth Son scoffed at this. "If that was the case, they should have struck while you were here alone, with even your voice turned against you."

"They tried. They failed." Wolf did not mention how near the assassination had come to succeeding. The brutal attack killed one of his *sekasha*, damaged one of his hands, and stranded him deep in Pittsburgh's territory just as it returned to Earth. If not for Tinker, the plot would have succeeded. "If the Ghostlands can be used to their advantage, they will wait for reinforcements."

"Wolf is right," True Flame said. "That they managed to stay hidden for nearly thirty years shows that they have patience. No matter what happens, we need you to ferret them out."

13: IGNORE THAT MAN BEHIND THE CURTAIN

Tinker sat high up on a towering cross, clinging to the crossbrace. Black was sitting at the very end of the crossbrace, sobbing quietly. The delicate-boned woman wore a puffy black mourning gown and a crown. Lying beside her was a long wand with a star attached to it. Her host of crows sailed overhead, cawing, "Lost, Lost!"

With a flurry of wings, Riki perched on the tip of the brace between Tinker and Black. He was wearing an odd red outfit. "There's no shame in being afraid of heights. Most people are."

"Oh, go away, monkey boy," she snapped.

"I'm not a flying monkey," the tengu said. "I gave that up. You melted the witch, so I got out of my no-compete contract. I'm working strictly as a freelance crow. The health benefits suck, but I make my own hours."

Tinker pointed to the sobbing Black. "Why is she crying?"

"She gave her heart to the Tin Man but she lost him," Riki told her. "Not even the wizard can fix that."

"Hey!" On the ground, Esme gazed up at them, wearing blue checked overalls and red ruby boots. "You can't get down. Your not smart enough. You're head is full of straw."

167

"I'll figure a way down," Tinker shouted back.

"Falling will work," Riki said.

And Tinker was falling.

The dream seemed to hiccup and she was safe on the ground then. Esme had a wicker basket and a little black dog. Pony was there, his hair loose and curly as a mane, whiskers, cat ears and tail to finish the cat look. Oilcan too, looking like he was made out of metal.

"You have Black's heart?" Tinker asked Oilcan.

"I have no heart." He thumped on his chest and it echoed.

"That was a different tin man." Esme butted between the two of them. "We need to find the wizard! Only he can solve all our problems."

"I can take you to the wizard." Oilcan squeaked as he moved his arm to point down a yellow brick road that led into a dark forest of black willows. "But we don't need to hurry, it's only six o'clock."

"We've murdered time." Esme took out a pocket watch. It seemed to be coated with butter. "It's always six o'clock—we have to run to stay in the same place."

"We will have to go through the trees." Pony's cat tail danced nervously behind him.

"I don't know if that's smart," Tinker said.

"Of course you don't, you have straw for brains." Esme picked straw out of Tinker's head to prove her point. "Look! See!" She held out the straw as evidence. "We have to get to the wizard. He's the only one who can give you brains so you can solve this problem."

"But the road ended with the tree," Tinker pointed out as they crept forward, clinging to one another.

"It's not the tree," Esme said. "It's the fruit."

The trees turned, their gnarled faces looking at them with wooden eyes. They were black willow trees but there were apples—red and tempting—in their branches.

"You need the fruit." Esme pushed Tinker hard toward the trees.

The trees plucked the apples from their branches and flung them like hard rain at Tinker.

⌐⟢═◉═⟣⌐

Tinker flailed her way out of her sheets to sit up in bed. It was very early morning by the pale light in the window—the birds hadn't yet started to stir. Windwolf was awake though, and dressing.

"I didn't mean to wake you." He came to kiss her. His shirt was still unbuttoned, and she burrowed into his warmth.

"I had another dream about Black, Esme, and the black willow."

"Esme?"

"I figured out who White was—she's Lain's sister."

"Ah, the one in white—you're dreaming that she's dreaming." He wrapped his arms around her, kissing her hair.

"Hm? Oh, yes, the Escher thing." Gods, it felt so right to be held by him.

"Have you talked to Stormsong?"

"Yeah. She—we fit."

He tipped her head back to gaze intently into her face. "You've accepted her? To be your beholden?"

She gave a tiny nod. It sounded like some kind of wedding vow. Was this what elf society was all about—getting married again and again, only without sex? "Yes. To be mine."

Windwolf gave her his smile that warmed her to her toes. "I release her to you. But—"

"But?"

"But that is not what I meant. You should talk to Stormsong about your dreams. She has some training in *yatanyai*. She might be able to help you determine what they mean."

"She does?"

"It was thought she would be an *intanyei seyosa* but in the end, she had too much of her father's temperament." Windwolf kissed Tinker again and slipped out of her hold. "I need to go. True Flame expects me. Why don't you go back to sleep?"

She eyed the bed. She was still tired, but to sleep would most likely mean another dream.

"I'll send Pony to you." Windwolf buttoned up his shirt.

"I'd rather have you." She settled back into the warm softness.

Windwolf smiled. "I am glad of that, but alas, you cannot have me, so you must make do with Pony."

Did he really know what that sounded like in English? She curled into ball and resolved to be asleep before Pony joined her. And she was.

Another day, another dress. She really had to do something about clothing. She picked out the Wind Clan blue dress and had the staff add pockets to it while she ate. Breakfast proved that Windwolf's household was still intent on mothering the life out of her. They stacked the garden table with plates of pastries, omelets, and fresh fruit. Tinker eyed the collection of dishes with slight dismay.

"If they keep this up, they're going to make me fat," Tinker complained.

"Eat." Stormsong pointed at a bench, indicating that she was to sit. "You and Pony have both lost weight since Aum Renau."

Pony nodded, acknowledging that this was the truth. "You should eat."

"*Pft.*" Tinker began loading a plate. "Fine, but you both have to eat too."

A sign of their "fit," they ate at first in companionable silence, then drifted into a conversation about which of the *sekasha* would work well with them. Of Windwolf's four Hands, they came up with a list of seven possible candidates to fill the three open positions of Tinker's First Hand.

"We can spend a few days pairing with others to see who works best with you." Pony meant Tinker. "Windwolf chose all of his *sekasha* so we work well together, and we've had years to learn each other's ways."

"What are your plans for today?" Stormsong asked. "Are we finished with that tree?"

"I don't know," Tinker whined. "I had another dream about it. Windwolf said I should talk to you about my dreams."

"You dream?" Stormsong said.

"I don't want to believe that I do," Tinker said, "but things keep showing up out of my dreams."

"Dreams are important," Stormsong said. "They let you see the future."

"Oh gods help me if this is my future," Tinker muttered.

"Tell me this dream," Stormsong said.

"Well, I had a couple, and they're all centering around two people, and the tree." Tinker explained the first dream and then the discovery of Esme's identity, and then last night's dream, ending with, "And I don't have a clue where all *that* weirdness came from."

Stormsong cocked her blue head with a faint disbelieving look on her face. "It sounds like *The Wizard of Oz*."

"What's that?" Tinker asked.

"It's a movie," Stormsong said.

Tinker had never heard of such a movie. "What's it about?"

"It's about—It's about—It's odd." Stormsong said. "Maybe you should just see it."

Since Tooloo rented videos, Tinker gave her a call.

"I'm looking for *The Wizard of Oz*."

"Well, follow the yellow brick road," Tooloo said and hung up.

Somehow, Tinker had totally forgotten how maddening it was to deal with Tooloo. She hit redial, and explained, "I'm looking for the movie called *The Wizard of Oz*."

"You should have said so in the first place."

"Can you set it aside? I'll be by to pick it up." And while she was there, she'd find out why Tooloo had lied to Nathan.

"No, you won't," Tooloo said.

Amazing that someone can give you an instant headache over the phone. "Yes, I will."

"You can come but the movie won't be here."

"Oh, did someone else rent it?"

"No."

"Tooloo!" Tinker whined. "This is so simple—why can't I rent the movie if no one has it?"

"I never had it."

"You didn't?" Tinker asked.

"It was fifty years old when the first Shutdown hit, and I

couldn't stand it after having to watch it every year for thirty years running."

Should she even ask *why* Tooloo had to watch it every year? No, that would only make her head hurt more. "So that's a 'no'?"

"Yes," and Tooloo hung up.

Tinker sat drumming her fingers as she considered her phone. Should she call Tooloo back and try to find out why Tooloo was telling people she wasn't married to Windwolf? Go and visit the crazy half-elf in person? She suspected that even if she could understand the logic behind Tooloo's action, she wouldn't be able to change it so the half-elf would stop.

She decided to focus on her dream. Where had she seen the movie? Her grandfather thought movies were a waste of time, so that left Lain.

"I don't have that movie," Lain stated when Tinker called and asked.

"Are you sure?"

"Yes, I'm sure. Esme insisted that we watch it every year after Thanksgiving. God knows why they picked Thanksgiving. It always gave me nightmares. I would be quite happy never to see that stupid movie again."

"Esme liked it?"

"She always identified too much with Dorothy, though she never understood why Dorothy wanted to go back home. Esme would go on and on about how if she were Dorothy, she would stay in Oz, which would make my mother cry. Every Thanksgiving we would have this huge family fight about watching it; Esme would win, Mother would cry, and I'd have nightmares."

They said their good-byes like polite people and Tinker hung up. Where had she seen this movie?

She called Oilcan. She never watched a movie alone, so he most likely had seen it with her. "Hey, I'm trying to remember something. Did you see *The Wizard of Oz* with me?"

"The what?"

"It's a movie called *The Wizard of Oz*. It's about Dorothy who goes to Oz." That much of the story Tinker had gathered from Lain, although she wasn't clear where Oz was. Africa?

"It's not ringing any bells."

She sighed. "If I track this down, do you want to watch with us?"

"A movie night? Cool. Sure. Meet you at your loft?"

She hadn't considered where to watch the movie once she found it. She suddenly realized it had been two months since she'd been home to her loft. Weirder yet, she didn't want to go—as in "don't want to go to the dentist because it would hurt" way. Why the hell did she feel that way? Her system made Oilcan's look like a toy, which was why they always used her place. But she was cringing at the thought of doing movie night at her loft.

"Tink?" Oilcan asked.

This was stupid—it was her home. "Yeah, my place."

"See you later then."

"Later."

She slumped forward onto the table, resting her cheek on its smooth surface. Three phone calls, she hadn't yet stirred out of the garden, and already she was emotionally raw and tired. Damn, she wished she could get a good night's sleep. Her exhaustion felt like it was teaming up with all her problems, conspiring to keep her off balance.

"*Domi*," Stormsong said quietly. "When I saw the movie, I rented it from Eide's."

At least something was working out in her life.

Eide's Entertainment was an institution in Pittsburgh, down on Penn Avenue in the Strip District. Established in the 1970s as a comicbook store, it had been one of the many landmarks that somehow not only survived but also flourished when transplanted to Elfhome. It was a mecca of human culture, which not only humans but also elves went on pilgrimage to. Tinker and Oilcan would always hit the shop once immediately after Startup to see what was new, and then several times a month to see what used music and videos were brought in by other customers. Besides music, videos, and comic books, the store was a treasure trove of collectible items: non-sport cards, magazines, Big Little Books, pulps, and out of print books.

Ralph raised his hand to them as they entered. "Hey, Lina,

long time no see. I've got that Nirvana CD you wanted in the back."

It wasn't until Stormsong touched hands with Ralph in a rocker's version of a handshake that Tinker realized he had been talking to Stormsong. Lina? Ah yes, *Linapavuata*, which was Elvish for "singing." Ralph looked past the elf, saw Tinker.

"Tinker-tiki!" Ralph used Tinker's racing nickname, which meant "Baby Tinker," "Look at you!" He ran a finger over Tinker's ear point, making her burn with embarrassment. "Like the ear job. Love the dress. You're looking *fine*."

Pony slapped Ralph's hand away and reached for his blade, but Stormsong kept him from drawing his *ejae*.

"Their ways are not ours," Stormsong murmured in High Elvish to Pony, and then dropped to Low Elvish to continue. "Ralph, this is Galloping Storm Horse on Wind, he looks to Tinker *ze domi*—and she is *very* off-limits now."

"Forgiveness." Ralph bowed and used passable Low Elvish. "Does that make you Tinker of the Storms?"

"Beloved Tinker of Wind," Pony corrected Ralph with a growl.

Ralph glanced to Stormsong and read something on her face that made him decide to flee. "Let me go get that CD."

Tinker turned to Pony, who was still glaring after Ralph. "What was that about?"

"He should show you respect," Pony said.

Stormsong clarified in English. "'Baby Tinker' is disrespectful, nor should he have touched you."

"I've known him for years!" Tinker stuck with Low Elvish. She didn't want to cut Pony out of the conversation. "Oilcan and I go to his parties. Tinker-tiki is what all the elves call me."

"Used to call you," Pony said. "No elf would be so impolite as to use it now."

"Only because they fear you would call insult," Stormsong implied, with a glance, that Pony would use his blade in dealing with anyone who insulted Tinker.

"Like—kill them?" Tinker asked.

"We have the right to mete out punishment as we see fit,"

Pony explained. "By the blood and the sword."

Oh boy. The little things people don't tell her. "You can't just whack the head off anyone that pisses you off!"

"If the insult is severe, yes, we can," Pony said. "*Sekasha* are divine warriors, who answer only to the gods."

"We have the right," Stormsong said. "Our training guides us not to take the options allowed to us."

"Look, if I'm insulted, I'll punch the guy myself. As far as I'm concerned, you guys are just here for oni and monsters with sharp teeth."

"Yes, *domi*." Stormsong gave an elaborate bow.

Pony looked unhappy but echoed, "Yes, *domi*."

Which didn't make Tinker happy, because she felt like she was somehow the bad guy for not letting them lop off heads right and left. Worse, she *knew* it was all really Windwolf's fault because her life gotten weird the exact second that he entered it. Suddenly she was very annoyed with him, but didn't want to be, which made her grumpier. She tried to ignore the whole confusing swarm of emotions and thumped over to the video rental section. The *sekasha* and stinging feelings, unfortunately, followed close behind.

She'd never actually rented a video from Eide's before and their categories confused her. There seemed to be two of every category. "Why two?"

"These are bootleg copies with subtitles in Low Elvish." Stormsong pointed out a sign in Elvish that Tinker had missed because a male elfin customer stood in front of it, flipping through the anime.

The elf noticed Stormsong with widening eyes, bowed low, and moved off with a low murmured, "Forgiveness."

"The other elves—they're afraid of you?" Tinker noticed that all the elves in the store covertly watched the *sekasha* and had cleared out of their path.

"If they do not know us, yes," Stormsong spoke quietly so her words wouldn't carry. "You are one that sleeps in the nest of dragons. You do not know how rare we are—or how dangerous."

"What makes you so special?"

"The Skin Clan did; they created the perfect warrior."

Tinker was afraid to ask how this gave them the right to preform indiscriminate head-lopping, so she focused on why they were here—to rent *The Wizard of Oz*. Knowing that Pony would be watching the movie with her, Tinker scanned only the translated videos. Unlike the originals in their glossy colorful boxes, the translated videos had plain white covers with Low Elvish printed onto the spines. She pulled out one at random and studied it. The movie was *The Wedding Singer* which had been translated to *The Party Singer*. Was it a bad translation or was there actually no Elvish word for wedding? How could the elves exist without the most basic of life ceremonies?

Tinker put the movie back, and scanned the shelves.

Stormsong had been searching too, and now pulled out a box and handed it to Tinker. "This is it."

The translator hadn't even tried to find Elvish to match the words *Wizard* and *Oz*. Instead, the title was phonetically spelled out.

Tinker turned and found Tommy Chang leaning against the end of the DVD rack, watching her with his dangerous cool. He was wearing a black tank top that showed off the definition in his muscled arms, a corded leather bracelet, and his signature bandana. Tommy organized raves, the cockfights in Chinatown, and the hoverbike races—the last being how she knew him best.

"Hi, Tommy." Somehow, the normal greeting sounded dorky. Something about his zenlike menace made her feel like a complete techno geek. If she didn't watch it, she ended up over-compensating around him.

He lifted his chin in acknowledgement. "I wasn't sure if they'd let you out." He glanced toward Pony. "They keep you on a short leash. In a dress, even."

"Piss off." That was a record.

"Aren't we touchy now we're an elf?"

"Excuse me, but I've had one fucked-over month."

"So I heard." And then, surprisingly, he added. "Glad you're still breathing."

"Thanks."

"You still going to ride for Team Tinker?"

She felt a flash of guilt as she realized that she hadn't thought about racing in months. Last she had heard Oilcan had taken over the riding. "How is my team doing?"

"It's been Team Big Sky's season since," he lifted a finger to indicate her appearance, "the whole elf thing."

That made sense. Oilcan was heavier than she was, had a different center of gravity, and was less aggressive on the turns. Team Banzai would have lost their edge when the oni stole Czerneda's custom-made Delta. That left John Montana, captain of Team Big Sky, with the only other Delta in the racing circuit, and his half brother, Blue Sky, a good match to her build and skills.

"So—you going back to riding?" Tommy asked.

"I don't know. A lot of shit has hit the fan that I need to deal with before I can think about that."

A flash of Wyvern red outside made Tommy look toward the store windows. "Yup, a lot of shit."

Her loft smelled of garbage. Months ago—a lifetime ago— she, Oilcan, and Pony had eaten, washed dishes, left trash in the can to be taken out, left, and never come back. Stormsong was too polite to say anything, carefully sticking to Low Elvish. Even after they'd opened the windows and let in the cool evening air, the place depressed Tinker with its ugliness. She had lived alone at human speed, always too busy cramming in what was important to her to deal with beautifying where she lived. Most of her furniture was battered, mismatched, used stuff that she had picked up cheap. The couch had been clawed by someone else's cats, the leather recliner was cracking with age, and the coffee table was scrap metal she'd welded together and topped with a piece of glass. The walls had been painted dark green by the loft's last occupant—not that you could see a whole lot of the color as her cinderblock and lumber bookshelves covered most of the walls and overflowed with her books. She had nothing beautiful—everything was just serviceable and in need of a good cleaning.

She knew it could be made pretty. She had time now, if she wanted to take it. The place could be cleaned, painted, and furnished. She could even hire carpenters to make her bookcases and kitchen cabinets. There was no room, though, for all the people in her life now. The place was for one busy person who was barely there or a married couple with no interests outside of each other. Windwolf would never fit—his life was too big—and she didn't want to live without him. Without Pony. And of late, not without Stormsong either.

She didn't fit into her old life anymore. This wasn't her home anymore, and it saddened her for reasons she couldn't understand. Perching on the couch's overstuffed arm, she tried to cheer herself up with an inventory of what had replaced her old life. A stud muffin of a husband with wads of cash who was crazy in love with her. A luxurious room at the best enclave. Fantastic food for every meal. A best friend who was even now sitting beside her on the couch, eyeing her with concern.

"What is wrong?" Pony asked quietly.

"I think I'm homesick," she whispered and leaned her forehead against his shoulder. "Look at this place. It's a dump. And I miss it. Isn't that the stupidest thing you've ever heard?"

He pulled her into his lap and held her in his arms. "It is not stupid. It only means you lived with joy here, and it is sorrowful to put joyful things aside."

"Bleah." She sniffed away tears that wanted to fall. "I was lonely, I just never let myself know how much. I made the computers all talk, just so I felt like someone else was here."

"You can grieve for something lost, even if it was not perfect."

The front door opened and Oilcan walked in. "Hey," he announced, not noticing that he had started Stormsong to attention. He balanced boxes and a carton of bottles. "I didn't think you would have anything to eat here, so I brought food." He settled the various boxes onto the coffee table. "Hey, what's with the sad face?"

"I'm just tired." She didn't want him to know how lonely she had been, or think that she was unhappy with her life now. "I've been having all these bad dreams. It's put me on edge. It's like I've been rubbed down to all nerves."

"Ah, yeah, that can happen." Oilcan had suffered from horrible nightmares when he first had come to Pittsburgh. For that first year, she'd climbed into his bed late at night, armed with boxes of tissues, to get him to stop crying. It was one of the reasons she led and he followed despite the fact he was four years older.

"Scrunches?" He asked her if she needed to be held, just as she had once asked him.

"Pony has it covered." She leaned against Pony. "What's in the boxes?"

"Chicken satay with peanut sauce." He lifted up the first lid to show off the skewers of marinated chicken. "Curry puffs, fried shumai, Thai roll, Pad Thai noodles, and Drunken Chicken."

He went into the kitchen to collect dishes and silverware.

"We'll get fat eating all this." She helped herself to one of the Thai rolls, dipping it in the sweet chili sauce. He must have come straight from the Thai place because the thin fried wrapper was still piping hot.

"Feed the body, feed the soul, you sleep better." Oilcan handed her one of the plates and found room for the others on the crowded table.

"Feed on spirits," Stormsong added as she examined the bottles of alcohol. "Hard cider, vodka coolers, and beer?"

"Beer is for me. Figured I'd bring a mix for you guys."

"These are good." Stormsong handed a cooler to Tinker. "The cider carries less of a punch, so Pony and I should stick to those."

"Ah, leave the hard drinking to me." Tinker twisted off the top. Half a cooler, a curry puff, and a plate of pad Thai noodle later, she realized that the rubbed-raw feeling had vanished, and the loft felt like home again.

Tooloo had mentioned that the movie was old, but Tinker was still surprised when it started in only sepia tones. Dorothy was a whiny, stupid, spoiled brat who was clueless on how to manage a rat-sized dog. When Tinker had been Dorothy's age, she had been an orphan and running her own business. Esme identified with this girl? That didn't bode well.

The Earth the movie showed was flat, dusty, and featureless. Tinker was with Esme—why would anyone pine for that?

"Is that what Earth is like?" Pony asked.

"I don't know—I've never been to Earth." Tinker groaned at yet another stupid thing that the girl did. "I'm not sure I can take a full ninety minutes of this."

"It—changes," Stormsong said.

And change it did as a tornado sucked the house up into the air and plopped it down in glorious color. Dorothy's dress turned out to be blue checked and she acquired glittering red high heels that they called "slippers," the source of Esme's overalls and red boots in Tinker's dream.

It took Tinker several minutes to realize how Glinda the Good Witch worked into her dream. "That's Black. She had the wand and the crown. And she was crying."

"I think I would cry if I was stuck in a dress like that," Stormsong said.

Tinker had to agree with that assessment. Tiny little people in weird clothes surrounded Dorothy and talked in rhyming singsong voices.

"Oh, this is so weird," Tinker whispered.

"Does this make more sense in English?" Pony asked.

"No, not really," she told him. "Do they ever stop singing?"

"Not much," Stormsong said as the munchkins escorted Dorothy to the edge of town and waved cheerfully good-bye.

"Oh, of course they're happy to see her go; she's a cold-blooded killer," Tinker groused as Dorothy discovered a talking scarecrow. "Oh gods, they're singing again."

Dorothy and Scarecrow found the apple trees that threw fruit, and then the Tin Man, whose first word was "oilcan." Tinker huddled against Pony, growing disquieted.

"What is it, *domi*?" Pony asked.

"How did I know? I didn't see this movie before, but so many things are just like my dream."

"Maybe we did see it and forgot," Oilcan said.

"Something this weird?" Tinker asked. "And we both forgot?"

Pony's lion showed up next. Tinker scowled at the screen. It annoyed her that she didn't understand how she had dreamed this movie—and that her dream self had cast Pony in such a cowardly character. "All these people are dysfunctional, delusional idiots."

Finally the foursome plus dog found the wizard, who turned out to be a fraud.

"What was this dream trying to tell me?" Tinker asked.

"I am not sure," Stormsong said. "Normally an untrained dreamer borrows symbols uncontrollably—and this movie is rife with them. Everything from the Abandoned Child archetype to Crossing the Return Threshold."

"Huh?" The only threshold crossing Tinker knew about related to chaos theory.

"Dream mumbo jumbo." Stormsong waved a hand toward the television screen.

The wizard/fraud had produced a hot air balloon, and was saying good-bye. ". . . am about to embark upon a hazardous and technically unexplainable journey to the outer stratosphere."

"Dorothy is taking a heroic journey," Stormsong continued. "She crosses two thresholds, one out of the protected realm of her childhood, and the other completes her journey, by returning to Kansas. If you were familiar with this movie, I would say you were seeking to move past your old identity and claim one that reflects growth. The tornado could be a symbol of the awakening of sexuality, especially suppressed desire."

Tinker resisted the sudden urge to shift out of Pony's arms. "I didn't dream about the tornado."

"Yeah, well, the odd thing is that you're not familiar with the movie. So the question is: Where is the symbolism coming from?"

"Don't look at me!" Tinker closed her eyes and rested her head on Pony's shoulder. "So, what should I do next?"

"Tell me your last dream again."

"I'm up high with Riki and he's a flying monkey. He's got the whole costume, and I'm the scarecrow. Riki talks about me melting the witch and setting him free. Then I'm on the ground, and

Esme is there as Dorothy, Pony was the lion, and Oilcan was the Tin Man."

The movie was obviously drawing to a close as Dorothy tried to convince people that her journey had been real.

"We wanted to go to the wizard," Tinker said. "But the road ends with the black willows, but they're also the trees in the movie that throw their apples. Esme keeps saying we need the fruit. I don't know. Do black willows even have fruit?"

Thankfully the movie was over and the credits rolled.

"I am not sure," Stormsong said slowly, "but I think, *domi*, finding out more about this Esme would be best."

"I'm going to have to talk to Lain about a lot of things." She went to her phone mumbling, "Fruit. Esme. Flying monkeys. Yellow brick roads. Munchkins."

She got Lain's simple unnamed AI. "It's Tinker."

"Tinker," Lain's recorded voice came on. "I'm going to be spending the next few days at Reinholds with the black willow. If you need me, you can find me there."

Tinker hung up without leaving a message. Sighing, she considered her home network. She should take it out before someone broke in and stole it. Pushing back from her desk, she lazily spun in her chair, scanning her loft. "I should really—you know—move out."

Oilcan glanced around, bobbing his head in agreement. "Yeah, unless you get divorced, I don't see you living here again. Well, I've got to go. I still have those last drums on the flatbed. I need to go dump them with the rest."

"See ya." She continued to spin, thinking of what she needed for the move. A truck. Boxes. People. As she considered how many boxes and how many people, she realized how little she really needed to move. Her computer. Her books. Her underwear. Most of her clothes were ratty hand-me-downs of Oilcan's, or too oil-stained to wear around the elves. Her battered furniture, her unmatched dishes, and all her other sundry things were just odds and ends she had picked up over time and weren't worth keeping. She could have a yard sale. She could make up a flyer and put an ad in the newspaper. They would need a way to tag all her stuff, a cash box with a starter kit of change, a tent in case it rained. They could sell hot dogs and sauerkraut to raise more money—except she didn't need money. Hell, a yard sale was a stupid idea.

She spun in her chair as plans came to mind and proved unneeded. And where would she move her stuff to? She supposed the computer could live in her bedroom at the enclave, but what about all her books? Her jury-rigged bookcases would clash horribly with the elegant hand-carved furniture. She could probably get bookcases. Snap her fingers. Make it so. But where would she put them?

Windwolf didn't fit into her life, but did she fit into his either?

She bumped into something and stopped spinning.

Stormsong stood beside her, looking down at her. "You're going to make yourself sick doing that."

"Pshaw." She stood up and toppled over.

Pony caught her and carefully put her back into the chair.

"I wish you guys wouldn't hover," Tinker snarled as they stood over her.

Pony crouched down so he was now eye level with her. "You are still upset."

She sighed and leaned her forehead on his shoulder. "I don't like being like this. This isn't me. I feel like I'm living without my skin. Everything hurts."

He put his arms around her and eased her into his lap. "*Domi*, I have been with you every day for some time now. I have seen you happy and relaxed. I have seen you bored. I have seen you snarling into the face of the enemy. And you were always yourself until two days ago. Something has changed."

"Do you think the oni dragon did something more to me than just draw magic through me?"

He considered for a few minutes, and then shook his head. "I do not know, *domi*."

"How do we check?" She asked.

He and Stormsong exchanged looks.

"Let's go to the hospice," Stormsong said. "And have them check you."

The hospice people poked and prodded and did various spells on her and shook their heads and sent her home feeling even more unbalanced. Her beholden fended off Windwolf's household, else she probably would have been doused again with *saijin* and put to bed. Ironically, the only place she had to retreat to was her bedroom, which didn't feel like home.

"There's no me in this room!" She paced on the bed just to get as tall as the *sekasha*. "This is not a room I live in. I need a computer. And a television. Internet connection! Is it any wonder that I feel like I'm going nuts when the most mechanical item in this suite is the toilet? Hell, I don't know even where to find my stuff! Where is my datapad? Where's—where's—shit, I don't even own anything anymore!"

The *sekasha* nodded, wisely saying nothing, probably thinking she was insane.

"I mean, how am I supposed to do anything? I know I have stuff. I had you put stuff in the car to bring home. Where did it go?"

"I will find it," Stormsong said and went off to search. While Tinker was still pacing the bed, she returned with the MP3 player Riki had left for her at Turtle Creek, the Dufae Codex, her grandfather's files on the flux spells and Esme, and a bottle of ouzo. Of course everything had been cleaned and given lovely linen binders tied with silk ribbons. Elves!

Tinker settled down with the file and a glass of ouzo. Smart female Stormsong. Must keep her. She tossed the player onto the nightstand where she might remember to take it to Oilcan, dropped the codex and the flux folder onto the floor, and opened up Esme's file. As she noticed earlier, the file contained general public information. NASA bios. Newspaper clippings. Interspersed into it, though, was detailed personal information. One paper was a genealogy chart of Esme's parents going back a dozen generations on both sides. Another set of papers chronicled medical histories for family members. Another sheet claimed to be account numbers for a Swiss bank account. Tinker weeded these unique papers out, wondering how and why her grandfather had such information on Lain's sister. Lain herself, she could understand. But Esme?

Last item in the file was an unlabeled manila envelope. She opened it up to find a photo of her father and Black wrapped in each other's arms, looking blissfully happy.

"Who the hell?" Tinker flipped the picture but the back was blank.

"What is it?"

"This is Black." Without her blindfold or hands covering her face, Black was clearly a tengu. She had Riki's black hair, blue eyes, and beaklike nose.

"This is Oilcan?" Stormsong pointed to Leo.

"No, my father." Tinker looked in the envelope to see what else was inside.

There was a handwritten note stating:

Two can play this silence game. I'm not going to let you pressure me into leaving her just so you can have grandkids. I've made a deposit at a sperm bank, just in case things change. I don't know what else I can do to make you happy. The next step is yours. If you don't call, this is the last you'll hear of me.

The attached form noted that Leonardo Da Vinci Dufae had deposited sperm to be held in cryo-storage for his personal use.

The last sheet of paper in the file was a form from a fertility clinic on Earth. Tinker read over it three times before its full import hit her. It was a record of her conception.

Esme Shenske was her mother.

She was still shaking when she found Lain at Reinholds. The xenobiologist was dressed in winter clothing and running the slim willow limbs through a machine. She glanced up as Tinker stormed into the big freezer.

"What is it, dear?" Lain paused to pluck something off the limb and place it in a jar.

"Look at this! Look!" Tinker thrust the form into Lain's hands.

Lain took the paper, scanned it, and said quietly. "Oh."

"Oh? Oh? That's all you have to say?"

"I'm not sure what to say."

Something about Lain's tone, the lack of surprise, her uneasiness got through, and after a stunned moment, Tinker cried, "You knew!"

"Yes, I knew."

"You've known all along!"

"Yes."

"How could you lie to me all this time? I thought you . . ." She swallowed down the word "loved," terrified to have to hear it denied. ". . . cared for me."

"I love you. I have wanted to tell you about Esme for so very long, but you have to understand, I couldn't."

"Couldn't?"

Lain sighed and her breath misted in the freezing cold. "You don't know everything. There's so much that I had to keep from you."

"What the hell does that mean?"

"It means what it means." Lain busied herself labeling the jar; the contents wriggled like worms. "Don't come storming in here all hurt and emotional about something that can't be changed."

"You could have told me!"

"No, I couldn't have," Lain said.

"*Tinker, my sister is your mother.* See how easy!" And then cause and effect kicked in. "Oh my gods, you're my aunt."

"Yes, I am."

"But what about those tests you did to show Oilcan and I were still related? You used your own DNA as a comparison."

"I didn't use my own. I used a stored test result. I wanted to make it clear that you and Oilcan are still cousins."

Tinker could only stare, feeling betrayed.

"Oh, put the hurt eyes away. I have been here for you, loving you as much as humanly possible. What does it matter that you called me Lain instead of Aunt Lain? I have always given you the care I would give my niece, no matter what you or anyone else might know." Lain snorted with disgust. "I always thought that Esme was a result of lavish parenting until you came along—daily

I've been stunned to realize it was all actually genetic."

"That hurts," Tinker snapped.

"What does?"

"That you could look at me and see my mother and never share that with me."

"Nothing about your birth and life has been cut-and-dried. I suppose that was one reason I wasn't that surprised when—out of the blue—you changed species."

A sound of hurt forced itself out of Tinker, and Lain came to fold her into a hug.

"Oh ladybug, I'm sorry, but I did my best."

"Can we get out of here and talk? It's very creepy and cold."

"Oh, love." Lain sighed, rubbing Tinker on her back. "This is the only time I'm actually going to be able to do this."

Tinker pulled out of her hold. "What are you doing that's so damn important?"

"I'm justifying all your hard work at preserving this." Lain gave her a hard look that meant that she thought Tinker was acting spoiled. "I'm scanning the structure of living limbs before this thing wakes up."

"What are these?" Tinker picked up one of the jars. Inside, small reddish-brown capsules had broken open, spilling out tiny, hairy green seedlike things, all wriggling like worms.

"Those are its seeds," Lain said. "It's possible that the Ghostlands somehow drained the tree of magic and made it inactive. It hasn't accumulated enough to wake, but the seeds need less magic."

"Seeds—are—fruit, aren't they?"

"Yes, dear." Lain focused on the limbs.

Okay, I have the fruit. Now what? Tinker eyed the seeds as they wriggled about. "I think—"

"Yes?"

"I think—Esme is trying to drive me nuts."

"Ah, that means you're family."

Tinker shoved the jar at Pony to keep while she continued her argument. "Why didn't you tell me? Why did you and Grandpa keep it a secret? Why Esme? Was she in love with my father?"

"I never knew why Esme did any of the things she did. She certainly never explained herself. I don't think she ever knew your father. I didn't think she knew your grandfather and yet—somehow—they managed to create you. She called me from a roadside pay phone right before she left Earth. She told me that she'd hidden clues to her greatest treasure in my house the last time she had visited but wouldn't say anything more. She kept repeating, 'The evil empire might be listening, and I don't want them to have it,' like she was some type of rebel spy."

"Huh?" Tinker felt as if the conversation had just veered around a blind corner. "What evil empire?"

"That's what we called our family; the empire of evil. Our stepfather was Ming the Merciless, his son was Crown Prince Kiss Butt, and our half brothers were Flying Monkeys Four and Five."

Tinker fought to ignore the sudden intrusion of *The Wizard of Oz* into the conversation. "I was her greatest treasure?"

"Yes." Lain went back to examining the limbs. "Although I'm stunned that she had the maturity to recognize that. I was expecting something more trivial like her diary, or bearer bonds she'd stolen off our stepfather. But no, it was a copy of that form, and your grandfather's address, and a note saying, 'Watch over my child. Don't tell the empire of evil—or a world away won't be far enough.' No please, no thank you, no why she had done it."

"So you're not happy that I was born?"

"Don't you twist that into something personal. I thought—and still think—it was horribly selfish and irresponsible of her, as if a child needed no more care than a dandelion seed. Throw it to the wind and hope for the best." Lain made a sound of disgust. "Which is so like Esme."

"I don't understand, though, why didn't you tell me?"

"I didn't think it was wise to trust such a secret to a child. Could you have kept it from Oilcan?"

"Oilcan wouldn't have told anyone."

"Tooloo?"

Tinker looked away. Yes, she would have trusted Tooloo, but who knew what Tooloo would have done with the information. Just look at what the half-elf was doing now—spreading lies

about her not being married. "You could have told me when
Grandpa died."

"Yes, I could have, but I didn't." Lain found another wriggling bundle and dropped it into a specimen jar. "My family are
takers. If there's something they want, they have the money and
power to take it. No one can stand against them for very long.
They go above, around, and sometimes through people to get what
they want."

"But—but—what does that have to do with not telling me
about Esme?"

"Until you met Windwolf and had seen the kind of power he
wields, I don't think that you could have possibly understood our
family. One word to the wrong person, and they could have
snatched you back to Earth, and nothing that you, your grandfather, or even I could have done would have stopped them."

14: A PARTING OF WAYS

Tinker fled the freezing cold of Reinholds and stumbled out into the baking heat of the summer evening. Oh gods, could her life get any more fucked over? Everyone she thought she knew was turning into total strangers. Tooloo was telling everyone she wasn't married, Lain was her aunt, and her grandfather had lied and lied and lied. He had always told her that her mother was dead at the time of her conception and that her egg had been stored at the same donor bank as her father's sperm. He maintained that he randomly selected the egg from a vast list of anonymous donors. He took the truth to his grave, not breathing one word that she had living family as close as Lain. He died and left her and Oilcan with no one to turn to. She'd gone nearly mad with fear and grief, and he had lied about everything, and then left them all alone.

"*Domi*, where are we going?" Pony asked quietly beside her.

She blinked and paid attention for the first time to where they were. They were walking up Ohio River Boulevard, halfway to McKees Rocks Bridge. The two Rolls Royces followed slowly behind her, effectively blocking traffic—not that there was any on this lonely stretch of road late in the evening. "I don't know. How the hell am I supposed to know. What day is it? I never know what day it is

190

anymore. Do you know how long it's been since I've seen a calendar? Thursday I destroyed the world and Friday I slept. Saturday we moved to the enclave and slept some more. Sunday a dragon used me for a straw. Monday I was on the front cover of the newspaper. Tuesday I got another person to follow along behind me and ask me impossible questions and I dreamed about my mother—who may or may not be dead—and this mystery person, Black. Wednesday. Today is Wednesday."

"If you say it is," Pony murmured.

"Tomorrow is Thursday. Thursday is the day I take scrap metal to the steel mill. They cut me a check. I drive downtown, deposit the check except for fifty bucks. I stop at Jenny Lee Bakery in Market Square and pick up a dozen chocolate thumbprint cookies. Thursdays the thumbprints are fresh. I head back to work and put in a few hours paying bills and filling orders. I cut Oilcan his paycheck and give it to him so he can go to the bank before it closes. We get together with Nathan and Bowman and some of the other cops at the Church Brew Works in the Strip. I get the pierogies or the pizza or the buffalo wings—I like being flexible—and try expensive beer. I liked beer. Now it just tastes like piss."

As if she'd summoned him, a Pittsburgh police cruiser pulled over on the other side of the road slightly ahead of her and Nathan got out.

"Tinker?" He came across the four lanes toward her. "What the hell are you doing?"

"How the hell am I supposed to know? I was never an elf before. I was never in charge of anyone. People left me alone. I could go all day without seeing anyone but Oilcan or you. I cooked my own food. Washed my own clothes. It's not like I blow up the world every day."

Nathan walked backward, staying a few feet ahead of her, scanning the bodyguards and the Rolls Royces. "Are you," he asked quietly, "trying to go home?"

"I don't know." And she didn't. She was nearly to the intersection where she could continue on Ohio River Boulevard or cross over the McKees Rocks Bridge or head up to Lain's house—not that Lain was home—but really, she had not a clue which direction she was going to go . . . although she was starting to suspect that it would be straight through, staying on Ohio River Boulevard until it hit the Rim.

"Do you want me to take you home? Or to Oilcan's? Lain's? Tooloo's? I can take you to a woman's shelter if you want. I am a cop; you can trust me to help you if you need help."

She made a rude noise. "How do you know who you can trust? How do you know when people are telling you the truth?"

"Tinker, I'm sorry about that—I know that doesn't forgive anything—but I'm sorry. I really thought you felt something for me. I thought that was why you said you wanted to go out on a date. But it's just like I offered a kid candy; I talked about dating and of course, you were curious. I should have known what you're like with something new. You don't stop until you know everything."

She hit the intersection and needed to make a choice. She nearly went straight through, but then realized that it was getting dark, and none of the streetlights worked out that way. She veered left, almost decided on going across the bridge, but realized that going to her loft would be depressing, and she didn't want to talk to Tooloo, not now, she'd probably strangle the crazy half-elf. She continued looping to the left. Nathan had a good idea; she should go talk to Oilcan. But that seemed silly, since the shortest way to Oilcan's was the way she'd come. Of the four ways out of the intersection, however, only going to Lain's house remained, and she didn't want to go there either.

She kept walking, now distinctly making a full circle in the center of the road. The Rolls Royces halted at the intersection, silver ghosts in the twilight. Pony ground to a halt behind her, watching her with a faintly worried look.

"Tinker, are you all right?" Nathan asked.

"Do I look all right? Seriously? I don't think so. Something has definitely come loose. But can they find out what's wrong? Nope. Can't do that."

"Tink." Nathan caught her by the wrist. "If you're not feeling right, walking around in the night isn't going to solve anything. Let me take you to Lain."

"No!" She tried to tug her hand free. "I don't want to see her. She lied to me!"

Nathan ignored her attempts to get loose, pulling her toward his police cruiser. "Then let me take you to your cousin."

"Pony!" Tinker cried, turning to the *sekasha*.

She saw the blur of the *ejae's* blade and was only registering its meaning when Nathan's lifeblood sprayed across her face. His hand tightened a moment on her wrist, and then his fingers went limp. She stared numbly as his hand slipped off her and his body crumbled to the ground with a heavy thud.

With the strength of a black hole, Nathan's body dragged her gaze down to it. He lay on his side, his wide shoulders canted back so she could see the thick column of his neck. The skin up to the sword cut was unblemished white, and then his neck stopped abruptly in a meaty collar of muscle, bone, and gaping pipes. Blood still fountained rhythmically from a severed artery.

She opened her mouth but couldn't form any words. She dropped to her knees beside Nathan and touched him—felt the warmth and solidity of his body. His heart still pounded, wild and frantic, pumping out his blood with lessening force until it shuddered to a stop.

What just happened? Nathan can't be dead—he was just talking to me.

She looked up to Pony and saw he had drawn his sword. Blood dripped from his blade. She whimpered, realizing she had cried out to Pony and he'd reacted as he'd been trained. She had gotten Nathan killed.

An oddly shaped object on the ground behind Pony caught her eye, and she gazed at it for a minute, puzzled, until she realized it was the back of Nathan's severed head.

She had killed Nathan.

A sound struggled up out of her chest. She pushed a hand against her mouth to keep it in and felt a sticky wetness on her face. She jerked her hand away from her face, stared at the blood covering her hand, and a loud, wordless keen forced its way out of her. Once free, it would not stop. She knelt there, wailing, as her stained hands fluttered about her as if they were trying to escape the sudden brutal reality.

"*Domi.*" Pony crouched beside her, gathering her into his arms. "Tinker *domi.*"

She rocked in his arms, keening, holding out her stained hands so he could see the blood on them. Anguish, dark and wild as flood-waters, poured into her.

Pony picked her up. Tears blinded her and she slipped into black swirling hurt, losing sense of everything but guilt and grief. Fear tainted the dark pain; she couldn't stop wailing. It was as if she'd been pushed out of her own body by the raw distress. Only Pony's warm, strong presence kept her from falling into complete panic. Slowly she became aware that he had carried her back to the Rolls, and they had driven back to the enclave. Voices of Lemonseed and others of the household came out of the darkness that she seemed to be trapped in.

When Pony sat her down and let her go, Tinker cried out and reached blindly for him.

"I am here, *domi*." He pressed close to her as he tenderly washed the blood from her face. "I will not leave you. Nothing could take me from you."

They were in the bathroom of her suite at Poppymeadow's. He'd stripped off his sharp-edged wyvern armor. She wrapped her arms and legs around him, clinging to him.

"*Domi. Domi*," Pony crooned. "*Domi*, please, stop crying."

She tried to push out words, but they came out strangled cries.

"*Domi*, please." Pony carried her into the bedroom and sat on the edge of the bed. "If I'm to understand you, you have to speak Elvish."

"I am!" She wailed, and choked out the words, "I—I wa-wa-want Windwolf," as if they were huge boulders. She needed him there, now, holding her, comforting her, making love to her, to drive away the pain.

"*Domi*, Stormsong is looking for him." Pony wiped the tears from her face. "We do not know if he will be able to come." The thought of being alone threatened to submerge her into anguish. "Oh, *domi*, please don't cry."

She buried her face in Pony's hair and breathed in his spicy musk scent, warmed by his body. She felt the play of his muscles under his fine cotton undershirt. Desire, suddenly monstrous in strength, surged through her. This time she didn't even try to resist, terrified of falling back into the dark gnawing pain. She abandoned herself to her need and kissed Pony.

He shifted his head up, giving her full access to his mouth. He tasted of cinnamon. She fumbled with his clothes, wanting to feel him, to anchor herself. The undershirt tore under her desperation, parting to reveal the chiseled lines of his body. He pulled the tattered cloth out of the way, giving her access to his warm skin and hard muscle.

While in the oni cell, she'd been so good, keeping her eyes and hands on a tight leash. Now, she nuzzled down his body to every point she'd resisted, sought out the parts of him that she had only caught glimpses of. He moaned as she freed him from his clothes and savored all his velvet hardness with her mouth.

He reached for her, pulled her up to his mouth, kissed her deeply. He rolled them so she was under him. His body eclipsed the rest of the world, blotting out everything else, so that all she could think of was him. His broad shoulders moving downward. His strong calloused hands sliding up her dress. His soft hair falling free of his braid to pour over her stomach like silk. His mouth on her, coaxing her into pleasure.

She came, gripping him tightly as her climax roared through her. It burned away the overpowering grief and pain that had been threatening to swamp her. Letting go of Pony, she slumped back into the sheets, feeling empty and fragile as a broken eggshell.

Worry filled Pony's dark eyes as he moved up to lean over her. His erection pressed against her, seeking her entrance. There was a quiet little voice, though, in the back of her head, saying it was time to stop this, that she'd already taken it too far.

"Pony," she whispered.

He froze. "*Domi?*"

She swallowed and stroked his check with a trembling hand. "I don't think," she whispered, "it would be wise to go farther."

"I never thought this was wise." He slid sideways so he was no longer pressed against her opening.

She laughed but her laughter broke in the middle and became a sob. "Oh, Pony, he loved me and I killed him."

"Oh, *domi*, please don't cry."

"I have to. If I try to keep it in, I'll just go under again." It still hurt, but it wasn't the drowning flood of pain.

She was still crying when the door opened and Windwolf walked into the bedroom.

"Windwolf!" She pushed at Pony so she could get up.

Windwolf's eyes widened at the sight of her on the bed with Pony. He shouted a command, summoning wind magic. It spilled into the room, the potential glittering at the edge of her teary vision.

Pony was jerked backward off her and thrown across the room. His shields flared seconds before he hit the wall with a crash—elaborate inlaid paneling splintering under him. He landed on the floor, coiled to spring, one of his swords miraculously in his hand.

"No!" Tinker leapt between Windwolf and Pony. Sword aside, she could guess which one was the more dangerous of the two. "Stop it, Windwolf! Don't hurt him! He did nothing wrong."

"It doesn't look like *nothing* to me." Windwolf glared furiously at the *sekasha*. "Did he hurt you?"

"No!"

"Why are you crying then?"

"I killed Nathan!"

Windwolf went still and quiet, gazing down at her. "You did?" he finally asked.

"Yes," Tinker said.

"No, she did not," Pony murmured. "I killed him, as is my right."

"He only did what I told him to do!" she cried and realized that, in the same manner, Pony had made love to her. He had thought it unwise, but he had done what she asked of him.

Oh gods, she had made love with Pony.

"Oh, shit," she sniffed. "I think I'm going to cry again. I'm sorry, Windwolf. I didn't realize Pony would do anything I told him. *Anything.* That he trusted me to do the wise thing—not the stupid. This is all my fault."

Windwolf sighed and glanced at Pony. "Leave us."

"*Domnae.*" Pony used the nonpossessive form, bowing slightly to Windwolf, but didn't otherwise move.

"Pony," Tinker murmured in Elvish. "Go, I need to talk to Wolf Who Rules alone."

Pony sheathed his sword and bowed out of the room.

That left her alone with her husband, wrapped in Windwolf's silence.

He reached for her and she flinched back. "I would never," he said huskily without dropping his arm, "strike you."

She closed the distance between them and allowed him to take her in a loose embrace. "I'm sorry. I was so hurt and confused. I've been through so much lately. Do you know that there's a slickie out there with pictures of me in my nightgown? That when I get attacked, it makes headlines in the newspaper? That women scream when they see me?"

He said nothing for several minutes and then whispered into her hair. "Are you unhappy being my *domi*?"

She hugged him then, suddenly afraid of losing him. "It's just—it's just . . ." she sobbed. "When humans get married there's a ring, and a church, and people throw rice at you and you get your picture next to the obituaries, and there's just the two of you, together, all the time, and nobody else to get in the middle and confuse things. There's no oni or royal princes or dragons or nudie pictures!"

"Beloved," he said after a minute of silence. "I'm not sure if that's a yes or a no."

"Exactly!"

He considered another minute and picked her up and carried her to the bed.

"I'm sorry," she cried. "I'm sorry. I've broken us."

"We are not broken." Windwolf eased her down and lay carefully beside her. "You are hurt and need healing—that's all."

Tinker was trying to write her full elfin name in the sand of the enclave's garden. She knew the runes but any time she went to scribe them out, the letters would creep and crawl oddly.

"You're dreaming," Stormsong stood beside her, a ghost of sky blue. "Those kinds of things never work. The part of your mind that processes them is asleep. You need dream runes. I could write what you want."

"No, no, I have to be able to do this. I'm the only one that can do this."

"Are you sure?"

"Yes, I'm sure."

Something moved in the darkness of the garden around them.

Stormsong activated her shields and they enveloped both of them, brilliant pale blue that was nearly white. "Go away. You're not wanted here."

"Give her to us." Esme prowled the darkness. She was the color of old blood. Black stood weeping in the woods with her host of crows oddly silent—only a rustle of many wings in the night. "We need her. We murdered time and now it's always six o'clock."

"No. I won't let you have her."

"You're not stopping us." Esme pressed a dark hand to the gleaming shell of Stormsong's shield, the light shafting through her spread fingers like solid spears. "You might be able to keep them out, but not me."

"You're hurting her!" Fear filtered into Stormsong's voice. "Leave her alone."

Esme moved counterclockwise around them, trailing her hand across the shield's radiance, a dark mote on pale brilliance. "There is too much to lose to worry about hurting her."

"Go away," Stormsong growled.

Esme had made a complete circle around them, testing the boundaries of Stormsong's protection. They stood as odd mirror reflections of each other—hair short and spiked—red, dark to the point of almost black versus blue paled to nearly white.

"I won't let you in," Stormsong said.

"We don't have time for this!" Esme balled up her hand into a tight fist of blackness, and punched into the light.

Stormsong's shield failed like a candle snuffed. Tinker fell into darkness.

". . . *focusfocusfocus* . . ." she whispered into the black.

A world snapped into being around her, but she ignored it to focus on the control panel in front of her. She punched a set of keys, ones she had practiced until her hands ached. Even as she entered the codes, and the world jerked hard to the right, alarms screamed to life.

She hit the intercom pad. "All hands suit up! Suit up!" She shouted, knowing what was coming. "Brace for impact!"

She looked up and found she hadn't seen the full truth. Instead of one colony ship looming in the great blackness of space, the feed from the front cameras showed several ships colliding together—heaving, twisting, and buckling. For a moment, she could only stare—stunned. Compartments of the ships were collapsing like crushed soda cans—their atmosphere spraying out in plumes of instantly freezing gushers.

She wasn't able to stop it. It was going to happen anyhow.

"We're going to hit! We're going to hit!" Alan Voecks screamed those hated words that had haunted her nightmares for months.

Something cartwheeled toward them, jetted on a haze of frozen oxygen. As it grew larger, she realized it was a human—without a space suit. There was time to recognize the face—Nicole Pinder of the *Anhe Hao*—before the body hit the camera. That screen went to static . . .

Tinker bolted out of the dream. She was tight in Stormsong's arms, panting from the remnants of her terror. "Oh gods! Oh gods!"

"It is over." Stormsong rubbed her back soothingly. "You are safe with us."

"Something went wrong," Tinker cried. "That's what they've been trying to tell me. Something went wrong."

"Well?" Windwolf spoke from the foot of the bed.

Tinker sat up to discover the room was full of silent people, all watching her sleep. In addition to Windwolf and Pony, Wraith Arrow and Bladebite stood guard. "What the hell?"

"There are other dreamers," Stormsong said, as if answering a question Tinker had missed. "One seems to be *domi's* mother. The others might not be able to reach *domi* alone, but her mother's blood connection is giving them all access to *domi*. *Domi's* mother is quite strong but untrained and with the morals of a snake; she does not care that what she's doing is hurting *domi*. They are crowding into *domi's* dreams, leaving her unable to cope with her own nightmares."

"Why now?" Windwolf asked. "It's been eighteen years."

"It might be that becoming an elf awakened latent abilities in *domi*," Stormsong said. "Or it might be something that happened when the dragon pulled magic through her at the edge of the Ghostlands. I can't stop them. United as they are, they are too strong. Something must be done or they will drive the *domi* mad."

"Will giving her *saijin* help?" Windwolf asked.

"Please, not *saijin*," Tinker whimpered. "I hate that stuff. The oni forced it on me."

Windwolf gave her a look full of raw grief.

"No, *saijin* will only make things worse," Stormsong said. "Now she can wake up from the nightmare, breaking its hold on her. Drugged, she would be trapped in her dreams."

"Oh please," Tinker cried. "Not that."

"There are some drugs," Stormsong said, "that she can take for a limited time that will keep her from dreaming completely. Someone more trained and gifted in dreaming would know better what to do."

"I like the idea of not dreaming." Tinker crawled across the bed to Windwolf, who took her into his lap.

"You need to dream," Stormsong said. "Dreams are how your mind heals you from emotional harm. The oni rode you hard, but you were able to heal yourself each night and stay strong. Your mother is raping the very core of you. She will destroy you if we don't stop this."

"Can we use some other terms for this?" Tinker asked. "Something nonsexual? This is my mother we're talking about. Ick."

"Find what she needs for now," Windwolf ordered. "I will send for a dreamer."

15: STICKS AND STONES

Wolf made time the next morning to pray at the enclave's shrine. Last night, he'd had the hospice deliver drugs for Tinker and sent a message to the *intanyei seyosa* caste in the Easternlands, but now there was nothing more he could do for his *domi* except pray. It filled him with helpless rage that the ones tormenting her were so far outside his reach. He had thought the time he spent wounded and helpless in Tinker's care was the worst possible torment, but this was far, far worse. Even when she had been held captive, there had at least been something he could do, the illusion of making a difference. Now he could only watch as the female he loved slowly went mad.

Worse, he could not even stay with her and comfort her. He needed to attend the formal negotiations between the clans. For the sake of everyone who counted on him, he needed to be centered and calm when he wanted to be raging at the universe. At least he had the comfort of knowing that his *domi* was in the care of Little Horse and Discord, who both loved her well, and they were supported by the rest of his household. He prayed to the gods that they too lend their aid to his *domi*.

Maynard was waiting outside the enclave when Wolf headed to the *aumani*. "We need to talk," Maynard said in greeting.

"I do not have time." Wolf headed down the street toward Ginger Wine's enclave. It had been decided before the Stone Clan arrived that Ginger Wine's public dining area would be considered neutral ground for the three clans. At that time he had liked the idea of keeping the sanctity of Poppymeadow's—now he wished he could stay close to Tinker, even though she was still sleeping.

"I have a dead cop missing a head on Ohio River Boulevard," Maynard continued in English, falling in step with Wolf. "And people are saying they saw a lot of *sekasha* in the area before he died. Tell me that this isn't what it sounds like. My people are scared enough without your people killing cops."

Wolf gritted his teeth to control his anger. Lashing out at his ally would not help the situation any. "You have a dead rapist missing a head."

"How could he have raped her? She doesn't go anywhere without her *sekasha*. Do you know how bad this looks?"

"It was after I transformed her. I left Tinker at my hunting lodge with a full Hand to guard her, but somehow, she ended up back in Pittsburgh with only Galloping Storm Horse." It put Little Horse in a difficult position as there was no way for him to communicate with the rest of the Hand, short of driving back to the remote lodge. "Your police officer forced his way into Tinker's home, stripped her nude, pinned her down, and tried to enter her."

Maynard looked like Wolf had just handed him a poisonous snake. "Tinker says that Czernowski forced her?"

"My blade brother does not know many English words, but he does know 'no' and 'stop' and 'don't.' My *domi* was threatening to gouge out Czernowski's eyes when Storm Horse intervened."

"Oh, fuck," Maynard whispered and then sighed. "That was two months ago. Why did they kill him yesterday?"

"The *domana* are forbidden to take lovers outside their caste other than their *sekasha*. I made Tinker *domana* caste because it was the only way we could be together. It also means she is now strictly off-limits to humans. Czernowski would not keep his distance. He stated at the photographer's that he would take Tinker back.

Last night, he attempted to pull her into his car."

Czernowski's intentions might have been innocent, but he had crossed the line of Little Horse's patience. Wolf could sympathize only with Little Horse. His blade brother, seeing Tinker spiraling downward, had been given the opportunity to take action—had been given a way to make at least one thing right—had been given a target. In the light of Tinker's imbalance, Czernowski's death had been inevitable.

"Stupid fucking idiot," Maynard growled, but it wasn't clear who he meant. Wolf chose to believe he meant Czernowski. "This was the last thing we needed, Wolf. My people are not going to trust yours after this."

"Did they truly trust us before?"

Maynard glanced away and ignored the question, which meant the answer was "no." "Which one of your people killed Czernowski?"

"*Sekasha* are exempt from all laws except the ones of their own making."

"So you're not going to tell me?"

"There is no need for you to know."

"What am I supposed to tell the police? Czernowski's family?"

"What is done is done and cannot be undone," Wolf said. "I have other problems to attend."

Maynard acknowledged the dismissal with a hard look but took himself away.

Ginger Wine intercepted Wolf in her front gardens, bowing low.
"What is wrong?"

Ginger Wine's face tightened and she glanced down the garden path. There were only her own *laedin* caste guards in sight. "These," she hissed in English, "conceited, pompous, arrogant Stone Clan pigs—that is what is wrong. I should have asked for four times my normal fee, instead of twice. The way they eat, you'd think they were hollow."

"I cannot do anything about arrogance and gluttony. Have they done anything wrong?"

She let out her breath in a long sigh, and then stood nudging a rock in the garden path. "It is just everything is—off; nothing seems right. Everyone is tripping over one another, plates are being dropped, laundry is being mislaid, and they eat and eat and eat." She looked pleadingly up to Wolf. "Everyone is frightened of them. We've lived so long with just you and your *sekasha*, I actually forgot how the world really is, what it is to live in fear."

"Do you want them out?"

She looked away, chewing on her bottom lip. Finally she shook her head. "No. Things are not that bad—perhaps it will settle down after another day or two—once we grow used to them." She laid her hand on Wolf's arm. "Please, *domou*, get rid of these oni so we can go back to our comfortable life."

He patted her hand. "We will work hard to resolve this quickly."

Ginger Wine gave Wolf a tight smile. "Thank you. Please, let me show you to the dining room."

As they entered the elegant dining room, there was a crash from the far kitchens, followed by loud sobbing. Ginger Wine sighed, begged his pardon, and hurried off toward the kitchen. A large round table with six chairs stood in the center of the room. All the extra tables had been cleared away, leaving the space bare and echoing. While only five *domana* were attending, there would be fifteen *sekasha* and a server from each clan.

Wolf considered the sixth chair. Tinker should attend the meeting, but she was in no mental state to do so. He ordered a chair to be removed. Unfortunately, Jewel Tear arrived as the chair was being carried out.

"Your *domi* is not attending?" Jewel Tear managed to put malice into the innocent words.

"No." Wolf warned her with a look that he did not wish to discuss it further.

True Flame arrived with a shifting of the *sekasha* and a new contest of rank between them. "So this is where we will be?"

"Yes, Your Highness." Jewel Tear appropriated the role of hostess. She bowed low, displaying her charms to the prince.

True Flame recognized her with a slight cold nod. Wolf's cousin never had approved of Jewel Tear. It had been a source of bitterness between him and Wolf, even afterward, as it had been hard to acknowledge that his cousin had been right all along. Wolf could only hope that his decisions with Jewel Tear wouldn't now taint True Flame's opinion of Tinker.

True Flame glanced at the table and then to Wolf. "Five chairs?"

"My *domi* will not be able to attend." Wolf wished Jewel Tear weren't standing there, reminding True Flame of his bad choices in the past. "She is—" He found himself at a loss for words. What was Tinker? "—not herself."

"An interesting choice of words," Jewel Tear murmured.

Wolf ignored her.

Earth Son arrived with Forest Moss in tow. They made their bows to True Flame.

All parties gathered, they settled at the table to start the *aumani*, a formal meeting of clans.

Windwolf was sure that if they captured any oni and needed to torture information out of them, an *aumani* would be perfect for it. He sat across from Earth Son, studiously ignoring the servants as they laid out the elaborate table settings. Between the Skin Clan's love of elaborate power icons, and the thousands of years during which the clans had needed to conduct meetings in secrecy, elves had had the use of symbology beaten almost out of them. There had to be some deep buried need left in them that seeped out at times like this. How else explain the pure white table runner, the scattering of bloodred roses, the black ceramic place settings, and the glasses of sapphire blue? The lit candle. The smoking incense. The polished pebble. All the colors and the elements of three Clans were subtly present on the table.

They sat in reflective silence until the servers withdrew from the table. True Flame sipped his tea, opening the meeting. They drank, waiting for him to speak.

"So that we can all be of one mind," True Flame broke the silence, "Wolf Who Rules Wind, tell us our past."

Wolf recounted the last few weeks since the meeting of the three clans at Aum Renau. Knowing that he would lose face with True Flame for holding back information, he tried to be as thorough as possible in Tinker's kidnapping, Lord Tomtom's killing, and the discovery of Sparrow's treachery.

"And what of the Ghostlands?" Earth Son asked when Wolf came to an end. "Is your *domi's* gate still functioning?"

"Perhaps," Wolf admitted. "Something is keeping Turtle Creek unstable."

"Stupidity upon stupidity," Jewel Tear scoffed. "She shouldn't have built them a gate."

"I defy you," Windwolf said, "unarmed and captive of a ruthless enemy, to do better."

"Defy, there's an interesting concept, indicating lack of cooperation," Earth Son said.

"Yes," Jewel Tear said. "I wouldn't have cooperated."

"She cooperated because it's now in her nature to be cooperative," Forest Moss said. "Wolf Who Rules remade her and blessed her with our mothers' curse—to be yielding. Why else would we need the *sekasha* to guard over us? We cannot stand against anything, especially our own nature. How can you, sitting there with never a moment of stark helpless fear in your lifes understand? Our mothers were bred to lie on their backs, spread their legs, and not whimper too loudly—unless their masters liked it when they screamed. If it wasn't for the steel of our fathers' ambition, we would be cattle in the field."

"You may count yourself one of the cattle, but I do not," Earth Son said.

"Yes, yes, let us not listen to the one that has been under the heated blade. No, he did not have his eyes forced open to the truth just before one was seared out," Forest Moss spat. "You cannot hope to understand what it is like. To lie there unable to move as they ready the tools of your destruction. The first time, oh, you can be so very brave because you don't know what is coming; everything in your imagination is just a pale shadow of the pain. It's the second time and the third, when you've been so well taught, that the very smell of hot metal makes your heart race. You see the torch only once, right before they strap you down, but the hiss of the gas flame haunts your nightmares for years to come. You lay there, listening to the invisible dance of their preparations, the scrape of boots, the rattle of the cutting blades in a metal tray, the creak of tightening leather restraints, and there's nothing, nothing you can do."

"She wasn't tortured," Earth Son pointed out.

"Clever female knew the truth," Forest Moss said. "The truth you're refusing to see."

"If she didn't do something the gate in orbit would remain functional," Windwolf reminded the others. "The gate we couldn't shut down. Yes, the result poses a threat, but it is now in *our* realm, where *we* can deal with it ourselves."

"We will solve this problem you caused," Earth Son said. "Damn these humans and their gate."

"We can't blame this on them," Wolf said. "We elves went to Onihida and led the oni to Earth. If we hadn't done that, none of this would have happened."

He did not bother to point out that it was the Stone Clan who had gone to Onihida.

Earth Son countered it as if he had made the statement aloud. "The humans built the gate in orbit."

Wolf shook his head. "The oni stranded on Earth used the humans to build the gate—and manipulated them to keep it functioning."

"Why are you defending them?" Earth Son snapped. "It's unlikely that they're all innocent in this."

"Yes, some might be guilty," Wolf allowed. "But not all of them."

Earth Son waved the truth away. "Bah, they're just as bad as the oni—breeding like mice."

"Fie, fie," Forest Moss whispered. "We were all blind beings even before the oni burned out our eyes. Why should such arrogant fools as we listen to the warnings of the human natives? Of course the cave was a mystical place with mysterious goings and monstrous comings. What importance to us that humans were forever losing their way to other worlds and rarely coming back? What did it matter that we recognized nothing of ourselves in their stories?"

"Oh, please, shut him up," Jewel Tear hissed.

"Oh! Oh!" Forest Moss leapt to his feet and wailed, waving his hands over his head. "It's all so ugly! No, no, who cares if perchance we might learn something important? We must close our ears to this wailing of a madman!"

"Forest Moss!" True Flame snapped. "Sit!"

The male sat so abruptly that Wolf wondered if the outburst had been yet another example of Forest Moss using his reputation of being mad.

"Does anything he has to say have any relevance to what we need to do here?" Jewel Tear asked. "It seems to me that our task is simple. Do findings to track down the oni nests and burn them out. Instead we are sitting here constantly being distracted by the mad one's ramblings. By his own account, he was shortsighted in his venture. So he was caught and tortured—but all that hinges on one gross error; on the first moment of discovery, his party have fought their way clear and returned to the pathway."

"I had dealt with discovery by humans many times," Forest Moss said. "A show of power, a few trinkets, and we would be safe enough to pass on. How was I to know that the oni were monsters under the skin?"

"I'm trying to determine what the Stone Clan brings to the table," True Flame said. "And what they will come away with."

Earth Son made an opening bid. "Since the Wind Clan is demonstrating that it cannot hold the Westernlands, we will take them over."

Wolf shook his head and begain to tick off his strong points. "We are providing access to the fire *esva*. Without our assistance, you would have to deal with the oni and a dragon with only defensive spells."

"You can't withhold the fire *esva* the crown," Earth Son stated.

Was he being naïve, or clumsy in his attempt to undermine the Wind Clan's position?

"I did not suggest that." Wolf used small words. "I'm only pointing out that we are providing attack spells on two fronts, plus my four Hands, and ten enclaves. The Wind Clan can hold its own here—the same cannot be said of the Stone Clan."

"Yet you called for help."

"Because we did not know then—nor do we know now—the strength of the oni," Wolf stated. "We would rather give up some part of our holdings than give the oni a stronghold here."

"Which the crown sees as a strength, not a weakness," True Flame said. "We are limiting the amount awarded to Stone Clan. The area in question will be Pittsburgh and the surrounding land. Excluded will be the enclaves owned by the Wind Clan households."

"We want both virgin land and that from Earth," Earth Son said.

"And I want the *sekasha*, Galloping Storm Horse on Wind," Forest Moss said.

Startled silence went through the room.

"Never," Wolf snarled.

"If you release him, he can serve me," Moss pressed on.

"He looks to my *domi*," Wolf said. "He is her First. She also holds Singing Storm on Wind."

"That cross-caste mistake?" Moss made a sound of disgust. "Your *domi* can release Galloping Storm Horse and keep the mutt."

"She will not release him." Wolf was sure of this. "She loves him dearly. The oni captured him because they knew he would be an effective whipping boy for her. All that she did was to protect him."

"It is a simple thing—" Forest Moss started.

The two Stone Clan Firsts, Thorne Scratch and Tiger Eye, and True Flame's First, Red Knife, stepped forward to loom over their *domana*'s shoulders. Wolf felt Wraith Arrow behind him, joining the other Firsts at the table.

"This is not for you to discuss," Red Knife said quietly. "No beholding will be broken in this manner."

Earth Son coughed and carried on. "We're asking for a hundred thousand *sen* of virgin land for each of us, plus half of the city, to be awarded immediately."

The land, ultimately, Wolf did not care about. The three hundred thousand *sen* was a small price to pay for the safety of his people—and perhaps all of Elfhome. He did not want, however, to put humans under the care of the Stone Clan. He shook his head. "I granted the humans an extension of their treaty to work out issues among themselves. I think at this time it would be unwise to start procedures on dividing up the city."

"Who gave you the authority to agree to that?" Earth Son asked.

True Flame glanced at Earth Son. "As viceroy, it was in his authority to do so. But I must ask, on what basis?"

"We're not entirely sure that the orbital gate no longer functions. If my *domi* failed to destroy it and only damaged it, it is possible Pittsburgh will return to Earth."

"Yes, dividing the city could be premature," True Flame said. "How soon will we know?"

"Shutdown was scheduled for two days from now at midnight," Wolf said. "But if the gate is only damaged, then the humans might delay Shutdown for weeks. Without communication with Earth, it is impossible to know."

"Are we truly going to wait for something that may never happen?" Earth Son asked.

"We are elves, we have time," Wolf said.

"Most convenient for the Wind Clan," Earth Son said.

"We will wait three days, and then speak again on dividing the city." True Flame took out maps of the area. "Let us discuss virgin land."

16: LITTLE MONKEY BRAIN

After a long, long cottony warm sleep, Tinker was able to view the last few days with a saner eye. Thinking of Nathan threatened to drag her back to the painful void of grief, so she considered the last dream with Esme and Black. Obviously, something had gone drastically wrong with Esme, but what did her mother think Tinker could do for her? Esme was in space—someplace—in another universe, far, far away. And who was Black? The tengu woman obviously had been on Earth to meet Tinker's father, but where was she now? Why was Tinker dreaming about her in conjunction with Esme? Was it because Black was a tengu colonist and on one of the ships that Esme crashed into?

The dreams of Alice and Dorothy—little girls lost far from home—held a sad irony; Esme thought Dorothy should stay in Oz—but obviously that wasn't what she wanted for herself now. So what did she want from Tinker? Even if Esme's ship had crashed, that would have taken place eighteen years ago, shortly before Tinker was born.

In the movie the yellow brick road started when Dorothy crashed the house into Oz—bringing a stain of sepia on a world of lush color. The Discontinuity appeared as a stain of blue. Tinker's nightmares had gotten out of hand the same day that the Ghostlands had formed—even if the first one with Esme and Black had come two days later. The first dream had been *Alice in Wonderland,* the second *The Wizard of Oz,* and the last was Esme going through the hyperphase gate; little girls crashing into other worlds.

Tinker sprawled in the enclave garden, watching the sun shift through the tree branches. As usual, she had a full Hand standing around, doing nothing but watching her think. They shifted to full alert as someone came through the gate into this private area. Lemonseed carried in a tray of tea and cookies—midmorning snack. Tinker started to sit up but Lemonseed *tsked* at her and crouched beside her to lay out a mini picnic. Exquisite china bowls of pale tea. Little perfect cookies. A platter of rich rosewood. A small square of printed silk.

Esme wasn't the only girl who fell into another world.

"Can you have lunch packed?" Tinker knew that the enclave's staff most likely had the meal half-finished. "We're going out."

"Yes, *domi.*" Lemonseed bowed and left to make it so.

"Where are we going?" Stormsong asked.

We? How did it get to this point that she was so comfortable with having all these people in her life? No, she guessed she wasn't really at ease—but the edges of her discomfort were wearing away. Like the fact that she could strip in front of Pony without thinking. That it took Lemonseed's arrival to remind her that an entire staff of nearly a hundred people were poised around her—waiting for her to do something. Anything. Be the *domi.* Save the world again.

"The scrap yard," she told Stormsong but thought "Home."

She drained the tea to be polite, gathered up the cookies, and went to change.

Two newspapers, still neatly folded and bagged, lay in the driveway of the scrap yard. She picked them up on her way in, wondering why Oilcan hadn't brought them in. Tinker expected to find her cousin at work and was both relieved and disappointed that he wasn't. She didn't know how he would take Nathan's death. To her, it was a dark well of guilt and grief with a crumbling edge. She was trying to keep her distance just so she could keep functioning.

Ironically, she was fairly sure she could deal with Oilcan being angry at her more than she could help him with his grief.

"You know—I just don't get it," Stormsong said as Tinker was puttering around her workshop, trying to get back into being herself.

"Get what?" Tinker asked.

"This place, you, and Windwolf—it just doesn't—doesn't make sense."

"Yeah, I've never understood why he fell in love with someone like me."

"I do. You can go toe to toe with him. It's this place that doesn't make sense. You two are too big for something like this."

"Big?"

"With your abilities—why did you limit yourself to this tiny corner of the world?"

That sounded like Lain—who had always pushed for her to go to college, leave Pittsburgh, do something more with her life. She thought her plans were big enough, but it suddenly dawned on her that they were plans she laid out when she was thirteen. They seemed huge when she was a child—certainly they were larger than what other people planned—but yes, she'd grown to fit, and then the limits started to chafe. Had Lain seen a truth that she herself was blind to?

She veered from that line of thinking and distracted herself by poking at her insecurities. "I think it's fairly obvious what attracted Windwolf to me: I look like Jewel Tear. She's his perfect woman. And I can't measure up to that—elegance."

"No. You only think that because you've never met Otter Dance."

"Pony's mother?"

"Ever notice that Pony is the shortest of the *sekasha*? Otter Dance is half Stone Clan *sekasha*."

Tinker turned to look at Pony standing beside Cloudwalker; he was half a head shorter yet wider in the shoulders and deeper in the chest than Cloudwalker. Pony was the most compact elf she'd ever met until the Stone Clan arrived. Now that she looked at him, she could see points of similarity. His eyes were brown where everyone else's were blue. The shape of his face was different.

"You mean we—Jewel Tear and I—look like Otter Dance?"

"To know Otter Dance is to love her. Personalitywise, you're much more like Otter Dance than Jewel Tear could ever pretend to be—and she did try."

Tinker wasn't sure how to feel about that. She cleared her iboard. She needed a project—something big and complex—to keep from thinking about Nathan and all the messy bits of her life. Something that would help keep Pittsburgh safe from the elves, the oni—and the dragon. Oh gods, in all the chaos she'd forgotten about the dragon. There was a worthwhile project, especially since she hadn't collected enough data on the Ghostlands yet.

She called up an animation program and created a quick rough model of the dragon, using a ferret body, a male lion's head, and a snakeskin to cover the frame. Dragging the dragon model out onto the iboard, she let it gallop across the white screen. There had been a spell painted onto the dragon's hide. She wasn't sure what the spell did. Was it how the dragon raised its shield or was it what the oni were using to control the dragon? It seemed to her that the wild waving of the mane might have triggered the shields—much like the *domana* hand gestures triggered theirs.

"What do you think?" she asked Pony. "How did the dragon raise its shield?"

Pony put his hands to his head and wriggled his fingers. "Its mane."

Stormsong and the others who had been in the valley with her that morning nodded in agreement.

Okay, so the mane worked like *domana* fingers. She paused the dragon, added a "shield" effect to her model, and restarted the animation. "Next question is—does anything breach the shield?"

"Our shields do not stop light and air, because we must see and breathe," Pony said. "There is a limit to the force they can absorb. They will take a hundred shots fired in a hundred heartbeats, but not a hundred fired in one heartbeat."

"So light and air." Tinker opened a window in the corner of the iboard and noted this.

"Spell arrows don't affect the dragon," Cloudwalker reminded her.

Tinker wrote: *Different frequency of light?* And then thinking of Pony driving his sword point through the shield, she added, *Speed of kinetic weapon?*

"Pony, can I see your sword?"

He drew his sword and held it out to her to examine. "Careful, *domi*, it is very sharp."

She knew that the *ejae* had magically tempered ironwood blades, but she had never examined them closely before. It was a single length of rich cherry colored wood with a bone guard. The very tip came to a fine point. There was no sign of the spell that had created the blade, which she supposed was necessary since the *sekasha* used their swords while their shield spells were active. The surface area of its tip was smaller than a bullet; if they both struck at the same speed, the *ejae* would have a greater PSI. Pony's slow push through the dragon's shield might indicate speed was more important than force.

She wasn't sure how they could use a "slow" weapon against the dragon. It would be unlikely that the beastie would ever stand still like that again. She considered a giant glue trap, sleep gas, and mega stun guns. They all had their drawbacks from "what do you use as bait?" to "would it do anything but just piss the dragon off?" That got her wondering about what would affect the dragon once they got past its shields. Where were its vital organs? Would poison necessarily kill it? Elves couldn't tolerate some of the food humans ate in abundance. The inverse could be true—what was poisonous for Elfhome creatures might not hurt the dragon.

Maybe the stupid dream was telling her that she needed to melt the dragon with a bucket of water. Waterjets had jet speeds around Mach 3 and could cut through several inches of steel. She didn't have any in her junkyard, but perhaps she could salvage one and modify it. . . .

The *sekasha* were rubbing off on her. She really liked the simple "hit it with a big gun" solution. Too bad they couldn't simply make the shield go away so "a big gun" was a safe bet.

Her stomach growled. She realized that she had spent hours in front of the iboard.

"What time is it?" Maybe she should take a break to eat the packed lunch.

"I'm not sure. That clock is broken." Stormsong pointed to an old alarm clock that Tinker had dismantled to use in a project.

We've murdered time, it's always six o'clock.

Wait—wasn't that a line from *Alice in Wonderland*? During the tea party, didn't they talk about time not working for them? She sorted through the things she brought from the enclave, found the book, and flipped through it. Under the drawing of the Mad Hatter, there was a footnote that caught her eye.

Arthur Stanley Eddington, as well as less distinguished writers on relativity theory, have compared the Mad Tea Party, where it is always six o'clock, with that portion of De Sitter's model of the cosmos in which time stands eternally still. (See Chapter 10 of Eddington's *Space Time and Gravitation*.)

"Oh shit." Tinker took out her datapad and pulled up her father's plans on the gate.

"Shit?" Pony asked.

"Excrement," Stormsong translated. "It's a curse."

"Shit," Pony echoed.

"That aside, what did you figure out?" Stormsong asked.

"I made a huge mistake in the variable for time on the gate equations. And if I did it—I bet the oni did too. These plans, as they stand—all the spaceships would have arrived at the same moment. That's why they collided."

"When did they go to?" Pony asked.

"I think . . . that they were *held in time* until the gate was destroyed. They finished their journey—all five ships—three days ago."

"Your mother found herself in great danger and you're her only link to home," Stormsong murmured.

"Yeah, at which point, she started to hound me with nightmares." Tinker tugged at her hair. "But what the hell am I supposed to do? I mean, the good news is that obviously she's alive—for now. The gods only know *where* she is. She could be on the other side of the galaxy. And which galaxy? This one? Earth's?

Onihida? We're talking a mind-boggling large haystack to lose a needle in. Even if she was in space over Elfhome, *what* am I to do? What could I *possibly* do?"

"Forget the egotistical she-snake," Stormsong said. "You have pressing duties here. Her problems are not your concern."

"But why then, do things keep turning up? Like the pearl necklace, the black willow, and Reinholds? The dreams relate to me and my world, somehow. Don't they?"

Tinker saw a troubled look spread across Stormsong's face before the *sekasha* turned away, hiding her unease.

"Oh, don't do that!" Tinker picked up the morning's newspaper, still tightly folded in its bag, and aimed a smack at Stormsong's back.

Stormsong caught the newspaper before it connected and gave her a hard look.

"I need help here." Tinker jerked the newspaper free. "This is part of the whole working together. I need to know what you know about dreaming."

Stormsong sighed. "That is a wound I don't like to dig into. Everyone assumed that my mother had some great vision when she conceived me—and no one invested more in that myth than I did. But I did not have the talent or the patience for it. I was too much my father. I like solving problems with a sword. And I don't like feeling like I'm failing you."

Tinker fussed with getting the newspaper out of its bag so she didn't have to face Stormsong's pain. "You're not failing me."

Speaking of failing someone, the newspaper's headline was "Policeman Slain."

Nathan's body was draped with a white cloth in the island of light on the black river of night highway. *Nathan Czernowski, age 28, found beheaded on Ohio River Boulevard.* She stood there clutching the newspaper as faintness swept through her. How could seeing it in print make it more real than seeing his body lying in front of her?

Stormsong continued, "As you're finding out the hard way, dreamers can join for a gestalt effect, but unless they share *nuenae*, the resulting dream is conflicted."

Tinker pulled her attention away from the newspaper. "What?"

"Dreams are maps for the future." Stormsong held out her right hand. "If the dreamers share *nuenae*—" Stormsong pressed her hands, matching up the fingers. "Then the two maps overlaid remain easy to understand. But if the dreamers don't share *nuenae*—" Stormsong shifted her hands so her fingers crosshatched. "There is a conflict. It becomes difficult, if not impossible, to tell which element belongs to which *nuenae*. The pearl necklace was from your *nuenae*. *The Wizard of Oz*, is from your mother's."

"*Nuenae* being . . .?"

Stormsong pursed her lips. "*Nuenae* reflects goals and desires. Among elves, it is one's clan and household. I'm not sure humans can share *nuenae* like elves can. Humans are more—self-centered."

The newspaper screamed at how self-centered Tinker had been.

"So, Esme, Black, and I are operating at cross-purposes." Tinker folded the accusing headline away and went to stuff it in the recycling bin. "And my dreams may or may not have anything to do with helping with the mess we're in."

"Yes, there is no telling. At least, I can't, not with my abilities. Wolf has sent for help from my mother's people. They might be able to determine something since they share our foci in regards to the oni."

"Whereas my mother could care less."

"Exactly."

As Tinker dropped the paper into the recycling bin, the top newspaper caught her eye. The headline read: "Viceroy's Guard Kill Three Snipers, Gossamer Slain." She lifted out the paper.

When did this happen?

The paper was dated Tuesday. Tuesday? Wasn't she awake on Tuesday? Yes, she was—she had spent Tuesday at Reinholds— why hadn't anyone told her? The paper also reported that the EIA had declared martial law, that the treaty had been temporarily extended until Sunday, and the elves had plans to screen everyone living in Chinatown. How had she missed all this? She dug through the pile of papers, uncovering growing chaos that she had been oblivious to. Wednesday's paper had stories on the lockdown of the city by the royal elfin troops, a wave of arrests of suspected human sympathizers, the execution of more disguised oni, and the start of a rationing system as fears of the Pittsburgh dollar collapsing triggered massive stockpiling. Above the headline was an extra banner proclaiming, "Four Days to Treaty End."

Four days? Was that today?

The other unread paper was dated Friday. She had lost at least a day to drugged sleep. The top banner read, "Two Days to Treaty End." The Pittsburgh police had called a "blue flu" strike when the EIA closed Nathan's murder case.

Oh, gods, what a mess.

"What day is this?" she asked Stormsong. "Did I sleep through Saturday too?"

"It is Friday," Stormsong said.

"*Domi*," Pony said from the door. "It is the lone one."

Lone one?

The *sekasha* escorted in Tooloo, who must have walked up the hill from her store. Tinker stared at her with new eyes. Not that the female had changed; Tooloo was as she had always been Tinker's entire life. There were no new creases in the face full of wrinkles. Her silver hair still reached her ankles. Tinker even recognized her faded, purple silk gown and battered high-top tennis shoes—Tooloo had been wearing them when Tinker and Pony helped her milk her cows two months ago.

Only now Tinker realized how odd it was for an elf in a world of elves to live alone. What clan and caste had she been born into? Why wasn't she part of a household? Was it because she was a half-elf? If she was half human, born and raised on Earth, how could she be so fluent in High Elvish, and know all things arcane? If she was a full-blooded elf, trapped on Earth when the pathways were dismantled, why hadn't she gone back to her people? Three centuries was a short time for elves.

Tinker doubted if Tooloo would tell her if she asked. Tooloo had always refused to be known. She went by an obvious nickname, neither human nor elfin in origin. Not once, in the eighteen years that Tinker had known her, had she ever mentioned her parents. She would not commit to an age, the length of time she had lived on Earth, or even a favorite color.

Tooloo squirmed in Cloudwalker's hold. "Oh, you murderous little thing! You had to satisfy that little monkey brain of yours. I told you, starve the beast called curiosity—but nooo, you had to play with Czernowski and now you've killed him."

Tinker felt sad as she realized she'd lost yet another part of her life. "I didn't mean for Nathan to get killed."

"Oh, you didn't mean to! Do you think those threadbare words will heal his family, grieving over his headless body?"

"I'm sorry it happened." Tinker swallowed down on the pain that the words caused her. "I—I wasn't paying attention when I should have been—and I'm so sorry—but there's nothing I can do. I was wrong. I should have listened to you from the very start—but I didn't see where all this was going to lead."

"*Pawgh*, this is all Windwolf's fault—killing my bright wee human and making a dirty Skin Clan scumbag in her image." Tooloo spat.

"This has nothing to do with Windwolf making me an elf."

"Does it? My wee one never had such superciliousness of power."

"Supercil-*whatis?*"

Tooloo glanced at Pony standing behind Tinker. "Giving you *sekasha* is like giving an elephant rollerskates—stupid, ridiculous, and dangerous."

Tooloo could say what she wanted about her, but now she was going too far to include the *sekasha* too.

"Yes, I killed Nathan," Tinker said, "but I'm not the only one to blame. I'm a stupid clueless little girl, but you've lived with humans for over two hundred years—you knew exactly how Nathan would react if—" And then it dawned on Tinker and she gasped with horror. "Oh sweet gods, you wanted him to think I was a whore! You deliberately misled him! You evil she-goat!"

Tooloo slapped her hard across the face, enough to make stars dance in her vision.

Tinker heard the *sekasha* draw their blades and threw out her hands to keep Nathan's death from repeating. "No! No! Don't you dare hurt her!" Once she was sure that she was obeyed, she turned back to the stranger who raised her. "Why? Why did you do that to Nathan? You had to see it coming!"

"Because nothing else would have slapped you out of wallowing in your own piss. The city is about to run with blood unless you do something. Czernowski was the sacrificial lamb to save this city."

"I was trying to! I don't know how!"

"Use that little monkey brain of yours! The elves are about to march all over this city with jackboots. I've lived with humans for hundreds of years. They are good, compassionate people. I lived through the America's Revolutionary War, its Civil War, the fight for women's suffrage, and the struggle for civil rights—and all those advancements for equality among humans are about to be flushed down the crapper. It's already started—they're searching through Chinatown, dragging people out of their homes, and testing them and killing them where they stand."

Tinker glanced to Stormsong since the rant had been in English. Stormsong nodded in confirmation. "Why didn't anyone tell me?"

"You've been too fragile."

She couldn't trust Tooloo's version of this; the "lone one" kept whatever truths she had to herself. Nor, as much as she loved them, could she count on the elves in her life to understand what it was to be human. Tinker gathered up the newspapers; she needed their human-biased facts. And Maynard—she needed to talk to Maynard.

Red was becoming a predominant color in Pittsburgh, like an early autumn. They encountered four roadblocks on the way to the EIA offices, all manned by *laedin* caste Fire Clan soldiers.

"If True Flame has this many warriors, why do we need the Stone Clan?" Tinker had let Pony drive, but she hung over the front seat to talk to him and Stormsong. The backseat was crowded with the other three *sekasha*.

"Stone Clan magic can find individuals in a wilderness and things hidden in the ground," Pony told her.

"It's like calling in bloodhounds," Stormsong said in English.

Tinker remembered the sonarlike spell that Jewel Tear had used. Yes, that should make finding the oni hidden in the forest easier. She wondered how the Stone Clan would fare, though, in the steel-riddled city.

"And if you cannot solve the problem with the Ghostlands," Cloudwalker added. "They should be able to. They closed the natural pathways after the first invasion."

Stormsong made a rude noise. "There is a difference between collapsing caves and dealing with whatever is wrong with the Ghostlands."

"The Ghostlands should collapse on their own." Tinker was growing less sure of that—she would have expected the rate of decay to be faster. This morning marked the fourth day since she had reduced Turtle Creek to chaos. Now there was something not everyone could claim: I reduced a square mile of land into pure chaos. It made her sound like a small atomic warhead—"someone dropped a Tinker on us!"

The EIA offices directed her back across the Allegheny River to Chinatown. There she found Maynard overseeing the testing of the Chinese population. A mix of *laedin* caste soldiers and Wyverns were systematically emptying a house, putting the occupants into a line to be tested by the EIA. As she approached, it became clear that the process was hampered by the fact that most of the elves and many of the Chinese didn't speak English. East Ohio Street was a cacophony of shouted instructions, crying, and pleading. The coroner van—identified by bold letters—stood at the far end of the street. Blood scented the hot summer air.   And for one dizzy moment, she was back on Ohio River Boulevard, splattered with Nathan's blood.

"*Domi*, are you all right?" Pony murmured into her ear as he supported her by the arm. He'd activated his shields at some point and they now spilled down over her.

She nodded and pulled out of his hold.

"It is clear!" One of the Wyverns came out of a nearby building shouting in High Elvish.

There was a pulse of magic, and she *felt* the house, from the pipes underneath it to the tip of the chimneys. There wasn't anyone inside. Apparently that was the point. On some unheard command, the Wyverns moved down to the next building. Annoyingly, because of her height, Tinker couldn't see through the crowd to spot the Stone Clan *domana* directing the search.

"Is Jewel Tear here?" she asked Stormsong, who could see over the heads of most of the humans.

Stormsong shook her head. "It is the mad one, Forest Moss."

"Oh, joy," Tinker muttered. "Where is Maynard?"

"This way." Stormsong started forward.

Tinker thought they would have to push their way through the crowd, but as they approached the humans and elves, the crowd parted as if shoved by an invisible wedge. In the human faces there was a mix of fear and hope. They wanted her to be one of them but were afraid she was wholly an elf.

The crowd was avoiding a section of sidewalk. As Tinker drew even with it, she saw that it was covered with congealing blood, thick with black flies. As the *sekasha* brushed past, some of the flies rose in fat, heavy buzzing. The rest continued to feed.

"I want this to stop," Tinker whispered to Stormsong, dreading her answer.

"This is by order of the crown," Stormsong said. "There is nothing you can do to stop it."

Maynard saw Stormsong first and then scanned downward to find Tinker. "What are you doing here?"

"I want to talk to you about this stuff." Tinker waved the newspaper at Maynard.

"I'm busy at the moment. Why don't you get your husband to explain it to you?"

"Because you're here. I have the power to pin you down and make you explain it to me. And you'll use words I can understand."

Maynard glanced at the paper. "What don't you understand? That article is fairly clear."

"What can I do?"

He gave her a long unreadable look before saying, "I'm not sure. Windwolf bought us some time, but without proof that the gate is in orbit and possibly repairable, that time runs out Sunday."

Figures, after everything she had gone through to destroy the gate, she now had to save it.

"So," Tinker said, "if I can prove the damn thing is still up there, would that help?"

Maynard's eyes widened in surprise. "You think you can do that?"

It was tempting to say yes, but she had to be honest. "I don't know. I can try. It's a fucking discontinuity in Turtle Creek, across at least two or three universes. If Earth is one of those universes, there might be a way to use the Ghostlands to communicate."

"The elves are keeping everyone away from the Ghostlands," Maynard said. "The scientists at the commune are ready to storm the place for a chance to study it."

"Keep them away from it," Tinker said. "At least until we can make sure the Fire Clan and the Stone Clan don't kill them on sight."

Maynard looked away, as if to hide what he thought. When he turned back, his face was back to its carefully neutral—nearly elfin—facade.

"What do you fucking want from me?" Tinker cried. "I was raised in a junkyard!"

"You're the only one in a position to understand fully what it is to be human," Maynard said, "and still be able to do anything about this situation."

"But I don't know what to do."

"I know you don't," Maynard said but didn't add anything more—which would have been a big help.

There was a pulse from Forest Moss and this time the building wasn't empty. She—and Forest Moss—picked up two people still inside on the second floor. A shout went up. Tinker turned to see the Wyverns swarm in through the door of a tiny secondhand shop. Like flashbulbs going off, she felt spells flaring the small rooms into brilliance, one after another. The Wyverns quickly worked their way to the room with the hidden couple.

"Oh, no." Tinker started for the store.

Stormsong pulled her short. "They are only killing oni."

Was that supposed to make it better? Much as she hated the kitsune, she didn't want to see Chiyo beheaded. She didn't want Riki dead any more than she wanted Nathan hurt.

"We can't go in there—it would be asking for a fight." Stormsong kept hold of her. "One we cannot win. Wait. Please."

Much as she wanted to protect the strangers, she couldn't bear the thought of sacrificing her *sekasha.*

Tinker nodded numbly and pulled out of Stormsong's hold.

"Let's get closer."

She lost sight of the storefront beyond the wall of backs. This time her *sekasha* had to clear a path, pushing people aside to make what they thought was a wide enough path for her. Maybe if she was an elephant.

The Wyverns muscled out only one person. They dragged him to a white-haired elf, announcing, "We killed one inside—it tried to run. This one is spell-marked, but it was with an oni."

It was Tommy Chang.

"Kill him," the male *domana* said.

"No!" Tinker plunged forward, forced her way through the towering Wyverns to Tommy's side. "Don't hurt him!"

The white-haired elf turned and Tinker gasped at the damage done to his face.

"Ah, what honest horror!" the half-blinded elf said. "You must be the child-bride. Not much to you—how did you come out in one piece?"

"Because they underestimated me." Tinker tugged Tommy's arm out of the Wyvern's hold. "Look, he's been tested. He's not oni."

"He might be mixed blood," said the half-blinded elf.

"Who gives a flying fuck?" Tinker snarled in English.

"*Domi*," Stormsong murmured behind her.

"He's not one of them." Tinker switched back to High Elvish.

"How do you know?" Forest Moss asked. "From what I hear, the tengu fooled you."

She was not going to let them kill someone she knew. She stared at Tommy, trying to remember something that would prove he was what she thought he was—to herself as much as to them. Maddeningly, he said nothing in his own defense, just stood there, wrapped in his bulletproof cool. Didn't he know that no one was swordproof?

True, she'd trusted Riki blindly, but she hadn't known oni existed, and had awarded him the trust she gave all strangers. Her world had been a different place not so long ago.

"I know because—" she started in order to stall them. Because she'd known Tommy half her life. His family had owned a restaurant in Oakland since before Startup. He'd been a driving force organizing the hoverbike racing, and most summers she saw him on a weekly basis. He wasn't a stranger. She wouldn't immediately say he was "good" people. He had a temper and a reputation of being ruthless when it came to business; that didn't make him any more evil than she was. She suspected the elves wouldn't accept those facts as a good argument for his humanity. Riki had proved her judgment was flawed.

What could she say as proof that these elves would accept? They were growing impatient for her answer.

"Because—" And then unexpectedly, Riki provided the answer. "Because when the tengu came looking for me, he didn't know where to find me."

That puzzled them, which was fine, as she needed to cram a lot into this argument to make it sound.

"Two years ago, Tommy bought a custom Delta hoverbike off me. He needed to write a check, and there were the pink slips—forms to show transfer of ownership for tax reasons. I told him my human name, which was Alexander Graham Bell." Which of course had triggered a round of teasing from Tommy, and occasionally afterward, he'd called her "Tinker Bell." "I even told him why I was called that." In truth, she had been trying to stem the teasing with a sympathy play since Tommy's mother had also been murdered. "And that my father was the man who invented the orbital gate. I told him—he didn't tell the oni."

That seemed to buy it for the Wyverns. They released their hold on Tommy.

Magic suddenly flared across her senses, like a gasoline pool catching flame. Tinker spun around but there was nothing to see. Forest Moss made a motion, and she turned to watch him call on the Stone Clan Spell Stones and use the magic to trigger his shields. Around them, the Wyverns and her Hand went alert.

"What was that? Did you feel that?" she asked Forest Moss.

"It was a spell breaking." Forest Moss cocked the fingers of his left hand and brought them to his mouth. "Ssssstada."

The spell Forest Moss triggered was a variation of the ground radar. A long, narrow wedge of power formed from the male elf to the river's edge. He shifted his right hand, and the wedge swept northward through Chinatown. At the heart of Chinatown, he hit an intense writhing of power.

"How odd," Forest Moss said.

"What is that?" Tinker noted that Tommy, being smart, had vanished while they had been distracted.

Forest Moss gave her an odd look. "It's a ley scry. It lets me see recent and active disturbances in the ley lines. I don't know what it was supposed to do, but a spell was just violently altered, and it's now acting as a pump on a *fiutana*."

"Oh shit. The black willow."

The great doors of the refrigerated warehouse stood open to the summer heat. Magic flowed down over the loading dock in a purple haze of potential. Tinker cautiously pulled the Rolls around, trying to angle the car so they could see into the cave darkness, but the dock was too high, and the door, facing the afternoon eastern sky, was cave dark. Tinker flicked on the headlights, but even the high beams failed to illuminate the interior.

"I want a closer look." Tinker put the Rolls into park. She wished she could leave the engine running, but it would be a mistake with this much free magic in the area.

She got out and the *sekasha* followed. Magic flooded over her, hot and fast. The heat tossed the chimes on the ley shrine, making them jangle in shrill alarm. A smell like burnt cinnamon mixed with a taste like heated honey. The invisible brilliance hinted at by the shimmering purple made her eyes water.

"Be careful." She blinked away tears. "The magic is all around us."

"Even we can see that." Stormsong's shields outlined her in hard, blue radiance. "Your shields, *domi*."

Yeah, now would be a good time for that.

Tinker set up a resonance with the spell stones and then triggered her shield spell. Once the winds were wrapped around her, she waded up the steps, making sure that she didn't disturb the spell by gesturing.

The padlock had been cut off with a bolt cutter. Her spell hadn't failed; someone had broken in and sabotaged it.

Violet sparkled and shifted in the black of the warehouse, casting patterns of shadows and near light. Tinker couldn't see anything that looked like the black willow. Stormsong tried the lights, but the switch had no effect.

"The flood would have popped the lightbulbs." There was no way Tinker was going in there blind. "Do we have a light?"

"Yes." Pony took out a spell light, closed his left hand tight around the glass orb, and activated it. He played a thin beam of searchlight intensity over the room.

They had left the black willow tied down on pallets. The restraints now lay in tatters. Splinters of wood marked the pallets' destruction. The forklift sat upended like a child's toy. Dead leaves rode convection currents, dancing across the cement floor with a thin, dry skittering noise.

"Where is it?" Tinker whispered.

"I don't see it." Pony's eyes swept the room again.

"Neither do I." Tinker glanced back to the street. Where was Forest Moss? That ground radar thing would come in handy just about now. "Let's turn off the compressor and at least stop this flood."

They moved through the warehouse to the back room. The small windowless room was empty of trees, with only the purring compressor to wreak havoc. A crowbar lay across the metal tracings of her spell, encircled with charring. Odd distortions wavered around the compressor.

Cursing, she started for the breaker box.

"*Domi*, no!" Stormsong caught her shoulder and stilled her. "Stay here at the door. Let Cloudwalker do it."

"The willow isn't in here." Tinker nevertheless stayed at the door as Stormsong asked while Cloudwalker crossed to the breaker box and cut the power to the compressor. "See, no dan—"

Her only warning was the ominous rustle of leaves, and then the forklift struck her shield from behind. She yelped, spinning around to see the forklift rebound back across the warehouse.

"Shields!" Stormsong shouted.

Tinker had let her shields drop in her surprise. She fumbled through the resonance setup as Pony's narrow light played off the suddenly close wizened "face" of the black willow. They had to have walked straight past it, somehow blind to it. It filled the warehouse now, blocking them from the door. It lifted a root-foot and replanted it with a booming sound that shook the floor. Its branches rattled as it blindly felt the confines of the room. A dozen of it's arms encountered the upended forklift, scooped it up again, and flung it at her.

Tinker snapped through the shield spell, already wincing, as the forklift sailed toward her. At the last second the winds wrapped tight around her and the forklift struck the distortion's edge.

"Shit!" Tinker swore as the forklift bounced back across the warehouse to wedge itself sidewises in the far door. "There's no other door, right?"

"No, *domi*," Pony said.

Tinker wasn't sure whether to be amazed or annoyed that Pony sounded so calm, as if she could pull doorways out of her butt. "Oh damn, oh damn, oh damn. Okay, I know I'm smarter than this tree."

The black willow lifted another root-foot and shook the world as it planted it back down, a few yards closer to them, instantly pulverizing the cement floor, digging roots down into the building's footing.

"But I have some doubts," Tinker admitted, "that brains are going to win over brawn this time."

What did she have to work with? She scanned the room of bare concrete block as the willow stomped ponderously closer. Crowbar. *Boom!* Compressor. Five *sekasha*. Five *ejae*. *Boom!* Circuit breaker box.

"Stormsong, what do you know about electricity?" Tinker asked the most tech-savvy of her Hand.

"Nothing useful," Stormsong said.

Boom!

"Nothing?" Tinker squeaked.

"It lives in a box in the wall." Stormsong detailed what she knew. "It goes away if you don't pay for it."

Boom!

Right—nothing useful. Scratch having Stormsong rig an electrical weapon. Just as well, good chance they'd just electrocute themselves.

The black willow stretched out its hundreds of whipping branches to scrabble at her shield. Tinker forced herself to scan the room again, and ignore the massive creature trying to reach her.

"The roof! It's only plywood and rubber. See if you can cut through."

The tree found the gap between the top of the tall doorway and her shield. The thin branches pushed through the space, caught hold of the doorjamb, and started to pull.

"Oh, shit!" Tinker cried. "If it makes the door larger, I'm not going to be able to hold it! It's coming in!"

There was a pulse of magic from Forest Moss, instantly defining the Stone Clan elf with Wyverns out by the Rolls, and themselves, pinned inside by the black willow.

"Forest Moss!" Tinker shouted. "Get it off us!"

The concrete walls buckled under the strain, tearing free to leave sawtooth openings, exposing twisted and snapped rebar. The branches flung the debris against the back wall of the warehouse like mad shovels.

"Forest Moss, get it—"

And suddenly the branches wrapped around her, cocooning her shield in living wicker, and lifted her off the ground.

"*Domi!*" Pony shouted.

The black willow heaved her up. Its branches creaked as it tried to crush her shields down.

Oh please hold! Oh please hold!

A dark orifice opened in the crook where its main limbs branched from it's massive trunk. As the tree tried to stuff her into the fleshy maw, she realized what the opening was.

They have mouths! I wonder if Lain knows that. Oh shit, it's trying to eat me!

Luckily the diameter of her shielding was larger than its mouth. It was trying to fit a golf ball into a beer bottle. She held still and silent, afraid to disrupt her shields. Smell of burnt cinnamon and honey filled her senses, and her vision blurred—the tree fading slightly—even as it repeatedly jammed her up against its mouth.

It has some kind of hallucinogen—that's how we missed it, she thought.

And then the tree flung her through the wall.

The street beyond was a flicker of brightness, and then she plowed through a confusion of small, dim, dusty rooms of an abandoned office building beyond.   She felt Forest Moss track her through the building.   His power flashed ahead of her, surged through the next building in her flight path, and locked down on all the load-bearing supports.

The white-haired shit was going to pull the building down on her! She'd be buried alive—shields or not!

Dropping her shields, she made a desperate grab for a battered steel desk as she flew over it.   She missed the edge and left five contrails across its dusty top.   A floor to ceiling window stood beyond the desk.   She smashed through the window into open sky.

I'm going to die.

And then Riki caught her, wrapping strong arms around her, and labored upward in a loud rustle of black wings.

"Riki!" She clung to the tengu, heart thudding like a motor about to shake itself apart.   Yeah, yeah, she was still pissed at him. She'd let him know that—after he put her down safely.

17: A MURDER OF CROWS

"Stop squirming or I might drop you," Riki growled through teeth gritted with the effort of carrying Tinker aloft.

She glanced down and went still in shock at being dangled midair forty feet up and climbing. "Shouldn't we be going down?"

"Down is good for you—very bad for me."

"Damn it, Riki, my people need me. Put me down!" Tinker found herself gripping his arms so he couldn't just drop her.

"There are so many things wrong with that statement that I don't have breath to explain it all."

Movement at the window she'd smashed out of caught her eye, and with relief she saw Cloudwalker pointing up at her. Moments later Pony and the others joined him at the opening.

"Oh, thank gods," Tinker breathed.

Riki rose above the roofline. The crown of the black willow bristled in the street beyond. Its booming footsteps echoed up from the canyon of buildings. She felt a great surge of magic and a massive fireball suddenly engulfed the tree. Whoa! Apparently Prince True Flame had arrived. No wonder the tengu didn't want to land.

Riki dipped down behind the next building, out of sight of her Hand. Black smoke billowed behind them. He flew straight west—

as the saying went, as the crow flies—faster than a man could run despite being weighed down by her. When he reached the Ohio River, he turned and followed its course.

Where the hell was he taking her? It occurred to her that he couldn't have been just passing by and caught her by luck.

"You planned this! You knew if you screwed with my spell, I'd come to fix it."

"Would you believe this had nothing to do with you?"

"No."

"Believe it not, the world does not revolve around Tinker the Great."

How far could Riki fly? Could he keep up this speed, or had that been a sprint? And what did he want with her?

She tried to form a plan to escape. Riki, though, wouldn't underestimate her—he knew her too well. Of all the people in Pittsburgh, he could match wits with her. Her first thought was to force him to drop her into the river. The large dark form of a river shark swimming under the water, following their passage, killed that plan. They followed the Ohio around its gentle bends, and Pittsburgh vanished behind the swell of the surrounding hills. Once the city was out of sight, Riki climbed the steep hill that once was Bellevue and crossed the Rim. There he dove into the ironwoods. The forest canopy rushed toward them, seeming to her a solid wall of green. Riki, though, flicked through openings she hadn't seen, darting through slender upper branches to finally land on a thick bough, close to the massive trunk.

The moment they landed, Tinker twisted in his hold and swung at him hard as she could, aiming for his beaklike nose.

"God damn it!" He caught her hand and twisted her arm painfully up behind her back. He leaned his weight against her, pinning her to the trunk. "Just hold still!"

Cheek pressed to the rough gray bark, Tinker saw for the first time how far up the tree they stood—the forest floor lay a hundred feet below. Normally she didn't mind heights—only normally she wasn't this high up with an enemy spy. She stopped struggling, fear trying to climb up out of her stomach. She swallowed down on it—she had to keep her head.

Riki grabbed her right wrist, caught hold of her left, and bound both hands behind her with a thin plastic strap. Once she was bound helpless, he turned her around. He wore war paint—streaks of black under his vivid blue eyes and shock of black hair. His shirt was cut on the same loose lines as the muscle shirt he wore often during her captivity by the oni, made of glossy black scale armor. On his feet, with their odd birdlike toes, he wore silver tips that looked razor-sharp.

"What do you want?" She was pleased she didn't sound as scared as she was.

"I'm not going to hurt you."

"Somehow I don't believe you." She wriggled slightly to indicate her tied wrists. It made her teeter alarmingly on the branch, so she carefully scrunched down until she straddled the thick limb. There, perfectly safe. Ha!

Riki watched her with a cocked head. "There's no shame in being afraid of heights. Most people are."

She stared at him with shock. That was exactly what he said in her dream—wasn't it? She glanced downward and felt déjà vu; they'd been up high in her nightmare.

"What do you want?" she asked. "Are you going to turn me over to the oni again?"

"No. When you killed Lord Tomtom, we tengu managed to break free of the oni."

"*I gave that up. You melted the witch, so I got out of my no-compete contract.*"

This was seriously weird.

"Riki, who is the wizard of Oz?"

"Huh?"

"I had a dream and you were in it."

"And you and you and you too," Riki quoted the movie.

"Oh good, at least you know the source. In my dream, I was trying to get to the wizard of Oz."

"Oookay, and I thought I was deep in left field. Oh this is sad."

"Do have any idea who he might be?"

"The wizard?" Riki pulled a pack of cigarettes out of his back pocket, tapped out a cigarette, lit it, and took a deep drag. "Hmmm, in the movie the wizard was the traveling performer that Dorothy met when she ran away from home. Chances are, then, he's someone you've met but don't recognize now."

Taking another drag, Riki vented the smoke out of his nose in twin columns as he thought. "His nature is changing; some perceive him as great and powerful, others see him as foolish, but he's the only character that fully understood both Kansas and Oz. Most likely, you're looking for someone with great knowledge, but his intelligence is disguised somehow." Riki gazed off into the forest, eyes unfocused, thinking. "Like Dorothy, he's a traveler between worlds, just as lost . . ."

Riki's eyes snapped back in focus. "Impatience. He's your wizard."

"Who?"

"Impatience. The dragon that you fought at Turtle Creek."

She tried to fit the name of "Impatience" with the countless jagged teeth and massive snaky body.

"See, intelligence disguised." Riki waved his cigarette, reminding her of the astronomer postdocs when they went into lecture mode. "Legends say that a dragon has a body and a spirit, and you can encounter the one without the other. Usually in the old stories, the dragons send their spirits out to cross great distances—but while they're doing it, it's a very unwise thing to approach their bodies. The lights are on, but no one's home."

"Running on autopilot?"

"Let's just say that there's more than one story about someone getting their head bitten off while a dragon's spirit is absent."

She remembered the impression that intelligence filled the dragon's eyes—its surprise at having a hand clamped into its mouth. "So you're saying the dragon was unconscious at the time he attacked me."

"Probably."

That would certainly explain how she'd managed to walk away with nothing more than a sore hand. "So where is this dragon now?"

"Even if I knew that, I wouldn't tell you. I want Impatience for the tengu. That's what I was doing at Reinholds. The oni had set a trap for it, using the fountain as a lure."

"The oni?"

"Impatience was one of two dragons the oni had waiting on Onihida for the invasion. The other is Malice, who is much bigger. Somehow Impatience managed to slip the oni's hold on him and escape."

"So, on top of the royal troops and the oni, we have an unaligned dragon running loose in Pittsburgh."

"Well, a party is only fun if you invite lots of interesting people."

She stuck her tongue out at him. "How do you plan to find Impatience?"

"I don't know. *You* apparently have to follow the yellow brick road."

In her dream, though, the road ended with the tree. This was going to drive her mad. In the silence between them, she heard a slight noise from Riki's hip pocket. He frowned, slipped out a cell phone, and answered it with a cautious, "Hello?"

As he listened, his caution changed to worry. "You're where? Jesus Christ, what are you doing there? Oh fuck. Yes I said that, what do you expect me to say? No—don't—don't . . ." Riki sighed. "Put your cousin on. No, no, not Joey! Keiko." Riki waited a moment until the phone could be traded off on the other side of the conversation. "Yeah, I'm here. What's going on?"

Riki listened for several minutes, grimacing as if what he heard pained him. "I'll be there in a few minutes. Hang tight." Riki tucked away his phone. "Change of plans."

"You're letting me go?"

"Sorry." He actually managed to look it. "I'll never have this chance again. I can't throw it away." He pulled out a silk scarf and tied it over her eyes. "I don't want you to know where we're going." He took firm hold of her and jerked her off her feet. "This time, don't wriggle so much."

She felt him leap, knew that he'd left the safety of the tree, and nearly screamed at the knowledge. His wings rustled out, caught the air, and they swooped upward.

Fifteen or twenty minutes later, Riki dove down and wove through light and shadows to land again. Numb from dangling, her legs folded under her. Riki lowered her down to a prone position and then knelt behind her, panting with exertion.

Their landing site seemed too flat to be a tree branch but it swayed slightly with the rustling of the wind.

"Damn it, Riki, where are we?"

Riki tugged down her blindfold. She lay just inside the door of a tiny cabin; only eight-foot square, it would have been claustrophobic if it had actually contained furniture.

"We're at a cote," he panted. "Emergency shelter."

The cabin seemed to be made of scrap lumber. The one small round window letting in light held glass, and the high ceiling bristled with nails, indicating that the roof was shingled, so the cabin was weatherproofed.

"Stay put." He stepped past her to pull something off a set of shelves on the back wall. "There's no safe way down to the ground. I'll be back."

Cabin, hell, it was a tree house. Under any other circumstance, she would have been entranced with the notion.

Riki took a deep breath and stepped backward out the door, spreading his black wings.

"Stay," he repeated and flapped away.

Not trusting his word, she struggled to her feet and went to the door. The view straight down made her step backward quickly. It was a place strictly for birds. If her hands weren't bound behind her back, she could get to the massive branch just outside the door, but there was nowhere to go from there. The tree was too wide, and the lowest branch too far from the ground to allow climbing down. She could see nothing but virgin forest through both the door and window, not even a glimpse of sun or river to give a clue which direction they had flown.

The cote was cunningly made. A brace along the back wall provided the one anchor point so the stress of the shifting tree could not tear the room apart. The front of the cabin rested on a beam yoked over side branches. A loft bed nearly doubled the floor space. A generous overhang meant the front door could hang open even during a rain shower to let in light without the weather. The outside of the cabin had been painted gray and black in a pattern that mimicked ironwood bark.

She kicked shut the door but the latch was too high for her to shift with her hands bound.

The shelves on the back wall were stocked with survival gear: warm clothing and blankets in plastic bags, extra plastic bags, rolls of duct tape, a serious first aid kit, ammo for guns, flashlights, two box knives, waterproof matches, bottled spring water, a water purifier kit, a small cooler filled with power bars and military rations, and even a roll of toilet paper. Judging by the shape of the bag, Riki had taken a set of clothes with him.

She fumbled with one of the box knives, blindly sawing at the plastic strap binding her wrists. The blade kept slipping, nicking her wrists, before she finally managed to cut through. She bandaged her wrists, looking at what she had to work with. A rope ladder from strips of blanket, reinforced with the duct tape? Or perhaps she should just try to jump Riki and take his cell phone. No, he'd gone to meet someone, so he could return with others.

As if the thought summoned the tengu, Riki kicked the door open. She snatched up the box knife and spun around to face Riki as he dropped in through the doorway. He wasn't alone. He had a child with him—a little boy in an oversized black hooded sweatshirt.

"Riki!" She started toward him, angry at the tengu, and afraid for the boy.

Riki looked up, saw the knife in her hand, and his face went cold. She had always suspected that the tengu treated her with kid gloves. Suddenly, it was as if a stranger was looking at her, one who would hurt her if she took another step forward.

She stopped, and reached out with her empty hand. "Don't hurt him."

Still tight in Riki's hold, the boy glanced over his shoulder at her, and blinked in surprise. He had the tengu's coarse straight black hair, electric blue eyes, and sharp features—though his nose wasn't so nearly beaklike as Riki's. "Oh, hello," the tengu boy said with no fear in his voice. "I'm Joey. Joey Shoji. Who are you?"

With a rustle of wings, two slightly older tengu children crowded the doorway. Wearing blue jeans and torn T-shirts, they would have seemed like human children except for the way they clung to the sides of the doorway with birdlike feet, fanning the air with black wings. The girl looked thirteen and sported the black war paint and sharp spurs that Riki wore. The boy was younger—eleven? Ten? Both had Riki's dark wild hair and sharp features.

"Hey, what's a girl doing here?" the boy asked in English and hopped into the cote.

The girl scowled and remained hovering at the door. "She's an elf—the fairy princess."

"What's an elf?" Joey asked.

"She's still a girl elf, Keiko," the boy insisted.

"What's an elf?" Joey asked again.

"It means I have pointed ears." Tinker tapped on her left ear. She used it as a distraction to put the knife on the shelves as casually as she could. The two younger kids studied her ear, but Riki and Keiko's eyes followed the knife.

The coldness left Riki's face, but he still watched her carefully. "This is Mickey and Keiko." He released the littlest one. "And Joey. They're my younger cousins."

"Should we really be telling her our names?" Keiko asked. "What's she doing here?"

Joey pulled off the adult-sized sweatshirt he was drowning in. Underneath he had a ragged T-shirt like the other two—the back torn open to reveal the elaborate spell tattooed from shoulder to waistline, in black. "Look, look, I have wings too!"

He spoke a word, and magic poured through the tracings, making them shimmer like fresh ink. The air hazed around him, and the wings unfolded out of the distortion, at first holographic in appearance, ghosts of crow wings hovering behind him, fully extended. Then they solidified into reality, skin and bone merged into his musculature of his back, glistening black feathers, all correctly proportioned for his thin, child's body.

"Wow," Tinker said. "Those are cool."

Keiko hopped into the cote to catch hold of Joey and pull him away from Tinker, giving her a dark distrusting look.

Riki said something in the harsh oni tongue that made the younger tengu look at Tinker with surprise.

"Her?" Keiko cried. "No way!"

Riki shrugged, making his wings rustle. "She's the one that

killed Lord Tomtom. The dragon went to her. I have to check."

"Wait," Tinker said. "This is all about the tattoo you think the dragon put on me?"

"Yes." Riki nodded.

"Are you nuts?" Tinker said.

"No, just desperate. Please, take off your dress."

"Oh, you have to be kidding." Tinker took a step back and realized how crowded the tiny cabin had just gotten with tengu wings. "I am not taking off my dress in front of all of you."

Riki touched Joey's shoulder. "Wings, Joey. Keiko and Mickey, you too."

The boys spoke spell commands and their wings vanished. Riki picked them up, one at a time, and swung them up to the loft bed. They sat on the edge, dangling down their three-toed feet until Riki said, "Nyah, nyah, all the way up. Quiet little birds."

Keiko crossed her arms, flared out her wings, and leveled a hostile look at Riki. "I'm a warrior."

Riki glared at the tengu girl until the girl added something in oni. "A witness? Yes, I guess you're right."

"Yeah, I'm supposed to act as if that's better?" Tinker asked.

"Take off your dress, let me look at you, and if you don't have the mark, I'll let you go."

Tinker scoffed. "Yeah, sure."

"I promise," Riki said.

Like that was worth anything.

"Don't be such a chickenshit!" Keiko said.

Riki slapped the tengu girl on the back of the head. "Hey, you're not helping. Would you want to take off your clothes in front of strangers?"

Keiko blushed and stuck out her tongue at her cousin.

Riki returned his attention to Tinker. "Come on. Just do it quick and it'll be over."

"I don't have any mark."

Riki's face went neutral, all emotion draining out, leaving only resolve.

Tinker considered whether she wanted her dress forcibly taken off. There wasn't any running away, and while Keiko was young, the tengu girl was as tall as she was. Probably if Tinker tried calling the winds she'd end up in a wrestling match before she got the spell off. "Fine. I'll take it off."

She struggled out of her dress, and as she feared, the bra had to go.

"It would be over her heart, wouldn't it?" Keiko looked as uncomfortable with Tinker's nudity as Tinker felt.

"It should." Riki took Tinker's hands and examined her arms carefully, even to the point of undoing the bandages and peering under them. It wasn't as bad as Tinker feared. She realized it was the kids' presence; she trusted Riki not to do anything with them there— watching. Hopefully she was right.

"Okay," Riki finally said. "You can get dressed."

"Does she have it? Does she have it?" Mickey called from the loft.

"No." Riki glanced down at Keiko. "Can you make it to the near cote without stopping? It's going to be dark and we'll need to move quietly and fast."

Keiko screwed up her face, torn between saying yes and admitting the truth. Finally she hunched her shoulders, looked away, and said, "No."

Riki tousled the girl's short black hair. "It's better that you tell the truth now. I'll take Joey and then come back to guide you two. Rest up."

"What about her?" Keiko asked, and then added quietly. "You promised her."

If it wasn't her freedom they were talking about, it would have been funny to see Riki realize how screwed he was. He could start to ferry the kids back home, but it would leave her alone with at least two of them. Taking her home meant all three kids would be alone for a much longer time—perhaps a very long time if he ran into trouble with the elves. He looked at her in sudden panic.

She sighed and waved her hand. "Take care of them first."

"Promise me that you won't hurt them."

She laughed. "Who is going to protect me from them?"

A wry smile came and went. "I'm trusting you two to behave. Understand?"

"Yes, Riki," Mickey said.

Keiko nodded, watching Tinker.

"Joey?" Riki motioned to the littlest tengu and the boy flung himself out of the loft into Riki's arms. "Ooomph! Settle down, you little monster. Here, sweatshirt on first." Riki knelt and pulled the sweatshirt onto the boy. "Remember, once we leave, no talking. Quiet little birds."

Joey mimed locking his mouth and throwing away the key.

"Good boy." Riki picked up the child and gave them a worried look. "Remember there are oni in the woods. Keep it down and no lights."

"Quiet little birds," Mickey said.

Riki wavered at the door, Joey clinging to his neck. "Tinker— I love them as much as you love Oilcan. Everything I've done has been for them. Please just—just wait for me to get back."

The tengu kids took the loft bed and Tinker settled by the door, her back to the wall so she could keep an eye on them. Keiko continued to stare at her. Mickey swung his legs. Dusk fell on the forest and darkness crawled into the cabin.

"How far does Riki have to go?"

Mickey started to say something but Keiko poked him.

"We're not allowed to say."

"What are you doing so far away anyhow?"

"Joey just got his wings," Mickey said. "We were on his first long flight and got cut off by a troop of oni moving through the area. We tried to go around them and got lost. When we hit the city's edge, Keiko said we should call Riki. I'm the one that remembered the number."

"Then all you would do was cry," Keiko said.

Mickey pulled up his legs, curling into himself.

Keiko gave him a look of remorse and then swung down. She rummaged through the shelves and then handed up a bottle of water and a power bar to her younger cousin. "Here. You can have the last chocolate one."

Keiko put a second bottle and bar up beside Mickey. Wordlessly, she left an offering of food and water for Tinker down on the floor, carefully staying outside of Tinker's reach, and then swung back to the loft.

Tinker hadn't had a power bar as an elf—she expected something tasteless. She was surprised how good it tasted. "Oh, these are yummy."

Mickey nodded in agreement, made instantly happy by Keiko's offering. "I didn't think elves could speak English."

Keiko pinched Mickey.

"Ow! What?"

"Don't display how ignorant you are. She was a human until the viceroy turned her into an elf a few months ago."

Mickey looked at Tinker, recognition dawning on him. "Oh, she's the Dufae girl?"

"Yes," Keiko said.

Fear filled Mickey's face.

"Why are you scared of me?" Tinker asked.

"We know what Riki had to do to you," Mickey whispered. "How he had to turn you over to the oni."

"Riki didn't want us to come to Elfhome," Keiko said. "He said that either the elves would find us, or the oni would. Better stay on Earth where we were at least free. But the oni came to our house and took Joey hostage. Riki sent us on ahead to be with our aunt, but he stayed to work for the oni—to try and get Joey back."

"He never told me about you."

"If he told you, then the kitsune would know, and then the oni would know. He couldn't tell you the truth about anything—or he'd put us in danger."

"You hate the tengu now—don't you?" Mickey whispered.

A few days ago, Tinker probably would have said yes. She knew that when she found the MP3 player, she'd been angry enough to beat Riki to a pulp again. Now, with the dead in Chinatown, and the children looking at her in fear, she couldn't hate all the innocent strangers. "No."

Keiko scoffed, disbelieving. "I'd never forgive anyone that did that to me."

"I saw what Lord Tomtom did to those that failed him—and it scared the living shit out of me." She shuddered with the memory of the torture; the flash of bright blades and white of bone stripped clean of flesh. "I was willing to do almost anything to keep the knives away from me."

"So you forgive Riki?"

There was something about the darkness that demanded honesty. "I'm still angry at him. But I was with the oni for nearly a month—I can understand why he did it and don't think I can hate him for it. He took my shit and never complained, and when he could, he protected me."

There was a sudden roar outside and a hoverbike—lift engines at full—popped up and landed on the massive branch outside the door. Its headlight flooded the room with stark white blinding light.

Tinker stood and called magic, wrapping the wind around her.

"Tinker *domi!*" Stormsong's voice came out of the light.

"Stormsong?" Tinker squinted into the glare.

The headlight snapped off. Stormsong sat on a custom Delta Tinker had done for a charity auction last year. Somehow Stormsong had managed to land and balance on the branch—it was going to take work to get it down in one piece. In her right hand the *sekasha* held a shotgun resting across the handlebars and trained at the cabin door.

"How the hell did you find me?" Tinker asked.

"I closed my eyes and went where I was needed." Stormsong glanced beyond Tinker to the kids. "They're tengu."

Tinker realized that her being safe meant the kids were now in danger. "I promised that they wouldn't be hurt."

"That was a silly thing to do," Stormsong said.

"They're just kids." Tinker moved to protect them with her shield.

"Kids grow up," Stormsong said.

Tinker shook her head. "I can't let you hurt them. I promised."

"Yes, Tinker *ze domi,*" Stormsong said in High Tongue.

Tinker released the winds. The kids huddled against the back corner of the loft bed.

"We won't hurt you," she told them, "but I need to leave."

"Hey," Keiko called. She pulled off a necklace and scrambled forward to dangle it out to Tinker. "Take this. It will protect you."

"From what?"

"Tengu."

Tinker looped the necklace over her neck and picked her way out onto the branch. "How the hell did you get a hoverbike the whole way up here? I know the lift engine can't do a hundred feet straight up—or down."

"Flying blind." Stormsong uncocked her shotgun and holstered it. "Hang tight to me—this is going to be tricky. And you might want to close your eyes."

Tinker clung tight to Stormsong, trying to let her trust of the bodyguard override her knowledge of the hoverbike's limitations. Stormsong didn't even turn on the bike's headlight, just raced the bike's engine and then tipped them over the edge. A squeak of fear leapt up Tinker's throat—followed by her heart—as they nose-dived. They hit a lower branch that cracked under the lift drive and suddenly they were corkscrewing madly. She gripped Stormsong tight. She felt more than saw the blur of tree trunks and branches as they kissed off them. Seconds later they straightened out and roared through the darkness—Pony on a second hoverbike waiting on the ground running alongside them.

"Thank you," Stormsong called back.

"What for? You rescued me."

"Yes, but you trusted me to do my job."

18: SEEK YOU

The *sekasha* suggested a bath and bed, but Tinker didn't want to unwind and take it easy. Things in Pittsburgh were bad, and getting worse, and like it or not, she was one of the few people who had the power to fix things. The only question was how.

She placated the *sekasha* by agreeing to dinner and took her datapad with her to the enclave's private dining hall. Maynard thought that opening a line of communication with Earth would be key. Yeah, right, just phone home. Riki had said that the dragon was the wizard of Oz, and implied that dragons understood how to move from world to world. She didn't know where the dragon was, however, and from the sounds of it, both the oni and tengu were searching hard for it. Follow the yellow brick road? What road? Ohio River Boulevard? I-279? The last lead she had was the black willow tree and last she saw of that, it was flambé.

Wait, she had seeds from the black willow. At least, she thought she did. She had Windwolf's staff track the small jar down, and the MP3 player. Watching the seeds wriggle in the glass, she listened to the songs recorded on the player. It was one of Oilcan's favorite elf rock groups, playing a collection of songs that her cousin had written for them. If you didn't know Oilcan, the songs seemed

to be about lost lovers. Tinker knew that they were about his mother. Odd how the words could stay the same but knowledge changed
the meaning.

Tinker laid her head on the table and remembered Riki in
another light.

Pony ran his hand across her back, a delicious feeling that
uncoiled a sudden deep need. On the heels of that, like cracking
open a bottle full of dark storm winds, a confusing wash of emotions.

"Don't do that." Tinker shifted away from his touch and tried
to cork the bottle. She was too fragile for that.

"Have I hurt you?" Pony asked.

She shook her head.

"All day, you have avoided me as if I had. I need to understand—
what have I done wrong? We are not fitting this way."

She had? She hadn't even been aware of it. "It's not you. It's
me. I-I've so totally—" Unfortunately there wasn't an Elvish match
for "'fucked up," so she stuck in the English, "everything and everyone."

"Fuck," Pony repeated the English curse. "Can you teach me
that?"

"No!" She realized he meant the word's meaning, not the actu-
al action. "It means intercourse." And once she saw the confusion
in Pony's face as he tried to plug in the meaning into her sentence,
she added, "It's a curse word generally meaning—well—anything
you want it to mean. It's one of the more versatile words we have."

"How do you conjugate it?"

"Fuck, fucking, fucked when used as a verb. It can be used as a
noun, indicate a person, place, or thing, generally derogatory." This
was the not the conversation she thought she'd be having with Pony
this evening. "It could also be combined—creatively—with other
words. Fuckhead. Fuck off. Fuckwad."

"I'm starting to understand a little more about human fascina-
tion with sex."

"Besides the fact that it's so damn fun?"

"What is damn?"

"Pony!"

"I feel that it is time that I learned English."

She felt a pang of guilt knowing that Pony hadn't understood any of Nathan's last words, that he had only seen her struggling in Nathan's hold and her cry for help. "Yes, that would be good."

"Why do you feel this way? That you have 'fucked up'? You have done the best you can against very difficult situations."

"Pittsburgh is stuck here on Elfhome. Nathan is dead. Half the people I know probably hate my guts now. I'm not sure even Oilcan or Lain will ever want to see me again. I cheated on my husband, and seduced you! How is that 'the best'? Gods forbid if I had done my worst!"

He reached out and pulled her back, into his lap.

"Pony." She wriggled, trying to escape him.

"*Domi,*" he whispered into her hair, his lips brushing the tips of her ears, sending a shiver of want through her. "Have I no will of my own? Am I your puppet?"

She stared into his dark eyes and felt cold dread take hold. "I don't want to talk about this."

"Because if you're in control, I am not to blame for my actions?"

"Pony, please."

"And if I am not under your control, does that make me a terrifying stranger? Someone that you do not know?"

She clung to him then, afraid that he would slip away from her. "Please, Pony, you're the only thing sane about my life right now."

"You are being unfair to both of us to say that what happened was only by your hand. I am not your puppet. You did not act alone. You can not be solely responsible."

"You do what I tell you to do. I told you I wanted sex and you gave it to me."

"I choose to do what you tell me." He took her hand and nuzzled her wrist. "I was pleased that you trusted me enough to turn to me and to stop when you changed your mind."

"I'm just supposed to use you? Get off and then throw you across the room? Like you're some kind of—" She was going to say "vibrator" but elves didn't have a word for battery-operated sex toys. Nor did she want to hurt him more by being crude. "—substitute for my husband?"

"That is what I am. I am to be here for you when Wolf cannot be."

"But—But— And you're okay with that?"

"I have lived my entire life knowing that as a *sekasha*, if I became a *domi's* beholden, she might take me to bed. And I knew, when I offered myself to you, that meant all of me. My life is yours. My love is yours. And I have watched you fight the demon spawn themselves to keep me from harm. Nothing happened yesterday that I did not know might happen, that I wanted to stop, and that I am sorry about—except the part about being thrown across the room."

If he thought this was going to make her feel better, he was wrong. She felt worse, and struggled to keep from showing it. Obviously she sucked at it as sadness filled his eyes.

"I did not realize until Stormsong explained that humans are so—singular—with their love. It is not our way." Pony used the inclusive "our," meaning that they both belonged to it: she was one of them. "That is why we *sekasha* are *naekuna*; so you can turn to us if you need us."

"Oh, Pony, I might have the body of an elf, but in here—" She tapped her temple. "I'm still a human. I can't commit to one person—heart and soul—and then take another one to bed, without feeling like I'm doing something wrong. I just can't."

"I know." He said it with quiet acceptance in his voice, and then nothing more. After a minute, she leaned against him and soaked in his calmness. It still felt wrong to stay so close, so intimate with him when she was married to Windwolf. Her logical side, though, was starting to recognize what Pony must know—that while she was emotionally fully human now, that in a hundred years or so, she would slowly grow to be elf inside as well as out. And to elves—a hundred years was a very short time.

Well, sitting wallowing in her own pain wasn't going to help Pittsburgh. Time to pull rabbits out of her butt. How could she communicate across realities when Earth wouldn't have a receiver for her transmitter? She'd already tested Turtle Creek for radio waves, and nothing recognizable was coming through. She entertained the idea of linking two phones together with a phone line and tossing one into the Discontinuity. No, a phone would sink like the gate had. So would messages in bottles.

She sighed and slid out of Pony's lap. "Time to get busy. I need to do some modeling."

Communication with Earth was a simple science problem. What was happening in Pittsburgh was a vast sociological problem that she didn't know how to solve. She didn't even know where she stood in regards to it. How far did her responsibility extend? Were the elves right in hunting down all the oni and killing them? The scientist in her could see the simple logic of it. Both races were immortal, only the oni were prolific and the elves weren't. If the elves did nothing, the oni would win eventually by default. Morally, genocide was wrong—but did the elves have a choice? It wasn't like the gods had put both races on one world. The oni had invaded, which put them in the wrong. It would be stupid to put them in the right simply because they failed to kill the elves first.

And what about the tengu, who seemed to be a race separate from the oni and on Elfhome against their will? What was her responsibility to them? Riki had betrayed her, but if the tengu children were telling the truth, he had been forced to choose between her and his cousins. She knew she would move the world to protect Oilcan; how could she hold Riki's betrayal against him when that meant putting the children in danger?

And how many tengu were there on Elfhome? Would she be protecting Riki, the three kids and the unnamed "aunt" or were there more? A dozen? A hundred?

Where did her responsibility begin and end? Could she protect all the humans and the tengu too? Or to keep the humans safe, would she have to ignore what was morally right?

And under it all was the dark suspicion that she didn't really have the power to protect anything, despite what Tooloo might think. True Flame thought she was a useless child. The Stone Clan was trying to kill her. Windwolf had lent her his power, but if she took a stand against him, would he take it back?

When Wolf asked Tinker to be his *domi*, he'd suspected that she would be able to lead. Certainly, when she spoke, people obeyed. She didn't seem to be aware that she had the quality, but the day she saved his life, everyone listened to her without quarreling. Time and time again since then there had been satisfying—although usually mystifying—proof that he was right about her. He found his *domi* deep in another mysterious project in the middle of the Westinghouse Bridge, overlooking the Ghostlands.

"What is this?" Wolf pointed to a large cylindrical machine beside his *domi*.

"This is an Imperial searchlight." Tinker patted the three-foot-tall light fixture. "It uses a Xenon 4,000-watt bulb to output 155,000 lumens. They say that the output is visible at distances of more than twenty kilometers."

Wolf eyed the wires snaking away to either end of the bridge. "Do you have more than one?"

"Three. I tried to get four, but these babies are hard to find in Pittsburgh—and a bitch to move. They weigh nearly two hundred pounds and then you need almost four hundred pounds of ballast so they don't tip over. I put the other two on either hill to get maximum spread."

Tinker settled at the table at the center of the bridge. "I've got them tied together to this control board. I'm trying to track down a manual on—" She paused to eye her screen closely. "Ah, there, Morse code."

Wolf crouched beside her. "You're going to use the light to communicate?"

She smiled and leaned down to touch her forehead to his. "Exactly. By the composition of the buildings inside the Ghostlands, it's clear that Earth is one of the dimensions intersected by this Discontinuity. The blue shift of the area seems to indicate that certain wavelengths of light are being absorbed and only the blue is reflecting back to us."

"So other wavelengths are traveling on through to the other dimensions?"

"I think so. If we communicate with Earth, we might be able to get them to help. I'm just a little worried that no one on their end will be paying attention—this will only work in the middle of the night."

"They're missing a city with sixty thousands souls. They're paying attention."

"Well—there is that." She kissed him and went back to work.

"Have you considered that the oni will see this too?"

"Yes, I know, that's a flaw in the plan. We'll have to consider any communication from another world as suspect."

He considered this problem as she typed. "It is unfortunate that the EIA had been compromised. Maynard might have had a way to verify any communication from the UN as authentic."

"Hmmm, hadn't considered that angle. Human agencies that have security protocols. Wait—I wonder—what happened to those NSA agents?"

"The human agents that tried to kidnap you?"

His tone made her glance at him and giggle. "Oh, don't look like that. They only wanted to protect me from the oni. They actually were nice, once they stopped trying to drag me back to Earth."

"Maynard will know where they are, if they are in Pittsburgh."

She took out a cell phone and made it beep repeatedly. "I would have never dreamed of having the God of Pittsburgh's phone number in my address book."

"He is not God of Pittsburgh. He is our servant."

"Somehow I doubt that he sees it that way." Her face changed as the call went through. "Oh, hi, yeah, this is Tinker. Say, do you know what happened to the NSA agents? Briggs and Durrack? Really?" She listened for a minute. "Oh cool! Can you send them out to Turtle Creek? I need them out here. Thanks."

As she hung up, Wolf wondered what Maynard made of the phone call. It was a perfect example, though, of his *domi's* leadership skills. She saw the need and did what was needed to fill it without guidance from him. All she needed was the authority of her title. And she probably did not realize how rare the ability was.

"They didn't leave last Shutdown, so they're stuck here." Tinker relayed what she learned. "They've been working with him. Apparently when they kidnapped me, he put them through a detailed background check. They're among the few people in Pittsburgh he could trust to be who they said they were. He was using them to weed through the EIA's databases to find altered files and recover the original data."

Her walkie-talkie beeped and one of the work crews reported in that the other two searchlights were in place and pointed down into the valley. The walkie-talkies tickled him to no end. That was what he wanted for his people—the ease of communication that humans had.

Tinker glanced up into the night sky. Dark lay full on the land and the stars gleamed brilliant overhead. "What do you think? Is it dark enough?"

"It will not get any darker without clouds."

"These lights are about two hundred times brighter than a normal lightbulb," Tinker warned him. "You shouldn't look directly at them when they're on. Okay, let's see if it works." Tinker radioed the other two units with "Turn them on."

The three beams of light cut brilliant down into the valley. Midway the light shifted to blue, somewhat muted, but still dazzling in the pitch darkness.

"Hmm, that's a good sign," Tinker murmured.

"Did you plan tonight because of the lack of moon?" Wolf asked.

"I'd love to say yes, but actually we just got lucky." Tinker clicked her keyboard, activating her program. The searchlights started to flash. "I've written a short script in Morse code—C-Q-C-Q-C-Q-D-E-S-1-K—and interspersed it with three minutes of darkness."

"What does that mean?"

"This manual says it means 'calling any station, this is designation station one, listening.' I'm not sure if that's totally correct Morse, but I figure it's close enough for horseshoes."

She saw his smile, and her eyes widened as she realized what she'd said, and then she smiled too. He'd asked her to be his *domi* after playing horseshoes with her.

The searchlights snapped off, plunging them into darkness, and Tinker slid down into his lap.

"Did you—" Tinker whispered to him. "Did you have lovers other than Jewel Tear—and the *sekasha*?"

"A few. Not many. I had my insane idea of coming to the Westernlands and establishing a holding here."

She made a small unhappy sound.

"If I had known you were in my future, I would have waited," he whispered. "Think, this way I came to you a skilled lover. This way one of us knew how it was done."

"I can build a hyperphase jump gate, I'm sure I could have figured sex out. Insert Tab M into Slot F. Repeat until done."

Windwolf laughed. "You delight me."

"Good. You delight me too."

They stole several minutes for themselves. With much regret, Wolf focused back on their many problems. "I think we'd better strengthen our position." he said. "We're going to stir the oni up doing this."

"Oh! I hadn't considered that," Tinker said.

He was learning that his *domi* became so fixated on a puzzle that she ignored the outside world. It meant that she could lock all of her brilliance onto finding a solution, but it left her open to being blindsided.

He kissed her brow and reluctantly left her to make the valley safe for her.

Despite their rocky start, Tinker actually liked the NSA agents. They arrived in a sleek grey sedan so out of place in Pittsburgh that it didn't need the D.C. plates to identify it as out of town. Nobody drove new cars because the parts were too hard to find, and no one knew how to service them. Corg Durrack and Hannah Briggs got out of the car cautiously, as if they were trying not to spook the heavily armed elves.

Both NSA agents, though, looked like they could hold their own with the *sekasha*.

The tall, leggy Briggs wore a clingy black outfit that looked like wet paint, and slid in and out of the shadows with feline grace. A Batman utility belt with small mystery packs had been added to her ensemble, slung low on her hips, holstering her exotic long-barreled handgun. Tinker couldn't tell if Briggs was now flaunting her weapon, or just displaying the one that was impossible to conceal.

Corg Durrack had a boyish face and the body of a comic book hero. He carried his usual peace offering of a white wax-paper bag, which he held out Tinker with a grin. "Your favorite."

"I'll be the judge." Tinker opened to the bag to find her favorite cookies—chocolate frosting thumbprint cookies from Jenny Lee. "This is spooky. How did you know?"

"It's our job to know." Durrack winked.

Briggs scoffed at this, and drifted back into the darkness.

"So what's our little mad scientist up to now?" Durrack settled down beside Tinker's chair where Windwolf had been a short time before. The searchlight flashed the work area with brightness as it cycled through the short message.

Tinker stuck her tongue out at him. "You know, I thought Maynard kicked you two out of Pittsburgh months ago."

"You were only the top of our to-do list. It took twenty-four hours of negotiations, but we stayed in this mud hole after the last Shutdown."

She laughed at the look of disgust on Durrack's face. "You don't like our fair city?"

"This isn't our world and the elves seem determined to remind us of that every chance they get. Besides, it's like getting stuck in a time warp; Pittsburgh is missing a lot of the simple conveniences of home. The television sucks here. And I would kill for Starbucks."

"Starbucks?" Tinker said. "Sounds Elvish. Who is he?"

Durrack gave her an odd look.

"What else is on your to-do list?" Tinker asked.

"Little of this, little of that," Durrack said. "Gather intelligence."

"In Pittsburgh?"

"You're got five or six races stuffed under one roof, it makes for lots of secrets floating around."

"How do you get six?"

Corg ticked them off on his fingers. "The elves, the humans, the oni, the tengu, the mixed bloods, and now a dragon—which the tengu say is a sentient being."

The searchlight fell dark, dropping them into blackness.

Tinker wasn't sure why, but she found it annoying that the NSA had apparently talked to the tengu about the dragon. "I didn't know you were so friendly with the tengu."

"Politics has nothing to do with friendship." Durrack's voice came out of the darkness. "It's doing whatever you have to do to protect what's yours. Pittsburgh might be under UN control, but its people are Americans and it's our duty to protect them."

"You realize the tengu lie."

"Everyone lies."

"The elves don't. They see it as dishonorable."

"They might not lie, but they dance around the truth. Like yesterday, during that little encounter you had with the tree. You analyze the events and it's fairly clear that the Stone Clan tried to kill you. Forest Moss withheld his support until you were captured by the tree, and the building you should have landed in collapsed for no apparent reason."

"I know."

"He made elegant excuses about why he was so slow, but it was all bullshit. He wanted that tree to kill you."

"I know. You don't have to rub it in."

"Are they trying to keep you from building another gate? If there is a way to travel back and forth between Pittsburgh and Earth, the treaty stays intact."

She hadn't considered that as the reason why the Stone Clan wanted her eliminated. "Nothing I could build would transport the entire city."

"At this point, I'd take a trapdoor back to Earth."

Tinker laughed. "And I'm not sure I can really build a gate that works right. Look at the mess I made with this one."

The searchlight flared on, bathing the Discontinuity with brilliance.

"Is it getting bigger?" Durrack asked.

Tinker nodded. "And oni are coming through it."

"Yeah, I saw the kappa you pulled out. The oni are sick puppies to warp their people into monsters like that. You know, the more I find out about the oni, the more I think the elves are right in wiping them out. The problem is collateral damage."

"I don't think the tengu are all that bad." Tinker whispered what she hadn't had the courage to say to Windwolf.

"The tengu aren't oni," Durrack said. "They were mountain tribes of humans living on Onihida, descendants of people that ended up there by mistake. The story goes that half of them were killed on a battlefield trying to resist the oni, and the greater bloods that defeated them merged the survivors with the carrion crows that had been feeding on their fathers and brothers. Twisted little tale, isn't it?"

"But it is true?"

"Their DNA supports the claim."

The searchlight finished its cycle and dropped them into silent darkness.

If the story was true, then the tengu had been screwed from the very start, the moment their ancestors lost their way and fell from Earth.

"I'm going to do everything I can to protect the humans of Pittsburgh," Tinker said. "But I don't know what I can do for the tengu."

"From what I've seen, there's not much anyone can do for the tengu."

"How long are we going to do this?" Durrack asked an hour later, when darkness fell over them yet again.

"Until the lightbulbs burn out, my husband loses his patience, I figure out something better—or they answer us."

"Want to bet which happens first?"

"My bet is that they answer us, or the bulbs burn out. The lifespan of these bulbs are rated at a thousand hours, but there's no telling how many hours they have left."

"And there are no replacement bulbs?" Durrack guessed.

"Nope, not unless Earth can sling them through the Ghostlands."

"Are we going to be able to tell if they're answering us?"

"I have a collection of detecting devices aimed at the valley to catch heat, light, sound, and motion."

"Where are you aiming the spotlights?"

"At the buildings. I'm not sure if the air over the valley is part of the Discontinuity, so I'm not positive if light passing through it will be visible in another dimension. The buildings though, will either reflect the light or absorb it, which in theory makes them visible on all dimensions—but I could be wrong."

"This just seems so basic. If it could work, then Earth should have—"

Blue slashed upward, out of the darkness, pulsing in the rhythm of Morse code.

"They're responding!" Tinker scrambled to kill her transmission program. Her detectors were already translating the flashes.

Calling S1, this is S2, listening.

"It's Earth!" she said.

"You don't know that. Here." Durrack nudged her away from the keyboard. "This is where I come in—remember?"

The searchlights flashed quickly through code and then went dark.

"What are you saying?" Tinker asked.

"I'm requesting verification. It might take them a while to dig someone up who can answer . . . or they might have someone standing by. Fort Meade isn't that far from the Pittsburgh border."

The valley went dark and then a reply blazed back.

"Someone standing by?" Tinker asked.

"No, they want to know if Pittsburgh is safe on Elfhome."

"Depends on your definition of safe."

Durrack laughed and typed. "I'm repeating my request. Never give info unless you're sure of who is listening."

"Most likely the oni on Onihida can see this."

"Exactly."

Wolf returned to his *domi* to find her looking unhappy.

"What is it?"

"We've verified we're talking to Earth. The gate is gone, just like we thought. Pittsburgh is stranded."

"You are still communicating?"

"We're comparing notes—seeing if we can use the Ghostlands to our advantage, or close it up somehow. From the sounds of it, though, Earth is still fighting over who has jurisdiction."

A runner from Poppymeadow's threaded his way through the *sekasha* to hold out a piece of paper. "A distant voice came from Aum Renau, relayed from court."

Wolf took the folded paper, opened it, and read the five English words within: *Follow the yellow brick road.* He frowned at the message and flipped the paper over, hoping for more. No. That was it.

"What does it say?" Tinker asked.

He handed it to her. "It's from Pure Radiance. I sent word to the *intanyei seyosa* caste asking for help with your dreams. I don't understand this."

"Follow the yellow brick road? Follow the yellow brick road? Just point the sucker out and I will. So far, I haven't found any road—bricked yellow or otherwise—figuratively, literally, allegorically."

"You understand her message?"

"No!" She sighed deeply. "But it looks like I have to figure it out."

19: SNAKES, SNAILS, AND PUPPY-DOG TAILS

Tinker kicked the blackened remains of the willow tree. It had died on the waterfront, leaving a burnt trail from the warehouse. Several buildings along its path had scorch marks where the burning tree had brushed up against them while staggering toward the river.

"Okay, let's take it from the top. We're off to see the wizard, the wonderful wizard of Oz."

"Because?" Pony asked.

"Because—because—because—because." Tinker didn't know. Did she ever know?

"Because of the wonderful things he does," Stormsong deadpanned.

Tinker glared at her. "In the dream, the yellow brick road led to the willow trees." She gave the tree another kick. "Which threw apples at us. Esme told me to follow the fruit to find the wizard—which is the dragon."

She followed the black path of soot and cinders back toward the warehouse. "Lain gave me one of the seeds, but I couldn't figure out anything interesting with it. Most of the times it doesn't even wriggle. So obviously fruit is something else. Whatever it is, it will lead us to the dragon. The dragon is the desired end product—not the fruit."

"I am not sure it would be wise to face the dragon again," Pony said. "We barely survived the last fight."

"I know, I know, I know. Riki did say that it needs magic to become sentient, and once it used me to tap the spell stones, it—" She paused. "Wait. Riki said that the oni messed with the spell to trap the dragon. What if the 'fruit' is just magic?"

"In the movie," Stormsong said. "The apples were gathered up by Dorothy, the Scarecrow, and the Tin Man."

"No, the Tin Man came in during the apple scene, Dorothy was picking—" Tinker stopped with sudden realization. "Oh, gods, Oilcan! He was hauling the overflow cans away—when was the last time anyone saw him?"

"The day we watched the movie," Pony said. "Wednesday."

Neither Oilcan nor the flatbed had been at the junkyard on Friday. He had left two days of newspapers in the drive. Feeling sick, she fumbled with her phone, picking his number from her address book. His phone rang three times and dropped to voice mail. Trying not to panic, she called the scrap yard and then his apartment, getting only voice mail. Where had he taken the barrels? Had he said? No, just that he had to dump them. Where could he have taken them? They had gone through nearly a hundred barrels before she got the spell repaired—a massive pool of magic to dump haphazardly, but Pittsburgh had lots of big empty places. Still, the barrels and the steel filings represented a good bit of money once the magic leached out—so he would probably leave them on land that they owned. That left one place—the barn.

She dialed the land line to the barn. She expected his machine to pick up after three rings, but it continued ringing. She clung to the phone, whispering, "Oh, please answer."

On the twelfth ring, the phone clattered off the hook, and Oilcan said breathlessly, "Yeah?"

"Oh, thank gods, are you all right?"

"I'm fine. What's wrong?"

She laughed, not even sure where to start on that question. "Did you take the barrels from Reinholds to the barn?"

"Yeah, they're here."

"Look, I think you're in a lot of danger. I want you to leave the barn."

"What's going on, Tink?"

"It's all rather complicated. I think my dreams are telling me to trap the dragon and do something with it."

"Trap it?"

"Yeah, the barrels are the fruit." That sounded sane! "Look, you're in danger there. Just go home and let me deal with it."

There was only silence from Oilcan.

"Are you okay?" Tinker asked again.

"I'm kind of in the middle of something. You know—I don't want to mess with the flow. Why don't you come out and we'll talk about what has gone down since Wednesday?"

Wednesday. Nathan died Wednesday. Did Oilcan know? If he didn't, she didn't want to tell him over the phone—not that she really wanted to tell him face to face, either.

"Okay, I'll see you in a couple of minutes."

Oilcan used a barn deep in the South Hills as a retreat. Just as she tinkered on machines, he played with art. It was a side of him that few people saw, as he seemed to think it revealed too much of his soul. Sometimes he welded bits and pieces taken from the scrap yard into mechanical ogres, other times he painted dark and abstract murals. Those he kept at his retreat and only friends got to see. She knew he kept journals with poetry that he never showed anyone, not even her. The only form of his art that he shared was music he composed, a fusion of traditional elfin music with snarling, angry human rock, which he didn't perform but sold to local bands under the penname of Orphan.

Art wasn't something that Tinker had patience for. She liked computer logic of true or false, knowing if something worked or didn't with a flip of a switch or a turn of a key. She could help Oilcan animate his ogres, but she could never see why the sculpture had to take a certain form, or move in a certain way, or make a certain sound.

She couldn't perceive what made one piece "right" despite how many times Oilcan tried to explain it.

It was midmorning when they drove up the driveway lined with wild lilac bushes. The flatbed was parked in the apple orchard, its bed littered with fallen apples. Across the road, the magic gleamed purple in the shadows of the tractor shed, stuffed full with the barrels.

Tinker had debated bringing two Hands with her. She wanted a small army between her and the dragon, but in the end, she decided that if Oilcan was fine, then most likely she was wrong about the barrels. Certainly, it was a stretch in logic to get from the black willow to the barn.

"Not that there's any real logic involved in this," she complained as she parked the Rolls away from both apples and magic. It had been easier to drive than constantly interrupt her thoughts to give directions. "It would be simpler to believe that the oni drove me stark raving mad than all this dream hocus pocus."

"You are not mad." Pony got out, taking point.

"My mother would have not directed us to 'follow the yellow brick road' if you were only mad." Stormsong kept close to Tinker as they headed for the large barn doors.

Denial, the most misshapen of Oilcan's animated ogres, lurched out of the lilacs. It moaned out its low recording of "nooo, nooo, nooo," as it wrung its crooked arms around its deformed head. Instantly her guard had all weapons out and leveled at the mechanical sculpture.

"Whoa, whoa, whoa!" Tinker cried. "Don't shoot it!"

"What is it, *domi*?" Pony kept his machine gun trained on it.

"It's a sculpture," she said.

Denial folded back down, stretching out a third hand to grasp in their direction. The guards backed up, unnerved by the thing as its recording changed to a wordless keening.

"It does not look like art to me." Pony reluctantly slung his gun onto his back and motioned to the others to stand down.

"Well," Tinker admitted, "sometimes it doesn't seem that much like art to me, either, but that's what it is."

She pointed out the motion sensor by the door; Pony had

tripped it as he moved ahead of her. "That activates it, though, that's new. I wonder . . ."

The big door rolled open, and Oilcan called, "Hey!" in greeting.

"Hey," she said back. "What's with Denial?"

"Just using him as a doorbell." He eyed the guards with their hands still riding their weapons. "Can—can we leave them here? I don't want them shooting anything by mistake."

Considering what else he had in the way of art, Tinker didn't blame him. She held up a hand to her *sekasha*. "Stay."

The *sekasha* peered into the barn. The back door was rolled the full way open, flooding the cluttered floor with light. They didn't look happy, but stayed put outside while Oilcan rolled the door shut.

"You really have to leave." Tinker followed him through the clutter. From the looks of it, he'd been camping out here for the last few days. "This might be a total long shot, but it's really dangerous here if I'm right. What did you do to your answering machine?"

Oilcan glanced down at the dissembled unit, the parts carefully arrayed on a blank canvas like a piece of art. "Ah, it got taken apart. What are you going to do with the dragon?"

She groaned as she hadn't considered that far ahead. "Gods if I know! He's the wizard of Oz."

"And that means?"

"Riki—Riki wove this whole theory that sounded so right about the dragon being the wizard, but it just hit me—Riki lied and lied about so much. Yeah, so his reasons were good, but he has this history of twisting things to suit his goals."

Thinking of Riki, she pulled the player out of her pocket. "Here. Riki says he's sorry."

As Oilcan stood looking at the player, the oni dragon snaked out of the shadows to stop beside Oilcan. Its eyes gleamed in the dimness, its mane flowing like a bundle of snakes.

"*Yanananam mmmooooootaaaa summbaaaa radadada,*" the dragon said with a deep breathy voice, the words rumbling against her skin like the purr of a big engine. "*Aaaaah huuu ha.*"

"Oh shit!" Tinker jerked back, fumbling for the pistol on her hip.

"It's okay!" Oilcan held up his hands to ward off her action.

"He won't hurt you. He's friendly."

"Friendly?"

"Yeah, see?" Oilcan patted the huge head butting up against him. "He scared the shit out of me. But he talked, and, well, I lis- tened."

She backed up regardless, wanting distance between her and it. "You can understand it?"

"Actually—no."

"*Mmmananan pooooo kaaa.*"

It was weird to watch such a huge thing speaking, but there was no mistaking the rumble of syllables and consonants for anything but language.

"So you have no idea what's it's saying."

"No." Oilcan shrugged with a sheepish grin. "Sorry. But come here, look at this."

After the surprise of the dragon, Tinker wasn't sure she want- ed to see what else he had to show her. Oilcan walked down the stone steps to what used to be the milking stalls. The dragon glanced back and forth between her and Oilcan. Apparently realizing that they were all to follow Oilcan, it finally bounded after him. Despite its short legs, and ferretlike humping run, its gait remained fluid.

"We've been working at communicating," Oilcan was saying. "We finally resorted to drawing. It's been—educational."

In the back was a little dragon nest complete with rumpled blankets, a barrel of drinking water, and a large dog dish of well- chewed bones. Drawings covered the walls. She recognized Oilcan's hand in the ones done in chalk. Scratched into the wall, the dragon's pictures were fluid and elegant and incomprehensible.

"Educational? Really?" she asked after several minutes of try- ing to understand the alien pictograms.

"It's just so different how he sees the world. Here—" He point- ed out his map of Pittsburgh, with the two rivers converging to make the Ohio River, and the many skyscrapers and bridges. "After I drew this, he made this."

Less stylistic than the other dragon drawings, it was a series of wavering lines, some lightly etched and others deeply gouged. She studied it for a moment, keenly aware of the huge monster shifting beside them. It seemed completely random, but she trusted Oilcan's intelligence. If he said this meant something, it did. If the dragon recognized Oilcan's Pittsburgh—was this how he saw the city? It was the deep pit on the north side, roughly at the location of Reinholds that triggered the recognition. "He's drawn the ley lines."

"Yes. I think it was the magic in the barrels that drew him here." Oilcan pointed out a blank area of the wall. "And look at this."

"At wh—?"

The dragon nosed her aside—jolting her heart into a fierce pounding—and raised a long, sharp claw to the wall. In a nerve-grating rasp, it lightly sketched a dot at the center of Turtle Creek and radial lines outward, carefully linking the radials up to existing ley lines. The dragon glanced up at her, making sure she was watching, and then flattened its great paw and smudged away the dot and lines, creating the same blank space.

"There's no magic," she whispered.

"Tooloo has always said the dragons can't exist without magic." Oilcan absently scratched the dragon's jaw, getting a deep purrlike rumble from it.

"So as long as we keep him saturated in magic, he's safe."

"Yeah."

Tinker thought of the barrels stacked in the tractor shed. They represented a huge pool of magic, but a leaky one, draining away. "He can't stay here, then. I have no idea how long the magic will last from the barrels, but it's an artificial environment. Sooner or later, it's going to be drained."

"Yeah, I know."

"Oilcan! This isn't some stray dog. Look what I found, Grandpa, can I keep it? It didn't work with the warg puppy."

"This isn't a warg, this is an intelligent being that can talk, and create art, and communicate. Look!" He pointed out a set of small pictures. "It has a written language!"

"How do you know? That could be—be—anything!"

He gave her an annoyed look. "Did it or did it not just communicate something meaningful to you?"

She sighed. "Yes."

The *sekasha* weregoing to just love this.

"What?" Stormsong asked for about the third time in a row when Tinker updated the *sekasha* on the current plan.

"We need to move the dragon to the scrap yard. It's got a strong ley line running through it, so the dragon will stay sentient there. But the flatbed is a double clutch manual transmission, so if none of you can drive manual, then I'm going to have to—"

Stormsong caught her by the hand, dragged her to the side of the barn into the old apple orchard.

"Hey, hey, hey, what are you doing?" Tinker cried.

"What am I doing?" Stormsong snatched up an apple and flung it at Tinker. "What am I doing?"

The apple smacked the barn wall, blossoming into a flower of rotten sweetness unnervingly close to Tinker's head.

"What fucking part of that don't you understand?" Tinker shouted at her.

"You—are—too—trusting!" Stormsong flung apples to emphasize her words—one apple per word. They whizzed past Tinker so closely she felt their passage. "And—too—slow—at—putting—up—your—shields."

There was now a halo of spattered fruit outlining Tinker.

"I get the point! I get the point!" Tinker called up her shield. "See, shield! Happy?"

"Happy?" Stormsong snorted, picked an apple from the tree instead of the ground, and polished it against her black jeans until it gleamed with promise. "Here!" She tossed the apple in a lazy arc toward Tinker.

Tinker moved her hands to catch the apple and her shield vanished.

"You're—too—trusting!"

The first apple hit Tinker in the shoulder in a painful splatter. The second and third were intercepted midair by other apples so that they exploded in front of her, spraying her with apple bits.

"Stop it." Pony had another apple ready. Part of Tinker was impressed that he could knock apples out of the air—the other part wanted to know where the hell he was for the first volley. "She is the *domi*. She leads us."

"She's going to get herself killed!" Stormsong growled.

"What she says is true," Pony said. "The dragon cannot stay here. The truck is the only vehicle that will carry it. She and Oilcan are the only ones who know how to drive it—and he will be focused on keeping the creature calm. The fewer people we involve in moving the beast, the less likely the oni will learn that we have it."

"How can you support this plan?"

"The *domana's* self-centered creativity is why we chose to obey them. We need their drive. Trust her, she will make it work."

"Or die trying," Stormsong muttered. "This is insanity."

"Is it? We have the Scarecrow." Pony pointed at Tinker and then tapped his chest. "The Lion. The Tin Man." He pointed at Oilcan's metal sculpture. "And the apple trees." He held up the apple in his hand. "And the apples being thrown at the Scarecrow."

Stormsong's eyes went wide.

"There, see!" Tinker cried. "It's crazy with a purpose."

"And that is supposed to make me feel better?" Stormsong snarled. "What are you going to do with the dragon now that you've found him?"

Tinker held up her finger, indicating they were to wait, and pulled out her datapad. "Give me a few minutes. I've been keeping notes on the dreams. Offhand, I don't remember anything. Wait— how about this—Esme said, 'He knows the paths, the twisted way, the garden path. You have to talk to him. He'll tell you the way.'"

"The way? To where?"

"Obviously where I need to go."

It was like having a *very* large, hyperactive five-year-old in her workshop. The dragon flowed in and out of the various rooms of the trailer, carrying on a running commentary in its rumbling voice, as it examined everything with its massive but manipulative paws. After rescuing her scanner, their radio base, and antique CD player, Tinker realized what had happened to Oilcan's answering machine and started to fear.

"Okay, okay, I think first thing in communicating would be—to—get a record of what it's saying." She snatched her camera from the dragon before he could disassemble it. She flipped out her tripod, snapped the camera to it, and caught Cloudwalker by the hand and dragged him to the camera. "Here, keep the dragon—the dragon's image—in this little window." Great, she was actually dealing with two groups of technology-challenged people. "And we'll build a dictionary of his words."

"I was trying to do that." Oilcan distracted the dragon from her computer systems with a flashlight. "But usually it's hard to tell where one word starts and another ends."

". . . *mmmenananannaaaaaaapoooookaaaammmamma-mamyyyyyyaaanananammmmoooo* . . ." The dragon rumbled while clicking the flashlight on and off, and then disassembled it and sniffed at the batteries.

"Yeah, I can hear that." Tinker had microphones planted in the offices so she could trigger her computers without a headset. "Sparks, are you active?"

"Yes, boss," her office AI answered.

"Filter audio pickup into separate voiceprints and put it up on the workshop screen."

"Okay, boss."

As she had hoped, Impatience's ramblings easily divided out. "Sparks, record this track." She tapped the bass rumbles of the dragon's voice. "Convert to phonetics and indicate all pauses and breaks."

Impatience stuffed the batteries back into the casing, screwed on the lid, and tried the switch. When the flashlight didn't light, the dragon took it back apart and eyed the pieces carefully. Apparently it had spotted the "this way up" diagram stamped on the plastic as it eyed the batteries closely, repacked them into the casing and turned it on. This time it was rewarded with a beam of light. "*Huuhuuhuuhuuhuuhuuhuuhuuhuuhuu.*"

One word down.

"Okay." Tinker pulled up the recordings she had made of Turtle Creek and directed them to her largest monitor. "Since I don't have a clue how I'm supposed to help my mother, let's see what he has to say about my biggest problem: the Ghostlands."

The great Westinghouse Bridge had fallen. The Ghostlands had lapped up against the centermost support column and toppled it. Two of its four great arching spans now lay in ruins on the valley floor, slowly leeching to blue. The remaining two spans would soon follow.

Wolf gazed down at the ruin, trying to not let dismay overtake him. "There's nothing you can do?"

Jewel Tear glared at the valley as if it personally defied her. "Not in time. At the rate it's expanding, it will involve the main river shortly."

She meant the Monongahela River, which flowed past the mouth of the Turtle Creek.

"The creek froze solid," Wolf said. "You don't think the river will freeze?"

"If I understand this correctly, the worlds are mirror images." Jewel pointed out at the river. "Where there is a river here, there is one on Onihida?"

"Yes."

"I can't predict what will happen when the force of the river meets this, but what I fear is that the oni can make use of it. As they are now, the Ghostlands are a deathtrap. The forces are funneling downward, like the pit of an ant lion. The river might allow the oni to pass unchecked through the Ghostlands."

"How soon?"

"Only a few more days." She turned away from the Ghostlands and him. "Something has to be done. They say your *domi* can work miracles. Since this is her fault, it would be good for her to fix her mistake."

Yes, he needed to talk to Tinker. He had faith that once she was given opportunity to study the situation, she would find a solution. He had brought a second Hand just so he could have one of the *sekasha* "babies" along to operate the walkie-talkie.

"Find out where *domi* is," Wolf said to Wraith and turned back to Jewel Tear. "I want Stone Clan to keep their distance from my *domi*. After what happened with the black willow, I do not trust any of you near her."

Jewel Tear looked away, giving a slight huff of indignation, but didn't deny the implication that they meant Tinker harm.

Wraith came back with unease clear on his face. Wolf bowed his leave-taking and headed for his Rolls.

"What is it?" Wolf asked Wraith once they were out of the Stone Clan's hearing.

"*Domi* is at the scrap yard. The dragon is there."

Wolf's heart leapt at the news. "She's fighting the dragon?"

"No. Apparently, she's—talking—to it."

"No, I'm not talking to it," Tinker said with much disgust in her voice. She smelled of apples, butter, and sugar, and her face had mysterious streaks of color paste on it—but otherwise she looked unharmed. "It's giving me math lessons—and I think my head is going to explode."

"Math lessons?" There were times he wondered if his English wasn't as strong as he thought it was.

His *domi's* workshop was normally ordered chaos, but it now looked like a storm front had passed through it. The digital wall boards were covered with elaborate designs and fluid pictures. Printouts were tacked to bare walls, extending the boards to each side and up onto the ceiling. A television cycled through pictures of the Ghostlands. Machines either half built or partially disassembled covered all the table surfaces and the floor was littered with magazines, engine parts, and chewed tires.

The only sign of the dragon itself was its long tail sticking out from behind the worktable, thumping against the floor with a force that shook the entire trailer.

"I think it's math." Tinker tugged at her hair as if she wanted to tear it out. "Whoever said math is the universal language should be hunted down and shot. Or maybe they thought that sentient creatures wouldn't have the attention span of a gnat."

"So you're safe with it?"

Tinker glanced toward Stormsong instead of the dragon for some reason. "I—don't know. It seems playful as a puppy, but it has sharp teeth—lots of them—in a big mouth."

Wolf shifted sideways until he could see around the table.

Tinker's *nagarou*, Oilcan, and the dragon stared at a television screen while they manipulated something in their hands. On the television screen, a small human female in a skimpy red dress fought a tall muscle-bound creature with energetic kicks and punches. The fight ended abruptly with the words "Winner" flashing on the screen and the female bouncing around cheerfully. Oilcan groaned and slumped to one side.

"He—he learns fast." Tinker shook her head. "I've never met anyone that intimidated me with their intellect before—but I always thought that the person that did would be more—"

"Human?"

Tinker waved her hand, as if trying to sift out a better word, and then nodded. "I suppose that would work. The language is a huge barrier to understanding what's he's trying to explain to me."

"Have you learned anything useful?"

"This was educational." Tinker caught Wolf's arm and pulled him to the kitchen. On the counter was an odd sculpture. A rainbow of creamy paste whirled upward like a tornado with paper plates dividing the various colors. It was supported by a silvery aluminum plate, which had been balanced on a base of soda cans.

The paste was the source of the color streaks on Tinker's face, and the smell of butter and sugar. Wolf smeared some off her face. "And this is . . . ?"

"Frosting. Long story. Doesn't matter anymore. This—" Tinker pointed to the structure. "I think this is a model of the Ghostlands. Look, he's sculpted the frosting into a Roy G. Biv spectrum and at each color shift there's a universe marker—the paper plates. Well—at least I think that's what they are."

Tinker took out a camera from her dress pocket, and flipped up the screen. "I filmed it all." She played a minute of the dragon building the sculpture, rumbling in a low steady tone. "What we need is someone that speaks dragon. But, until then—" She folded the camera back up and stuffed it into her dress pocket. "This is what I think it's trying to tell me. Look, can you see down into the middle of this? He made a big production of dropping a lug nut down into there, and did a lot of pointing and talking. He took it out and dropped it a couple of times. And then the math started. I think—he's trying—maybe—to say that my gate is still active."

"Can you stop the Ghostlands from expanding?"

"If I can figure out a way to remove my gate, yes, I think it might close the Ghostlands completely. What I think is happening is this." She dragged him to the whiteboard.

Tinker swept her hand across dragon writing and the English words "save: yes no" appeared. She touched the "yes" and the board went white. Drawing a straight horizonal line, she turned to him. "This is Turtle Creek before the chaos started. According to Stormsong, when you originally surveyed this area a hundred years ago, there was a *fiutana* here." She added a large purple oval under the line. "Now, Lord Tomtom talked about protective spells that the oni had cloaking their compound, so I think this is why the oni were based here—which also might indicate where their other camps are and why you can't find them."

Yes, that would explain much. "If the other springs in the area are cloaked, then we know that the oni are using them. Look for what is missing instead of what is there."

"Huh? Oh, yes, that would work. Now, my gate was here." She drew in a black circle above the line, and then added a second black circle at the bottom of the board. "And that's the gate in orbit. I set up a resonance between then." The resonance was represented by a wavy line connecting the two black circles that ran through the heart of the purple oval. "I think what Impatience is telling me is that along this line, a discontinuity emerged, which immediately affected the land under my gate."

She turned and typed on a keyboard. The television, which had been cycling pictures of Turtle Creek, stopped on a blur of blue. "This is thermal readings of the Discontinuity. It's hard to see, but this area here—" She tapped a circle at the heart of the screen. "That's the same size and shape as my gate, lying on its side."

Tinker turned back to the whiteboard, and drew a series of black circles stacked inside the pool of purple. "See, as it sinks, the area affected by the gate would expand." She stepped back from the board, gazing at it. "I'm not a hundred percent sure this is an accurate model, but it explains why the effect is growing."

"Even though the gate in orbit was destroyed?"

"Each gate was designed to operate independently."

"So if we remove the gate, the Discontinuity will heal?"

Tinker sighed. "I don't know. If I'm right, and we can get the gate out, it will at least stop the Ghostlands from growing."

Wolf considered what Jewel Tear claimed about the current forces working in the valley. "That would be good enough for now. We need to do something quickly."

"Well, I'm not getting anything done here." She picked up various items and slipped them into her pocket. "I can get to work on the retrieval now."

20: FOLLOW THE YELLOW BRICK ROAD

Stone Clan chose to wait until the next morning to protest Wind Clan's actions. Wolf wasn't sure why they had delayed, so he stood and listened to Earth Son rant on about protocol and etiquette.

"Wind Clan is insulting us at every step. Look." Earth Son pointed up the tall ironwood scaffolding to where Tinker stood, overseeing the installation of her scrap yard crane. Little Horse was up in the scaffolding with her, but the rest of her Hand were keeping to the ground. "Wind Clan's *domi* hasn't come down to hear our complaints."

Wolf made a show of glancing around. "We did not know this was to be a formal *aumani*. I see the rock, but where is the incense and the flame?"

Wolf surprised True Flame into a smile, but the prince caught himself and gave him a hard look.

"Do we need to call an *aumani?*" True Flame's look warned him not to make light of it.

Wolf spread his hands to show that he didn't know. "Jewel Tear came to me and stated that the Stone Clan could not solve this problem before—"

"It was not her place to make that decision!" Earth Son

snapped. "I will say when the Stone Clan can or cannot do something."

Wolf glanced at Jewel Tear but she had her court mask on, letting none of her emotions show. There was no way to judge if this was an honest miscommunication within the Stone Clan, or a contrived situation. If it was the latter, then politically it had been a mistake to act.

Wolf would have to salvage the situation by forcing True Flame to disregard political protocol for the sake of military imperative. "If the information she gave us was accurate, then what is important is that the oni are prevented from using the Ghostlands—"

"Are you saying that I'm lying?" Earth Son seemed eager for Wolf to slander him.

Wolf considered Earth Son for a minute. Was he that blind to the dangers that they were facing? "I'm saying that there are tens of thousands of oni and an oni dragon on the other side of the Ghostlands, and it would be good to keep them there."

Earth Son waved that concern aside. "Your untrained *domi* and her Hand survived the first dragon."

"Do not mistake that creature for a true oni dragon." True Flame had studied Impatience at Tinker's workshop. The prince pointed out that not only was the "dragon" much smaller than the creatures he had fought; it also had one more digit per foot.

Tinker theorized that since the spell painted onto Impatience's scales had been washed or rubbed away, the dragon might be free from the oni's control. Regardless, they still didn't know how to cage or effectively fight the beast. All options weighed, it was decided to leave the creature in Oilcan's care as an ally instead of treating it as a foe. According to the tengu, however, and confirmed by some mysterious means by the NSA agents, there was a second, larger dragon by the name of Malice still on Onihida. Plans to update the Stone Clan on the dragons, however, had been waylaid by Earth Son's attack on Tinker's operation.

Wolf pushed the conversation back to the military implications. "Jewel Tear stated that if the Ghostlands expand to the river, there will be a shift in forces that will allow the oni to push their army through."

Jewel Tear's mask slipped and she gave him a look of pure hatred.

Earth Son scoffed. "They'll be pinned between the river and the Ghostlands. With five *domana*, seventy *sekasha*, the dreadnaught, and the royal troops, we can easily deal with the oni as they emerge . . ."

True Flame lost his patience. "If the oni send a dragon across first, we will be too engaged with it to block the oni. We will do whatever it takes to close the Ghostlands before anything more can come through."

Earth Son recognized that he was treading on an edge with the prince and retreated with, "I am not saying we ignore the Ghostlands. I am saying that this is a Stone Clan specialty—"

"Are you being hampered by the Wind Clan *domi*?" True Flame snapped. "She will not be using magic, since, as you pointed out, she is untrained."

Earth Son smoothed his face to court mask to consider his options. Finally he said, "No, we will not be hampered."

True Flame nodded and turned to Wolf. "Have you found the maps?"

"Yes. There are four possible sites not counting the *fiutana* that was located here and the one at the icehouse."

"What maps?" Earth Son growled.

"My *domi* believes that the oni are camping on *fiutana*. I had my people pull up the original survey maps for this area, showing the *fiutana*."

"Have you scryed out any *fiutana*?" True Flame asked Earth Son.

"No."

They waited for Earth Son to elaborate, but he didn't.

Behind them were shouts and the crack of splintering wood.

Wolf turned to see a massive oni dragon surge up out of the Ghostlands. It shouldered aside the scaffolding, shattering it to pieces. Tinker and Little Horse were falling from their high perch. Little Horse had been near the ladder and was falling with the tumble of heavy timbers. Tinker, though, had been far out at the end of the boom, over the liquid blue.

"No!" Wolf shouted as a call on the Wind Clan spell stones thrummed across his senses.

Tinker hit the ground, sending up a spray of blue, and then sank down into the ground. Ripples spread out from where she disappeared. And then all sense of her vanished. The Ghostland went smooth and her call on the stones broke off abruptly.

"Wolf!" Stormsong struggled with Little Horse, who had fallen to the "shore" of the Ghostlands and was now trying to fling himself into the blue. "Stop him! He'll only die! She's gone already."

Wolf gasped, feeling her words stab through him. No, Tinker couldn't be gone.

The dragon scrambled out of the blue, clawing up the shore with feet as large as the Rolls Royce. It shook dirt from its massive head, growling low and loud as thunder. Its seemingly endless body heaved up out of the chaos.

"Wolf!" Stormsong had Little Horse pinned, but it left her vulnerable to the dragon now turning its attention to the small figures at its feet.

Wolf called the wind. The dragon's head whipped toward him as if it sensed the magic gathering around Wolf. He aimed a force strike on the dragon and flung the spell at the beast. As the magic arrowed at the dragon, it crouched low and its mane lifted. A shield effect shimmered into existence. The force strike slammed into the shield and was swallowed up.

Jewel Tear flung up a force wall between the dragon and the elves, curving it to include Stormsong and Little Horse. A fire strike from True Flame hit the dragon's shield; the blaze curled harmless around it.

The dragon sprang away, landing among the rubble of the fallen bridge.

Wolf started to summon lightning when it leaped again, landing this time on the far section of the bridge still standing, high above the valley. A third leap took it out of sight.

Since the call-lightning spell took both hands, he couldn't cast a scrying spell.

Beside him, Jewel Tear cast a ground scry. "It took flight. I can't track it through the air."

True Flame cast his more inclusive, weaker scry of flame. "It's out of your range already, Wolf."

Wolf locked his jaw against a growl of impatience, forcing himself to remain silent as he canceled the lightning call. The spell was too dangerous to leave in a potential state. The power neutralized, he started to call the winds to fly after the dragon.

True Flame caught Wolf's wrist, stilling his hand. "No, I will not allow you to fight it alone. It's too dangerous."

"It killed my *domi!*" Wolf snarled.

"No." Stormsong dragged Little Horse up to Wolf, as if she was afraid to let the young *sekasha* go. "*Domi's* on the yellow brick road." Stormsong's eyes were soft and dreamy. "She's talked to the wizard. She's gone now to steal the flying broomstick from the witch and the flying monkeys."

Tinker fell into the cold blue air. She shouted the trigger to her shields seconds before plunging into the dark blue mass of out-of-phase ground. The blue deepened to midnight black, and then all sensation fell away, as if she had no longer had a body. Was she dead? She had felt the shields form around her in a flood of magic, and the deepening cold of the Ghostlands, but now she sensed nothing.

Suddenly, something hit her from her left. Startled, she lost her shields, and she smacked into a flat, hard surface and then slid *down* it, to land hard on something perpendicular to whatever she had struck. Pain shot up from her left leg. She lay panting in darkness. The air was hot, dry, and tainted with smoke. Nearby, water gurgled through unseen pipes. A distant hammering was muffled as if carried through a thick wall.

What had she hit first? Sliding her hand along the smooth floor, she found a right angle that rose up in a wall of steel. But how did she hit a wall sideways when she'd been falling down?

And where was she now?

She sat up and pain jolted up her leg again. Wincing, she felt down to her ankle and discovered that she was bleeding. "Shit." And then she remembered—she hadn't been alone on the scaffolding. She searched the area around her with blind hands. "Pony! Oh, gods, Pony!"

There was a loud, metal clank and then the squeal of hinges as a door opened somewhere out in the darkness. Someone was coming. It dawned on her that that might not be a good thing; the Ghostlands had been the oni compound. She groped at her side and found her pistol.

A flashlight flicked on some fifty feet away, its light a solid beam in smoky air. As it swept the room, her eyes adjusted, and she made out the figure of a being standing in the open doorway. The shock of hair, the sharp beak of a nose, and the tall lean body suggested a tengu.

She covered her mouth and nose to muffle her breathing.

The tengu moved toward her, shining his flashlight onto pieces of equipment on either side of the room—large tanks, pipes, pumps, and pieces of computer monitoring stations.

Go away, go away, go away, she thought hard at him.

The tengu paused at one of the monitoring stations, checking the gauges there, and then moved to the second one. Grunting at what he found, he turned and ran his light high along the back wall. The beam swept over her head, moved on, stopped, and returned to a point a few feet above her.

Gripping her pistol tight, she glanced up to see what caught the tengu's attention. A smear of fresh blood led down to her.

Don't look. Just move on. There's nothing here to see.

Inexorable, the light slid downward to shine on her.

Squinting against the brilliance, she pointed her pistol at the tengu. "That's far enough."

"Well, well." The tengu spoke English with a heavy accent, the flashlight obscuring his features. "You're what's down here making so much noise."

"Where is Pony? What have you done to him?"

Confusion filled the tengu's voice. "We don't have any ponies here."

"Where am I?"

"You don't know?"

"Answer me, damn it!"

"Water storage."

That explained the tanks, pipes, and liquid sounds. "Okay,

you're going to walk me out of here."

"Walk?" He closed the distance between and crouched down in front of her, twisting the flashlight's base so it became a lantern, bathing them both in soft light. He was an older version of Riki, from the electric blue eyes under thick unruly black hair to the birdlike cock of his head. "Walk where?"

She tried to hold the gun steady but reaction from her fall was setting in, making her tremble. "Out of this place."

"You—you want to go outside?"

"Yes."

"Where exactly do you think we are?" He seemed more puzzled than alarmed, ignoring her gun to search her eyes.

"Water storage."

"Which is . . . where?"

"What is so hard to understand about this? I've got a gun and I'm willing use it. You either get me out, or I'll shoot you."

"Okay, okay, my English, it's good but not perfect. I don't understand what you want, princess."

"Oh, please, don't call me that; technically I am not a princess."

"Oookay." He acted like this was a hard concept to wrap his brain around. "What should I call you?"

"Tinker. Of the Wind Clan."

"I'm Jin Wong."

Tinker knew she had heard the name before, but she couldn't place it. "Jin, I want to go home, and you're going to take me."

He sighed and shook his head. "I'm sorry, Tinker, but you're going to need to give me the gun before I can take you anywhere."

"Like hell."

"You're hurt."

"I'm fine." And she scrambled to her feet to prove it. When she tried to put weight on her left foot, though, pain jolted up her ankle.

Jin had stood with her—as to be expected, he was at least a foot taller than she was. He wore a dark polo shirt with his name embroidered over his heart, dark nylon pants, and white socks, all stained with soot, oil, and blood. He stepped to her as she sagged back against the wall, hissing against the sudden agony.

"Don't touch me." She stopped him by raising the pistol.

"I'm not going to hurt you."

"Are all you tengu liars at birth?"

"No," he said after a moment of surprised silence. "Our mothers give us lying lessons so we can tell when someone is lying."

He looked down at her foot to indicate what he thought she was lying about.

"My ankle is just twisted," Tinker snapped.

"Just to point out the obvious, if you shoot me, you're going to have to crawl out of here." He held out his hand. "And I'm not going to let you out of this room with the gun. So just give me the pistol, and I'll do what you want."

"I give you my gun and you'll turn me over to the oni."

"There are no oni here."

"Liar."

"We lie, but tengu still have honor. I give you my word—you won't be harmed."

They stood there at an impasse, half in shadows, the gun growing heavy in her hand. She had fought to the death before, but she'd never shot someone in cold blood. She wasn't sure she could actually do it and live with herself afterward—certainly not after exchanging names and carrying on a civil conversation.

"I'm so screwed." Sighing, she unloaded the pistol, pocketed the clip, checked the chamber, and handed him the empty gun.

"I'll take care of you." He tucked the pistol between two pipes near the ceiling, way out of her reach. "I promise."

"Bleah." She wished she could believe him. Had Riki broken his word? Or had he actually never given her any promises, knowing full well that he couldn't keep them? She couldn't remember.

Jin produced sterile bandages out of his pocket and dealt with the shallow, bleeding cut on her ankle. He slipped an arm around her, then helped her up. As he supported her, they headed toward the door.

The room was a maze of tanks and pipes, gurgling ominously. At the end of the room, they stepped through a low steel door, reminiscent of old submarine movies, and into another low-ceilinged room of mystery machines. What the hell did the oni have buried under Pittsburgh? She seethed with anger that Riki hadn't warned her about this.

"What the hell is this place, anyway?" she asked.

"This is life support."

She scoffed at that. Life support made it sound like a damn spaceship.

At the far end of the room, she could see there was a narrow, tall window. It gave her pause. Who put a window in an underground area? She forced Jin to detour through the equipment to look out it. At first she only saw night sky, above and below them, which confused her more. When had she fallen? It was midmorning—wasn't it? And how do you fall *into* the ground and end up above it? The stars were more brilliant than she had ever seen them. And they seemed to be moving—which really meant she was.

A planet rose on the horizon, filling it completely.

She'd seen enough photos of Earth from orbit to recognize the luminescent blue swirled with gleaming white clouds. The sight of it punched the air out of her; she stood gasping, like a fish finding itself out of water, trying to get her breath back. The planet rose, filling the window, evidence that the ship she was on was rotating to maintain artificial gravity.

"No—we can't be—this isn't possible. This is a trick. I can't be in space. I was in Pittsburgh. You don't fall in Pittsburgh and land in orbit." She couldn't be in space. Could she? "You don't fall in Pittsburgh and land in orbit," she whispered again. But she hadn't fallen to ground, but into the Discontinuity—who knew what all was tied into that knot of realities? "Oh gods, where am I?"

"Apparently quite lost." Jin tightened his hold on her, as if he expected her to collapse. Considering how weak she suddenly felt, it was probably a good idea.

"Lost! Lost!" cried the crows in her dreams.

She realized where she must be. She had fallen straight to Esme. "You're part of the tengu crew of the *Tianlong Hao*."

"I was the captain."

"Was?"

"This is the *Dahe Hao*." Jin leaned over her shoulder to tap on the window, drawing her attention back outside. "There's the *Tianlong Hao*."

The ship had continued to rotate and a vast debris field of broken ships slid into view. The great long cylindrical ships were shattered to pieces. Parts were folded like soda cans. The space around them hazed and glittering from frozen moisture and oxygen trapped in the same orbit as the ships. The bodies of astronauts tumbled in among the litter.

She covered her mouth to keep in a cry of dismay. Still her shock came out in low whimpers.

"The *Dahe* managed to rescue most of my crew minutes after the accident," Jin said quietly. "We saved crew from the *Zhenghe Hao* and the *Anhe Hao*, but the *Minghe Hao* reentered before we could get to it, along with parts of what we think was the gate."

"Jin!" A female voice called from beyond an open hatch. "Did you find what the hell made the loud bang?"

"Yes!" Jin shouted. "We somehow picked up a visitor."

"What kind of visitor?" the female snapped.

"The gun-waving elfin kind," Jin shouted.

"Have you fucking flipped?" The female voice drew closer. "An elf?"

"Yes, an elf," Jin called.

"Jin." There was something familiar about the female's voice. "There were no elves on any of the crew lists."

Jin cocked his head at Tinker and made a slight noise of discovery. "You did fall from Pittsburgh."

A purple-haired woman appeared at the door and Tinker recognized her. It was Esme. She hadn't changed from when Lain's photo had been taken, with the tiny exception of the bandage on her forehead. On her temple was a pink line of recently healed flesh. Like Jin, she was marked with soot, blood, and exhaustion.

"Well, I'll be fucked." Esme had Lain's voice, only slightly more raspy, as if she had shouted her throat raw. "Well, it's about time you got your scrawny ass up here."

"You had a gun-waving elf princess on order?" Jin asked.

"Not exactly. I had a dream. And you were there." Esme pointed at Jin and then Tinker. "And you."

"I'm starting to understand the appeal of Kansas," Tinker grumbled.

Jin looked at Tinker in surprise. "You forgot your little dog."

"I'm Dorothy," Esme corrected him. "She's the Scarecrow. So, how the hell did you get here?"

"I fell," Tinker said.

"Down the rabbit hole?" Esme asked.

"More or less," Tinker said.

"Great, you can get us out of this fucking mess," Esme asked.

Tinker could only laugh bitterly. "I'm not even sure *where* I am, let alone how to get out. What planet is that? Elfhome? Onihida?"

Esme glanced at Jin with narrowing eyes. "Onihida?"

"The tengu homeworld," Tinker said. "Or don't *you* know about the tengu?"

"We've covered that little speed bump," Esme said dryly, still looking at Jin. Then she shrugged. "All things considered, finding out that half the crew isn't human is just all part of the weirdness."

"It doesn't matter which planet it is," Jin said. "We've lost all our shuttles in the crash. We can't land. Normally that wouldn't be a problem, the ship is designed to support its crew for decades—but we've got the survivors of four ships onboard."

"I think its Elfhome." Esme turned back to Tinker. "At least, Pittsburgh is down there. Every now and then, we pick up an FM station." Esme named a couple of Pittsburgh radio stations. "It sounds like a fucking war has broken out."

"More or less," Tinker said.

"Oh joy." Esme indicated that they should start in the direction she had come from. "Hopefully you have something other than straw in that head of yours, because I've got a mess for you to fix."

"Aren't you supposed to be the expert?" Tinker let Jin pick her up and carry her. All the little speed bumps, as Esme would put it, had finally gotten the best of her.

"Yes, I am." Esme led them through the next section of the ship. Smoke hazed the air here, and red lights flashed unattended. "But you're the Scarecrow."

"What the hell does that mean?" Tinker asked.

"It means what it means." Esme opened a hatch, stepped through, and closed it after Jin. The light was dim in this section, but the air was clean. The floor was cluttered with crew sleeping. At a glance, at least half of the sleepers were wounded. "All fucking logic went out the window about seven days ago."

Stormsong had said the same thing when her dreaming powers had told her that Impatience was no longer a danger to them. Esme sounded like she was operating on the same skewed logic— she wanted Tinker to fix the mess that the colonists were in because the dreams said she would.

Oh great, yet another group of people expecting me to pull rabbits out of my hat.

For the first time in her life, Tinker felt intimidated by a piece of hardware. She knew that a spaceship was a delicate balance of systems, a spiderweb pretending to be a simple tin can, with the lives of everyone inside dependent on it. "Look, I really don't know a whole lot about spaceships."

"I'll use terms you can understand," Esme said. "My ship is sinking and I can't bail fast enough."

"Okay," Tinker said. "Exactly how does a spaceship 'sink'?"

"The jump did something to my computers." Esme stopped beside a workstation with a monitor showing static. The front panel had already been pulled, and the boards inside gleamed softly with magic. "I'm getting—all sorts of weird errors—and I'm starting to lose systems completely."

"Well, doh." Tinker dug through her pockets until she found a length of wire and her screwdriver set. "Magic is causing your systems to crash."

"Magic?" Esme echoed, looking mystified.

Tinker realized that none of the colonists could see the magic. "That's Elfhome and this universe has magic. Your computer systems aren't shielded for it."

"Oh fuck, it is blindingly obvious, isn't it?" Esme pressed her palm to her forehead, took a deep breath, and let it out. "I should have thought of that when I started to dream true again. Okay. This system controls my engines. Right after the crash, I pulled into what should have been a stable orbit and started up the rotation that allows for the artificial gravity. We're drifting, though. If I don't correct our orbit, we're going to enter the planet's atmosphere—and my ship is not designed to survive re-entry."

"Okay." Tinker took the lantern from Jin and started to strip it for parts. "We need to first siphon off the magic, and then create shielding for the system. Here's what I need . . ."

Tinker had never worked with astronauts before and was amazed how quickly they learned. While Esme had fired the positioning jets to stop the ship's rotation and pulled them back into a stable orbit, Jin drafted a team of people to drain excess magic from the computer equipment. Despite Esme's "you're the Scarecrow" statements, everyone seemed hesitant about Tinker actually working with the ship's systems. After Tinker trained the astronauts, she found herself in a supervisory-only position. She floated in place, stranded by the lack of gravity, with an ice pack strapped to her ankle.

For some reason—whether it was because Tinker had missed the event, or because she was the ultimate outsider as an elf, or because she had magically appeared—the astronauts started to tell her their stories. They had gone through a harrowing experience, filled with confusion, death, lucky chances, small miracles, and a great deal of heroics. At the core of it all was Esme, riding roughshod over rules and logic, ruthless in purpose, making one lucky guess after another. Esme, everyone agreed, forged a miracle, salvaging what should have been complete disaster.

Even Esme opened up to Tinker when they found themselves alone together. "One summer, while I was in college, I went to visit my older sister on Elfhome. Two months on another world— it seemed like an exotic vacation. Then the dreams started—like I had some third eye that had been forced open and I was made to see. Some of what I had to do was so very clear, like changing my master's degree to astrophysics and applying to NASA. Some of it was—blind faith—that it would matter. Somehow."

"I hate to tell you this, but I have no idea how to help you beyond this."

"This buys me time, which is what I needed most, Scarecrow." Esme scowled at her screens. "It gives me a chance to figure out what the fuck to do next."

"Don't call me Scarecrow. I rented the movie and watched it. Everyone in that movie was a dysfunctional idiot."

"You didn't read the books? The Scarecrow is the wisest being in Oz and rules the kingdom after the wizard and Dorothy leave."

Tinker found the news vaguely disturbing. "That doesn't help."

"It's like flying blind in the clouds—you have to have faith in what instruments tell you. The dreams told me that I needed you. Things are still iffy—but I have a chance now to make everything right."

Tinker was torn between relief and annoyance that Esme seemed to think Tinker's part was done. She didn't want to be responsible for all the astronauts, but she didn't want to be stuck in space either. She didn't know what else to do. She couldn't even stay decent. Without gravity to constrain it, the skirt of Tinker's red silk dress developed a life of its own, determined to show off her panties as often as possible. Still, she had hoped they had gotten past all the dream bullshit. She hated not having an obvious direction to go, a clear-cut problem to solve. The path here had been so convoluted, the clues so obscure, that she would never have guessed where it was taking her. She supposed that she could only do everything she could imagine, and hope that one of them was the right thing.

Sighing, Tinker nudged one of the magic sinks. "These are just makeshift. They'll fill quickly and then leak. We'll have to burn off the magic until we can create a large, permanent storage tank."

"How do we do burn it?" Esme asked.

"You burn it off by doing spells," Tinker explained. "It can be used to create heat, light, cool things off, do healing—"

"Healing?" Jin seized hold of the word, proving that her "private" conversation with Esme had been just an illusion.

Tinker pulled out her datapad and made sure it worked. "Well, I have spells for healing but I don't know much about—"

Jin didn't let Tinker finish. He scooped her up and they flew through the ship as if Jin had wings. "We've got so many wounded that we've wiped out the *Dahe*'s supplies. Most of the medical supplies on the other ships were destroyed."

"I really don't know much about healing," Tinker finally managed to finish her statement.

"We're desperate. Some of our people—we can't do any more for them."

"Are they tengu?" Tinker asked.

He stopped and looked down at her. "You won't help us?"

"I didn't say that—although a 'please' would go a long way. It makes a difference what spells I use. Some won't work on humans—but they might work on tengu."

"Please, help my people. I beg you. They're dying."

She felt shame and anger at the same time that he would think she would let a wounded person die merely because of some biological difference she could barely see. "I'll do what I can. I just don't know how much that will be."

The infirmary was a tiny cramped place stained with blood, filled with people hooked to machines. The beds were more like cocoons with nylon bags holding the patients flat. Jin paused at the first bed to gaze at a blond man lying there.

"What happened to Chan Way Kay?"

"Sorry, Jin, we lost her," a man said from back of the room.

"This is Wai Sze Wong." Jin turned Tinker's attention to the patient to her other side. "She's tengu."

Wai Sze was Black from Tinker's dream. More a sparrow than a crow, she was a little female with delicate wrists and fingers. Massive bruising on Wai Sze ran the range from deep purple to pale yellow. Apparently they had run out of surgical tape, as black electrical tape held splints on Wai Sze's left arm and leg in place. The monitors on her showed an unsteady heartbeat.

Tinker gasped in the shock of recognition and the extent of

Wai Sze's injuries. "I—I—can only guess at how to help her."

"So guess." Jin gave her a look that spoke of trust and confidence. "We have done all we can, and she's only getting worse. If you can't save her, then we're going to lose her."

Tinker sighed and tried to think. Riki had recuperated quickly from the savage beating Tinker had given him, so the tengu probably had recuperative powers similar to the elves'. Tinker had saved Windwolf's life with a spell that focused magic into his natural healing powers. The ambient level of the ship, while enough to wreak havoc on the unshielded computer systems, was actually quite low. If the tengu's ability was close enough to the elves', the same spell might save Wai Sze. She searched the memory of her datapad and found that she did have the spell downloaded.

"Do you have transferable circuit paper?" Tinker asked.

Jin nodded.

"Okay," Tinker said. "I need the first magic sink we set up, some power leads, and a computer connection so I can print on the circuit paper."

One of these days she had to learn bio magic. She hated gambling with people's lives. Hopefully today wasn't going to be the day that she guessed wrong.

She explained to the doctor how she needed Wai Sze prepped while Jin sent people off to fetch the sinks and leads, and then Jin took her to print off the spell.

"If this spell works, we can use it on all the tengu." She explained to Jin how it focused magic on the tengu's natural abilities. "But it's useless on humans. For them, I'll need to see if there is a spell for their specific injury in my codex. It will be a much slower process."

"Let's save the spell onto this system; that way, if Wai Sze shows improvement, I can come back and print off more spells while you start working with the humans."

When they returned, they found Wai Sze stripped bare to her waist. Burning with embarrassment, Tinker peeled the protective sheet from the circuit paper and pressed the spell to Wai Sze's small chest as Jin watched her intently. It required a lot of fiddling to make sure it was smoothed down over the hills and valleys of Wai Sze's breasts. On the female's hip was a tattoo of a lion overlaying the Leo star constellation, Leo's heart—the star Regulus—a blaze of blue-white in its chest. Tinker used it to change the subject. "She's a Leo?"

"Hmm? Oh, that, no, it's for Gracie's husband, Leo. He got a tattoo for her in the same place, a little bird."

Gracie was obviously the Americanization of Wai Sze's name. Leo was the name of Tinker's father, killed by the tengu before she was born. "He's a tengu?"

"No, Leo was human. He was my college roommate at MIT—and my best friend for many years."

"Was?"

Jin glanced at her sharply. Whatever he saw on her face made his hard look softened. "Leo and Gracie were like Romeo and Juliet. They fell madly in love at first sight. Their families didn't want them to be together. They got secretly married. And it all ended in senseless tragedy. Leo was killed in an accident, and for the last five years, Gracie has been suicidal with grief. Crows mate for life."

"Leo's family didn't want him to marry her?" Tinker asked. "They knew she was tengu?"

"No. We were Chinese—that was enough."

Yes, that would have been enough. Much as she loved her grandfather, she knew the truth of his bigotry. She had been wondering why she dreamed of Gracie. Now she could only remember how the little tengu female had endlessly wept in her dreams.

Tinker had taped the leads to the power-distributor ring of the spell and hooked the other ends to the battery. "You check to make sure all the metal is clear of the spell. It would distort the effect of the spell, which could be deadly. The activation word is pronounced this way."

Jin listened closely, and then nodded as the outer ring powered up, casting a glowing sphere over the rest of the spell. The healing spell itself kicked in, the timing cycle ring clicking quickly clockwise as the magic flowed through the spell in a steady rhythm. "How long before we can tell if it's going to work?"

Tinker shrugged. "On an elf, I could tell immediately."

As they watched, color flushed back into Gracie's face and her breathing grew deeper. The machines monitoring her health verified that her heart was stabilizing.

Jin clapped his hands, just like an elf would, to summon the attention of the gods to him, and then whispered a prayer. Tinker floated in place, gazing at the female who would have been her mother, if everything had gone differently. Had it been chance that put Gracie on the same ship as Esme—or some dream-inspired plan of Tinker's real mother?

Jin finished his prayer and turned to Tinker. "Thank you. Truly you must have been sent by the gods to us."

"No, just the wizard of Oz."

21: NO PLACE LIKE HOME

Wolf was ready to kill something. They should have been reacting quickly, but instead they stalled with negotiations. Wolf had
demanded that one of the Stone Clan return to the enclaves to
guard the noncombatants. Earth Son assigned the task to Jewel
Tear but then tried to maneuver True Flame into qualifying it as
a failure on Wolf's part to protect the enclaves.

"I can choose to protect the enclaves," Wolf said, "and leave
you to face the dragon."

"We will have the dreadnaught," Earth Son pointed out.

"No, we won't," True Flame snapped. "Human weapons
can't pierce the dragon shielding. The dreadnaught is good at
spotting and attacking ground troops. It would be an aerial ban-
quet table for the dragon."

"We should travel light," True Flame continued. "One Hand
each. The fewer we have to protect, the better."

Wolf let Wraith choose which of his *sekasha* would remain.
Wolf drew Little Horse and Stormsong aside; of the *sekasha* returning
to the enclaves, they were the ones best suited to interacting with
humans. "Call Maynard. Let him know what his people might be
facing. They need to know that their weapons won't work on this."

-*-=◉(=-*-

Even as Jewel Tear and the extra *sekasha* left, Earth Son was still arguing against True Flame's decision. "We should wait until it comes to us. Running around looking for it will only weaken our position."

Wolf scoffed at this idea. "Sit here on our hands while it does what it will to the city?"

"Property damage can be fixed later," Earth Son said.

"And what of the humans?" Wolf said.

Earth Son had the gall to say, "I do not know why you fuss so. They are short-lived anyhow."

"I think we should go and be the heroes." Forest Moss struck a heroic pose. "Females are attracted to males of action."

"What females?" Earth Son cried.

"Poor Earth Son, I might have one blind eye—" Forest Moss tapped his cheek under his ruined eye and then reached out to tap both of Earth Son's. "—but apparently you have two."

Earth Son slapped away Moss' hand. "I am not blind."

"Then you must see that this city is filled with fertile young females? There are so few *domana* females, and they are a choosy lot. The law prevents us from taking lovers outside our own caste who are not *sekasha* with *naekuna*, and the *sekasha* frown on us making another caste into *domana*—that would be too much like our Skin Clan fathers. Would not the *sane* plan be to follow Wolf Who Rules' path, winnow out the perfect female from the thousands and thousands of humans, and make her elfin?"

"No!" Earth Son flinched back from the mad one. "Are you capable of even recognizing sanity?"

Forest Moss thought a moment and then shrugged. "The sad truth is: I am not sure. But neither am I sure I care. I have found a certain freedom in madness. Ah, but it is oh so lonely. I do not wish to be alone anymore. Unfortunately, I have fallen into a paradox. As *domana*, I cannot attract a household without *sekasha*, but the *sekasha* no longer trust me. I failed to protect what was mine. What a small mistake led to my downfall, and I did not make it alone. At our first encounter with the oni, despite their displays of friendship, we should have fought. One miscalculation and all was lost. Lost forever."

"I fell in love," Windwolf stated coldly. "Do not mistake my honest passion for calculated convenience."

Forest Moss made little flicking motions with his hand. "Feh, feh, I will love her. She will, after all, win me what I wish for the most. I tried to show my responsibility and leadership by holding dogs and monkeys, and small birds. Surely keeping safe such fragile packages of life shows some ability to protect? Alas, no elf has offered themselves into my keeping."

"And this mad plan would bring you respect?" Earth Son looked puzzled.

"Beloved Tinker holds two *sekasha*. I'm told that she lacks a full Hand merely due to the limits of time. Even the renowned Bladebite offered to her. Surely there is another female of the same caliber in this city."

"No," Windwolf growled. "My *domi* is a rare and treasured find."

Forest Moss refused to be distracted from his plan. "Ah, well, I will have to settle for some lesser gem then. Let us be off. There are dragons to kill, and females to impress."

With the elder Stone Clan male strutting off, Earth Son had no choice but to agree to go after the dragon. It made sense now that Forest Moss had tried to use the *aumani* to gain Little Horse. Although young, Little Horse's bloodlines meant young *sekasha* would be willing to look to him as First. There was some sound reasoning to that—as well as this current plan of Forest Moss. Both, however, were equally distasteful.

Hopefully Malice would cut short Forest Moss's plan.

Tinker spent hours in the infirmary, choosing spells out of the Dufae Codex, modifying them to work with the batteries, printing them off, and casting them. She was learning that she wasn't cut out to be a doctor; having to touch strangers so intimately was still unnerving.

Being weightless was at once a joy and a constant reminder that she wasn't on Elfhome. What had happened when she fell into the Ghostlands? Pony had been up on the scaffolding with her. Had he fallen into the deadly cold and died? Or had he fallen through, like her, and was now lost on another world, or out in space? The possibilities terrified her. She wouldn't allow herself to even consider what that might have happened to Windwolf. There was, however, the dreadful knowledge that Windwolf would put himself between Malice and Pittsburgh, and continue until either he or Malice was dead. She had to get back and help Windwolf—somehow.

The largest drawback to being weightless was that you didn't fall down when you fell asleep. One moment she was drifting in a niche, waiting for some crew to move past, trying to think of a weapon that could kill Malice. The next she was wondering if there was enough black willow left to make lively maple-flavored ice cream. Dragons, Oilcan was telling her over the phone, had a weakness for sweets.

"You're going to have to make it." She became aware that she had made the phone from two tin cans and a long string of red thread strung between them. The thread vibrated as they talked, a blur of red, resonating to their voices. Resonation was the key to everything. "It's really easy to make. Just follow Grandpa's recipe."

She realized then that the ice cream had been what they needed all along—but she had taken the recipe with her. While she considered this, she drifted through the wall of the spaceship. Space, it turned out, was all sticky, sweet black treacle. Here was all the molasses they would want. She could make the ice cream out of this—only how did she get it back to Pittsburgh? Fling it from orbit? No, no, it would all burn up before it hit Pittsburgh.

"*Domi?*"

Tinker looked up. Stormsong was drifting toward her, a flowing angel of hazy gleaming white. The *sekasha* had one hand on the red thread and was following it to Tinker's tin-can phone. "Stormsong, I'm stuck in the treacle."

"No, you aren't." Stormsong held out her hand and Tinker caught hold of it. It felt warm and intangible as a sunbeam. "Remember."

"Remember what?" Tinker cried as Stormsong hazed to a nebulous gleaming form.

"There's no place like home," Stormsong whispered, brilliant now.

Tinker blinked against the brilliance. Stormsong had transformed to a shimmering ghost of Impatience. She clung to some of his snaky mane.

"*Sssssaaaammmmmmaaananana.*" Impatience's voice rumbled against her skin.

A loud gasp made Tinker turn her head. Jin floated a few feet away, gazing at her with amazement. They were back in the infirmary, the wall beside her lumpy and cold and the smell of smoke and blood omnipresent.

Am I still sleeping? Tinker looked back at Impatience.

"*Huuhuuhuuhuuhuuhuu,*" Impatience rumbled and faded away.

Jin drifted toward her, his eyes still wide as he gazed at her. "Remember what?"

Tinker scrubbed at her face. Was she awake or still asleep? Her right hand felt warmer than her left—like she had held it over a open flame. "There's no place like home."

"That's it?"

Dragons have a weakness for sweets and space is treacle? "Maybe." Tinker realized that she was awake now—yet somehow Jin had experienced part of her dream. "Did you hear Stormsong?"

"The dragon's name is Stormsong? That doesn't sound like a dragon name."

Was pinching yourself an accurate test to see if you're awake? If it was, then she was awake. "You *saw* the dragon?"

Jin nodded. "And I heard it. It said, 'Remember.'"

"You understood what it said?"

"I'm Providence's child."

"You're what?"

Jin cocked his head in his birdlike inspection of her. "You walk with the dragons but don't know their way?"

"No."

Jin crossed to her side and settled beside her. "Providence is the guardian spirit of the tengu. Each generation a tengu child is born with the mark of Providence upon him." The tengu undid his shirt buttons to expose his chest. Over his heart was a red birthmark that looked like the flowing outline of a dragon. "We're taught the language of the dragons."

A whole mysterious part of her life suddenly made sense. "This is what he was looking for."

"The dragon?"

"No, Riki. He kidnapped me and made me strip. He wanted to know if Impatience marked me but he didn't tell me what the mark was for."

"Who is Riki?" Jin asked.

"A tengu—stuck between a rock and a hard place. Apparently he tried to stay out of oni control, but they took his younger cousin, Joey, hostage. It put us on opposite sides, which is too bad, because I think we could have been good friends."

Jin reached out and touched the necklace Keiko had given her. She'd forgotten she was even still wearing it. "Did he give you that?"

"No, his younger cousin Keiko did. She said it would protect me from tengu."

"It will." He tugged it out of her neckline so it laid overtop. "But you've got to keep it out where it can be seen. That way we can tell you're under the protection of the Chosen blood."

"The what?"

"I'm the Chosen one. The spiritual leader of my people. I decide the path for my people and they follow me. Riki and his cousins are all my nieces and nephews. In my absence, my people are turning to them."

"Which made them targets for the oni wanting to control the tengu."

Jin nodded.

Having experienced people turning to her for leadership, Tinker felt sudden sympathy for Riki. "One thing I don't get. These people are astronauts and still buy 'the chosen one' bullshit?"

"When you're born a mythical creature, you tend to have a different mind-set on these things."

"Wait—so—all this colonization—going back to Onihida stupidity was your idea?"

Jin looked away. For a moment, Tinker thought he wouldn't answer, but he sighed, and said, "We're half bird—we can't breed with humans—not without magic. Yes, a couple hundred of us came to Earth before the elves destroyed the pathway, but it wasn't a big enough gene pool. For generations we've been careful not to interbreed, but we were coming to a dead end. We had to find some way to get back to Onihida and the rest of our tribe. You have no idea what it's like to see genocide bearing down on you."

"If Riki was looking for a chosen one, then that means the tengu don't have a leader."

"It seems like it."

Tinker yawned. "When this is all over, I think I'm going to sleep for a week. Are we going to get gravity back?"

"We did another course correction, but it seems like something is pulling us down toward the planet. It's already pulled all the debris into reentry. We're not spinning up this time to save fuel."

"So—if we don't do anything, eventually the ship will be pulled out of orbit?"

"It seems like it."

Tinker groaned. She didn't want to deal with dreams! "No place like home—that's what Dorothy says to get home. The stupidity was that she had the means to get home the entire time; she just didn't know it. I have no idea how that Glinda bitch gets away with being the 'good' witch. What do I have on me?"

She unloaded her pockets, letting the items float in orbit around her. Although the dress had limited pocket space, she still managed to fit a large amount of stuff into them. Not only did she have her datapad, she also had her camera with the recording of Impatience trying to teach her—something.

"Oh my, these could be my ruby slippers!"

Tracking Malice proved difficult, despite his size. The massive dragon leaped and bounded and shifted through buildings like he was a ghost, leaving a shattered trail. Wolf chafed at the slower speeds that others traveled, but True Flame would not relent, and Wolf had to acknowledge that the older elf had battle experience, whereas he did not.

The trail led up the Monongahela River valley to beyond the Rim, and then disappeared without a trace.

"There is something wrong here," Wraith whispered to Wolf as his Hand gathered close. "Smell the blood?"

Wolf gazed at the still, boulder-strewn forest around them. There was a slight blurring to the trees, as if a mist hazed the air. He would not have noticed it if the *sekasha* hadn't called his attention to it. Pulling out a survey map for the area, he confirmed his suspicions.

"I think this might be an oni encampment, covered by an illusion."

The sekasha pulled their *ejae*, readying themselves for a possible ambush.

Forest Moss did a ground scry, took a few steps, and repeated it several times until he stopped beside an ironwood sapling. "Wolf Who Rules, break this tree."

Wolf aimed a force strike at the sapling and unleashed it.

The sapling vanished when the leading edge of his blow struck it. A tall square stone, inscribed with spells, replaced the sapling for a heartbeat before disintegrating into rubble. An oni camp sprang into being around them. The boulders changed into rough cabins. Mossy logs became well-gnawed humanoid carcasses. Blood soaked the ground and everywhere were dragon tracks.

"All the magic flowed toward the sapling." Forest Moss nudged the remains of the crude oni spell stone.

The *sekasha* moved out to search the cabins.

"Malice has wallowed in magic and feasted on oni." True Flame used his sword tip to point out that the skulls were horned. "Maybe it slipped its bonds, like the little one did."

"There were no spell markings on Malice." Wolf wondered too the significance of the dragon's name. Tinker had called Impatience "hyper." If the dragon's names reflected a personality, perhaps one named Malice needed no prodding to wreak havoc.

"I am not sure what the other beast is, but there is no mistake here, this is an oni dragon." True Flame pointed out a four-toed print in the dirt. "The little beast has five claws like the hand of an elf."

Red Knife reported for the *sekasha*, saying that the cabins were empty of oni and any evidence of what they planned. "There were, though, a hundred oni here only hours ago."

"It is a good thing that we delayed, then." Earth Son earned a sharp look from even his First, Thorne Scratch. "We would have had to face both oni and the dragon at the same time."

Instead both had vanished away after having time to lay cooperative plans.

The dragon tracks led down to the river.

Earth Son made a sound of disgust, eyeing muddy water. "None of us will be able to track it in that."

"If Malice was sent by the oni on Onihida to distract us, then he will circle back to the city and attack." Wolf was glad that Jewel Tear was protecting the enclaves. While the Stone Clan was weak on attack spells, they had the strongest defensive spells. "We should return."

Tinker and Jin found a working computer station and with some jury-rigging managed to get her state-of-art camera interfaced with the two-decade-old systems.

"I recorded about six hours so this is going to take a while." Tinker started the playback.

"*. . . we'll build a dictionary of his words,*" her recorded voice started out the recording. Cloudwalker had been filming the dragon but had trouble tracking it as it moved through the scrap yard's offices.

"Riki says the dragon's name is Impatience," Tinker said, "but Riki has lied to me—a lot."

Jin attention was on the recording. He said nothing but he frowned slightly at this.

"*. . . mmmenananannaaaaaaapoooookaaaammmamma-mamyyyyyaaanananammmmoooo . . .*" Impatience rambled on the recording.

"I'm not familiar with the name." Jin paused the recording after another minute of the dragon's monologue. "Dragons usually use a lot of words to say anything. Like 'a pleasantly warm but not too warm, sunny, cloudless time of the day that isn't dawn but the sun hasn't quite reached its zenith' for 'good morning'. It is considered rude to get to the point too quickly. When you talk to a dragon, you're supposed to elaborate as much as possible."

"Dragon Etiquette 101?" Tinker asked.

"Historically, rude tengu are dragon snacks. This dragon, however, is being very to the point. He might come across as impatient to other dragons, which would explain his name."

"So you understand him."

"Yes, so far he's said, 'What is this object? Oh, this moves. Ah, it makes light. I wonder how. This part twists. What are these? I see. It does not work without those. Why does it not make light? Have I broken it? It seemed as if it was supposed to come apart. A diagram. I must have them backward. Ha, ha, ha.'"

"Yeah, I got the laughing part."

A female astronaut flew into the cabin with tengu grace, "Wai Sze is awake and wants to see the Scarecrow."

The tiny tengu woman was awake and looking surprisingly well compared to how awful she had been before. She gasped as Tinker swam into the infirmary. "Oh my, you *are* here! Oh, look at you! You're so beautiful."

Tinker blushed. As a female elf in a deep jewel-red silk dress in zero gee, she was attracting a lot of attention from the crew. "It's the dress."

"Ah, yes, it not so practical in space, is it, my dear? Xiao Chen, can you find her something to wear?"

Xiao Chen had been the crew member who summoned them to Gracie's side. The tengu female nodded, cocking her head to study Tinker's size before moving off, graceful as a bird in flight.

Jin looked at Tinker as if noticing the silk flowing around her for the first time and then smiled. "I don't know. It's good for morale. At least with the guys."

Tinker smacked him and found herself floating backward.

He laughed, and caught Tinker before she could hit something. "I am only joking."

"Shoo, shoo!" Gracie waved Jin away. "I want to talk to her without your noisy squawking."

Jin smiled fondly at his cousin and flew away.

Gracie held out her unbroken hand to Tinker. "Let me look at you." Gracie had tears in her eyes, which Tinker expected, but not the brilliant smile that the fragile tengu bestowed on her. Tinker found herself smiling back. "You've got Leo's eyes and his smile."

"Yeah, I guess. The patented Dufae face."

"I'm so happy to see it. It hurt so much that I hadn't been able to give Leo a baby. It made losing him all the more horrible. He was a wonderful, wonderful man and he was utterly gone."

It occurred to Tinker for the first time how awful to lose your husband—never see him again—and a sudden fear took root in her. What if she couldn't get back to Windwolf? What if she never saw him again?

"There, there, my love." Gracie wiped Tinker's tears away. "We'll get you back to him somehow."

"Yeah, I know, we're working on it." Tinker sniffed.

"Let me see your leg. I know Jin, he probably didn't think to clean that cut. He might be Dalai Lama of the crows, but he's hopeless with first aid."

Gracie deftly took off the bandage, gently cleaned the wound and applied an antiseptic, and rebandaged the cut.

"Are you a medic?" Tinker asked her.

"I'm the ship's xenobiologist," Gracie said.

"You're kidding."

Gracie looked up in surprise, and Tinker found herself talking about Lain, and then about Esme. "Have you told her? I don't think she's realized who you are yet."

Tinker shook her head. "Right now, it's all too weird. I don't even want to think about it. Besides, I'm kind of ticked at her. Not about leaving me. About everyone having to lie to me about it because—I don't know—some strange family stuff. I didn't know the truth for eighteen years. She can go on not knowing for a couple of days. I'll tell her later."

Xiao Chen flew into the area, carrying a set of clothes. "These should fit our Scarecrow."

"I don't know if I like that nickname." Tinker took the clothes and drifted awkwardly as she checked the pant size against her waist.

Xiao Chen laughed. "I am sorry. For so long, we did not know your name, just that you were the Scarecrow."

"Did you tell everyone about your dream?" Tinker asked Gracie.

Xiao Chen, though, answered. "All of us that slept that night shared Wai Sze's dream—that is her ability. She is our dream crow."

"In some ways, we are more bird than human," Gracie said.

"Can you see the future?" Tinker asked "How am I going to get us out of this mess?"

Gracie shook her head. "Where one person can determine the future, the way is clear, but we're in a tangle of possibilities. Many people can push the future one way or another. This is a time when everyone will determine the end."

Since there were no private places, Tinker turned her back and they pretended to ignore her, talking in Chinese, as she changed. She tried not to feel like they were talking about her. Certainly with the ship falling out of orbit, they had plenty of things to discuss. At least with the dress on, she was able to change panties and pull on her pants without flashing them. The pants were a little loose, but Xiao Chen had included a length of nylon cord to serve as a belt.

Tinker turned back around and pulled on the knotted cord.

"I look the part of the scarecrow now."

The tengu laughed.

"I've been greedy." Gracie reached out and squeezed Tinker's hand. "I've kept you here too long. Thank you for letting me see you."

Tinker hugged her good-bye and returned to the task of finding out how to get them back home to Windwolf.

Impatience, it turned out, had been trying to teach her a spell. It incorporated math, something that Elvish spells didn't do, and used magic to manipulate time and space. It took everything she knew and pushed it in a new direction using an entirely new symbol set. Jin translated the words and then, later, the number system that Impatience used but looked mystified by most of what he was saying.

"You understand this?" Jin asked.

"Yes, yes. The roots of elfin magic are here, but taken to another order of understanding. This is recognizing the quantum nature of magic and its effects *across* boundaries of realities. My god, I really screwed up. I never considered that I could warp the fabric of space and time on this kind of scale."

"What?" Jin cried in surprise. "*You* made this mess?"

"I had help. Okay, here's what happened." She found a marker in her pocket and drew a planet on the nearest wall. "The oni forced me to build a downsized gate on Elfhome. I set up a resonance between my gate and the orbital gate." She drew both gates in their proper positions and the wavy resonance line between them. "Now, Leo's gate was flawed. The time coordinate was never set." She drew the ships entering the orbital gate. "So the default time coordinate became the moment of the gate's destruction—or around midnight Eastern standard time, seven—eight days ago."

She had totally lost track of time since she landed on the spaceship. What day was it now?

Jin understood the result. "Thus the collision."

"Yeah. Old news. This is the important part—all the ships, when they passed through the gate, must have picked up the resonance signature." She drew a ship on the other side of the gate, labeled it *Dahe Hao,* and continued the wavy line to it. "As long as there are objects in orbit, the resonance will continue, which is why the Discontinuity hasn't collapsed. It's because of this link, that when I fell into the Ghostlands, I ended up onboard. For every action, though, there is an equal and opposite reaction. Basically the power spike originates here on Elfhome and travels in this direction—" She drew an arrow parallel to the wavy line through the planet. "—the multiuniverse is trying to drag the *Dahe Hao* back along this line." She drew a second arrow from the ship running beside the resonance path toward the planet. "Again, as long as the Discontinuity continues, the *Dahe Hao* will be affected by this force."

She turned and was startled to find her audience had grown from Jin to about twenty crew members. "Um, well, this isn't all bad. We can use this force to our advantage. The entire ship and everyone on it is keyed to *this* location." She underlined Turtle Creek. "Now, if you look at this section of the text..." She pointed to the screen. "This is a spell. It creates a sphere of hyperphase. All we need to do is cast this spell which will step the ship into hyperphase and follow the line of force back to Pittsburgh."

"That's *all?*" Esme said.

Tinker turned back and found her audience had grown again. Esme and another twenty crew members crowded the small area. "My biggest concern is power. If the amount of magic we feed into the spell is too small, it will just punch a hole in the middle of the ship. We need enough power that we can guarantee that the entire ship goes. Even if we think we have sufficient magic, we probably should gather everyone close to the spell, and close all the hatches between the sections of the ship."

"What we've collected isn't enough?" Esme asked.

"I don't think so, and access time on it is slow. The spell is set up to mimic how the dragons cast magic with their mane. With elf magic, there's a timing ring around the spell that controls the power coming in. It gives the magic a slow steady burn. This spell takes all the free magic and converts it in one burst." Tinker sketched the ship and put an "X" at roughly the center of the ship. "It's kind of like dropping a stone into a pool of water. Splash!" She drew in the initial impact in a large circle around the "X". "That's the rock hitting the surface. There seems to be some resulting ripples in the fabric of space." She added larger circles around the first, and then shaded in the space between the circles. "I'm not sure what the ripples will do, but I can't imagine the delay factor will be good for the structural integrity of the ship."

"In other words," Jin sought to clarify what she said, "part of the ship returns to Pittsburgh seconds before the next section goes?"

"Yes. Leo's gate, however flawed, did transfer all the ship to the same second. These ripples would have a different time coordinate, so probably we're looking at pieces of the ship arriving in Pittsburgh—unless we hit it with a damn big rock."

"So where do we get it?"

"I don't know. If we could tap the spring under Turtle Creek, that would work, but I don't see any evidence that power is seeping through."

There was no sign of Malice in Oakland when Wolf and the others returned to the enclaves. Maynard had set up a command center in the building across the street from Poppymeadow's. He and the NSA agents had set up lookout posts across the city, linked by radio.

"Unless it can go invisible, it hasn't appeared in the city yet." Maynard tapped three points on the map. "Between the Cathedral of Learning, the USX building, and Mount Washington, we can see for miles—and Stormsong said that this thing was huge."

Wolf nodded. "Unfortunately, it will be dark soon."

Someone was hammering upstairs. The hammering stopped, and something large moved overhead accompanied by an odd rhythmic clicking noise.

Wolf cocked his head, trying to place the sound. "What is that?"

Stormsong glanced toward Earth Son standing in the street, just outside the open door, and lowered her voice. "*Domi's nagarou* brought the little dragon, so the humans can see what we're fighting."

Interesting how one afternoon could change your perspective on size.

Maynard had caught Stormsong's caution and spoke quietly in English. "Briggs and Durrack are seeing what works against it."

Wolf couldn't decide if this was ingenious or unwise. He found the stairs leading up to the one large open room taking up the entire second story. The windows had been boarded shut and mattresses leaned against the walls. The dragon and others were in the far corner, standing around a computer set up on the floor. While Oilcan and Durrack were focused on the screen, Briggs and Little Horse and Cloudwalker were standing back and watching the dragon.

All beings—dragon, humans, and elves—looked up when he arrived with his Hand.

"*Domou.*" Little Horse acknowledged his arrival.

"What are you doing here?" Wolf thought he had sent his blade brother back to the enclaves.

"There is nothing I can do for *domi*, but she would want her *nagarou* safe. Surely, the oni will try and take back the little dragon."

Wolf glanced at his *domi's nagarou*. There was so much of Tinker in Oilcan's appearance that it hurt—her mouth, her eyes, and her haphazard haircut. In the hectic last two months, Wolf had not spoken once to the young man. Wolf realized now that Tinker was Oilcan's only family; he was now quite alone. Wolf could not imagine it; an elf only found himself alone if he was exiled from his clan. Clans were so vast that natural disaster could lay low entire households and families and there would still be someone left to be responsible for the orphans.

Wolf had been lax toward Oilcan because he was an adult— if he had been an elf, Oilcan would have chosen a clan that super- seded all family responsibilities. That had been wrong of Wolf. Even if he lifted Tinker out of her species, it did not completely free her of her culture's obligations—and as her *domou*, her responsibilities were his own. But beyond that, it been wrong of him to be a stranger to the one human that Tinker loved as much as life.

Oilcan cautiously separated himself from the dragon, as if he didn't fully trust either the dragon or the warriors from either race. "Wolf Who Rules." Oilcan gave a proper bow. "I heard about Malice on the scanner," he said in High Tongue. Sorrow filled his eyes as he spoke, and then was firmly put aside. "I thought we might learn something from Impatience."

"Thank you, *nagarou*. That was wise of you." Wolf dropped to Low Elvish, and put a hand to the young man's shoulder.

A smile flashed over Oilcan's face, then vanished as he sighed. "Unfortunately, most of what we've found out so far isn't good."

"I did not expect anything else. What have we found out?"

"Well, there was a question if Impatience and Malice are both really dragons, given their size and various other differences. From what we've pieced together, we think they are. In Chinese mythology, the four-claw dragons are considered common dragons but the imperial dragon has five claws. We think the variations are racial instead of species differences, and possibly represent political differences too."

"Tengu worship five-claws—they—compassionate guardians of tengu in past," Durrack spoke very rough low Elvish. "Four-claws—they have bad reputation—they work with the oni without being enslaved. Malice is not enslaved."

"Now, the dragon can't maintain its shields all the time." Oilcan patted Impatience on the head, showing that the little dragon's shields were currently down. "It takes them approximately thirty seconds to raise their shields."

Durrack abandoned Low Elvish, to add in English, "If we could catch Malice completely unaware, a sniper might be able to take him out with a well-placed bullet. But once his shield goes up, things get tricky."

Oilcan murmured a translation to Little Horse and Cloudwalker, and then added in Elvish, "The shields, while they use ambient magic, are very efficient and translate all kinetic energy—including the motion of the dragon's body—somehow into magic. Bullets, rockets, baseballs—" Oilcan nudged a ball on the floor that they apparently had been using in their experiments. "—anything you can throw at them—will only make them stronger."

"And they can keep the shields up while they phase through walls." Durrack patted a wooden partition erected next to him.

Impatience took this as a request to demonstrate his phasing abilities. His mane lifted up and he shimmered into a ghostly haze and leapt through the wall and returned.

"Good boy!" Oilcan produced a large gumball from his pocket and gave it to the dragon, who chewed it with obvious relish. "We believe your lightning will cross the barrier because it's composed of a different type of energy particle."

"Electricity works." Durrack lifted up half a cattle prod. "We established that."

Impatience snatched the cattle prod out of the NSA agent's hand and phased it into the wall. When the little dragon let go, the cattle prod remained as part of the wall. The other half, Wolf noticed, was already part of the wall. Apparently the little dragon didn't like that test.

"As a one shot deal, pepper spray will work." Durrack picked up an aerosol can. "Of course, it only annoys the hell out of them, and then the dragon changes its shields so that gas won't penetrate."

"I'm stunned you are all still alive." Wolf realized that Impatience had to be remarkably forgiving to put up with these experiments.

"We talked first," Oilcan said.

Briggs scoffed, "We drew pictures and did a lot of pantomime."

"He seems to understand what's going on," Oilcan said. "He seems to hate both Malice and the oni, but he's made it clear that he can't beat Malice in a fight."

"How do oni enslave the dragons in the first place? Do the tengu say?"

Durrack shook his head. "No."

Wolf wondered if this was the truth. While he trusted Oilcan to be as forthright as Tinker, the NSA clearly saw themselves as separate powers, with all that implied.

After the accident, and the various course corrections, the *Dahe Hao*'s low orbit didn't put them within range of the Wind Clan spell stones at Aum Renau. After discussing their fuel situation and the reliability of their engines, they decided to look for stones elsewhere within a *mei*. The spell stones were large enough and distinctive enough that the pattern recognition software found several sets. It was impossible to distinguish which clan the stones belonged to, but they found four grouped together in the place the crew nicknamed Giza.

"There are four major clans—Wind, Fire, Water, Stone—so I think it's a safe bet that it's one set for each major clan." At least, Tinker hoped it was. She knew there were lesser clans, but she didn't know anything about them. "At this speed, though, we're already out of range, so I'll have to wait until next orbit to check."

"You've got about an hour and a half then." Esme murmured a curse as something flashed red on her monitor. "But we're drifting again. We're going to have to do another course correction."

"Try and keep us in this orbit," Tinker said. "A *mei* is only a thousand miles, give or take a couple hundred miles. If we drop much closer to the equator, we'll be out of range."

Tinker then retreated to work on printing out the spell. Jin tracked her down a short time later.

"Gracie wanted to be sure you got something to eat." Jin held out a container.

"*Pft.*" Tinker waved away the offering. "If I eat, I'll have to figure out how you go to the bathroom up here, and I figure that's not going to be a pleasant activity."

Jin laughed, still holding out the cup-sized container. "You have to eat."

"What is it?"

"Cream of tomato soup."

"Oh! My favorite." She took the container and found that it was warm. As she snapped it open and sipped the rich creamy broth, Jin swung up to perch across from her.

"It was your father's favorite too." Jin sipped his own soup. "I can see Leo in you. Hear him in the way you talk. It makes me happy."

"Why?"

"Leo was my best friend for many years. I'm glad that in a way, he is living on through you."

"If he was such a good friend, why did you kill him?"

She expected him to deny it, but he only gazed at her, sorrow filling his eyes.

"I—I made a mistake. We never told Leo that we were tengu. And he never told us—at least, not until it was too late—that he was elfin. We kept our secrets from one another, and in the end, it killed Leo."

"I don't understand," Tinker said.

"Leo and I met at MIT. We both had radical ideas, ones that made us unpopular. We believed that magic existed—that there were other realms that could be visited via magical portals. Of course, we had the proof in our very blood, but we never told anyone that, not even each other." Jin sighed, shaking his head. "It seems so obvious now. Dufae. How did we miss it?"

"What really happened? My grandfather never told me the details."

"When Leo showed us his gate design, a possibility opened up to us. A paradise for the tengu. It became the flock dream, a bright promise at the end of a path through dark woods full of unseen danger. To be able to choose one's mate out of love, and not a carefully ordered breeding plan. To be able to fly. To walk under the sun in our true form, and not to be always hidden. I went to the kitsune, who are powerful in the Chinese government, and talked to them about funding. They involved other parties. It was dangerous, I know, but I thought I understood all the factors. What I didn't know was that Leo was an elf—that he knew exactly what the oni were—and that he wouldn't cooperate with them."

"Halfway through the meeting with the investors, Leo just freaked. He told them that he would never help the oni build a gate. And worse, he told them why. As much as the elves feared the oni, the oni of Earth feared the elves. He stormed out of the meeting. I went after him. We were arguing—" Jin fell silent for a minute. "It happened so fast. One moment he was standing beside me on the street corner, arguing with me, and the next he was dead in the middle of the road.

Jin sighed. "I wasn't driving the car. I didn't push him out into its path. But I brought death to him. And I can only say I'm sorry. And I truly am. I loved him like a brother."

All Tinker could imagine was Nathan out on the road, his blood on her. Oh gods, she didn't want to cry again. She squeezed her eyes tight on the sudden burn of tears. "How do you deal with knowing that you fucked up so bad? That you killed someone who loved you? Who trusted you?"

"Accept the truth of what happened, and then forgive your-self. They would if they could."

She laughed bitterly. "Why would they?"

"Because they loved you."

She pressed the palms of her hands into her eyes, and struggled to get back in control of herself. The truth of what happened? The truth was that she had ignored all the warning signs with Nathan. She had to pay attention, think about the consequences of her actions. Like now—she was desperately trying to get back to Pittsburgh, but what if she was totally wrong? With sudden terror, she saw the implications of her actions. She was taking *Dahe Hao* to Pittsburgh. She might be saving the human crew, but she was dooming the tengu crew to genocide.

"I'm worried about what will happen to the tengu when we reach Pittsburgh. The elves are killing people that they just sus-pect are oni. And I know they *will* see tengu as oni."

"You still don't think of yourself as one of them?"

"No, not really. Wait—how do you know?"

"For the last week, all we've dreamed about is you—all the weird twists and turns your life has taken." Jin picked up the camera. Cloudwalker had had trouble tracking the hyperactive dragon through the trailer and caught her and Pony in the viewfinder instead. "We've seen what you've done to keep your *sekasha* safe."

"You know everything?" She wondered if this was why she had been having such horrible nightmares lately.

"Enough. Your fight with the Foo dogs. Your transformation from a human. Your fight with the oni lord." Jin played a few seconds of recording as Pony acknowledged one of her requests with a slight bow. "This is just proof of what we already knew. You're the Wind Clan *domi*, guarded by a Hand of *sekasha*, one of which is another dreamer."

"Her name is Stormsong."

"You told me."

"I don't know what to do about this," Tinker admitted. "If we don't do the spell, I don't think anyone will survive. If we do the spell, then you end up in the mess in Pittsburgh."

Jin reached out and tapped Tinker's forehead, reminding her of the *dau* marked onto her forehead. "You have the power to protect us. You could make us part of your household. We could be yours, as these *sekasha* are yours."

"Mine?" Tinker squeaked. "Why would you want that?"

"Because we trust you more than we trust the oni."

That wasn't saying much.

"I don't know if that would work," Tinker said. "The elves make a big thing about beholding. The *sekasha* promise to serve in exchange for protection. That everyone fits into society—someone above them responsible for them, but they are answerable to."

"It seems fairly simple. I will promise that the tengu will obey you and you promise to protect us."

"You're serious? You would listen to what I told you to do?"

Jin nodded.

"Are you sure your crew is okay with obeying some snot-nosed kid?"

"Leo's daughter who talks with dragons? Yes, I am sure."

She opened her mouth and then closed it, reminding herself to think about implications and complications this time. She supposed that the tengu could make up a household like Poppymeadow's, where the crew would be under Jin and the tengu captain would be under her, yet they wouldn't be directly part of her household. She wished that she knew more about how the enclaves worked, but she suspected that they were like all things elfin, where an exchange of promises were enough to bind both parties. But how would the tengu fit into her life? There was a terror deep inside her, one she didn't want to look at closely, that if she promised the tengu to protect them, it would have to be against the people that she loved the most. What would she do if Windwolf refused to acknowledge her claim on the tengu? She didn't want to think about Windwolf systematically killing the tengu she had gotten to know. She didn't want him to be the type of person who could do it. Yet she couldn't stop thinking of Nathan dead in the road because she was married to Windwolf. Of the bloody streets of Chinatown. Of Tommy Chang within moments of being cut down.

If she committed to the tengu, then she might have to fight even Windwolf to keep them safe. *I can't. I can't.*

She pressed trembling hands to her mouth. But if she didn't protect them, who would? How could she stand aside and let them be killed and do nothing to save them? "I'll do my best to protect you, but you have to remember to do what I say, or I won't have the power to stop the elves from killing you all."

"I promise. You will have the obedience of the tengu."

Her life had so many strings attached that she felt like a puppet.

"Hey! Scarecrow!" Esme called over the ship's intercom. "We're getting close to your mark in five minutes!"

Tinker swam back to the bridge, blinking on the salt burning in her eyes.

"Two minutes," Esme announced.

They waited in tense silence, bathed in the soft earthshine.

"In ten," Esme said quietly.

Tinker made sure she had her fingers in the correct position.

"We're in range."

Tinker brought her hand to her mouth and said the trigger word. Nothing happened. Her heart jolted with the sudden spike of fear. "Daaaaaaae." Still nothing. She checked her finger positions and carefully announced the trigger word. Zip. "Daaae. Daaaaaae. Dae. Daaaaaaae."

"And we're out of range," Esme said.

"Oh, fuck," Tinker said.

"Just checking—it didn't work?" Jin asked.

"No." Tinker rubbed the heels of her hand into her eyes.

"Well, you better think of something else, Scarecrow," Esme said. "We only have fuel for one more burn."

"How's it going?" the tengu Ushi asked. Tinker was finding that while the humans treated her with slight condescension after the initial novelty wore off, the tengu regarded her with an odd mix of awe and affection. The ratio of worship versus familial warmth seemed to be dependent on how well they had known her father. Either way, they kept seeking her out, wanting to know if she was comfortable, or needed anything. It was driving her to distraction.

"I'm still thinking." Thinking she needed to find a hiding place. "We're at about two hundred miles above Elfhome's surface, crossing over spell stones in Giza around eighteen miles per second. The reach of the spell stones are one *mei*, which is approximately one thousand miles, which means that theoretically we're within their reach for about a minute and a half."

"Why are they important?"

"They're a source of a lot of magic. If I could pull on them, then I could use the magic to trigger the spell."

She covered her eyes to think. Apparently Ushi took the cue that he was distracting her; when she opened her eyes again, he was gone. Too bad all her problems didn't solve themselves so neatly.

Why couldn't she call the spell stones? They were in range, for more than a minute, nearly two, and a call took less than one. Something had to be interfering with the call. Was it that there wasn't enough ambient magic to fuel the initial call? Tinker ran her hand across the wall of the ship, focusing on her magic sense. She could feel the latent magic. It was as strong as a ley line, but with a strange texture. It was like the difference between silk and wool. Magic on Elfhome flowed, smooth and quick. The magic here buzzed with static. If the call was supposed to be resonance of magic across the DNA signature of the *domana*, then perhaps that chaotic nature of the magic on the ship was creating too much static for that call.

Perhaps if she could filter the background magic to one frequency—oh, gods—how the hell did she do that? She groaned and pulled at her hair. The *sekasha* had magic stored in the beads woven into their hair, which guaranteed that if they were in a magic-poor area, they still could trigger their shields and have a few minutes of protection. She never had examined them but knew in essence that they were metal balls, insulated with glass, that acted like her power sinks. She believed that storing the magic in a "clean" enough medium would reduce the static. So, she should be able to use a sink just like they used the beads. The problem probably would be eliminating the background magic so only the stored magic was active.

Wait, if she modified the Reinholds spell based on Impatience's theorems, she might be able to trigger a magic equivalent to a wide-scale electromagnetic pulse. It would basically clean the slate. The danger would be that, if the pulse worked, not only on the magic wavelength but also included the electronics of the ship, she could accidentally kill all the computers maintaining the ship's life support. That would be bad.

But if she wiped out the buildup, and then used one shielded source to do a call on the Wind Clan spell stones—would that be enough magic to trigger the jump? It might. Too bad she couldn't pull from a second set . . .

Or could she? She had felt the Stone Clan magic. She had watched Forest Moss call on the Stone Clan's spell stones. Did she remember the hand positions and vocalization? Yes, she was sure.

She was nearly quivering now with possibilities. If she could pull on both stones at once—wait—*at once*—that kind of meant at the same moment. Since the vocalization was different she couldn't do both. She wished she could pace. She thought better pacing. She settled for bouncing between the walls, flying through the air.

"Whoa, whoa, whoa!" Jin suddenly caught her, and brought her to a stand still. "You're going to hurt yourself doing that."

"I can't say two things at once! I suspect that the genetic key equates to vibrations in the quantum nature of magic—and I'm at a loss as to how to test that theory. There isn't time for me to invent a device that can sample how the magic interplays with matter at the molecular level, or the equipment we would need to recreate that resonance. And according to my last dream, resonance was the key to everything. And if getting home isn't the full ball of wax—"

"Shhh." Jin put his finger to his lips.

She frowned at him and then put her finger over his lips. "Do that again."

"Tinker, listen."

"No, do the 'shhh' thing again."

"Shhhh," Jin repeated and then said, with her finger still in place, "We're picking up the radio from Pittsburgh again. They say that Malice is attacking Oakland."

"I need to get home. And I think I know how."

True Flame drew Wolf aside to speak quietly with him. "You and I have the only attack spells that have a hope of hurting Malice. We need to pair off with the Stone Clan. They'll provide defense while we focus on attack. Which do you want? Forest Moss or Earth Son?"

The mad one or the male who hated him? Both had good cause to see him dead. If they were wise, they would hold their political maneuverings until after the dragon was dead. Where Forest Moss lacked sanity, Earth Son lacked political savvy; Wolf did not think either was rational enough for wisdom. While he trusted Jewel Tear to defend the enclaves, he was not sure he could entrust their safety to the males.

"I would rather not stake my life—and the lives of my people—on the Stone Clan." Wolf spoke the blunt truth.

"I realize that," True Flame said. "But we will need both hands for our most powerful attack spells, which means no shield."

"In that case, I don't want to take *Sekasha* into this battle. I do not want to leave them at the mercy of the Stone Clan."

True Flame nodded. "That would be wise."

"I'll take Earth Son." When faced with two evils, Wolf would rather deal with the known.

When True Flame announced the pairing, Earth Son shook his head.

"I do not like this pairing," Earth Son said. "Forest Moss will go with Wolf."

"You will go with Wolf," True Flame said.

"As clan head I should be with you," Earth Son said.

"I have given the choice of partners to Wolf since he is in disadvantage," True Flame said. "We don't have time for this. You are to pair with Wolf."

Thorne Scratch stepped forward to murmur in Earth Son's ear. The Stone Clan *domou* cast a dark look at his First and then smoothed his face to the unreadable court mask. Wolf wondered what Thorne had to say to Earth Son.

"Fine, I will pair with Wolf Who Rules," Earth Son said. "But my mewling infant of a cousin, I swear that was the last time that you'll twist matters to get an unfair advantage."

The wind shifted, blowing hard from the east. Clouds boiled over Oakland as weather fronts collided. Wolf could sense something alter the wind flow.

"I think the dragon is coming." Wolf motioned that the non-*domana* should retreat to the enclaves.

"Wolf." Stormsong held out something. "This goes in your ear. It's like the walkie-talkie but smaller. *Nagarou* wanted you to have it. You should be able to use it without it interfering with your magic—I tested it with my shield."

Wolf took the small bud of plastic. "How does it—"

Stormsong fitted it into Wolf's ear. "*Nagarou* has gone to act as a spotter with the NSA. He is in the cathedral. He will talk to you."

"Windwolf, this is Oilcan," the young man stated calmly in Wolf's ear. "The dragon is in southeast Oakland, at the intersection of Bates Street and Boulevard of the Allies. It seems to be leveling houses."

Which meant it was less than a mile away.

Wolf did a wide range scry and caught the passage of something large in that area. Earth Son finished his spell and as he shook his head, Wolf lost the scry on the dragon.

"This way." Wolf started to walk. Forbes Avenue was a major street in Oakland, with multiple lanes leading from the downtown out to the Rim. The EIA had stopped traffic in the city, erecting barriers. To his right, at the center of its lush lawn, was the towering Cathedral of Learning with Oilcan at its summit. To his left was the massive stone Carnegie museum.

"Tell me how to get to Bates," Wolf said.

"Go through that parking lot on your left." Oilcan started into the directions.

True Flame indicated that he would continue down Forbes Avenue, following his scry.

The boil of clouds had darkened to angry grey, with streaks of black where thunderheads were starting to build. When Wolf reached the top of Bates Street and looked down the hill it climbed, he saw that the shield around the massive dragon created a miasma that was forming the clouds. He understood now why the humans thought his lightning would be able to strike—it was perfect lightning weather. Cloaked by his shields, Malice moved within the misty darkness, showing only flashes of himself.

"Call your shields," Wolf told Earth Son. "Keep him back, otherwise the lightning will arc to us."

Remember, you can't trust Earth Son, Wolf thought to himself, and called on the winds in order to summon his lightning.

The darkness shifted, as if Malice had turned, and the gleam of his eyes appeared in the miasma and then vanished.

"He's shifting to your right." Oilcan's voice was flat with the effort to keep the information concise. "He stopped just around the corner, behind the brick house."

Wolf didn't know how Oilcan could tell from his perch above the miasma, but Wolf knew the humans had their ways. Magic thrummed around him, ready to be used. He shifted through his call-lightning spell. His right hand primed the clouds as his left hand readied the ground. Magic flooded the street on a hot wave of air that flared out his duster. The hairs on his arms lifted as the magic shifted into potential. He felt it reach critical point and he brought his hands together, aiming the channel through which the lightning would run. The faint leader flashed downward out of the belly of the clouds, and then the return stroke leapt from behind the brick, up to meet the leader with a deafening clap of thunder. The blinding column of light flared the dark miasma to white haze, and the thunder rumbled as the stroke climbed up into the sky.

Malice roared in pain and anger. The lightning licked the

sky, as leader and return stroke danced back and forth over the open channel.

"He's coming at you!" Oilcan said.

"Keep him back!" Wolf shouted at Earth Son and started another call.

Earth Son locked into place, both hands set into shields. He was holding a force wall set half a block around them and another shield wrapped tight around himself. The lightning flared again and again. Wolf could feel the thunder in his bones. Malice stepped *through* the brick house, coiling like a ghost snake. His eyes gleamed bloodred. Down Malice's left flank was a massive smoking wound.

Wolf felt twin spikes of magic flash through the area and a moment later a fire strike bloomed around the ghost Malice. The dragon ignored the flames, rushing toward Earth Son's force wall. Wolf focused on the growing potential, waiting for it to hit the critical point. He could only cast the spell, though, if Earth Son kept the dragon at a distance.

The lightning died and darkness closed in around them.

"He's through your shield!" Oilcan cried. "He's through your shield!"

Malice must have stepped through Earth Son's shield the same way he had walked through the house. There was no time for Wolf to change spells.

"Earth Son, cover me, damn you!"

In the dark, the ghost Malice was a presence felt, not seen or heard, bearing down on him. A fire flare went off, lighting the area. Malice loomed over them, transparent as smoke. As the dragon snapped into solid form, a shield wrapped around Wolf. Forest Moss was protecting him.

The dragon struck Wolf. The shield held, but the ground underneath didn't. The pavement under Wolf's feet lifted, and he was airborne.

He had a dozen heartbeats to realize that Forest Moss had lost track of him. He had no protection. And then he smashed down through the skylight roof at the museum. He tumbled painfully downwards through the building. Unseen layers broke

under him, as if he was falling through a house of cards. He landed hard on a marble floor, surrounded by construction materials.

"Windwolf! Windwolf!" Oilcan shouted over the radio.
"He's still after you! Can you hear me! Malice is coming for you!"

Gasping for breath he tried to get up. Pain shot up from
Wolf's right hand. Hissing, he looked down and found his fingers
bent at impossible angles. He cursed, hunching over his hand.
He could attack or defend, but not both now.

"Windwolf?" Oilcan called to him again.

"I hear you."

"The oni are attacking the dreadnaught."

Wolf cursed. "Get a message to True Flame. Tell him to
deal with the oni. I'll keep Malice busy."

A backup source of magic was shielded, the spells were
printed off and floated in place, the computers were turned off,
and the crew was gathered around her. Tinker cast the magical
magnetic pulse spell and it flashed through her like a cold wind,
leaving her feeling strangely empty. With sudden panic, she
realized that her body might be a living computer.

Oh gods, I hope that didn't destroy my ability to call the stones!

Esme powered up the workstation beside her. "Well, it didn't
kill our computers. We're coming up to spell stone range in two
minutes."

Tinker triggered the first spell that pumped the filtered stored
magic out. It was a relief to feel the magic start to pool around her
feet. Tinker had told the astronauts that she needed silence, and they
had taken her seriously. They watched now, silent, fearful. More
than one had their eyes closed, and lips moving in prayer.

Esme indicated that they were at the one-minute mark.

Tinker made sure her fingers on both hands were in the correct position, and then stood, waiting.

Esme held up her fingers then and counted the last ten
seconds down silently. When she nodded, Jin—with Tinker's
right hand nearly touching his mouth—and Xiao Chen—on
Tinker's left—pronounced the activation words for the Wind and
Stone Clans.

Magic flooded through the connection. Tinker let it run for thirty seconds by Esme's silent count. She could feel the purity of it, but the edges were starting to tangle, caught by the magnetic field of the ship. She dropped her hands and the tengu went silent.

The activation word for the dragon spell was simple. She spoke it into the tense silence.

The universe went dark and formless.

It wasn't the sense of falling that she always felt during Startup and Shutdown. This was like death. All Tinker could feel was growing terror that she had just pulled her greatest fuckup. She had killed herself and all the astronauts. Then light and sound and gravity returned, tumbling Tinker and the others into a pile of bodies. The "floor" now formed walls up to the matching bulkhead ceiling. They untangled themselves, laughing with relief.

"It worked." By the tone of her voice, Xiao Chen hadn't expected it to.

Tinker wanted to say, "Of course," but the way her life had been going, the mind boggled as to all the ways it might have screwed up. "We're on a planet, but which one?"

Esme glanced upward to the window far over their heads. "Don't know yet."

"We landed well." Jin headed up the ladder. Tinker followed.

"That was not a landing," Esme called after them.

"We're on the ground," Tinker said. "Engines down, bridge up. That's good enough for me."

"You do realize that this ship is nearly a half mile long?" Esme said.

Oops.

Jin reached the window. He turned his head this way and that, studying the view intently, before announcing. "Trees. Nothing but trees."

"It's not Onihida or Earth then," Tinker said. "I hope it's Elfhome, or we ended up someplace totally new."

"That was the point of the colonization program as far as the humans were concerned," someone said from below.

"There's an airlock at midsection." Jin kept climbing upward. "We might be able to get a better view."

Tinker only gave the window a passing glance. The trees looked like ironwoods but it was difficult to tell. They were ten or twenty feet above the canopy. If this was Turtle Creek, then she had just erected the tallest structure in Pittsburgh—for however long it remained standing.

The airlock opened to summer dusk. There was a narrow ledge that wrapped around the ship. Tinker carefully picked her way around and found what she most wanted to see—Pittsburgh. Clouds boiled over Oakland, but no lightning flashed from them. Was that a good sign or bad? Had Malice killed Windwolf?

They had "landed" in Turtle Creek, neatly replacing the Ghostlands with the massive bulk of the ship's engines. The *Dahe Hao* would have taken out the center section of the Westinghouse Bridge if it hadn't already fallen. The remaining spans of the bridge butted up against the side of the ship just ten feet down from the ridge she stood on.

And like one of her impossible dreams, Pony stood on the bridge, looking up at her. He lifted up his arms and motioned for her to jump to him. Relief flooded through her like a weakness. Her legs started to buckle, so she leapt to him.

Pony caught her and pulled her close. "*Domi.*"

"Oh, Pony, I was so scared that you were killed." She hugged him tightly, burying her face into the warmth of his neck, smelling his scent.

"I thought I lost you." His voice was husky with emotion.

She kissed him on the strong line of his jaw. He turned his head and captured her mouth with his and kissed her deeply. He tasted of the enclave peaches; the sweetness poured through her like warm honey; she clung to him, letting the feeling push out the fear and worry.

Tinker realized that Stormsong was beside her. She burned with sudden embarrassment at the way she was acting. Knowing that neither elf would see it as wrong didn't help.

She broke the kiss but couldn't bring herself to let go of

Pony. With one hand, she reached out to Stormsong to pull her into a three-way huddle. "And you too. I was worried sick about both of you."

"What? I don't get a kiss?" Stormsong teased.

Tinker laughed and kissed her quickly on the lips. Then holding them close, she whispered. "Is Windwolf all right? Where is he? What's happened?"

"We can not get close enough to the museum to look for Wolf," Pony said. "Malice, though, appears to be searching for something, so we think that Wolf has eluded him."

"The oni have stolen the dreadnaught and taken it down river," Stormsong said. "Our greatest fear has been that while Malice kept us busy, the oni would push an army through the Ghostlands."

"Well, I stopped that." Tinker gave a weak laugh.

As Pony and Stormsong updated her, Cloudwalker, Rainlily, and Little Egret joined them at the end of the bridge. She greeted them with hugs. It felt good to be surrounded by her people.

The *sekasha* shifted to face crew members picking their way around the edge of the ship. It was Esme with Jin and a handful of the tengu crew members.

"It's okay. I've taken the tengu as my beholden."

"Are you sure that's wise?" Pony asked.

"Yes." She took a deep cleansing breath. She pressed her palms to her eyes and considered current obstacles and possible tools. If Malice was hunting Windwolf, then they would have to hunt Malice. The EMP spell that she had used to clear the ship should work on Malice. They needed, however, a big gun to take advantage of it—a very big gun. She could think of only one place they could get such a gun. "Okay, we're going to need the dreadnaught."

"What's a dreadnaught?" Jin asked.

"I suppose you could call it an attack helicopter on steroids," Tinker said. "It's more a flying fortress. It's armed with a variety of heavy guns, from machine guns to cannons, and can carry a large number of troops into any location. The elves built them with magic in mind—so they're very low tech, and thus extremely clunky."

"And you want us to take it out?" Jin asked.

"No," Tinker said. "We need it to take on Malice."

"Take it over?" Stormsong said. "Are you fucking insane?"

She held up her hands to ward off Stormsong's objections. "While we were at Aum Renau, I got inside of the dreadnaughts. I think it was part of me being the pivot—they didn't know what I would need to stop the oni, so they told me anything I wanted to know—full access to everything."

"Yes," Stormsong hissed, her eyes going soft and vague. "The pivot keeps turning until the door is fully shut."

Tinker shivered. "Oh, that creeps me out. I took detailed notes and I scanned them into my datapad – I was thinking of making a few for the Wind Clan."

"You would," Jin murmured.

"The big question is—do we have anyone that knows how to fire the guns?" Tinker expected that they would need to track down some the Fire Clan crew. Surprisingly, all the *sekasha* pointed to themselves.

"We were all taught how when we were in Aum Renau," Pony explained. "After you showed an interest in the airship."

"They didn't miss a trick with me being the pivot, did they? How the hell did I miss—never mind, don't answer that."

"We will need a pilot," Stormsong said. "The oni killed the dreadnaught's crew."

"How close is it to Earth's aircraft?" Esme had worked her way down to the bridge. She spoke Elvish, which surprised Tinker and also made her realize that Jin had been speaking it too.

"The controls are modeled after a helicopter's," Tinker said.

"I'm your pilot then." Esme noted Tinker's surprise. "I'm the best fucking pilot you're going to find. It's the magic. On Elfhome, I can fly blindfolded." Tinker remembered Stormsong's ability with the hoverbike and realized that Esme probably had the same type of talent. "Taking over controls midair might be tricky—but should be a piece of cake compared to some of the NASA simulations."

"You know," Durrack called out of the gathering twilight, announcing the NSA's arrival. "We're going to have to reclassify you to 'force of nature.'"

"Oh good," Tinker said. "We're going to do an assault on the dreadnaught and we could use your help."

Briggs laughed as she joined Durrack. "And she's not even trying to be scary."

Tinker kept losing count of their numbers. They would need a tengu to get every non-tengu up to the dreadnaught while it was in flight. The problem was that she kept forgetting to count herself, or she added herself to both elves and humans. It was really starting to bug her.

"Eighteen," she hissed to herself. "Nine tengu and nine people without wings."

While the elves and the NSA agents arranged transportation and weapons, and the *sekasha* magical supplies, she and the ship tengu gathered high-tech gear.

"I found the dreadnaught," Durrack called as Jin winged her down to the bridge. Dusk was deepening into night. "The oni took it downriver to Shippensport and took over the nuclear power plant."

"Without power, the humans will be crippled." Pony pointed out the logic of the oni's attack.

As if we didn't have enough to worry about. "Did they damage the nuclear plant?"

"No, they haven't. They just took it off the grid. EIA has dispatched a team to take it back, but they don't have any way to fight Malice. They're leaving him to us."

"Did you find everything?" Getting a nod, she motioned toward the yellow delivery truck that the NSA had produced. "Let's go."

Malice cocked his head, as if listening carefully.

Suddenly there was a massive boom, loud beyond description. A shock wave of air suddenly blasted through the streets, and a moment later, there was an echo under foot.

What was that? Wolf wondered.

Someone looped an arm under Wolf's and pulled him to his feet.

"Shhhh," a male hissed, and then added in English. "Don't use magic."

The male was an Asian human. He tucked in under Wolf's arm, supporting him.

As Malice crashed loudly through the rubble, the man guided Wolf backward, unhurried. Malice scanned the room, swinging his head back and forth, as if searching for them without seeing them. What magic was this that the man had?

A cold chill went down Wolf's back as he realized that the male's ears were furred and pointed like a cat's. This was an oni like Lord Tomtom. Judging by Malice's seemingly blind search, the oni was keeping the dragon from seeing them. But why was the oni helping Wolf?

Malice stilled and the oni froze in place. The dragon cocked its head again as if listening closely. The oni male tightened his hold on Wolf as if worried that Wolf could act. Wolf, however, was under no illusions as to how useless his magic was at the moment.

The great beast grumbled, its voice like thunder, and it sniffed deeply. The massive head turned toward them and Malice stared long at where they stood. The oni stared back, gripping Wolf tightly.

Was the dragon truly fooled, or was Wolf the one being deceived? It was an uncomfortable thought—as was the awareness that the oni had hold of his good hand, making him totally helpless.

Malice stalked forward, muttering deeply. The dragon stopped again, now only a dozen paces from them. Malice rumbled out, seemingly in disgust; its breath washed over them. The oni pulled a container of red powder out of his pocket, and silently emptied it onto the floor. Malice sniffed deeply again, forming runnels in the dust at their feet breathing in the red powder. The dragon flung back its head, gave a series of deep coughing roars, and shuffled back suddenly, away from them.

The oni jerked Wolf backward and they hurried to a staircase at the corner of the room, and down the steps into darkness. Behind them, Malice smashed loudly, roaring, but Wolf couldn't tell in which direction the dragon was heading—after them or away. In the complete darkness, they made a series of quick turns. Either the oni could see in the darkness or was running blind with one hand on the wall.

"What is that red powder?" Wolf asked.

"Cayenne pepper."

They turned again, and the black gave way. A grate stood half-open to a dimly lit tunnel crowded by three pipes thick around as an elf. The oni pulled Wolf into the tunnel and shut the grate.

"This way," the oni male said.

The floor was curved, making walking difficult. A hundred feet down, the tunnel joined another. Wolf knew that they couldn't be inside the museum anymore.

"What is this place?" Wolf asked.

"You ask a lot of questions."

"I like knowing where I stand."

"Yeah, nice when you can get it." The oni kept walking. "These are the old steam tunnels that used to heat all of Oakland."

"Who are you?"

"My name is my own to have," the oni said.

"That makes it awkward to thank you."

The oni paused to look at him. Finally, he said, "You can call me Tommy."

"Tommy," Wolf bowed. "Thank you."

Tommy grunted as if surprised.

"You are Lord Tomtom's son?" Wolf asked.

Tommy started down the tunnel without seeing if Wolf followed. "His bastard. Don't think that you did a disfavor to me by killing him. Quite the opposite. I would have killed him myself if I thought I could have gotten away with it."

"I see."

"No, you don't. You have no idea. He raped my mother just to see if he could get a human pregnant. It took him months to get her knocked up, and he kept her tied to the bedpost the entire time. Even after I was born, he'd come to our place and beat the snot out of both of us and rape her again, just because he could."

"Is that why you helped me?"

Tommy glanced at Wolf, ears laid back. At the next intersection, he paused to ask quietly, "What am I?"

"You? You're an oni."

"The fuck I am. I'm a human."

"Your father—"

"Was a sadist pig." Tommy stalked off. "So my good, kind,
beat-to-death mother doesn't count, even though she contributed
half my genes, gave birth to me, and raised me to be a man? A
human man. I'm *not* one of them. Not that that means shit to
you elves."

Wolf had never considered that the half-oni would think of
themselves as human. How could he refute the difference that
mind-set made in a person? Making Tinker an elf had not
changed her basically human outlook. If the half-oni had the
capacity for human compassion, then it had to be logical that they
could be revolted by the oni's lack of it.

"It means something to me," Wolf told Tommy.

Tommy stared at him again, as if trying to see into the
inner workings of his mind. Perhaps he could. "We know that
the plan is to kill all of us mixed-bloods alongside of the oni, but
we're more willing to gamble on you elves being humane than
the oni."

How ironic, that both sides were looking for humanity in
the other.

"We don't want to be their slaves," Tommy continued.
"We've had thirty years of that shit."

"Then why didn't you leave? There's a whole planet for you
'humans' to go to."

Tommy made a sound of disgust. "It's all so black-and-white
to you elves? I don't get how you can live so long and not realize the
world is full of grey. We didn't leave because we couldn't."

"Why couldn't you?"

"You can't just walk out at Shutdown. The UN has fences
and guards and you have to have the right papers or they throw
you in prison. And even if you get past the guards, you need a
birth certificate and social security numbers and high school

diplomas to live in the United States. And you need money, or you're out on the street and starving."

"And you don't have these things?"

"The oni are masters of keeping power to themselves. They've got all the paperwork. They try to keep us from learning how to speak and read English. They know how much money we're making, and they'll beat us half to death if they even suspect we're trying to keep a little on the side. We don't know how many oni there are in Pittsburgh—who is a disguised oni and who isn't—so we can't even turn to the humans for help. The oni spy on us as much as they spy on you."

Wolf wasn't sure if Tommy was telling him the truth, but certainly it would explain how the oni kept control of the half-breeds. He could see ways around the oni enslavement—until he remembered that all the half-oni would have been born and raised in the oni control. A child could be kept ignorant, molded into believing it was helpless.

Tommy stopped him with a hand on his shoulder. The half-oni's ears twitched. Wolf caught an echo of harsh voices. He would have to accept it as real.

"There are oni ahead of us," Tommy whispered. "We can't go this way. I can only cloud their sight and they have noses like dogs."

Wolf nodded, and followed Tommy back to a tunnel they'd passed before. They went through a maze of turns and up a flight of stairs to go through another grate into a basement stacked high with cardboard boxes. The labels indicated that the boxes once held cans of food. Just as Wolf wondered whether they still contained their original contents, Tommy opened a door and the smell of cooking food flooded over them.

Beyond the door was a large kitchen filled with Asians. A low right-angled counter divided the kitchen off from the restaurant's dining room. The long leg into the dining room was a bakery display case filled with buns and breads.

"What are you doing here, Tommy?" one of the cooks, an old man, asked in Mandarin as he took a tray of buns from the oven. "Bringing him here?"

"The oni are in the steam tunnels," Tommy answered in the same tongue.

"Ugh!" the old man grunted. "You'll get us all killed."

Wolf looked at the crowded kitchen. "These are all mixed bloods?"

"No." Tommy wove through the cooks. "These are all humans. That was my great-uncle."

A herd of children galloped into the kitchen from a back room. Some could pass as human—might even be fully human—but mixed in were children with horns and tails. With cries of dismay, in ones and twos, the adults yanked the children out of Wolf's path, leaving only one child standing alone.

The little female looked up at him fearlessly and he knew her. Zi.

"Hi." She cocked her head, puzzled by his presence. She had a cookie in either hand. She held one up to him. "Do you want a cookie?" And when he hesitated, she added, "I didn't drop it or anything."

"Thank you." Wolf took the cookie with his left hand and bowed slightly to her. "That is very nice of you."

"Come on." Tommy caught him by the left wrist, and said in rough Low Elvish, "If oni find you here—they kill everyone."

"What is she doing here?" Wolf resisted being moved. He had demanded that the little female be kept away from people that would poison her against elves.

"No one else would take her. The humans are afraid of the oni and the oni don't give a shit. Look at me, I'm Lord Tomtom's son, and even I don't get a disguise to protect me."

Wolf scanned the kitchen, seeing this time that the children were in the arms of only small-framed, battered women. There were only two males, men made fragile by time. They used Mandarin in their fearful cries, and it was Chinese written on the signs posted around the room. The Skin Clan had used this kind of slavery—transporting women out of their homelands to places they couldn't speak the language and then tied them down with children.

He understood now Tommy's hate. It was the same hate that had fueled the genocide of the Skin Clan.

Tommy suddenly pushed him back against the wall. "Stay still! I don't have my father's talent—I can't mask a moving object from multiple watchers. They will kill *everyone* if they find you here!" He glanced to his uncle. "Mask the scent!"

The uncle opened the fridge, took out a container, and flung the contents on the grill. An eye-watering reek filled the air. "Onions! Pepper!"

While some of the women quickly herded the children upstairs, others took out knives and attacked onions and bright red peppers. Tommy's focus was on the door. Moments later, it opened, and oni warriors crowded into the restaurant. There were a dozen large, red-haired, horned males. They had war paint on their faces and carried machine guns and swords. They snarled in Oni, wrinkling up their noses against the assault of smell.

The leader was the tallest among them. He set four of the warriors to watch the street and barked orders to the others. Three warriors raided the bakery counter. The rest moved into the kitchen and back rooms. The leader picked out a female, shoved her face down onto one of the tables, tore away her skirt, and forced himself into her with brutal casualness. The woman pressed knuckles into her mouth, stifling whimpers. No one else appeared even to notice, but Tommy locked down hard on Wolf's good arm.

The bakery raiders stuffed their mouths and pockets and then flung the buns to other warriors.

Outside, a deep roar from Malice echoed up the street.

"He sounds hungry." The leader spoke Mandarin so that the humans could understand. "He's probably looking for something to eat."

The warriors bayed with laughter and gestured at the frightened women. "We can feed him one of these fat sluts. That one looks like it has a fat ass."

The leader finished with the woman he was raping and slapped her buttocks. "Yes, a nice fat ass."

Their hunger satisfied, the warriors pelted each other with bread. The leader barked an order. The warriors gathered again at the front of the restaurant. The last one out of the back room, though, was carrying a whimpering, squirming Zi.

"Look what they have." The warrior held the little female out by the back of her shirt.

The leader took her by her throat. He turned and shook the child at the human like rag doll. "What is this doing here?"

"The EIA—" Uncle stuttered. "They imprisoned her crazy mother."

The leader grunted. "If the elves find this here, they'll know that this place belongs to us."

"We'll move her." Uncle held out his arms but moved no closer to the warriors.

Without word or warning the oni leader broke Zi's neck.

Everyone had told Wolf about the oni savageness—but he hadn't comprehended it fully until too late. He gasped out in shock as the oni leader dropped the child's limp body onto the floor.

"Malice is coming. Throw this out onto the street for him to eat."

Wolf breathed in and anger burned through him like fire. Nothing mattered but to see these monsters dead. He jerked his arm free of Tommy, summoned a force strike and slammed it into the back of the oni leader. The front of the restaurant exploded out as the strike drove the oni male across the street. He made a bloody star on the far building. The warriors scrambled for cover, pulling out their machine guns.

"Hold still, you stupid elf fuck!" Tommy growled.

Wolf braced himself as he flicked through a fire burst. The oni bullets chewed through the other side of the restaurant. Apparently between Wolf's sudden attack and Tommy clouding their minds, the oni were disoriented as to where Wolf was really standing. The fire burst went off, igniting three of the oni into columns of flame.

Wolf slammed a force strike at the last oni. A second bloody star joined the first.

"What the fuck was that?" Tommy screamed. "She was dead! This does nothing but make you feel better! All those women and children are now dead because you had to be a hero!"

Someone as young as the half-oni couldn't understand that to be immortal was to have forever to regret. Wolf knew if he had let the oni walk away unpunished, he would not be able to live with himself. But Tommy was right. He had brought danger down on the rest—the human mothers and half-oni children.

"I'll see that they're safe until this is done."

"Yeah, that will make the kids safe! Until you kill them for no other reason than their mothers were raped by the wrong species."

"I give you my word—they will not be harmed."

Tommy caught himself from saying anything else, and stood, fists balled, panting.

"Windwolf?" Oilcan murmured in Wolf's ear. "If you're the one that just took out the Changs' restaurant, Malice is coming your way."

Wolf glanced out into the street where the oni still burned like massive candles. "Malice is coming. Get the others. We need to move to someplace safe."

Tommy's cat ears flicked. "Oh fuck. He is coming." Tommy went off to gather the women and children.

Wolf gazed again the wreckage he was leaving behind. Tinker was rubbing off on him.

22: END OF THE RAINBOW

Briggs drove while the rest of them sat in the back. Tinker had grabbed a flex screen from the ship and now spread it out on the floor. Downloading the dreadnaught's layout and defenses, they planned the assault.

"The dreadnaught's biggest weakness is that it wasn't built with an aerial attack in mind. It's like a turtle, with lots of service hatches down in through its shell. Also it tends to be blind in the butt. I was going to fix that with a turret on top."

"Prince True Flame said that it was useless for fighting the dragon because it couldn't defend against from attacks from above," Pony said.

"That's true," Tinker said. "So we're going to have to kill Malice before he has a chance to close."

"Oh, fun," Esme muttered.

"But the airship is vulnerable to the tengu," Tinker said. "I think if we fly up behind it, we can approach it unseen—but it leaves a very choppy wake."

"We can handle it, *domi*." Jin waved off the worry.

Domi. That drove her commitment to them home and left her a little breathless. *I'm responsible for them—and I'm taking them straight into danger.* But what recourse did she have? Just as the elves were not about to let the oni live, the oni couldn't leave any of the elves alive either.

"We need three things." Tinker forced herself to focus on the plan and not how badly it might end. "We need to keep the ship in the air, pick where it goes, and fire the cannons. So, that means we need to secure the fore and aft engine compartments, the cannon turrets, and the bridge."

Pony gazed at the plan for a moment, and then pointed to the access hatch nearest to the rear, which opened to the aft engine compartment. "We'll enter here. Once we've secured it, we'll break into teams. These tengu are good with machines—yes?" Getting a nod from Tinker, Pony continued. "There are three doors to this area including the hatch, so Little Egret and four tengu will stay."

Jin assigned Xiao Chen and three of the other tengu to the aft team.

"The rest of us will then move to the fore engine compartment and take it." Pony traced a route across the top of the airship to the forwardmost service hatch. "Four doors open to this area, but we'll control what's beyond these two doors. Rainlily and four of the tengu will hold this position. We split here. *Domi* and Cloudwalker will take the bridge with Esme, Jin, and Durrack—which should be lightly manned and will have only one door not controlled by us. Stormsong and Briggs will come with me. We'll take the main cannon turret—which will be heavily manned."

Tinker explained how she planned to kill Malice. "Now when this spell goes off, you're going to lose your shields and it might take a minute or two before a normal level of magic is restored," she warned her Hand. "Your beads should be protected from the spell effects, so if you save the power in them, you can recast your shields immediately."

The *sekasha* nodded, indicating that they understood.

Durrack pressed his hand to his ear and listened to it intently. "Okay. Understand." He knocked on the partition to the driver's cabin. "Briggs? Where are we?"

"Nearly to McKees Rocks Bridge," Briggs answered.

"The dreadnaught is here." Durrack tapped the map just downriver of Neville's Island, and then ran a finger up the Ohio River toward Pittsburgh. "They're following the river."

"If we're carrying others, we won't be able to climb fast," Jin said. "We should start high, like at the edge of a cliff or on top of a building."

"They'll come over the bridge," Pony pointed to the bridge. "We can wait on the supports. The bridge will give us cover, and then the tengu can take us aloft."

"That will work," Jin said.

Nearly a mile and a half long, the McKees Rocks Bridge stretched across the wide, flat Ohio River valley in a complex string of structures—more a chain of bridges than one single bridge. The part that actually sat above the river was a seven hundred feet long trussed-arch bridge. On each side of the elegant steel curve were two massive stone pylons. They hid the truck in the shadows of the western pylon.

The cloudy night was on their side—it cloaked them in darkness.

"I hear it." Jin put out a hand to Tinker. "I'll take you up."

The other eight tengu paired off with the humans and elves.

It was a short spring up to the arching steel. They crouched down, tucking themselves in the crossbeams.

The roar of the dreadnaught grew louder.

"There! See it?" Jin whispered.

Twin searchlights appeared in the distance, slashing downwards; the cockpit was a pale gleam between them. The dreadnaught moved up the broad valley, keeping between the hills that flanked the Ohio River. The searchlights played back and forth in a narrow arc, directly in front of the airship.

Durrack glanced upriver toward the darkened city and then back to the oncoming dreadnaught. "They're probably following the river because it's the most recognizable landmark they can see with the power out."

"Lucky for us," Jin said. "They're going slow so they don't hit anything. That will make it easier for us to get to it."

In the dark, the true size of the dreadnaught was lost. It was a wedge of darkness behind the searchlights' brilliance. They crouched in the bridge's shadows as the gleaming spots moved across the shimmer of the water, encountered the bridge, and played up and over the network of steel struts. Tinker held still, heart hammering, trying not to think about the machine gun cannons. Her luck on this kind of thing had been so bad lately.

The cockpit slid overhead, and the belly of the dreadnaught followed, the air throbbing. Ushi with Pony leapt upward, the rustle of his black wings spreading lost under the rumble of the dreadnaught's engines. As he took his first downstroke, Xiao Chen with Stormsong vaulted after him. Niu and Zan rose together. Tinker lost sight of them in the dreadnaught's eclipse.

Jin took hold of Tinker and murmured, "Hang on." And then they were airborne.

Amazingly, in some strange heart-stopping manner, winging upward was fun. In her flights with Riki, she had been so concerned about their end destination that she never noticed the thrill of flying. Did it say something about her that as long as she knew where they were going, she could enjoy the ride?

Jin landed them between Ushi and Xiao Chen.

"I think I envy you," Stormsong murmured to Xiao Chen.

Tinker smothered a laugh, and whispered. "Yeah, once you get used to it, it's fairly cool."

"It's wood!" Jin whispered, running his hand over the hull's surface.

"Of course," Tinker whispered. "These are elves."

Her Hand activated their shields. Pony asked a question with blade talk. Getting a nod from the others, he opened the hatch and the *sekasha* dropped down into the dim engine room.

She had never seen the elves really fighting before. Not a full Hand against hordes, unconcerned for her protection because she was safe behind her own shield. She hadn't expected it to be so beautiful. Their swordplay became a fluid dance, the oni seeming like paper cutouts instead of real opponents. The dreadnaught, though, was buzzing like a kicked beehive, and they had spread themselves thin.

On the bridge, Tinker used her shield to back the oni warriors away from the door. Cloudwalker slipped around her on the right and Durrack went left.

"Don't shoot any of the instruments!" Tinker had her pistol out, but was afraid to fire. She rarely hit what she aimed at and all the controls were vital to their success.

"I—don't—miss." Durrack picked his shots with deliberation. "Someone get the pilot before he crashes us!"

Two warriors blocked Tinker.

"Esme, the pilot." Jin spun on one heel and kicked one of the warriors out of Tinker's path. Tinker edged sideways, covering Esme as her mother scrambled into the low cockpit.

The ship banked hard to the left, rushing toward the hills that lined the valley, Esme struggled with the oni pilot.

"Tinker!" Esme cried. "We need to lift! Pull up on the collective."

Dropping her shield, Tinker scrambled into the cockpit and grabbed hold of the collective control stick and pulled up. The engines roared louder and they started to climb.

"Tinker!" Jin shouted warning, and she ducked instinctively.

Bullets sprayed the windshield just over her head. A dozen bullet holes reduced the Plexiglas to a haze of cracked glass.

The oni pilot kicked Tinker backward. She hit the cracked windshield; it held for a moment then gave way. She screamed, flailing, and caught hold of the pilot's leg as she fell. Her weight jerked him half out the cockpit. He grabbed the edge of the cockpit before he fell the whole way out. They dangled far above the last mile of I-279 before it ended at the Rim, the oni pilot holding onto the airship and Tinker onto his leg.

"Jin!" Esme shouted, struggling to keep the airship aloft and reach for the oni pilot at the same time. "I can't reach her!"

Jin shouted; his words resonated against Tinker's senses with magic.

The oni pilot clawed at the edge of cockpit, trying to pull himself up. He grasped the windshield wiper and started to pull himself up.

The wiper snapped and he fell—and Tinker with him.

Tinker screamed and Esme, staring down at her, cried out in dismay.

Then someone caught Tinker's wrist, and she was jerked hard in both directions.

"Let go of him!" Keiko cried, flapping madly. "I can't catch you both; we'll all fall."

"No! No! No!" the pilot wailed, dangling upside down by Tinker's grip on his leg. But she wasn't strong enough to hold his weight by one hand. He slipped out of her hold and plunged downward again. The clouds had slid away and moonlight gleamed silver on the pavement below. The pilot dwindled to doll size but still hit the road with a loud carrying thud, a sudden burst of wet on the grey pavement.

"Shit, shit, shit!" Keiko cried as they continued to slowly fall. "You're still too heavy."

Xiao Chen swooped down and tried to intercept them.

Keiko hissed in anger, bringing up her razor-sheathed feet. "She's charmed by the Chosen's blood. She's not to be hurt!"

"You heard her," Riki glided in. "She's charmed by my line!"

"It's only Xiao—" Tinker yelped as Keiko suddenly passed her to Riki in a mid-air fling.

"I got you," Riki said it as if this was supposed to be comforting. "Keiko!"

The tengu female was heading for the airship. "I was called! He's here! He called!"

"Keiko!" Riki shouted, chasing after the teenager. "Wait! Damn it, Tinker, who is on that dreadnaught?"

"Your uncle Jin."

"That's not possi—" Riki gasped as they swept back in through the shattered windshield and he saw Jin. "Uncle Jin?"

Jin reached out and pulled Tinker out of Riki's hold. "Are you okay?"

"I'm fine." Tinker fought the need to cling to Riki, or Jin. *I'm safe inside. I'm safe inside.*

"What the hell is going on? Where did you come from?" Riki gazed in stunned amazement at the tengu, elves, and humans.

"We got her. She's safe." Durrack had found the speaker tubes to the gun turret and engine rooms. Cloudwalker and Keiko were holding the door that boomed with the oni's attempts to break it down. "Tinker, your cousin says that Malice has Windwolf pinned down in Oakland. If you don't want to be a widow, we better get going."

It took Tinker a second to realize that Durrack had received the last part via his earbud radio and not the speakertube.

"What?" Riki cried. "You're taking on Malice? Are you nuts?"

"I've got a plan." Tinker wondered if that sounded remotely reassuring. She couldn't stop trembling. *Yeah, yeah, I'm fine.* "Do we have the guns?" she asked.

"The Storms are holding the guns." Durrack meant Storm Horse and Stormsong.

Tinker hugged herself, panting, trying to remember said plan. She was missing something important. "Oilcan? Wait? Where's Impatience? I don't want to take him out with this spell—he'll revert to a wild animal and kill anyone near him."

"He's in the cathedral with your cousin," Durrack said.

"Okay, I *really* don't want Impatience in the spell range then." Tinker thought a moment. "Tell Oilcan to put distance between him and Impatience—just to be on the safe side. Esme, let's do a strafing run on Malice."

"And NASA thought it covered all possible flight simulations." Esme banked the ship hard back toward the city.

Clouds continued to clear, and the city resolved out of the darkness. Their shadow ran on ahead of them. Esme climbed out of the river valley, and crested over the Hill District to the flat plain of Oakland.

"Where is Malice?" Tinker asked Durrack.

"See that dark cloud?" Durrack pointed at a billow of darkness that looked like smoke. "That's him."

"Oh, good, he's at least a half mile from the cathedral." Tinker started to unload her bag, setting up for the spell. "Let's get his attention. Esme, get ready to run. Pony, can you hear me?"

"Yes, *domi.*"

"Shoot Malice with one of the cannons. He's going to come fast, so get ready with the other cannon. Fire the second cannon when my spell takes your shield down."

"Yes, *domi,*" Pony said.

Esme had edged sideways so that they hung over Fifth Avenue where it spilled down the hill toward the flood plain of Uptown. The cannon thundered, deafening at close range. The shell whistled away. It hit the edge of the miasma and the black deepened. Something stirred in the darkness. Massive eyes gleamed at the heart of the cloud and then Malice uncoiled and lifted from the ground.

"Here he comes!" Tinker cried.

Esme scuttled the airship backward, roaring out over Uptown, keeping the cannons pointed toward the onrushing dragon. "Come on, come on."

Suddenly Malice dove into the ground.

"Where the fuck did he go?" Esme cried.

"He's phased!" Durrack shouted. "He can move through solid objects!"

"Oh, you've got to be shitting me!" Esme flung the airship forward and they raced up Fifth Avenue, into the heart of Oakland.

"Where are you going?" Tinker cried.

"You said run." Esme put all power into forward motion, tilting the airship to fit down the narrow space of Fifth Avenue. They lost something—hopefully not vital—as they took out one of the red lights over the street.

"Not this way!" Tinker cried, pointing at the towering cathedral that stood over Oakland, where Oilcan was with Impatience.

"It had to be this way!" Esme snapped.

Tinker looked behind them. Malice rose out of the ground where they would have been if they had continued toward Uptown. "Okay, this is good."

"He'll come after us," Esme said. "Trust me. When you run, it's like you put out a sign that says 'free lunch.' It's an easy way to make even the smartest ones get stupid."

Perhaps she was right; Malice was giving chase, coiling through the air like a snake in water. Esme banked around the curve of the Hill, nearly clipping the tops of houses.

"It's like trying to drag race in a Volkswagen," Esme complained.

Tinker had been watching the cathedral dwindle behind them. She realized now that they were heading into Downtown, the most densely populated area in Pittsburgh.

"No, not this way either!" Tinker pointed away from the city. "I don't want to open fire in the middle of the city!"

"I don't either," Esme said as they skimmed across the Veterans Bridge and ducked into the forest of skyscrapers. "But we need time for me to get turned around and face him."

They wove through the tall buildings, the gleam of the cockpit reflecting in the glass walls as they streaked by.

"Okay, keep going west." Tinker pointed out west just in case Esme didn't know. "After you get out of the city, try to get Malice south of us, up against Mount Washington. It's a blank slate. We can open fire on him there."

Esme suddenly squeaked in surprise and banked hard to the right. A moment later Malice came *through* a skyscraper and fire jetted out of his mouth. The night went bright with the flame, the light reflecting off the canyon of glass around them.

"Oh shit!" Esme banked again, somehow dodging both the flame and the PPG tower. She clipped the side of the Fifth Avenue Place. "Oh shit—we lost our front right props." She fought the ship to keep it from careening out of control. "No one said anything about him breathing fire!"

"He's a dragon," Jin said. "That's what they do!"

"We've got a fire up here!" one of the tengu shouted from the front engine room.

"We're running out of city," Durrack warned.

"I know, I know, I know." Tinker was loath to open fire in the city, but if Malice took the airship down, they'd lose the guns and then they'd all die. Point Park was going to have to do. "Get ready, people!"

Esme wrenched the airship about as they roared over the empty expanse of the park. Malice flew at them. Tinker watched him come, spell in hand, waiting for him to get clear of the city.

When he cleared the highway dividing the city from the park, she cast the spell.

The coldness flashed over her. The wings vanished from the

tengu's backs. Cloudwalker's shield winked out. The miasma of
Malice's shield vanished and he fell, twisting madly as he plunged
out of the sky. The cannon roared. The shell caught him in the
left eye, blasting his head backward.

"I'm losing it!" Esme shouted as the dreadnaught slid sideways toward the massive Fort Pitt Bridge. "We're going down!"
Tinker called for her shields and nothing happened. The ambient
magic in the area hadn't recovered from the flux spell yet. "Oh shit."

And then they hit the bridge.

Wolf braced himself for the worst. He had trusted that
Tinker would somehow kill the dragon, but he was afraid she had
leapt one too many times into the void. As he hurried toward the
downed dreadnaught, his fears only deepened. The airship had
struck the first span of the twin-decked bridge and then crashed
into the Monongahela River. The crumpled wreckage lay half in
and half out of the water. Human emergency crews gathered on
the shore and on the water, trucks and boats with bright flashing
lights.

Wolf pushed through the tightest knot of people to find
Little Egret lying unconscious on the pavement. A pair of soaked
tengu were giving the young *sekasha* CPR. As he watched, Little
Egret coughed and sputtered weakly back to life. Oilcan had told
him that the astronaut tengu were helping Tinker kill the dragon.
He assumed that these two were part of that crew.

"Where's Tinker?" Wolf asked the two tengu.

"We were in the aft engine room." The tengu female indicated the submerged section of the dreadnaught and then made a
vague motion at the part smashed up against the bridge. "She was
in the cockpit."

He left a healer from the hospice with Little Egret and moved
on, working his way around the airship. One section was still
burning, and the humans were frantically trying to douse the
flames. Wolf caught snatches of their conversations that focused
on the live ammo still on board the ship.

There was a body under a white sheet. He paused to draw
aside the sheet. A male tengu, badly burned.

Little Horse, Discord, and Briggs were on the other side of the wreckage. They worked with the Pittsburgh fire fighters and more tengu, hacking at the splintered wood hull.

"*Domi* was on the bridge with Cloudwalker." Little Horse hacked at a section of the hull with his *ejae*. "Rainlily took in too much smoke, but she got out without being burned. Two of the tengu with her were not so lucky. You were hurt?"

Wolf held up his spell-covered hand, careful not to flex. "Just this but it's healing." Wolf glanced over at a row of dead bodies covered with sheets. "How many tengu did you take with you?"

"Those are oni." Discord was favoring the leg bitten by the dragon earlier in the week. "Most we killed taking the dread-naught."

Blood on the pavement showed that there had been fighting after the crash too.

A cry went up and people were lifted free of the wreckage. A tengu male and female, both young, faces painted for war. They were battered but alive.

"Were they with you or against you?" Wolf asked.

"They caught *domi* when she was knocked from the dread-naught," Little Horse said.

"*Domi* promised that all tengu would be under her protection," Discord added.

"All?" Wolf indicated that the war-painted tengu were not to be harmed. "How many does that include?"

Discord shrugged and then gave a wry smile. "I do not think *domi* bothered to find out."

More survivors were lifted out. Durrack, a woman, and another pair of tengu, these from the spaceship.

"I can see shielding!" Little Horse cried. "Cloudwalker has his shield up!"

"He and *domi* should be the only ones left," Discord said.

They cut carefully through the shattered wood and broken instruments to the young *sekasha*. Despite his shield, he'd been knocked unconscious. He still protected Tinker, however, in his loose hold. Wraith leaned into the hole they had cut and whispered to Tinker the word to deactivate Cloudwalker's shields, which needed to be spoken close to the *sekasha*'s heart. It felt like eternity before the hurt and dazed Tinker understood what was wanted of her and the shimmering blue of the shields vanished.

The healers from the hospice cast spells to make sure they could be safely moved, then the two were lifted carefully out of the womb of twisted wreckage. Only then could Wolf hold Tinker in his arms and reassure himself that she had emerged once again safely out of the void. She seemed so small and fragile without her normal vibrant personality.

"Oh, thank gods, I was so worried about you," she murmured as if it had been him in the airship. "The others?"

"Your Hand is safe." He spared her the news of the dead tengu.

She cried in dismay at the extent of the damage to the airship. "Oh, I crashed True Flame's dreadnaught! He's going to be angry."

"He will not care. It is a thing. All things wear out—just usually not in such a spectacular fashion."

Tinker groaned.

"Do not worry, beloved. He will only be concerned that you and yours are safe and that the dragon is dead."

Tinker whimpered against his shoulder. "Windwolf, I've made the tengu mine."

"So I've heard."

"Please, don't hurt them. I promised them that they will be safe."

"They are safe."

"You won't hurt them?"

"I will protect them for you." He kissed her carefully. "Rest."

True Flame and the Stone Clan were arriving, so he reluctantly, gave Tinker over to the healers and the protection of her beholden.

True Flame stopped on the edge of the roadway where he could see the dead dragon, the crashed dreadnaught, and in the distance, like an exclamation mark in the weak morning sky, the towering spaceship.

"You were right, Wolf."

"I was?"

"She's surprisingly destructive for one so small. I am starting to see why you love her so—she is the right size for you."

"Yes, she is."

A shout caught his attention. Little Horse and Wraith Arrow were holding the Stone Clan *sekasha* back from the tengu.

"What's going on here?" True Flame stalked down to the river's edge.

"These tengu are still alive." Earth Son stood behind his First, Thorne Scratch. He pointed at the battered and soaked tengu who had given Little Egret CPR.

"Yes," Wolf noticed that the Wyverns were watching. A whispered discussion was being passed through their ranks. "And they are staying that way. My *domi* has taken the tengu as beholden."

"They are oni," Earth Son snapped. "We must eliminate the monsters before they can breed to dangerous numbers."

"The tengu and the half-oni are no different than the elves," Wolf pitched his argument to True Flame and the silent *sekasha*. "We were created by the Skin Clan, as they were created by the oni. They are turning on the oni as we turned on the Skin Clan. Yes, the oni are as evil as the Skin Clan—but we merely need to look at ourselves to know that good can come from evil."

"Tengu flock together." Forest Moss drifted into the conversation, his tone light, as if he was discussing clouds. Wolf could not tell how the mad one felt on the issue. "Their loyalty to one another will supersede any claim that they make to you. If you act against one of their brethren, they will turn on you."

"Tinker *ze domi* holds all the tengu," the astronaut tengu named Jin said.

True Flame looked at Jin. "All? How many are all?"

The war-painted male stepped forward, apparently speaking for the Elfhome-based tengu. "We don't have a full count. It has been too dangerous to count, lest the oni ever found out what we were doing."

"Which was?" Wolf asked.

"We hoped to be free here on Elfhome," Riki said. "So in the last twenty-eight years, all of the tengu of Earth and Onihida have come to Elfhome."

"All?" True Flame glanced over the ten living tengu. "Are we speaking hundreds? Thousands? Millions?"

"Several thousand." Riki glanced to Jin to see if he should be more specific and got a nod. "We believe around twenty thousand."

Which meant they greatly outnumbered the oni now trapped on Elfhome.

True Flame turned to Wolf. "How does your *domi* possibly think she could hold all of them?"

"Through me," Jin said, "I am Jin Wong. I am the heart and soul and voice of the tengu. I speak, and all will listen."

"I doubt this greatly," True Flame said.

Jin raised his hands and gave out a call toward the east. It resonated with magic, as if his voice alone triggered some spell. He turned to the north and called. He faced the west and called. Even as he faced the south and called, a rustle of wings announced the arrival of a great flock of tengu. The sky went dark with the crow-black feathers. Warriors all, faces painted, and feet sheathed in sharpened steel. They carried guns holstered on their hips. They settled silently on the bridge trusses, the tops of buildings, and streetlights.

When the last tengu went still, Jin called again, magic pulsing out from him. It echoed off the buildings and the hillside across the river. He turned, gazing at them, as if he too were stunned by the massive numbers of them. "I am Jin Wong! I have returned to our people!"

And the tengu flock shouted back, "Jin! Jin! Jin!"

Jin raised his hands and the flock fell silent. "We are entering into an alliance with the elves. We are taking Tinker *ze domi* as our protector. Under her, I hope that for the first time our people will live in peace, security, and prosperity."

The flock roared in approval, a deafening sound that washed over them. Jin raised his hand, commanding silence, and received instant obedience.

"Jin offered his people," Wolf said in the silence. "*Domi* offered her protection. Such an oath, once made, no other person can break."

"This is true," True Flame said.

Earth Son had cast his shield, encompassing only him and his *sekasha*. "She can't hold them. This is preposterous."

"They fit the model of a household with Jin as the head," Wolf said.

"Only clan heads can hold that many people," Earth Son said. "And she is nothing but a—"

"She is my *domi* and we are the clan heads of the Westernlands," Wolf growled. "Forest Moss is right. You are blind. Tinker has closed the Ghostlands." Wolf pointed to Malice's massive body. "She killed the dragon that four of us could not harm. She has made a peace with a force that we didn't even know existed. Do not assign her your limitations. We can hold the tengu."

"They are monsters!" Earth Son shouted.

Wolf shook his head. "They were once human, forced into their shape by cruel masters. They have fought beside my *domi* to kill the dragon. They have protected my youngest *sekasha* from harm."

"You are a traitor to your people," Earth Son spat the accusation and then looked to True Flame, as if challenging the prince to refute it.

True Flame said nothing, waiting to see the outcome of the debate.

Wolf directed his argument to the Wyvern and the Stone Clan *sekasha* because he knew that his Hands had already decided on the issue—they wouldn't have defended the tengu otherwise. But their decision was based on their trust in him. The others would need convincing. "My people are those that offer me their loyalty, be they elfin, human, tengu, or half-blooded oni. It is my duty as *domana* to extend protection to those weaker than I am."

"It is our duty to keep our race pure," Earth Son said.

"That is our Skin Clan forefathers speaking. Kill the misbegotten children. Eliminate the unwanted genetic line. Ignore trust, obedience, loyalty, and love in the search for perfection. It was the Skin Clan's way, but it is not ours."

"This is insanity. They breed like mice. All of them do. The oni and the humans. This is our world. If we don't eliminate them, they will overwhelm us."

"If they offer their loyalty and we give them our protection—do they not become one of us? They do not lessen us—they make us greater."

Earth Son worked his mouth for a minute, and then finally cried. "No! No, no, no! They are filthy lying creatures. I am Stone Clan head of the Westernlands, and I say that the Stone Clan will never accept this!"

"I do not care what the Stone Clan accepts." Wolf cocked his fingers, wondering if Earth Son would be as stupid as to actually start a fight with all the tengu assembled. Since Earth Son was holding shields, he could strike quickly. "Know this—the tengu are Wind Clan now. I will protect them."

Earth Son made a motion. It was a start of a spell. What spell Wolf would never know. Wolf snapped his hand up to summon the winds, even though he would be too late to block the attack. Thorne Scratch reacted first. With deliberate calm, she struck out and beheaded Earth Son. His lifeblood sprayed his Hand, but none moved against their First. They watch impassively as his body toppled to the ground.

"We will not follow the path of the Skin Clan." Thorne Scratch cleaned the blood from her *ejae*.

Red Knife, True Flame's First, nodded. "Those that offer loyalty will be protected."

Jewel Tear gazed down at Earth Son's body. "As temporary Stone Clan head of the Westernlands, I recognize that non-elfin can be beholden."

23: PEACE

⟡⟢

Tinker woke slowly. She had been dreaming, but for once, it was a pleasant dream of the new viceroy palace being complete. She had walked from room to room to room, marveling that all this was hers. Theirs.

When she opened her eyes, she knew instantly she was in her own bed at Poppymeadow's because Windwolf lay beside her, his black hair poured like silk across the cream satin sheets. Contentment poured through her like warm honey. She snuggled closer to him. For once the taffy thickness of the *saijin*-induced sleep didn't seem threatening. If she was with Windwolf, then everything was right with the world.

And then with sudden dark coldness, she remembered the tengu. She had promised to protect them but then had let the elves drug her. What had she been thinking of? The elves would have only seen the tengu as enemies.

She sat up, hands to her mouth to hold in the cries of dismay. What had happened after she was carried away? Were Jin, Grace, Xiao Chen, and all the others already dead?

"Beloved?" Windwolf sat up beside her.

"Oh gods, I failed them! I promised Jin I would protect the

352

tengu! I failed them."

"You did not. You are my *domi*. Your promises are mine. I protected them. It was, after all, the right thing to do."

She knew, in a way she wouldn't have known a week ago, what she had asked of him, and how different he had to be from other elves to understand. There been a secret fear hiding inside her that he wouldn't understand, that instead of being a powerful protector, he would be in truth a ruthless killer. That cold knot of fear dissolved.

"Oh, thank you!" She hugged him tight. She didn't need anything else but to be in his arms and hear his heart beating. She snuggled closer, wanting to drown in the *saijin*-laced honey contentment. She never wanted to let him go; never wanted to risk losing him forever again.

"It was the least I could do after you solved that small dragon problem I had." He said it with complete seriousness, but there was laughter in his eyes.

She laughed, tangling her fingers in his hair and pulling him down to kiss her. She delighted in his taste, the feel of his hands on her, finding the hem of her nightgown to slide up her bare skin.

"I love you," she murmured. "I'm never letting you go."

His gaze went serious and deep. "I am going nowhere, my love."

Only later, after a proper renewal of their relationship, did she think about another small dragon problem.

"What happened with Impatience when we did the flux spell? Is Oilcan okay?"

"He is fine." Windwolf smoothed away her fear. "Your spell did not affect the little dragon. And the tengu have been quite useful already. With their help, we had a long discussion with Impatience about creating a pathway to Earth. The question is where to put it."

"What about the Squirrel Hill tunnels? They go nowhere now."

Windwolf considered for a moment and then nodded. "Yes, that would be expedient."

Using the tunnels would open four travel lanes between Elfhome and Earth and yet be easily controlled. "Wow."

"I told you, beloved, you and I would shake the universe until we found a way."

EPILOGUE: CUP OF JOYS

Elves may live forever, but their memories do not. Every elfin child is taught that any special memory has to be polished bright and carefully stored away at the end of a day, else it will slip away and soon be forgotten. The eve of Memory was past, but Wolf wanted to share the ceremony with his *domi*—even if somewhat belatedly. They had time now. He wanted her to know how to save the memories of all that had happened in the last few days, the good along with the bad.

Wolf settled before the altar of Nheoya, god of longevity. His beloved sat down beside him.

Tinker took a deep breath and let it out in a deep, heartfelt sigh. "This is going to be like being dragged through thorns—there's so much I regret. So many ways I've fucked up."

"This is not to punish yourself, beloved. Nothing is gained from that. The worth comes from reflecting on the events—removed from the passion that blinded you at the time—and learning from the mistakes."

"Easier said than done."

"Think of it as something that has happened to someone else— the person that you used to be and not the person you are now."

She nodded and lit the candle of memory. Together, they clapped to call the god's attention to them and bestowed their gifts of silver on the altar. They sat in companionable silence, waiting to reach perfect calmness before starting the ceremony. Wolf reached his center quickly, but waited until Tinker was ready to pick up the cup of tears and taste the bitter memories.

He allowed himself to reflect on his failure with Jewel Tear and the bitter things she had to say to him. There was some truth in what she had to say. He had allowed silence to create a gulf between his heart and hers, so that their dreams took different forms. He would have to remember this, remind himself to keep his heart open to his beloved, so that they could share their dreams.

Dawn was breaking, and the cups of tears were drained, so they set aside their bitter memories. As light spilled into the temple, they lifted the cups of joys.

All Wolf's new moments of happiness centered on Tinker. They were scattered through his days, bright like diamonds. As he took them out, played them close, and stored them away, he found a pattern to them. In every occasion, he had known he had at last found the one who could not only understand his vision, but see possibilities that he hadn't considered, and had the ability to make them real. He found at the root of it all a loneliness he hadn't allowed himself to acknowledge, an awareness that he had been totally alone while surrounded by people, an emptiness now completely filled.

"Are you okay?" Tinker asked him in English.

He smiled. He had told her that he felt most free speaking English, and by her answering look, she remembered. "Yes, I am very content at this moment."

"Good. So am I." But then unease seeped into her eyes.

"What is it, beloved?"

"You probably have someplace to go, something you need to do."

He held out his hand to her, and she took it, interlacing their fingers. "What I need is to sit here with my *domi* and talk about what we want to do next."

The End